I0817856

SERRA ROSE

The Shadow Within

First published by Serra Rose 2023

Copyright © 2023 by Serra Rose

First published in 2023 by Serra Rose in Melbourne, Australia.

Editing: Ellen Klowden

Cover design by Miblart

Map Illustration by Alyssa Hurlbert

Chapter Headers by Lauren Xena Campbell

For permissions, inquiries, or further information, please contact through:

www.serrarosewrites.com

First edition

ISBN (paperback): 978-0-646-88790-6
ISBN (hardcover): 978-0-9756102-0-6

This book was professionally typeset on Reedsy.
Find out more at reedsy.com

For Mum, who has always encouraged my writing.

Contents

Content Warning

This story contains some heavy themes that may trigger some readers.

Police brutality/interrogation

Death of a child

Religious themes

Anxiety

Alcoholism

PTSD

Abuse

Pregnancy

Childbirth

Birth trauma

This is the origin story of the Grim Reaper, so there is A LOT of death/murder.

Remember, always be kind to yourself. Your mental health matters.

The Shadow Within has been read by a sensitivity reader.

Note to Readers

To my readers:

Thank you for giving this book a chance. I hope you enjoy it as much as I enjoyed writing it. These characters and this story have been with me since 2010. The journey has been full of obstacles, but finally, here they are. My characters, from me to you.

To my American readers.

This story is set in Medieval England, and to stay faithful to my characters and the world they inhabit, I've written the book in British English rather than American English. You may notice words like "colour," "honour," and "realise." These are not errors but reflect the unique English of a different time and place.

Map

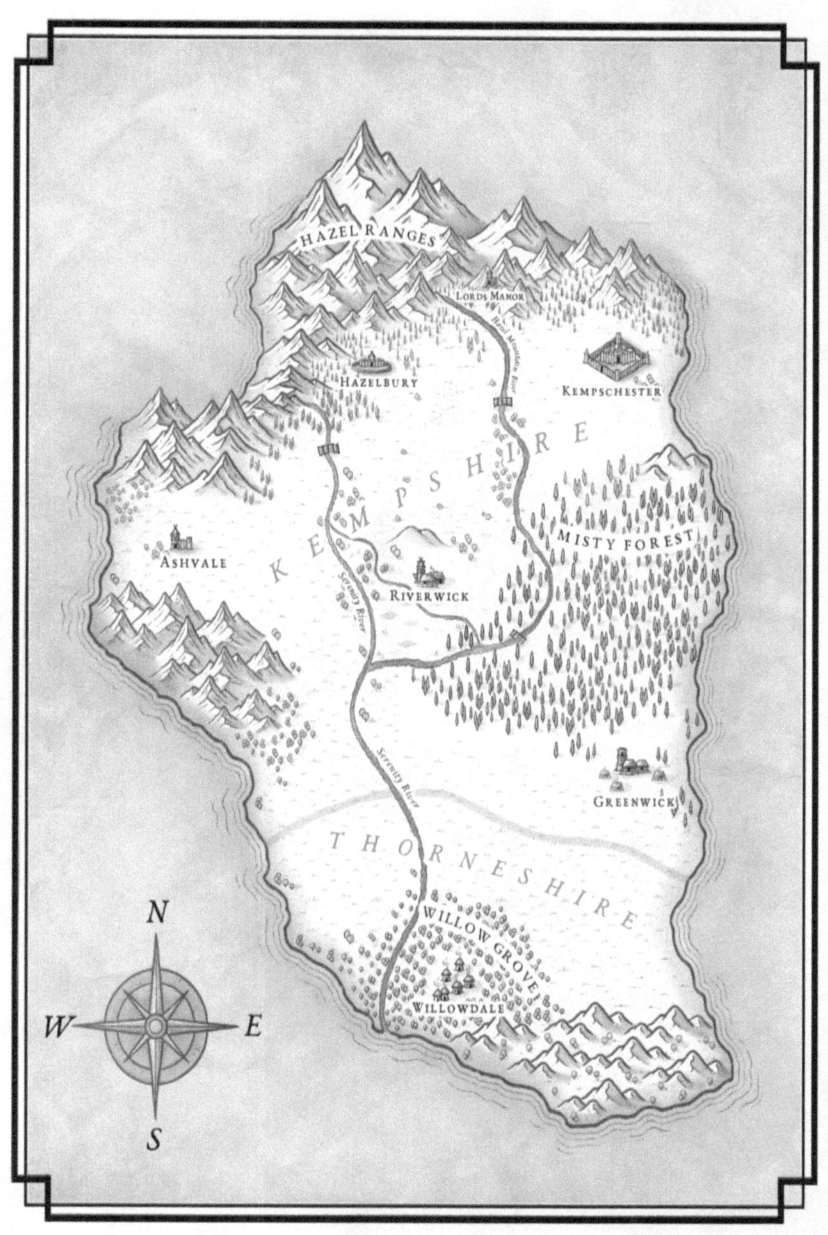

Map of Kempshire

Chapter 1

Moments ago, The Shadow had been elsewhere. Echoes of voices sparked recognition, and fractured memories clawed at him. He took in his surroundings. A realm clouded by fog, bathed in the blue light of the moon. Red lightning tore across the night sky. Haunted by another place beyond his grasp, The Shadow found himself unable to hold on to a life no longer his. The last memory faded, and loss engulfed him. Any connection he had to his former self was gone. All that remained was emptiness.

He belonged to this realm of shadows, yet a tether bound him to the life of another. He'd been sent here with a purpose he could not refuse. A primal need awakened, ending The Shadow's struggle to remember his forgotten life. Only one thing would satisfy this new hunger: to kill. Bloodlust arose from within, becoming all-consuming. Alert, he was ready to heed the command but needed a weapon. A sickle forged from Darkness took shape before him. He accepted the offering, closing his fingers around the handle.

The moans of dying mortals reached across the veil before their souls became trapped in this realm, their essence burning deep red. Tormented whispers of the dead seeking a way back were drawn towards him, his spark of life. Something dark watched him from the shadows, but he did not fear its presence. The two worlds were separate like night from day, connected only by the veil. Unlike the lost souls, he possessed the power to pass through.

It was time to hunt. The sickle in his hand thrummed with energy. As he passed through the veil, a strange beating began in his chest. This moon shone silver from a star-filled sky. The otherworldly glow cast light on a puddle at his feet. His murky visage gazed up at him. A figure in a hooded cloak. Eyes that gleamed white, a small smile. There was something familiar about his face, almost recognisable. Not a ghost, nor entirely human, but something in between. A being of shadows and Darkness.

Walls of stone towered over him, and a large wooden gate lay open. 'Kempschester' hung above the archway in metal letters. He walked through the gate and entered the town. Houses lined the street, built with wooden frames, woven sticks, and mud. Windows flickered with the light of lanterns as early risers emerged from their slumber. Dawn was close, and they would soon fill the streets with life. The odour of human and animal faeces and wet household waste mixed with the faint scent of burning wood in the air. In the still morning, a horse's hooves on cobblestones echoed. *That way!* Pulled towards the rider, he followed.

The dead's unmistakable scent stopped him at a woman's corpse. The blackened skin of the pestilence was present in her nose and fingers. A shivering child lay on the ground next to her. By the light of the moon, grey eyes shone from a grubby, round face. A radiance glowed from within the child, but in his centre, a black flame dimmed the light it touched. His future: nothing but death. The approaching winter would claim this one, if not starvation or the same affliction as his mother. Pity flickered through The Shadow but was dispelled in an instant. Nothing more than a familiar sensation from forgotten memories. This child held no significance to him. The Shadow left the boy to his fate, drawn again in a specific direction.

A crash from behind had him turning, his weapon raised. A scavenging dog had knocked over a clay pot that shattered as it hit the ground. The dog sprinted away with its tail between its legs. Laughter bubbled from The Shadow's chest, a strange sound in the morning's quietness.

"Who goes there?" a voice ahead of him called out with a ring of authority. "Show yourself!"

A surge of energy deep in The Shadow's being compelled him towards the voice. Anticipation stirred a sense of retribution. *Kill him!* Finally, the command he had been waiting for. This was the one who would die at his hands.

"I am Lord Philip Kemp of Kempschester. I command you to show yourself."

A Lord? The Shadow had been hunting a Lord. Philip's hair was thinning, and he had battle scars on his face. The mouth under the beard was pressed in a hard line. With his head held high, Philip's hand rested on the hilt of his sword. His tunic had the sheen of silk, and his cloak was fur-trimmed. There was no escape for the ill-fated Lord of Kempshire. His soul shone pale orange with a similar black flame to the child at its core, dowsing the glow of life. Despite Philip's air of power and privilege, this man's time had come. The Shadow stepped into the light, closing the distance between them.

Philip was off his horse in an instant. "Who are you?"

The answer needed no thought.

"I am your death."

Weapon in hand, The Shadow prepared to attack. Lord Philip drew his sword, brows furrowed, eyes watchful.

Kill him, a voice whispered inside him.

The man who stood before him held a relaxed stance.

Kill him! The command was more insistent this time, compelling him forward.

"Lord Philip." The Shadow drew the words out.

Flooded with only one desire, he embraced the shadows. A curtain of Darkness stood between him and the lord.

"What is this trickery? Where are you?" Philip spun around, sword in front of him.

Kill him! It was no longer a whisper or the voice of another, but his own.

There was nothing in The Shadow that fought against this urge to kill. Exhilaration flooded his chest as he stepped into view. Philip swung at him. The sword whistled through the air and connected with his sickle. The Shadow's own weapon was forced towards him, the curve of the blade at his throat as the lord drove forward. A sliver of fear surged, and The Shadow fought to keep the sharp edge from going any further. A cruel glint in Philip's eyes conveyed the lord's belief of victory. Unsure whether defeat would mean his own death, The Shadow gripped the man's wrist, forcing it back.

I will not be bested by a human whose end is the reason I'm here. He burned with rage and kicked hard enough to shove Philip back.

Before Philip could catch his balance, The Shadow advanced. One quick motion opened the mortal's throat. His eyes bulged, and a gasp turned into a gurgle. Blood sprayed, covering the face and neck of The Shadow. Lord Philip's sword slipped from the dying man's grasp, clattering on the ground. The Shadow's blade had cut deep, and the lord could only choke on his blood as he clutched at his throat. A fire blazed in those eyes as he wheezed for air, fighting for his life. The futile struggle of a man not yet ready to accept his own death. Finally, he fell, and one last wet breath rattled from his chest.

As The Shadow stood over Philip's body, the ember of life faded until it extinguished completely. His soul, however, wrenched free of the body, only to be pulled into the Shadow Realm. Deep red replaced the orange as Philip joined the many trapped behind the veil.

There was a whimper behind him as a peasant in muddy brown trousers and a torn tunic gaped at the body of Philip, eyes darting to The Shadow and his weapon. His essence shone brightly. The frightened man bolted, and The Shadow did not stop him. An alarm would be raised, but they could not capture him. He was not bound by this world, but to one beyond their reach. The body at his feet was the reason he had come forth, and his foothold in this world was waning. The Shadow Realm wanted him back. A smile tugged at his mouth as he raised his eyes to the town. Darkness had settled over Kempschester. Many would soon meet their death.

Someone was watching him. Fingers of ice sent shivers through him, and ripples of uneasiness travelled down his spine. With his jaw clenched, he glanced around, but the empty street offered nothing. His only escape was to pass through the shroud and return to the Shadow Realm. Lost souls whispered frantically, disturbed by a new arrival, alerting him of the presence. Wrapped in Darkness, like him, a silhouette in the fog. A shade? It had seen him. As suddenly as it had appeared, it was gone.

Chapter 2

The first beams of light inched across the land as Thomas struggled against the rising sleep that threatened to take him. Not yet! He had fought to stay awake to evade nightmares for three days and was not ready for that battle yet. The slow journey from the front lines of France had only added to his weariness from war. Despite his fatigue, overwhelming joy brought tears to his eyes. After four years, he was almost home.

The walls of Kempschester were a familiar sight that brought out his excitement. He couldn't stop the grin from spreading across his face. Thomas took the path around the town instead of through it. The streets would be filling by now as the market opened and people started their day.

It would not be long before he could surprise his twin brother and embrace his wife and son.

Thomas caught the smell of rotting meat with a faint hint of fruit. Two men emptied bodies from a cart into a trench just outside the town walls.

He addressed the men. "What is this?"

Corpses piled up in the trench, the odour so overwhelming that Thomas covered his mouth. This wasn't a new smell for him, but he would never get used to it. The two men looked up, their dark blond hair and green eyes showing they were related. The older man looked to be in his forties; the younger, in his twenties.

"It is a grave for the many who have fallen," the father informed Thomas.

Gravediggers. Another cart lay nearby, and two more men lay beside it, dead.

"You're throwing them into a hole? Do they not get a funeral?"

The father almost laughed. "Have you been asleep? The pestilence has taken too many lives for funerals."

The pestilence. He had passed signs of it in port-side villages. But before that, there had been word of an illness spreading across Europe. "I didn't realise it was this far inland."

"It is. I would be careful if I were you," the son said. "Lest you fall too, and we'll be throwing you in this trench."

Being thrown into a hole was not something he wanted to think about. Thomas pointed at the dead gravediggers.

"Who buries you if that happens?"

The father shrugged. "We'd be dead. I do not think we would be very concerned."

Thomas left them behind, in a hurry to get away from the rotting corpses. He returned to the road, the urgency to get home growing. What if the illness has reached Riverwick?

Urgency drove him forward. The idea of his family meeting such a grisly end tightened his throat. But as he approached the river, his heart stopped. Wooden barricades blocked off the stone bridge, and Enforcers stood in front, waiting to turn anyone away. Thomas clenched his jaw. *Damn.* He had very little to do with Enforcers, but their presence was enough for dread to set in. The men known for cruelty enforced the law of the lord. It didn't look good for him that they had taken station on the bridge. One had a greying beard, the other a receding hairline. Black horses grazed nearby. A regal breed that could only come from Lord Philip's breeder. Both Enforcers carried swords, dressed in their uniform: black leather armour under grey cloaks.

"Stop," Greybeard told him. "The bridge is closed."

"But I need to get home," he replied. "I live in Riverwick."

The two Enforcers glared at him.

"I said *the bridge is closed.* I don't care where you live; you are *not* getting past," Greybeard scowled, his tone sharp.

"Please, I've just returned from France."

"That isn't our problem." Greybeard rolled his eyes.

Thomas's hand twitched, and he resisted the urge to draw his sword. These men would not hesitate to take him to the Lord of Kempshire for an unprovoked attack. They could just as easily dispatch him themselves.

"Why is it closed?" Thomas asked.

"That's Enforcer business." Receding Hairline shifted his weight. "Now be on your way."

"Is Riverwick…?" He couldn't finish the sentence.

"Is Riverwick what?" Receding Hairline mocked Thomas. "I don't know or care about whatever peasant village you're from."

"I haven't seen my family in four years." It wasn't the complete truth, but they didn't know that.

Greybeard drew his sword. "You should leave on that dirty horse of yours before I kill you myself."

Thomas eyed the Enforcer. If it were just the two of them, he could win in a sword fight. But Receding Hairline would be a problem.

The beating of hooves on the hard road approached. More Enforcers. Taking that as his sign to leave, Thomas glanced at Greybeard one last time before turning his borrowed horse around. He would only be creating more problems for himself if he angered that many Enforcers. Without a word, he rode his borrowed horse away from the bridge. Their voices drifted after him with high-pitched urgency.

Thomas followed the road back towards Kempschester. His uneasiness grew as he choked with fear for his family. Thomas needed to find a way home. What had earlier been tears of joy turned into tears of frustration. He stopped in the middle of the road and rubbed his temple. To be this close only to get turned away had disrupted his return home.

Graeme! The connection had been silent for four years, but this was the time to invoke the bond with his twin brother. He would feel it if something bad had happened. The very reason he had shut it off in the first place was so Graeme wouldn't share his experience at war. Thomas sought out the bond that linked the twins together. *Nothing.* It had been too long since he had sensed his brother, and couldn't find the slightest flicker of Graeme's presence.

Dizzy, with a knot in his stomach, Thomas considered the forest that led towards Riverwick. He and Graeme had built their own bridge years ago. It could still be there despite the damage of flooding. He held on to an ember of hope and nudged the horse into a fast gallop towards the treeline. No Enforcers gave chase or called out.

In the forest, the horse slowed to a walk. Sunlight shone through the treetops, bringing rays of light to an otherwise dark forest. Thomas ran a hand over the rough bark of the nearest tree. Many of the trees of this forest were green all year round, but some showed bright reds, yellows, and oranges. Branches overhead creaked and leaves rustled in the breeze. Moss covered the ground, and as the horse's hooves pressed in, a damp, earthy smell filled the air.

Thomas rode towards the river. Stupid Enforcers. It was possible they would take it out on someone else or seek to make an example of him another time. They weren't known for being forgetful or forgiving. The forest held no warmth, so he pulled his cloak around him. Paths that had once marked an easy way towards Riverwick were gone. With his hope dying, he kept an eye on the river for an easy crossing.

Trees became more spread out. Thomas reached a small, roughly made bridge over the narrowest part of the river. He steered the horse across. This one appeared new, possibly Graeme's doing. The hooves made a sharp thud on the wood. Below, the hiss of the river was a comfort. The last time he had seen this river, it hadn't been this peaceful.

Thomas tried again to connect with his brother. Their link had been there as long as he could remember, and his inability to find Graeme added to the growing pit of worry in his stomach. *What if the pestilence had hit Riverwick?* In all his excitement to be home, that had not occurred to him. *What if he's dead? No, surely I would know, with or without the ability to sense him.*

Graeme's energy flooded in as Thomas finally unlocked their connection. His stomach flipped; Graeme's presence was close by. *He's hunting, just as we always have on this day.* The familiar cold surged within his heart, and he flinched, putting a hand to his chest. He had forgotten about the suffocating Darkness in his brother. Thomas considered again whether Graeme knew it was there. Like a black cloud passing in front of the sun, yet no one else seemed aware of its presence. After years of absence, the gloom settled around him once more.

To be this close to home filled him with both joy and dread. Graeme would likely ask him questions he wasn't ready to answer. But the look on his brother's face would be everything. Finally, he reached a more familiar part of the forest. Thomas emerged from between the trees into a large clearing and pulled hard on the reins.

In the middle of the clearing, Graeme spun around, raising a bow and drawing back the string. Thomas's heart leapt into his throat as he held his hands up. Graeme's narrow face was an almost identical reflection, except his black hair was shorter, his beard tidier than Thomas's own. Recognition flickered in piercing blue eyes, a contrast to the dark blue of Thomas's.

"Tom?"

Graeme's emotions engulfed Thomas. Surprise, joy, curiosity. Unable to block them out, Thomas forced a smile. The bow was still raised, arrow trained on him. As if realising what he was doing, Graeme lowered the bow. Thomas relaxed his arms. Exhaustion washed over him again as he dismounted from the horse, tying the lead rope to a tree. On the ground, he winced as pain shot up his injured leg. Forcing the discomfort down, he limped towards Graeme. He wrapped his arms around his brother in a hug. Graeme didn't stiffen as he normally would, but also didn't hug back. Thomas started to pull away. Only then did his brother's arms wrap around him, dropping the bow. Laughter rumbled through the both of them. Overwhelmed by the warmth in his chest, Thomas tightened his own arms.

They stepped back. Silence stretched out, each of them waiting for the other to speak. He was home.

"Hello, Grim," Thomas said.

Chapter 3

"You know I hate that name." Graeme rolled his eyes, yet a smile crept in. "When did you get back?"

"Now. Just in time to join you on a hunt."

Graeme's smile faded. "Please tell me this is not like the last time you returned. I'm not sure you realise how difficult that was, especially on Emma."

Thomas had returned a few months ago, bearing the bad news of Emma's brother dying on the front lines. "It wasn't easy for me, either. I didn't want to leave my wife while she still grieved. Or any of you."

Graeme picked up his bow. "Then you're here to stay?"

"Yes. I'm home, Grim." Thomas took a step back. "I thought you'd be happy to see me."

"I am."

"Then stop frowning; I feel like I'm being interrogated."

"Sorry. I am happy to see you. I just wanted to make sure you weren't leaving again," Graeme commented.

"I'm not leaving," Thomas said.

"I'm surprised Emma let go of you to join me for a hunt."

Thomas averted his eyes.

"You haven't been home yet?" Graeme sighed, shaking his head. "Tom. . ."

"I would have gone home first if I could have gotten through. The Enforcers have blocked off the bridge. I had to come through the forest."

Graeme frowned. "They have? Why?"

"I don't know, but something's happened. They probably won't be happy about me getting around their barricade, either." Thomas motioned to his horse. "I have a bow. Let's hunt." He raised his eyebrows at Graeme.

"But your wife…"

"She will understand." Thomas shot his brother his biggest grin. "It's been four years, Grim, come on. It is our birthday tradition."

Graeme shook his head, giving in with a smile. "It *is* our tradition."

Thomas walked back to the horse to retrieve his bow. "I'll make it up to Emma. She never stays angry at me. Is she well?"

"She is."

Being in the forest with his brother gave him a feeling of home. The war was behind him, and he could avoid all that had happened. As he turned, he caught Graeme staring. His stomach dropped. The limp was likely to raise some questions. Instead, Graeme's eyes darted over Thomas's face.

"You look awful," Graeme said in a hushed tone.

Thomas was all too aware of his appearance. His eyes were probably red, and he was in need of bathing.

"Are we here to hunt or talk about how bad I look?" he asked quietly.

Graeme gestured to Thomas's bow. "Do you mean to hunt without arrows?"

"No, I mean for you to give me one of yours." Thomas pointed to the quiver at Graeme's waist.

Graeme passed two arrows to Thomas. Thomas wouldn't need a second shot, so he gave the spare back to Graeme before nocking the arrow.

"Be careful, there's been an increase of raiders recently," Graeme said.

"Raiders? Here?"

Graeme nodded. "I've lost to them twice already, and Uncle James has lost to them three times. We sometimes pair up when we can. Numbers usually deter them, but they're getting bold."

Thomas tightened his fingers around the grip. "It's difficult enough. Now you have to fight them for food?"

"It's only going to get worse. I think we're in for a cold winter."

"What about scouts?" Thomas asked.

Hunting was always a risk. This forest belonged to the king, and to be caught hunting would put them both in trouble. They could be arrested or killed on the spot.

"I haven't seen any for a year. I'm always on the lookout, though. I thought you were either a scout or a raider."

"So you raised your bow?" Horror squeezed Thomas's throat. "Grim!"

"I thought I was caught. Might as well take them out, too."

Thomas walked beside Graeme and nudged him with his shoulder. "Are you any better of a shot yet?" he asked, attempting to change the subject.

That familiar rivalry was just as strong as ever. A challenging light sparked from behind Graeme's eyes.

"Well, I almost shot you," Graeme replied. His smile faded and he stopped walking.

Thomas rolled his eyes. "Ha! You did not hear me until I was almost right on top of you."

But Graeme's mood had changed. Words meant in jest turned to heavy dread, which reached through their bond. The stone in Thomas's chest made it difficult to breathe.

"But you didn't shoot me," Thomas reminded his twin. "Please stop worrying about something that didn't happen."

Graeme's stare was fixed on him, unblinking. Thomas relaxed the bow and snapped his fingers in front of his brother's face. "Grim!"

Graeme blinked. "What?"

"You're doing it again. Stop panicking. Nothing happened. Let's just focus on the hunt."

It had been a long time since they'd hunted together. Graeme slowed his step to match that of Thomas's, the limp impeding his natural stride.

"You were hurt." There was concern in Graeme's voice.

"I was," Thomas confirmed.

"Do you want to talk about it?" Graeme asked

"No, I do not." Thomas would talk when he was ready. If he ever was.

As they both shifted their focus into tracking, their conversation halted. The gentle swishing of leaves rustling above and the whistle of birds were the only sounds in the quiet forest. Graeme moved off to his left, and Thomas kept his eyes on the ground looking out for tracks.

The heavy hoof falls of an animal, followed by splashing in the river made them both freeze. His whole body tensed as he met Graeme's eyes. Deer or horse? Scout or raider? Thomas mouthed the word *hide* to his brother and scanned his surroundings. He took shelter against the trunk of a tree. Thomas held his breath, waiting, sick with fear and worry that was either his, Graeme's, or both. His fingers twitched, resisting the temptation to reach for his sword. He strained for any sound that didn't belong.

There was no more sound and no sight of anyone, so he let out his breath. "All clear," he said in a low voice.

Graeme stepped into his eyeline, and without a word they resumed the hunt, but Thomas's calm was gone.

Finally spotting deer tracks, he hissed through his teeth to gain Graeme's attention and pointed. Following the trail, he led the way. His brother's footsteps behind him stopped. *What?* Graeme was transfixed on something at his feet, eyes blazing. That's a lot of excitement for droppings or more tracks. The forest darkened. Thomas glanced up, but there were no clouds.

The Darkness in Graeme rose, and Thomas watched his brother's face. Every part of him wanted to run, but he resisted the urge. To forsake his brother was unthinkable. *I will face this Darkness one day and free my brother from its grasp.* Thomas tried to put up a mental shield to block out the overwhelming presence, but was out of practice, and the energy was too strong for his feeble attempt.

The footsteps he'd been following were fresh; the animal should be nearby. As Thomas searched the forest around them, a twig snapped. Graeme cursed under his breath. Something moved fast. A stag came out of nowhere and ran straight for Graeme, its head lowered. Graeme raised his bow, but Thomas was quicker, bow already raised and string drawn. The bowstring twanged as he loosed the arrow.

The stag dropped. Thomas's vision blurred and his heart raced.

"You bumbling clod, were you not watching where you were going? We're at war, you complete halfwit. You want to announce to everyone that we're here?" he said in a loud whisper, his face hot.

"At war? What are you…? Tom, you're *home,*" Graeme said in a quiet voice.

Thomas took a deep breath and stepped back, rubbing his face with one hand.

"Sorry." Thomas attempted a smile. "I am tired. It has been a long journey home."

Graeme studied Thomas's face. "You're tired? I think that's more than tired."

The stag's musky scent was strong as he advanced. "Let's get this back." Thomas strained to pull the arrow from the stag. When he freed it, his brother heaved the animal onto his shoulders.

"It was my kill. I can carry it," Thomas offered.

Graeme shook his head. "No, I've got it."

They walked in silence. Thomas's mind wandered back to what he'd said. It wasn't his way to lose control of his anger. His time on the front lines had had more of an effect on him than he'd thought. Not only in losing his temper, but he'd been convinced he was still at war.

Chapter 4

Thomas's limp and the burden on Graeme's shoulders made the trek back to the horse slow. Graeme's breaths were shallow, and Thomas matched his brother's breathing as if he were carrying the stag. It was a cold morning, but small beads of sweat began to trickle down his face and neck.

Every few steps Thomas caught a falter in Graeme's step. Being so near to one another strengthened their bond. Pain and emotions mixed, making it difficult to separate his own from Graeme's.

"You're not trying to shield yourself," Graeme noted.

"I can't. It's been years since I had to."

They walked in silence for a while.

"If we are to share pain," Graeme panted, "at least tell me the cause of it."

This was the question Thomas had been waiting for. To tell the cause of his injury he would have to think about that day. Swords clashed. Screams. Caleb's pleas. Thomas's throat closed and his vision swam. Finally, he shielded himself to suppress the strength of their link. The connection shifted from a clamour to a whisper.

"Very well," Graeme conceded. "Keep it to yourself, then. Can you at least tell me why you're nervous? I thought you'd be happy to be home."

Reality set in that Thomas was about to see his wife and son. His heart soared, yet his stomach was in knots. Despite a brief visit home when he had been granted special leave a few months ago, Thomas was a stranger to his son. He had the chance to make up for lost time now, with both Isaac and Emma.

"I am." Thomas gave Graeme his best smile.

"But?" Graeme asked.

"But…. you said it yourself. The last time I was here…" Thomas let his sentence trail off.

"It was difficult for her, losing her brother to the same war you left to fight in — not just once, but twice." Graeme raised his eyes to Thomas.

Thomas could find no words.

"A lot has happened in the past few months. I think she will just be overjoyed that you're back." Graeme's eyes glinted as he turned away, but Thomas didn't miss the strange smile.

His brother was hiding something. "What aren't you saying?" Thomas demanded.

Graeme turned, his eyes widened as his tone rose. "Nothing!"

"You're a terrible liar," Thomas teased. "That innocent look didn't work when we were children, and it won't work now."

"Just don't put off seeing her more than you already have," Graeme advised him.

They walked in silence. The hush and familiarity of the forest was a comfort, but Thomas couldn't help but notice the significant differences to the noise he was used to. In the trees above, the content chirrup of birds replaced the death screams of horses and men. The hiss and whispering river were calming, unlike the roar and crackle of fire as buildings burned. Some distance away, a wolf howled, its long, soulful sound resonating through his chest, raising the hairs on his arms. The answering howls, amplified by the surrounding forest, were different from the snarls of scavenging wolves on the battlefield that were drawn in by the scent of blood.

The snort of his horse was a welcome sound. They had reached the clearing.

"Put the stag on the horse," Thomas suggested, and he untied the lead.

"You're going to walk?" Graeme asked.

"Yes. We're not that far from home."

"I would rather you didn't," his brother said with raised eyebrows. "I'm more comfortable without that pain in my leg. Even dulled, it's bothersome."

His sharp honesty shouldn't have taken Thomas by surprise. Whatever it was that lived inside Graeme affected his ability to be compassionate at times.

"I see you're still as sensitive as ever to the pain of others," Thomas responded with anger in his voice.

Graeme let out a sigh. "I'm sorry, I shouldn't have said that. You ride, I can carry this to Willow. She isn't too far away."

Why didn't you say that before? Thomas kept silent as he mounted the horse. As he no longer bore weight on his injured leg, the relief was both his and Graeme's.

They left the clearing, and Thomas resisted the urge to close his eyes. His horse's ears twitched. Watchful and now wide awake, Thomas whistled at Graeme, who looked up and a crease formed on his forehead.

The horse below him whinnied.

Thomas's bow was still strapped to his back with the string against his chest. He pulled it over his head.

Thomas held out his hand. "Give me some arrows," he said in a low voice.

Graeme handed arrows to him.

"Stay alert," Thomas instructed, his voice barely audible as they started up the hill.

The silence of the forest made the hairs on his arms rise. This was a little too familiar.

At the top, Graeme's white horse, Willow, lifted her head at their arrival. Thomas surveyed the forest around them once more.

"There's no one there," Graeme said, easing the stag onto the back of his horse. He flexed his shoulders. "I don't know what you were so worried about."

"Animals adapt to war. When they react to something you can't see in enemy territory, it's best that you listen."

"Enemy territory?" Graeme scoffed. "Do you hear yourself? This is our territory."

Thomas let himself relax. An arrow flew past him screaming, striking the stag with a dull thump. Reflexively, Thomas fired back in the direction the arrow had come from.

Three men stepped into view, bows drawn.

"You!" Graeme's voice seethed with hostility.

"Which one of you fired at my brother?" Thomas demanded.

"It was a warning shot, he knows what we're here for," the leader of the trio said. He looked from Thomas to Graeme. "Twins?!"

Thomas half turned in his saddle to meet Graeme's eyes. "These are the raiders?"

Graeme's eyes flashed, and fury blazed through their connection.

"Grim," Thomas warned. *Please, don't do anything stupid.* "You were following us, weren't you?" he asked the raiders.

"Just give us what we came for," the leader said.

"What kind of a man cannot hunt for himself?" Thomas scoffed. "You have to steal another man's kill?"

The raiders approached, their bows trained on Thomas.

"I've heard that sometimes twins feel each other's pain," the leader said, shifting his gaze from Thomas to Graeme and back to Thomas. "Is it like that with you two? If I shot him, would both of you die?"

With a roaring in his ears, Thomas raised his bow. "If you're going to threaten my brother, you better make sure you kill me."

"We don't want to kill anyone if we don't have to."

Two of the raiders approached Willow, putting down their bows. The taller of the two moved around the horse so they could take the stag. As he did, Graeme stepped forward, the tip of an arrow at the raider's throat.

"That's *ours*," Graeme said, barely containing the malice in his voice.

Waves of fury radiating from his brother battered Thomas. His impulse was to let Graeme kill the raider and to shoot the leader who still held a bow on him. The other raider retrieved his bow.

"Grim." Thomas fought against the rising black rage. "Stand down, let them take it."

A piece of food wasn't worth either of them dying over. Thomas lowered his bow. Graeme didn't move. *He's going to kill him.* Black spots danced in front of Thomas as he feared what that could awaken in Graeme.

A second arrow was released, hitting the tree behind Graeme.

"Let him go, or the next one goes in your throat," the raider said.

Graeme's face was a mask of fury.

"Grim. Stop."

God, please don't let my brother die right in front of me. Thomas's instincts screamed at him to kill the leader for firing at Graeme again. With no other way to snap Graeme out of his haze, Thomas pressed the tip of an arrow into his hand. Graeme turned his eyes towards Thomas.

"Let him go," Thomas pleaded.

At first there was no change. Graeme had pressed the arrow in enough to draw blood. Finally, the savagery receded. "Take it." He lowered his makeshift weapon.

The thieves were hasty to retreat with the carcass, quickly escaping further into the forest.

"What's wrong with you?" Thomas demanded.

"I'm tired of them stealing. Why did you stop me?"

"Because I would like to go home, and I didn't feel like dragging your body through the fields. How do you think Amelia would have taken that?"

Graeme climbed onto his horse. "I wouldn't know. You would have to ask her that."

They're still struggling.

He rode in silence. As they reached the edge of the forest, Thomas caught sight of the farm and the thatched roof of their house. A lot had happened in the months since he had been granted leave, and what should be a comfort felt dream-like instead.

Most houses in the village were smaller in size, square with sloped triangular roofs. Their two-level cruck house, alongside James's next door, was somewhat larger with an arched roof. Between them was a large stable. In front, there were strips of freshly harvested fields, and to the side of his home were pens filled with pigs, cows, and sheep. Chickens roamed around freely. On James's side was an orchard of apples and pears. The subtle perfume of fruit reminded Thomas of the days he and Graeme had roamed the orchard, eating pears. He could almost taste the pear, both sour and sweet, crunchy with juice running down his chin.

As they approached the farmhouse, emotions Thomas had shut off at war came rushing back, his heart bursting. Emma...

"Welcome home, brother," Graeme said.

The words rang in his ears. *Welcome home.* Rightfully, he should not have come home. There were many times his death looked inescapable. To be here was beyond all expectations, a miracle. They passed a peasant who worked in the fields during harvest season.

"You go inside," Graeme offered. "I need to warn Uncle James about what happened before I go to the cemetery with Father."

The mention of Father brought back a forgotten resentment. The drunken outbursts and shielding Graeme from beatings. *I could go another day without seeing him.*

Thomas tied the horse and opened the door, walking inside.

In the kitchen, Emma and Amelia spoke in low voices. The rich aroma of pottage lingered in the air, his mouth watering. Unsure how to announce his arrival, he paused in the doorway. His five-year-old son, Isaac, had Thomas's narrow face and dark hair. Warmth spread throughout every part of him as he watched the boy eat, his legs swinging under the table. So many went to war, never to see their children again, but here he was.

Thomas had stood in the same place the day he'd left. Watching his family, filled with ideas of honour and duty. A very different man from the one who stood there now. He almost didn't recognise that man he had been.

Finally, he shifted his gaze to Emma, and everything slowed down. Seated at the table, she had her back to him and laughed at something Amelia said. The absence of her usual wimple revealed a long braid. Emma's laughter reminded him of the first time he had heard it.

Eighteen-year-old Thomas stopped at the blacksmith and picked up a sword, swinging it.

Graeme joined him. "Don't hurt yourself. You're a farmer, what need do you have of that?"

"There is a war in France. It's only a matter of time before we're summoned. Perhaps you should have one, too." Graeme picked up a sword, and the idea of him at war filled Thomas with dread. "Don't hurt yourself," he repeated his brother's words.

Peals of laughter drew his attention to a woman walking towards them, with another who could only be her mother. Brown, wavy hair framed her face, with dark eyes that crinkled as her lips curved into a smile. Thomas gave her a once-over, before raising his eyes back to her face. Their gazes locked and she lowered her head. A deep blush coloured pale cheeks as she tucked loose strands behind her ear. He put the sword down, turning as she passed by.

"That's the Blake twins," the woman's mother whispered loudly. "You'd do well to have children with one of them, Emma."

Emma groaned. "Mother, they can hear you," she warned, in a voice no quieter than her mother's.

Thomas shook with silent laughter.

"I'm betrothed," Graeme spluttered.

Emma glanced at Thomas over her shoulder. Before Thomas could help himself, a wide smile crept across his face.

"You're staring, and you have that stupid grin." Graeme nudged Thomas with an elbow to the ribs. "Has something caught your eye?"

Thomas followed Emma's movement as she walked away. "Something has," he murmured.

Emma's voice brought Thomas back. The sight of her in the marketplace had taken him by surprise. He had been summoned to war so soon after the birth of their son. To leave her at such an early stage in their marriage had been painful for both of them. Guilt squeezed his chest, closing around his throat.

"Graeme?" Amelia noticed him. "What are you—" Her eyes dropped to the sword at his hip, and realisation sparked in her eyes. "Not Graeme."

Amelia's round face lit up and she nudged Emma's hand, pointing. Emma looked around and froze. "Thomas?"

"I'm home, Em."

His rapid heartbeat thundered as he waited for Emma's reaction. First, her eyes clouded over before she blinked. She whispered something inaudible, and Amelia moved around the table to help her to stand. Thomas dropped his gaze to her belly, then back to her face.

"You…" *How long ago had it been since I came home? January? February? I was only here for two weeks.* "Did I…?" He was at a loss for words.

"You left something behind when you returned to France." Emma rushed for him.

"Grim didn't tell me."

"Graeme knows better," Amelia said. "Thomas, it truly is good to see you." Her eyes met his over Emma's shoulder. "Your return is a welcome one."

"Thank you, Amelia." Thomas smiled. "It is good to see you, too."

"I'll leave you three to your reunion," Amelia whispered to him as she left the kitchen.

Emma's hands clung to the back of his neck. Careful not to squeeze too hard, Thomas wrapped his arms around the middle of her back, pulling her to him. He breathed in; her scent of fresh lavender and lemon filled him with bliss. He lifted her chin, pulling her mouth towards his. Emma's hands slid down to both sides of his face, her kiss fierce. As they pulled apart, Thomas wiped a tear from her cheek with his thumb. All doubt from earlier melted away, and he lowered his forehead to hers.

"My wife. My heart," he whispered. "I'm home."

As Emma's hand dropped to rest over his chest, the other remained on his face. "My joy. Are you here to stay?"

Thomas wrapped his hand around hers. "I am," he murmured, kissing her hand.

She beckoned to their son. "Isaac, your father has returned to us."

The boy approached Thomas with hesitance, his brown eyes wide with curiosity.

Thomas pulled himself from Emma's embrace and knelt. "Hello, Isaac."

Chapter 5

"It has been a long time since I had a meal like this," Thomas said between mouthfuls.

The pottage was rich with meat, cabbage, carrots, and turnips, flavoured with rosemary and sage. He followed it down with ale. With Emma next to him, and Isaac on the other side of the table, Thomas couldn't hold back the wave of joy. His hand held Emma's, resting on her leg.

As his head dropped, he jerked awake. and Emma couldn't stop her smile.

"You look exhausted," she said.

Thomas squeezed her hand. "I am."

"I think Amelia would be happy to watch Isaac for us while we rest."

Tired of fighting what his body needed, Thomas nodded. His head pounded. He had seen the effects of withheld sleep and would be plagued by apparitions if he didn't rest soon.

A heavy step thumped on the stairs.

"Grandfather is awake!" Isaac said, looking up from his food.

Thomas pushed away the bowl of pottage, and his shoulders stiffened. A tankard of ale sat in front of him, and he swallowed a mouthful. Sweet, with a honey flavour, the ale barely calmed him. Thomas ground his teeth together as the footsteps got closer. Father stood in the doorway, regarding Thomas. On his feet immediately, Thomas gave a tight smile.

"Hello, Father."

Father narrowed his eyes and grunted. Without a word, he left. Thomas sank back onto the seat. It was as if he were a child again, unable to do *anything* to please Father.

"My sweeting, I'm sure he is happy to see you." Emma reached for his face.

"Don't do that. Forget him."

"Can I go outside?" Isaac asked. "I'm finished."

"Go find Amelia," Emma instructed.

Isaac ran from the kitchen as Graeme entered.

"You have a visitor," Graeme said to Thomas, and left, taking the stairs.

"Who knows you're back already?" Emma asked.

"It's probably James. Grim would have told him. I'll see what he wants." Thomas shot Emma a wicked grin. "Then we can have that rest you spoke of." He released Emma's hand, sliding his further up her leg and pressing in between her thighs. She sucked in a breath and let it out with a sigh.

"No, not that kind of rest," Emma said as she pulled his hand away with reluctance. "Help me up. I'll speak with Amelia."

Thomas held Emma's arm, easing her from the seat.

Graeme thumped down the stairs. "Where is he?"

"Father? He left. Did you not see him?"

Graeme's eyes flicked skyward, and he huffed. Thomas followed Graeme. Thomas froze at the doorway. Samson Kemp, son of Lord Philip, stood a little distance away, his back to him. Samson turned at his arrival.

"Samson. When did you get back?" Thomas closed the door, and Graeme walked in the direction of the cemetery.

In his late twenties, Samson had blue eyes, with shoulder length, dark-blond hair and a full beard, and he was taller than Thomas. His fur cloak was finery that did not belong in Riverwick. He had been in France when Thomas left. Thomas moved away from the house as the two of them walked towards Samson's horse.

"Not long after you," Samson replied.

Samson's departure from the front lines, followed by a visit to Riverwick, meant something had happened.

"You left? Is the war over?"

Samson's gaze clouded over. "Did you not…?" His eyes cleared. "Of course. You were already gone when they halted the war."

"They halted the war?" Thomas's mind raced.

"The pestilence claimed too many soldiers."

Thomas absorbed this. "Why are you here? Is there something you need?"

"Thomas, address me correctly."

"Address you…" Thomas frowned. "I don't understand."

"My father has died. I am the Lord of Kempshire; address me as such."

"Sorry, Lord Samson," he said. "My sympathies for the loss of your father."

Lord Samson smiled, with no warmth, and reached a hand towards Thomas. He held a message, the letter K pressed into a wax seal. Thomas's heart sank. He had received a similar message before.

"What is that?"

"What does it look like? A summons," Lord Samson breathed out a sigh of impatience.

Thomas checked around him to make sure no one could hear, and lowered his voice. "But I was dismissed. Why would you summon me to a halted war?"

"This isn't a summons to war, Thomas."

He took the summons, his hands shaking as he broke the seal. The soft parchment had a hint of yellow.

Lord Philip has been killed in the town of Kempschester. You have been summoned to hunt down his killer. In your service to the king, you have proven to be a valuable asset to Lord Samson. The King's Law states that you will answer any summons by His Majesty or those he delegates to represent his affairs.

"You came all this way because you want me to help you find a murderer?"

"I came all this way for your hunting expertise. It is your duty to answer a summons," Lord Samson reminded him.

"I need no reminder of my duty. Have I not shown my commitment to that? You granted me leave on the condition that I bring back more soldiers for the king's war. I led those men to their deaths," He waved the summons. "Don't you have Enforcers for this?"

Lord Samson's face was blank, but the flicker in his eyes filled Thomas with dread. *No. Not that.* His blood ran cold.

"This isn't just a summons to find a murderer, is it?" he rolled the parchment.

Isaac ran to Thomas and stared up at Lord Samson, a wooden sword in his hand. Lord Samson barely glanced at the boy.

"No," Lord Samson said.

Thomas pulled Isaac towards him. "I *can't* leave my family so soon. Can I not have *one* day with them before I leave them again?"

"You have one day. I will expect you at my manor tomorrow."

Tomorrow? How am I going to tell Emma I'm leaving again? This will break her heart.

"I'm a yeoman. I can't be an Enforcer. Why would you ask me this?"

"Your actions in France show otherwise."

Thomas's skin crawled. His intention of putting France behind him collapsed. The echoes of war were trying to pull him back.

"I can't do that," Thomas argued. "Not again."

"Have I led you to believe you have a choice? You know what it means to deny a summons. I can't help you if you choose to do that. You have your duty, and I have mine."

Lord Samson climbed onto his horse. "I have matters to attend to, but I will see you tomorrow. If you're not there, and I have to send for you—" he sighed. "just be there." He reached for the lead rope on the horse Thomas had borrowed, towing it behind him.

The summons rustled as Thomas crumpled it. Weak in his legs, he slumped to the ground. To be an Enforcer would mean committing to brutality, and wielding a power that only nobles and their sons held. Thomas wasn't nobility or cruel. To be chosen for such a role would only bring shame to his honour. With a rushing in his ears, the world around him faded and he sank into hopelessness. *I can't do this to my family.*

Voices reached Thomas from far away. His name. Through his haze someone was talking to him. A hand gripped his shoulder tight, shaking him.

"Tom?"

Thomas blinked. He was sitting on the ground. Graeme and Uncle James stood over him, their cloaks a reminder of the cold. He suppressed a shiver, his arms and body chilled.

Thomas forced himself to his feet. "Grim? I thought you went to the cemetery."

"I did, but Father didn't want me there." Graeme's eyebrows drew together. "Where is your cloak? Are you not cold?"

Struggling to pull himself from his dread, Thomas had difficulty breathing. The summons was still tight in his hand. Uncle James had a fixed smile on his face, yet worry shone through. With dark brown hair and grey eyes, James looked nothing like his elder brother. He certainly didn't share Father's temper, but was a man of compassion who had often sheltered Thomas and Graeme. Now, those eyes fixed on Thomas, and he winked.

"Give your brother some space," James told Graeme.

Graeme stepped away from him.

"James," Thomas said at last, his voice raspy.

"Uh oh, I know that look all too well," James said.

"What look?" Graeme's eyes moved from Thomas to James.

"*Shock*. Time at war does that." James's attention focused on Thomas. "Have you slept yet?"

Aware of Graeme's curiosity, Thomas made sure he was well shielded from his brother. He was not ready to discuss Lord Samson's visit yet.

"No. What are you working on today?"

"Well, it's been a few weeks since the fire. I think we need to commit to pulling the church down so we can finally start to rebuild it."

"There was a fire?" Thomas glared at Graeme. "You didn't tell me that."

"I did not think to bring it up while we were hunting," Graeme shrugged.

"Was anyone hurt?"

"Father Rohan died," his brother said.

Father Rohan. Thomas had known the priest his entire life.

"May he rest in peace," Thomas frowned. "How have people attended church?"

"Until recently, we've travelled to Greenwick or Kempschester." James shook his head in despair. "But now, the pestilence has many hesitant to leave Riverwick."

"Will the church assist with the rebuild?" Thomas asked.

James's eyes were pained. "They have rejected our plea for help."

A village of two hundred people is without a place of worship.

"This village isn't important enough. But if the church in Kempschester were to fall, it would have been rebuilt already," Graeme grumbled.

James's son, John, called out from the direction of the orchard.

"Excuse me." James looked Thomas up and down. "I'm happy to see you, Thomas. But make sure you get some sleep. You're dead on your feet." James walked towards the orchard. "You boys should come over for dinner next week. Susanna and John will be happy to see you both. Bring your wives."

Thomas was left standing with Graeme.

"He's right," Graeme said. "Amelia has Isaac. You need sleep."

In his exhaustion, Thomas almost missed Graeme pushing against his shields. He gave Graeme a mental shove. "We have never done that to each other. You cannot do that."

"Sorry, I am just wor—"

"Worried. Yes, I know, I can feel it. There is no need to be. Please, Graeme, give me time. Don't pry, not like that."

Thomas hurried back into the house. Graeme was right to be concerned, but he wasn't ready to discuss his consignment into the Enforcers.

Thomas took the stairs slowly, the bannister rough against his hand. Every step burned as if he were being shot with an arrow again. By the time he reached the top, he was gripped by the need to wrap his arms around Emma and never let go.

Emma was still awake, and her face lit up when he entered their bedroom. He removed his sword and belt, placing them on the wooden chest at the end of their bed, tucking the summons into the scabbard. After removing his clothes, Thomas dumped them on the floor.

"I had given up on you returning," she said as he climbed into bed. "What did James want?"

"We're invited over for dinner next week." Thomas clamped down on the guilt that rose from his lie. She would find out soon enough that Lord Samson had been here, and why, but for now she didn't need to know.

The comfort of his bed was a stark contrast from the hard ground of France. Embracing Emma, he pulled her close, making sure his hold was tender. Her warm skin against his sent jolts of heat through him, and his heart skipped. Their lips almost touched, his gaze locked on her face.

"You need to tidy your beard," Emma murmured.

"You don't like the beard?" he asked, brushing his chin against her.

Emma squirmed. "Stop," she laughed, scrunching her nose up, trying to pull away. "You look like a wild man who's been living in the forest too long."

"Wild? You liked it when we first met."

"It wasn't this unkempt then, and you had only just started growing it."

Thomas leaned his head forward, pressing his mouth to hers. *I'm home.* Emma's lips were soft and sweet. She made a satisfied sound and nestled into his chest. With his chin resting on the top of her head, warmth engulfed him. Drowsiness set in, and Thomas closed his eyes, descending into sleep.

Faces emerged before him. Screams of rage. The pleading cries of those who met his sword. Blood. Caleb.

Thomas opened his eyes, peace abandoning him. His entire body shook, and Emma pulled away.

"What is it?" she massaged at the tension between his eyes with her thumbs.

"Shhhh. Nothing. Go to sleep." Thomas rolled over to hide his horror from her.

Emma's hand lay against his back, her touch a comfort. "Thomas, you're shaking! That isn't nothing."

He took a deep breath, willing himself to calm. "It's nothing," he repeated.

"I prayed for your return," Emma whispered. "Don't turn away from me now. Thomas, please."

With reluctance, Thomas turned to face her again.

Emma cupped his face. "You're here with me. Let that soothe your troubled heart. I will not ask you to talk about it. You'll have enough of that from your brother."

Warmth flooded him. He tightened his arms around her once more. "What did I do to deserve you?"

"Oh, you think you deserve me?" Emma teased.

Emma's eyes remained on his. Before long, hers fluttered closed. Sleep started to creep in again, followed by the ghosts. As soon as he closed his eyes, they were there, waiting for him.

Chapter 6

Thomas's eyes shot open. In a cold sweat, he pulled away from Emma. Her gentle breathing meant she was asleep. The war and everything he'd done washed over him. The first time he had taken a life. Men dying, far from their families. Fear that he would die in the mud far from his own. The roar of men as swords clanged together. Swords piercing flesh. The scent of blood, so strong it left a coppery taste in his mouth. Caleb's death.

His throat constricted and his chest burned. He sat on the side of the bed, head in his hands. Gasping for breath, he forced down the urge to retch. *Calm yourself, Thomas! You're home! You're home.* The words repeated themselves, and he could scarcely believe it. *I need fresh air.* He pulled on fresh clothes before leaving his room.

The warmth of his wife and bed would not keep those lurking nightmares away. He hesitated before descending the stairs. When he took the first step, pain shot through his leg as he bore weight on it. It was an agonising climb down the stairs, worse than ascending them earlier.

Outside, his hands shook. Thomas moved towards the stable, hopeful that a ride around the village might help calm him. Something normal, boring, safe. The breeze on his face was cold, ruffling his hair as he took in deep breaths.

"Are you leaving again?" Isaac's voice surprised him. "Please don't go," his chin trembled.

Thomas knelt to the boy's level. "I'm not going anywhere. Aren't you supposed to be with Amelia?"

"But that man said—"

He wrapped his arms around Isaac. "I'm going for a ride around the village. Do you want to come with me?"

Isaac looked at him, and a smile broke out. "Can I?"

Thomas's chest lightened. "Of course you can. Have you ridden a horse before?"

"Yes, Uncle Graeme lets me ride with him."

My brother has seen more of my son growing up than I have. Bitterness crept in.

"Uncle Graeme? On his horse?" Thomas asked.

"Yes."

"Today, you ride *my* horse," he ruffled Isaac's hair.

"Why do you walk like that?" His son's eyes were on Thomas's leg.

"My leg hurts."

"Did someone hurt you?"

Not wanting to frighten or lie to his son, he paused at the stable door. "They did. But I'm all right. I will heal."

Isaac made a stabbing motion. "Did you hurt them back?"

His mouth fell open. Stifling a laugh, he led Isaac into the stable.

"I did."

"Good. I hope you stabbed them in the leg and that it hurts like yours. Or you chopped it off."

The vehemence in Isaac's tone was unexpected. A little boy should not have dark joy over such things. A possible effect of Graeme's influence. His brother had displayed the same glee when they were children. He would have to put a stop to that.

"Isaac, we do not take joy in the pain of others." Thomas lifted his son to his shoulders as he approached the horse stalls.

There she was. His beauty, Guinevere saddled and waiting. A magnificent black mare with a white mane and tail. A unique horse, one he had seen nowhere else.

A stable hand glanced up from brushing her down. "I have just taken her out as your brother instructed."

Thomas stepped into the stall. "Thank you. I will be taking my son for a ride."

The peasant simply nodded and stepped out of the way. Thomas rubbed Guinevere's neck.

"Hello, my girl, did you miss me, then?"

Guinevere nudged his side, her mouth searching. Two pieces of fruit had been placed in the trough, likely from James.

"Do you want to feed her?" Thomas held half an apple to Isaac.

"Will she bite me?"

"No, she eats fruit, not fingers." Thomas smoothed out Isaac's hand. "Hold it out, flat like this." He lay the fruit on Isaac's open palm.

Guinevere lowered her muzzle to the apple.

Isaac giggled. "It tickles!"

Guinevere crunched on the apple.

"See, all your fingers are still there."

Thomas lifted Isaac into the saddle, half-expecting the boy to have no balance. But as he led Guinevere from her stall, Isaac sat high and well-balanced in the saddle. His heart burst, swelling with pride. Graeme had taught Isaac well, but it should have been Thomas teaching his son how to ride. Hollow inside, Thomas hauled himself onto the horse behind Isaac.

To be called away as an Enforcer, he would only miss more of his son's life. His brother was the father figure *he* should be, and Thomas could do nothing about it.

There was a familiarity, riding past the homes of his neighbours. Many waved at him, their faces lighting up when they saw him. To them, he was Thomas Blake, taking his son for a ride. They didn't see an imposter, or the disgraced soldier who waved back at them with a forced smile. To them, he was the same Thomas who left four years ago, ready to earn his place among heroes. He was the boy they had generously farewelled on a sunny day just like this one. That pride was no more, his life forever changed while theirs remained the same. There was nothing heroic about war.

Thomas stopped in front of the burned-out church and climbed off his horse. He lifted Isaac, placing him on the ground. A cemetery lay in the shadow of the church, with a large tree in the corner. He found James standing over the graves of brothers lost during a war from before Thomas had been born.

"Uncle."

James looked around. "Thomas, you've rested already?"

"No."

James shot Thomas a look of understanding. "I remember what it was like."

A figure stood under the tree, watching him. *Caleb?!* Thomas closed his eyes. When he opened them, the figure was gone.

"Did you have nightmares?" he asked.

James hesitated. "I did. So did Ethan. But he had a farm to run and wasn't permitted time to hide from such things."

Thomas made his way over to James, Isaac trailing him in silence.

"What were they like?" he asked.

"Thomas, your namesake, was a lot like your brother. Just as his namesake was a lot like you."

"He was the best brother, then. Funny, charming, good-looking." Thomas couldn't resist the grin.

James chuckled. "Brazen, unsightly, wouldn't shut up." James's eyes were unfocused as if he were remembering. "He always watched out for me. For all of us. Just as you do for your brother."

"You told me to protect him."

"You never needed my telling you that," James studied him. "You took that on long before I said anything."

"I always will."

"But now you need to let Graeme be while you recover. I know what you are doing, and it will not work for long. Nightmares are your mind adjusting to what you've endured. Face them so you can move on. It's the best way to leave war behind." James pointed to Thomas's chest. "Let those scars heal." James raised his hand, pointing to Thomas's head. "And those ones."

Unable to say anything, Thomas nodded.

James's gaze remained on him. "Come on, let's look at the church. I know you're curious."

Thomas followed James, but stopped at a grave he usually visited in private.

Isobel Blake, a devoted wife. 1304 - 1323. Rest in peace.

This was the day she had died, giving birth to him and Graeme. Or rather, him. She was already dead by the time they cut Graeme from her corpse. His brother's presence had been unknown until a midwife had found life inside while tending to the body.

"This is where your grandmother rests," he told Isaac.

The boy stared at the grave. Thomas kept watch for Father.

"Hoping your father won't find that you still visit her?" James asked from behind him.

"I prefer to avoid reminding him that I'm the reason she's here," Thomas said.

"You still believe he blames you for that?"

"Doesn't he?"

James looked down at the grave. "I lost my brother the day she died. It's as if she took all the light with her. Now he's..." James stopped.

"An angry drunk," Thomas finished for him. "Who doesn't know how to be a father."

"You're too hard on him," James said.

"He was too hard *on us*. You have been more of a father to us than he ever was."

"Thomas, stop. Ethan may not be perfect, but he is still my brother."James glared.

Thomas motioned to Isaac. "I will never treat my children that way."

"From son to father, you have learned what you needed to from him." James folded his arms. "You're more like your father than you realise."

James said that often, and it still annoyed Thomas. In silence they walked to the church.

The thick odour of smoke and ash clung to the building. As he opened the door, it creaked, the charred wood flaking and black grit smeared on his hand. He wiped it on his tunic.

"We cannot go in there," Isaac said, his voice high. "It might fall down."

"It will not fall down, not yet," James said to Isaac. "But we are going to knock it down so we can rebuild it."

"How did this happen?" Thomas asked.

"Grandfather said God was angry," Isaac said. "Is He angry at us? At me?"

Thomas lowered himself to Isaac's height, brushing the boy's hair out of his eyes.

"Your grandfather says that about everything," he said.

The church was once a humble building, with a small cross at the front, wooden pews, and plain windows. Now, with the roof completely gone, the wooden walls blackened and half of the back wall caved in, it was hardly recognisable. The cross at the front had fallen over. This would help him readjust to being home.

"Welcome home, Thomas," yet another villager called out.

This time he could barely manage a smile. Tired of being on public display, he needed to be away from prying eyes and forced pleasantries.

"I will come by later," Thomas said.

All he wanted was quiet, but he wasn't ready to go home yet. Despite his best efforts, war had followed him home and waited for him every time he closed his eyes. Perhaps a drink would help drown out the noise. The tavern was close, and hopefully it would be quiet enough to get away from the attention.

"Don't forget what I said," James called out as Thomas returned to his horse.

He lifted Isaac into the saddle, and discomfort nudged at him. A notion that he should tell someone where he was going. Shrugging it off, he led Guinevere from the church.

Chapter 7

A wooden sign with 'Leo's' in large letters stood in front of the tavern. The owner was Leopold, but everyone called him Leo.

"What are we doing here?" Isaac asked.

Thomas opened the door. "Getting some quiet," he replied as he nudged Isaac inside. "We will not be here for long."

After the bright sunlight outside, the candlelit room appeared dark as his eyes adjusted. He made his way to the nearest table, the empty room quiet and calm. With Isaac seated at the table, Thomas signalled to Leo. The innkeeper had lost hair since Thomas last saw him. He was tall and brown-skinned with crinkles at the corner of his eyes from always smiling. Leo glanced down at Isaac.

"Milk and bread for him. I'll have ale," Thomas said.

Moments later, a tankard was placed on the table in front of him. Gulping back the drink, he tasted honey with an earthy flavouring. The ale washed away his low spirits. He set the empty vessel on the table. Leo returned and placed bread in front of Isaac. The boy looked at Thomas for permission.

"It's all right, you can eat, Isaac."

A fire in the corner enveloped the room in a cosy bubble. Leo returned with another tankard. The scent of the burning wood mixed with ale coaxed Thomas into happiness.

"It is on the house," Leo said. "A thank you to a war hero."

Thomas clenched his teeth together, his peace receding. *So much for getting away from the fuss.* But he couldn't say no to a free drink, so he graciously accepted.

"Are the rumours true? About the truce with France?" Leo asked.

Thomas nodded. The last thing he wanted was to talk about war. Or the truce. "The pestilence brought it to a halt… for now."

Leo let out an impressed whistle and placed a small tankard of milk in front of Isaac. The boy gripped his drink, beaming up at Thomas. He ruffled Isaac's hair, unable to hold back the wave of warmth and pride. He downed the ale, and a new drink immediately replaced the empty tankard. Thomas took a deep breath, and let his shoulders relax.

"Thomas!" Graeme's raised voice burst through the dark.

With a racing heart, Thomas rose, swaying on his feet. What? Where am I? The tavern! Isaac had lain down on the seat, asleep.

"Grim." His voice was thick. "Come to join me for a drink?"

Thomas reached for the tankard, only to find it empty. Oh. When did I finish that?

"Don't call me that, I thought you were resting."

"I was." For once there had been no nightmares, a blessing of the ale.

Graeme's eyes narrowed as Thomas dropped his weight to the seat.

"I was just…"

"You were taking Isaac to a tavern so you could get drunk? Emma's worried sick," Graeme informed him.

Oh, right. He had taken Isaac without a word to anyone.

"Does she at least get an explanation? Or Amelia since he was in her care?"

"Please, Graeme, I just need..." *What? More ale? Sleep? To be left alone?*

His brother knelt beside him. "I may not know what you're going through, but this isn't the way to deal with it."

"It is a good way to stop the nightmares." The words slipped out, and Thomas winced. The ale had made him a little too talkative.

Graeme's face was expressionless. "That's why you're here? To avoid dreams?"

Thomas put his head in his hands. "All I want is to drown out the noise. I see the same faces every time I close my eyes."

His brother squeezed his shoulder. "Dreamless sleep is not as pleasant as it sounds. It won't stop what's chasing you."

Thomas raised his head. "Like what chased you?" Graeme averted his gaze.

Memories of what happened when they were eight washed over him. Thomas's nightmares had been a lot different then. Graeme's inability to dream had manifested into something that haunted them both for many years.

Thomas awoke from a nightmare, cold and shaking. As he caught his breath, fear squeezed inside his stomach. It was coming from Graeme. Thomas left his bed and sought out his brother, finding him whimpering in the kitchen with unblinking eyes.

"Grim, what are you doing here?" Thomas ran to his brother. "If Father finds you, he'll be angry."

"It's coming to get me," Graeme whispered, his whole body trembling. "Don't let it take me, Tom."

Thomas followed Graeme's stare, finding nothing there.

"Are you having a nightmare?" Thomas asked.

"This is not from a dream. It is watching me in the dark."

"But there is nothing there." Thomas put his arm around his brother's shoulder. "Are you sure it wasn't a nightmare?"

"I don't have dreams."

"You don't? Then what do you see when you sleep?"

Graeme's hair fell into his eyes. "Nothing. Only black, until I wake."

Thomas led Graeme upstairs to the bedroom. "Maybe your dreams show when you're awake. There was nothing there."

"There are things watching us, Tom, shadows from a dark world. They whisper to me. It wants to take me with it." Graeme shivered.

Chills moved up Thomas's arms. He'd had this dream, of the shadows. The very nightmare he had just woken from. A dark presence waiting for something, whispering to him.

"I won't let it take you," he promised. "I'll protect you."

But as he walked his brother to his bed, Thomas sensed the same presence from his dream. Fear became a cold fist within his chest, and he fought the urge to run. It was in his brother.

"Tom, are you listening to me?" Graeme's voice pulled him from the memory.

Thomas suppressed a shudder. His dreams now were not the result of whatever shadowed presence lay within his brother. He battled against a Darkness of his own.

"I know you want me to talk about it, but I can't. Not yet," he couldn't meet Graeme's eyes.

Graeme rose. "Then you need to sleep. You may think you're shielding yourself, but I feel your anguish, Thomas. And your exhaustion. You can't keep this up." He lifted Isaac. "Are you coming?"

His brother was right; he needed to sleep. But now he had a way to hold off the nightmares.

"Not yet."

Thomas waved at Leo. The innkeeper brought him another ale as Graeme made his way out with Isaac. A figure stood in the doorway, eyes on him. Unsure if he was seeing an apparition or being haunted, Thomas downed the entire tankard, signalling for another. The ghost disappeared.

Chapter 8

It was much later in the day when Thomas finally found his way home. The temperature had dropped, and clouds had settled over Riverwick. At the front door, Emma's lips were pressed together, her cheeks flushed as she put her hands on her hips.

She spoke quietly. "You took our son to the alehouse?"

"Graeme, I heard your brother is back," a voice cut in. "Is he going with you to the manor tomorrow, or will you be taking workers?"

Emma clicked her tongue at the interruption, her eyes narrow. Thomas held his hand up, then faced the owner of the voice. The man speaking was among a handful of peasant farmers who didn't work for the lord of the manor. Thomas's family often hired him during harvest season.

"That's something for you to take up with my brother," Thomas said. "I'm sure he would appreciate your help, though."

The peasant did a double-take. "Thomas. Sorry, I thought you were your brother. It's not easy telling you two apart."

Emma huffed.

"So I've heard," he said. The peasant didn't leave. "I'll tell Grim that you offered your service. Is there anything else?"

"No. Thank you." The peasant hurried away, leaving Thomas to Emma.

"I didn't know where he was, Thomas," she said.

Rubbing her arm, he met her cold stare. "He was safe with me, Em."

She pushed his arm away. "But you fell asleep!"

"Not something I intended to do."

Her anger was like icy water. She held her chin high. "That doesn't make it better."

Thomas tried to move around her. His focus drifted, and keeping his eyes open became more difficult. "Can we please talk about this later?"

Emma blocked his way. "No, we're not finished here."

With effort, he leaned in to kiss her.

Emma turned her head away from him. "Ugh. Your breath stinks."

He held his hand up to his mouth, breathing into it. His hot breath returned, the slight scent of ale.

Her eyes welled with tears. "What were you thinking? You're back half a day, and you take our son and fall asleep at the alehouse. What's the matter with you?"

Swaying, he bowed his head. Everything in him desired to lie down. Unsure he could stand without support, he put his hand against the doorframe.

"Emma, please let me pass. I cannot have this conversation right now."

"Why not? Because you're drunk? Is that not what you hate about your *own* father?"

He tensed, and a flash of irritation spread throughout him.

"One afternoon hardly compares to a lifetime of it," he said. "I'm sorry I took Isaac with me. I only sought to spend time with him. I didn't think."

"You don't think. That's the problem! Thomas, you haven't been here. I've always known where Isaac was. He never leaves the house without me or Amelia. She and Graeme were just as worried as I was."

Thomas faked a yawn, hoping she would back down and let him go. In doing so, his eyes watered as he let out a real yawn.

"Don't think I don't know what you're doing. You're not actually listening to a word I'm saying, are you?"

When did Emma get so stern? They had argued before, but she'd always given in. Now, she met his eyes without flinching.

"No!" he snapped, his voice rising. "I'm not listening, because you're standing in my way while all I want is to go upstairs and sleep. Let me pass, woman!"

Amelia appeared behind Emma and shot him a warning look.

"Just say you're sorry," Amelia said. "While you were drinking yourself into a stupor, we were scared someone had snatched him."

Graeme's anger earlier made sense. Thomas's thoughtlessness had put that on his family. "Oh." He put his hand to his chest. "I'm sorry, I'll do better."

Emma moved aside. Thomas kicked off his shoes and made his way upstairs. Behind him, Emma straightened his shoes, the women murmuring too low for him to hear what they were saying.

Thomas jolted awake, sitting up. An ache in his stomach told him something was wrong. It was too quiet as he strained to recognise where he was. Nothing appeared familiar in the dim room, and he let his eyes adjust. Where am I? I'm in a bed. How did I get here? Have I been taken prisoner? His breaths echoed in his ears, loud and gasping. A prickling sensation crawled up his back, and he broke into a sweat.

"Thomas."

He jerked his head towards the voice. A figure stood in the doorway.

"Who's there?" he croaked. *Where's my sword?*

"It's Amelia. Are you hungry? Come down for food."

My bedroom. I'm at home. The racing of his heart slowed down, and he flopped back onto the bed with a loud breath. He fought the urge to close his eyes again.

"Thomas?" she pressed.

"I'll be down," he said. "I just need a moment."

She left the doorway, and the stairs creaked as she descended. Gone were the all-too-familiar sounds of swords clanging and cries of pain and the smell of the dying. Yearning for the open sky and the warmth of the fire took him by surprise. Sitting amongst his brothers in arms, drinking and sharing stories of their homes. He had become too accustomed to war, and now his bed and home were strange and unfamiliar.

The wild smell of venison trailed up the stairs through his open door. With his stomach rumbling, he followed the mouth-watering scent downstairs. His insides churned. It had been a long time since he had sat opposite Father at the dinner table, and if this morning's unpleasant reaction was anything to go by, this would be just as awkward. He had faced his father's constant disappointment and judgement his entire life. The only time Father had shown pride was the day the summons had arrived. But it was not out of pride for Thomas. It meant glory for the Blake name. Whether he died in battle or came back a hero, it would reflect on Ethan Blake. Isaac would never experience that. He would grow up knowing his father was proud of him no matter what.

Thomas entered the kitchen. Amelia and Emma were sitting at the table, waiting, Isaac at the end with a look of impatience. Candles had been placed at the centre of the table, their light giving the room a soft, warm glow. Food lay spread across the table. His mouth watered again.

"Where did you get the venison?" he asked.

"James gave us his," Emma told him.

The aroma of freshly baked bread and vegetable pottage filled him with warmth. In the centre of the table sat a large pie, probably chicken. Amelia stood, pouring ale for everyone.

"What is this? Are we expecting guests?" Graeme asked, entering the room.

"We are celebrating your day of birth, and Thomas's return," Father said from behind Graeme. He gestured for Graeme to move, before turning his attention to Thomas. Dread gripped Thomas as he met Father's eyes, waiting for the vitriol.

"Are you waiting for an invitation to sit?" Father asked as he took his place at the head of the table.

Numb, Thomas sat next to Emma. Graeme mouthed the word *James* to him. *Yes, this is James's doing. It would be better if he were here.*

The food smelled heavenly. On the front lines, he had eaten the same thing for the last four years. Bean soup, apples and berries, cabbage, carrots, and radishes. Occasionally they hunted game or received a donation of cattle. Emma beamed at Thomas, and he took her hand, squeezing it. Their argument from earlier seemed forgotten. *Has she forgiven me, or will I hear about it later?* Raising her hand to his mouth, he kissed her fingers.

Father watched him. Thomas's apprehension had returned, his face hot under Father's hard stare. In his childhood, he had taken Father's treatment of him to be hatred. Blame for Mother's death. Being summoned to war had been a relief, a chance to experience the world beyond. Time away from Father to cool his bitterness. As he stared across the table at his father, refusing to shrink away, it all came rushing back. The never-ending expectations and demands.

Graeme had taken his seat next to Amelia on the opposite side of the table. Father finally averted his gaze, bowing his head. Everyone followed suit, and Father led them into the prayer.

Emma served up their son's plate and placed it in front of Isaac. She let out a slight gasp as she returned to her seat, her eyes lighting up. Reaching for Thomas's hand, she placed it on her belly. A flutter moved under his hand. His face broke into a wide smile. Pushing a strand of hair behind her ear with his free hand, he waited for more.

"That's all you get tonight," Emma laughed.

Thomas kissed the back of her hand and caught Graeme watching. The pain Graeme and Amelia had endured at the loss of their daughter clearly remained. The urge to feel sympathetic for his brother was outweighed by the pride and elation singing in his heart. He didn't want to feel his brother's grief. This was his and Emma's moment..

The radiance in Emma brought him joy. Thomas caressed her cheek. "You're beautiful," he murmured. He leaned forward to whisper in her ear. "When I get you alone tonight—"

"Enough of that. Not while I'm trying to eat." Father ordered.

Thomas gave Emma a smirk before turning back to his food.

Remember what you did. You don't deserve happiness. There it was. His heart pounded. Gone were the joyful tears, replaced by shame and remorse. The food tasted like dirt, the warmth stifling. That peace he desired would never be. The violence of war would not let him go; his duty meant he was not free. His actions would always be close by to steal any moments of happiness. There was no peace for him, no release from his obligation to the king and to Lord Samson. He forced a smile to hide the pain from his family.

Chapter 9

The blade almost got past his defence. Metal thudded against his sickle, and The Shadow stepped back to steady his footing. But his opponent followed through, striking hard. Pain shot through his arm as metal sliced flesh. With a grunt, The Shadow struck back.

"Not going how you planned?" the man in front of him taunted. "What do you expect when you attack someone more skilled than you?"

The Shadow remained silent as he tried to find a way past the man's defences. He had been awoken and drawn back into this cold, bleak world, leaving behind the comfort of the Shadow Realm. Street cleaners had run from him when he appeared in their midst. Driven towards a new kill, he'd quickly found this mortal, who was not ready to die.

He sliced down with the sickle, satisfied to hit something other than metal. But it wasn't deep enough. The fighter didn't pause as he scuffled forward, attacking with a forward thrust. The Shadow's sickle glided over steel as he pushed the blade out and away from his body.

Kill him, the familiar command urged.

"If you're going to try to kill me, at least tell me who you are."

"I am your death," The Shadow said.

Amusement shone from behind his opponent's eyes, followed by a snort. Quick footsteps thudded against stone. A sword thumped with each step as someone drew closer, running. He was about to be outnumbered. The cries of the street cleaners had drawn unwanted attention.

Stop stalling. Kill him, the voice thundered against the inside of his skull. Time was running out to fulfil his purpose. His connection to the Shadow Realm was fading. *Will I cease to exist, or return to the life that was taken from me?* Not wanting either, he gave in to the Darkness that lived deep in his heart. Empowered, he let the shadows close around him.

"Where are you?" The mortal's words had a quiver to them.

Shivers crawled over the back of his neck. The Shadow spun around. Someone was watching him. It was possible that a lost soul drawn to his energy had seen his fight. Unwilling to be distracted from the hunt, The Shadow forced himself to cross through the veil again. He emerged behind the confused mortal. With a quick movement, the outside of his sickle pressed into his throat, forcing the man to kneel.

"Drop your sword." A burst of triumph made him smile as the sword clattered on the ground.

One-handed, The Shadow picked up the discarded sword. He had wanted to savour the kill, draw out the fight, to give his quarry hope that he had a fighting chance.

"If you're hoping for begging, you'll not get it from me." The man's defiance in the face of death was a failed attempt to stretch out his miserable life.

"It was your fate to die tonight," he whispered.

The Shadow sliced across the exposed throat. The body slumped to the ground, staring up at the sky. The light faded from those eyes, his final breath barely audible. Another soul for the Shadow Realm.

"Drop your weapon," the armoured runner had arrived.

He spun around, holding the stolen sword high just as a downward strike hit. His new attacker wore black leather armour and a grey cloak.

"You're too late."

"You are the one we're hunting. You killed Lord Philip."

"I am. I did."

With his chin raised and hard, cold eyes he met The Shadow's. "You're going to burn. Maybe they'll torture you first."

"That may be so, but not tonight."

He waited for the command to kill. But it was silent. With a heavy heart, he lowered his weapons, throwing the sword to the ground.

"It is not your time to die. You live another night," The Shadow said.

It was time to go back, yet he hesitated. There was no call to kill this man, but with blood newly spilled and the thrill of the hunt still energising him, he wanted to. The need to return to the Shadow Realm soon exceeded his desire to take another life. Finally, he withdrew. The presence from earlier remained. This was not a lost soul, as he had first suspected, nor a shade, but a man. His watcher had emerged during a hunt, just like last night. From behind the fog, he caught sight of piercing blue eyes, in which shadows lurked. While human souls blazed with radiant colours of light, the energy that shone from this one did not. Beneath the surface was a great void, as if Darkness itself had claimed the mortal.

"Are you the one who called me forth?" The Shadow asked, only to be met with silence.

The figure in the fog vanished.

Perhaps next time I can push him to embrace his darker self. Invite him to the hunt. If that fails, I'll just kill him.

Chapter 10

Thomas lay in the grass, hands behind his head. Above him, stars and a full moon shone from the clear sky. Echoes of laughter, conversations, and the crackle of fire swirled around him. Unsure if in the village or just phantoms, Thomas's attempts to dismiss the sounds only heightened them. He sat up, removed the wooden cork from a leather flask, and took a drink.

The summons hung over him like a noose. What he wanted most was to stay with his wife. To be a father to Isaac and the new baby. War had taken him from his family, and he had missed so much of their lives. He could be there for his brother again. Thomas had never wanted to be a farmer as Graeme did, but after the horrors he had seen and committed, the quiet life now seemed more appealing.

But to ignore a summons would mean imprisonment or death. To be an Enforcer — *I do not belong in such a dishonourable duty. The people of Riverwick and Kempschester should not have a reason to look upon me with fear. I've never wanted this.* Thomas lifted the flask to his mouth again, wishing the ale would numb the pitching in his stomach. There was only one reason Lord Samson had called upon him for this. With a groan, Thomas lay back again, one arm behind his head and the other over his eyes.

The creak of the door opening, followed by a thud as it closed, alerted Thomas that someone had walked outside. Graeme's anguish crowded his own. A loud, shaky sigh forced him to sit up. The silhouette of his brother stood at the doorway.

"Grim?" Graeme jumped at his voice. "That was a serious-sounding sigh there, brother." Thomas laughed.

"Tom? What are you doing out here?"

"You're going to pretend you didn't know I was out here?" Thomas held up the flask and shook it.

"Should I be worried?" Graeme asked.

"Calm yourself, will you?" Thomas said.

"Is this still about you not being haunted by dreams?"

Another gulp of ale. "I may have left the war, but it isn't done with me."

"Does it work?" Graeme asked as he sat.

"Mostly," Thomas admitted

His brother grabbed the flask and drank from it.

"Why would you need to stop? You don't dream." Thomas took the ale back.

"It seems I do now," Graeme said.

Thomas scratched his jaw. "How long has this been going on?"

"A few weeks."

"What does the man who never dreams dream about?"

There was a hush as Thomas waited for his brother to reply. Darkness seethed within Graeme. A sense of dark hunger and fear flickered through.

"Are you going to talk about receiving another summons mere hours after you returned? Or were you planning on telling us as you waved goodbye?"

Heat flamed in his cheeks and ears. Thomas opened his mouth, but no words came out.

"Do you think I am an idiot?" Graeme asked with a gruff voice. "What is the summons for, Thomas? Are you going back to France? I thought we had a truce with them."

Thomas scoffed. "No, I'm not going back to France."

"Then what is it? I'm guessing you haven't told Emma yet, either."

Graeme took the flask from Thomas's hand.

"It's not long-term. Lord Philip was murdered—"

Thomas's words were cut off by Graeme choking on ale.

"Give me that!" Thomas seized the drink from Graeme's grasp. "No more for you. Amateur. What's wrong with you?"

"Lord Philip was murdered?" Graeme asked, his voice quiet.

"Lord Samson wants me to help bring in the killer, serve him justice."

"Justice?" Graeme repeated.

"Why are you echoing my words?" Thomas asked.

In the moonlight, Graeme's eyes almost appeared black, his expression unreadable. Thomas's skull prickled, as a cold breath of air ran across his neck and sent a shiver down his spine. Something was out of place. The Darkness was watching Thomas through Graeme's eyes, its presence crushing his chest, suffocating. Just as quickly, it receded, and Thomas could breathe again. *Is it stronger? Why would it be stronger?*

"Why you? Is that not what Enforcers are for? Leave it up to them. Lord Samson didn't need to ride out to a farm for you. He's got men trained for that," Graeme reasoned.

Words escaped Thomas. Of all people, he dreaded telling his brother the most.

"You?" Graeme's voice rose. "An Enforcer? With all they do, you cannot want to be a part of that."

Light-headed, Thomas finished the last of the ale. "You know it's not something I would ever *want* to do. I don't want to leave Emma again, nor Isaac. Nor you. I belong here. If it was you summoned, you'd have no choice but to go, just as I don't."

Reality sank in for Thomas. He didn't have a choice. There was no escape from joining the Enforcers. Numb, he took in a deep breath.

"But they didn't summon me. They summoned you," Graeme turned away from Thomas. "Again." The word was under his breath, but Thomas caught it.

"Are you pouting?"

Graeme didn't answer.

"You hate Enforcers as much as I do. But you are offended you did not get recruited as one?" *Unbelievable!*

Graeme cleared his throat. "I seem to elude these things. Do they think me incapable?"

"Be glad. War was unpleasant, just as this will be."

There was a reason Graeme had not been summoned to war. He would never find out.

"What will you say to Emma?" Graeme asked.

The question made Thomas wince. "I do not know."

"Is that the real reason you are out here? To avoid her?" Graeme's voice shook as if he were suppressing laughter.

"If you must know, yes. I'm avoiding the argument that it will raise. I don't want to do this to her again," Thomas replied.

A slight breeze ruffled Thomas's hair, and a dog barked in the distance.

"You have to tell her," Graeme said.

"This is your fault, you know," Thomas accused.

"How is this my fault?" Graeme demanded, his voice tight.

"You let Amelia behave wildly. She is an influence on Emma. The way she speaks is not—"

Graeme jumped to his feet. "Don't blame my wife for the reason you're too scared to tell yours that you're leaving again! As an Enforcer!"

The door opened. "You're leaving again? You promised me you were here to stay!" Emma spoke softly.

Thomas rose to his feet. Emma stood in the doorway, her features in shadow. Behind her, Amelia held a candle, yellow light reflecting on her face.

Emma held up parchment, and his heart sank. He had left the summons where she could find it.

"You better go," he told Graeme in a hushed tone.

Graeme patted Thomas on the back as he walked past. Emma, still in the doorway, let Graeme through. Graeme mumbled something to Amelia as the door closed, and her response was just as low.

"You should be in bed," Thomas said.

"Do not try to change the subject, Thomas!" Emma cried. "You thought you could hide this from me?!" She waved the letter at him.

Thomas squeezed her hand. "Emma, please, the baby."

"The baby is not causing me distress; it is you." A sob in the dark almost brought him to his knees. "Why would you not tell me?" she pleaded. "If I'm to watch you leave again, tell me the reason. Why you?"

Thomas couldn't find the words his wife needed. Emma pulled her hands away. Heaviness pressed against his chest.

"When I saw you in the kitchen this morning, I thought it meant we could finally be a family. I was so relieved to have you home," she said, and took a deep breath. "Since then, you have lied, kept secrets, taken our son without anyone's knowledge, taken him to a tavern, and told your brother before me that you're now an Enforcer."

"You're angry that I told Grim first? I could not keep anything from my brother if I tried." He swallowed down frustration.

"I'm angry that you had the whole day to tell me. When were you going to say something?"

Her voice rose, and Thomas fought the urge to raise his own.

"I didn't want to accept the summons," he said. "All I wanted was to return to what I left behind. You. Isaac." He placed a hand on her belly, and she tensed. "Our family. I want you, Em."

Thomas cupped her face with both hands, finding her cheeks wet. He wiped her tears away, leaning his forehead against hers. Emma's hands hovered over his as if she were struggling to let go of her anger. Finally, her fingers wrapped around his wrists. A shuddering sigh forced her warm breath against his mouth and she pulled his hands down, and turned her face to the side. She moved away, putting distance between them.

"You claim you want these things, yet you still lied to me. What am I supposed to say to that? Not only do I find out in your failed attempt to hide it, but from a conversation not meant for my ears," she cried.

Thomas took a step towards her, but Emma held up a hand to stop him, stepping back. Everything he had dreamed of was slipping away. *Four years of fighting for my life, only to now be fighting for a woman I've only been with for two of the six years we've been married.*

"I've hurt you," he acknowledged, his own heart aching.

"You have," she agreed. "I want what's best for us. All of us. But I cannot do this if you have such disregard for me. Maybe you leaving is for the best."

Fresh tears reflected on her cheeks in the moonlight. Emma left him alone in the dark. Breathless, Thomas reeled from her words.

Chapter 11

Thomas ran a hand over Emma's empty side of the bed, finding it cold. The sun having barely risen, he fought the urge to roll over and go back to sleep. But Lord Samson had made it clear that Thomas was to be at the manor. Still unwilling to accept his life as an Enforcer, he considered running. *No. Lord Samson will have me hunted no matter where I go, and Emma will never leave Riverwick.*

With effort, he forced himself from the bed. As he pulled on clothes, Emma's words repeated themselves. To prove her wrong, he would make sure to come home with haste. He grinned. If the murderer was captured, he could return. Overwhelmed with the hope that burst within him, his mood lightened.

Footsteps thudded up the stairs, and a door opened to the bedroom next to his. Amelia's muffled voice speaking to Graeme on the other side of the wall, followed by silence, filled Thomas with sympathy. The loss of their daughter had put a strain on their marriage. But to still be struggling after all these years made it seem as though they would not mend what they had. The footsteps trailed from Graeme's room downstairs again.

Graeme's strange behaviour from last night and his mention of dreams returned. Thomas knelt at the bed, pulling out a wooden box. James had given him the box years ago when Thomas had told him about the nightmares. Filled with leather-bound books, the box had remained hidden. Grabbing a journal not written in, he put the box back where it belonged.

He knocked on the door to Graeme's bedroom. "Grim?" he called out. "Are you awake?"

A groan sounded through the door.

He took that as an invitation and opened the door as Graeme sat up, hair hanging over part of his face. Dark circles shadowed his eyes. Thomas threw the journal onto the bed.

"What's that?" Graeme asked, eyeing the book.

"What does it look like?"

Graeme kept his head down. "Why are you giving me this?"

"Write in it. It might help with those dreams of yours."

Graeme climbed from the bed, putting the journal on his desk. "Thank you. Maybe it will help." He turned back to Thomas. "How did it go with Emma?"

Thomas flinched.

"Was it that bad?" Graeme asked.

"You were right; I should have told her," he said.

"She didn't take it very well?"

Thomas shook his head. "It was one of our worst fights yet. She's never been this way before." Thomas sat on the side of Graeme's bed.

"Been what way?" Graeme prompted.

"So unyielding."

Graeme sat beside Thomas. "That bothers you?"

Thomas leaned forward and bowed his head. "No. The fighting does, though. I hate to see her so upset."

"At least you fight."

"Grim, you cannot believe that Amelia's silence is because she doesn't care. She's hurting as much as you are." Thomas sat next to Graeme. "The two of you are caught up in your own pain. You both lost your daughter in an awful tragedy. I cannot begin to know what that's like." The memory of the river carrying away his niece would never leave him. "For all we know, your silence has convinced her that you don't care. Talk to her. I don't know why you haven't tried already."

Graeme gave him a small smile. "Is that elder twin wisdom?"

"If you want to call it that."

Silence stretched out. Thomas tapped his foot.

"I still hear Mary's cries. Every morning," Graeme said

Thomas's heart broke for his brother. He put a hand on his brother's shoulder. "That's what you need to share with your wife. Let your grief bond you together, not tear you apart." He stood, taking in Graeme's night attire. "Now get changed so we can go downstairs. I don't want to be down there alone with those two. I am not good at awkward silences."

"Is it that bad?" Graeme asked as Thomas opened the door.

He raised his eyebrows as Amelia's and Emma's voices echoed up the stairs. "Oh yes."

CHAPTER 11

They entered the kitchen, and the chatter stopped. Their wives' eyes turned towards Graeme and Thomas. Side-eyeing each other, they took their places at the table. Emma and Amelia put wooden bowls of porridge in front of them. The sweet aroma of nutmeg and cinnamon made his mouth water, and his stomach grumbled.

"I'll ride with you when you go," Thomas said to fill the silence. "Did you get villagers to help you?"

"They've already started loading the cart," Father said, appearing at the door. Graeme and Thomas were immediately on their feet. "Which is what the two of you should be doing. Get going. When you get back I need you to dig a new well."

"Father, I will not be back today," Thomas said.

Emma lowered her gaze, clasping her hands.

"Why not? Have you got somewhere else to be?" Father glowered at him.

"I'm joining the Enforcers," Thomas informed his father.

Father's lip curled. "You'd do anything to get out of farming."

Stunned into silence as Father left, Thomas bit back his anger. A flicker of sympathy radiated from his brother. Thomas rushed his way through breakfast, aware that Graeme was rushing too.

"I should go," Thomas said, pushing his bowl forward. "I do not want to be late."

"Me too," Graeme followed him as they made a hasty exit.

It was freezing outside, and a thick fog hung over the village.

James waved at them from his cart, as he and John started their journey to the manor. Their own cart was being loaded by three harvesters who worked for his family. Father's horse was secured to the front of the cart.

Isaac, dressed in a small brown cloak, was watching the workers. When he noticed Thomas, he ran towards him.

"Please don't go, Father!" Isaac cried, wrapping his arms around Thomas's legs.

Amelia and Emma followed them outside. Amelia handed Thomas his sword before giving them both cloaks. To Graeme, a black cloak, and Thomas grabbed his brown one, the wool soft against his skin as he put it around his shoulders.

"Make the most of that. You'll soon be wearing grey," Graeme muttered.

Thomas and Graeme stepped in to help load the cart. Wool, eggs, pails of milk and cheese, wheat and grain from the harvest.

"Saddle Guinevere," Graeme said to one of their workers. "my brother will be going to the manor today."

"I want a sword like yours," Isaac stared wide-eyed at his sword.

Thomas sat on the edge of the cart, motioning for Isaac to join him, and lifted the boy up. He drew the sword, resting the blade on his hand.

"You will need to learn to use one first. I will teach you to fight when you are old enough."

"I am old enough!" Isaac declared.

Laughter burst from Thomas. "No Isaac, not yet."

Isaac pointed at a scythe engraved on the blad. "What's that?"

"That is the tool of our trade. Grim's sword has this; so do the swords of James and your grandfather. Farmers. Reapers. My grandfather worked hard to earn his freedom. He purchased this farm so that we can be free men."

"Will I have to fight in a war, too?" Isaac asked in a trembling voice.

The question was unexpected. The silence was deafening as Isaac waited for an answer.

Amelia stepped in. "Your father went to war so that you will not have to."

Isaac didn't seem satisfied with the answer. "So, it's over? We won?"

Thomas re-sheathed his sword.

"The war stopped temporarily. I was released from my duty so I could come home to you."

"Released?" Graeme asked.

Thomas avoided his brother's eyes and stood. "If I don't leave now, my absence will be considered a reason to come looking for me." He searched Emma's face for any sign that she had thawed after last night's anger. "Emma?"

Emma wrapped her arms around him, and her face pressed into his shoulder. "I'm always saying goodbye to you. I will be glad when your duty has ended."

"I'm only in Kempschester," he told her. "I hope to finish this hunt within the week so I can come home."

"Can you take Isaac to the manor? Graeme can bring him back when he returns."

Isaac was still on the edge of the cart, legs dangling.

"You want me to…?" Thomas frowned.

"It will give you time with him, and me time to rest," Emma said.

Isaac had been watching them and smiled with excitement. "I can go with you?"

"Only to the manor. Not when I go to town. You'll return with Uncle Graeme."

Father approached from the stable.

"But why can't I go to town, too?" Isaac asked.

"You want to be an Enforcer, but you don't want him to see?" Father asked.

Thomas crossed his arms. *This was not a conversation I wanted to have with my son. Why are you always ruining things?*

"Ethan! Why would you say that?" Amelia's voice was elevated, her eyes narrow. "You would have him fear his father?"

"Amelia," Graeme warned, paling.

Despite the moment, Thomas held back laughter. Amelia's manner was usually frustrating. Her habit of speaking boldly and out of turn had influenced Emma somewhat. But she stood up to Father, and it was satisfying to watch the old man spluttering and red-faced. She was originally from Willowdale, an isolated village in Willow Grove. There was a spark of defiance in her that Graeme clearly could not rein in. Knowing Graeme, he had probably been attracted to her for it. Her lack of fear showed that she had been allowed to say as she pleased in her home. Thomas glanced at Father. The old man likely regretted the agreement he'd made with Amelia's father. He did not seem to appreciate Amelia speaking the way she had. He turned his icy stare on Amelia, then to Graeme, as if expecting him to reprimand her.

"Isaac, time to go," Thomas urged.

"Are you an Enforcer?" Isaac's voice wavered.

Father chuckled. "Your father will have to let go of his precious honour to be an Enforcer. But most men eventually do. It comes with the job. No man can resist the corruption of that power."

Thomas attempted to force down his burning rage and lost.

"Father, stop! Amelia was right. I will not stand for you scaring my son the same way you scared us." His voice came out more aggressive than he would have liked in front of Isaac. Father's thunderous glare that once terrified Thomas only enraged him more. "Go. Go back inside and drink yourself stupid. It's what you do best. You do not speak that way in front of my son."

Graeme's mouth was open as Father stormed off. "What did you do that for? He's only going to take it out on me."

"Then stay out of his way. You too, Amelia." He did not doubt for an instant that Father would find reason to intimidate Amelia after her words. "Come, Isaac, we are leaving."

Isaac hid behind Emma then, peeking at Thomas from behind her dress. As he took a step forward, the boy ran, afraid.

Cursing under his breath, Thomas scowled at Father's back. He took a step after his son. "Isaac! Hurry up!" He faced Emma. "I don't have time for this."

"Isaac, your father called you," Emma said, her voice gentle. "Time to go."

"No!" Isaac said, voice shaking. "He's an Enforcer! Don't let them take me!"

"No one is going to take you," Thomas insisted. "Come here, we need to leave now!"

Chilled by fear, Thomas tried again to reach for Isaac. *Now is not the time for this. I should have left already*. The longer he delayed, the more likely his arrest would be called for.

Isaac ran out of his reach. Emma followed to comfort him. His flash of irritation spiked, and he sighed. "Isaac, come here *now!*" Thomas's voice boomed across the farm. His head rang from the pounding in his ears.

The edges of his vision darkened.

"Thomas, what are you...? Thomas, stop!" Emma screamed at him, but her voice was far away.

"Thomas!" Graeme's words were quiet as he reached for Thomas's wrist, pulling Isaac's arm from his grip. "Thomas, you're hurting him."

As his vision began to clear, he met Graeme's eyes. How many times had Graeme uttered those words to Father? He released his grasp on his son's arm. Isaac's lips and chin trembled; his eyes squeezed shut.

"What's the matter with you?" Graeme asked.

Isaac ran to Emma. She wiped his eyes, kissing his forehead.

"Shhhh, it's all right," Emma cooed.

He was no better than his own father. Shaking his head, he turned, but Graeme stopped him with a vice grip around his upper arm.

"If you run from this now, you are like Father."

Despite the growing urgency to leave, he lowered himself to his son's level. Emma wrapped her hand around Isaac's and started to walk away.

"No, let me talk to him."

There were tears in Emma's eyes as she gazed at him. "I think you've said enough. You should go."

He rose, stepping into her path, his jaw tight as frustration surged. "Remember who you're talking to."

Her eyes bored into his. "I know who I'm talking to. Your son fears you right now. So do I. You've *never* raised your voice like that. Please, just let us go."

She was right. Thomas had sworn to never turn his anger on his wife and child. He turned his eyes to Isaac. The boy was staring at his feet, but glanced up at Thomas, his eyes wide. He was terrified. Of Thomas.

"I'm sorry, Em. You know I didn't mean that."

Emma sighed. "Never again."

Just two words, spoken quietly. But they burned into his mind. Stepping out of her way, he let them go.

Chapter 12

T*his is it. There is no turning back now.* Cold with dread, Thomas pulled his horse to a stop. The gates to the manor emerged from the fog, blocked by guards. A large archway towered above the road. He fought the impulse to turn and ride the way he'd come. Back to Emma and the farm that he'd once despised so much.

"Are you ready for this?" Graeme asked from the front of the cart.

"No."

Fealty and service would always be weights on his shoulders that he could not escape, taking him further from where he wanted to be. This new duty would take him to a dark place if he let it.

"Do not let this claim you," Graeme said. "You can never be like them."

Graeme's words were hollow. Enforcers might have started out with good intentions. They were created to protect the people, serve justice to those who broke the law. But the nobles soon dominated whose interests took priority. It did not take long for the sons of nobility to lay claim to the Enforcers, filling their ranks with their distorted views, privilege, and corruption. Those inducted were swept up in the notion of justice, only to find themselves against those they sought to protect. Now known for their brutality, interrogations, and prejudice, their search for Kempschester's latest threat would likely lead to senseless bloodshed.

Graeme prompted Father's horse forward.

"State your name and business," a guard demanded. He had a bent nose and eyes that showed boredom.

"Graeme Blake. Uhh, taxes."

The guard held up a book, reading through until he found what he was looking for. "Riverwick?"

"That's right."

The guard pointed to the two men sitting behind Graeme. "Them?"

"They work for me," Graeme said.

"Go through," The guard directed him.

The guard glanced up at Thomas and did a double-take, staring back at Graeme.

"Thomas Blake. I'm here by summons."

"Show me."

The summons! He had not thought to bring it with him. "You want to see it?"

"That's why I asked," the guard's tone was sharp.

"I do not have it," Thomas admitted as Graeme passed through the gate.

"Then you're not getting in."

"Can you not tell Lord Samson I'm here?" Panic turned to stone in his stomach. "I'm to report to him, and he does not tolerate delays."

"Then you should have brought the summons. You are not getting in without it."

Frustration rose, choking Thomas, and his hands tightened around the leather reins.

"You let my brother through," Thomas pointed out.

"He's on the record of farmers expected this week."

On the other side of the gate, carts filled with various supplies fell in line in front of a large stable. The open door revealed tributes already left by other farmers. Enforcers gathered in the middle of the courtyard, many familiar faces. The manor itself, made of stone, was three levels built for luxury and comfort.

Three men bearing the Enforcer uniform approached and were waved through.

Thomas held out his hand, palm up at the retreating Enforcers, raising an eyebrow.

"They're Enforcers. I've been instructed to let them pass," the guard said.

"I'm with them. I'm an Enforcer." Uncomfortable with the admission, Thomas shifted in his saddle. The words gave him an overwhelming sense that his life had forever changed.

The guard looked him up and down. "Then where is your uniform?"

"I don't have one," Thomas muttered, losing hope.

"Get off your horse," another guard approached Thomas, hand on sword.

Two more stepped in, the four surrounding Guinevere. One grabbed the reins where they joined the bridle. Guinevere whinnied, ears twitching. Soothing her, Thomas rubbed her neck.

"What are you doing?" he asked. "I'm supposed to be in there."

"Get off your horse now, or I will *force* you off." The guard who spoke to him had a large forehead and a chipped tooth.

With no choice but to comply, Thomas gritted his teeth and dismounted. The very thing he had been trying to avoid was happening, and it was no fault but his own.

"On your knees."

People turned towards him out of curiosity. Thomas caught Graeme watching with his jaw slack. His brother mouthed something and started to rise, but Thomas shook his head. With his heart in his throat, he sank to his knees, gasping as pain shot up his thigh.

"Please..." *Please what? Don't arrest me?* Light-headed, with his ears hot, he dropped his gaze to avoid eye contact with anyone.

The rattle of chains and shackles from behind him awoke an all-consuming rage, burning away any calm he was trying to maintain. Thomas forced himself to hold still as the metal closed around his wrists.

"What is this?" Lord Samson's voice boomed from behind him. "Release him."

A shaky laughter boiled inside as Thomas slumped, relief rushing through him.

"What are you doing?" Lord Samson asked the guards.

"He claimed to be an Enforcer, but had nothing to verify his claim," one of the guards replied.

"He speaks the truth. Shackles? Whose idea was that?" Lord Samson demanded.

The shackles were removed. Voices mumbled behind Thomas as he climbed to his feet, legs weak.

"Get back on your horse," Lord Samson commanded before returning to his hushed conversation with the guards. "Let him through. You go back to Kempschester's gates for that."

Hands shaking, Thomas returned to his saddle. He glimpsed concern in Graeme's eyes, mixed with a spark of cold anger through their connection. Graeme's focus shifted to the guards with an icy glare.

Unsure whether he was relieved or not, Thomas nudged Guinevere through the gate. He paused, not ready to be seen among the Enforcers. Farmers from other villages he had known his entire life now watched with curiosity.

"You're late," Lord Samson said, riding up beside him. "Any later and I would have sent a search party. Next time I expect you on time. Try not to get arrested again. You're an Enforcer now — you do the arresting." Lord Samson's eyes darted to Thomas's cloak and up to his face. "I will have a uniform arranged for you. Tidy the beard and hair. You look like you've been lost in the wild for three months."

Together, Lord Samson and Thomas rode towards the waiting Enforcers.

One face stood out that turned his blood cold. A nobleman named Patrick with a particularly cruel reputation. He was referred to as the captain, but it was unknown whether that was a promotion, or if he had claimed the title for himself. As if sensing eyes upon him, Patrick turned his head. He grinned with contempt, showing crooked teeth.

"You all know why we're here," Lord Samson's voice drew everyone's attention. "My father, Lord Philip, was murdered. Last night, another was found. I have called upon men I know will do whatever it takes to find this killer. There will be no mercy."

There will be no mercy. Lord Samson's voice faded as the words stirred a memory in Thomas. A flash of faces surrounding him, eyes filled with bloodthirsty rage. Thomas forced it down. *Not here!*

"Amongst you are seasoned Enforcers and newer faces, some recently returned from the war in France. These men have served the King well, and your duty is not a light one. You are to bring the murderer to face the King's Law."

Lord Samson pointed at a large structure being built at the far end of the courtyard. A pyre waiting to burn who they found guilty of the murders.

"Ride out," Lord Samson commanded, leading the Enforcers towards the gate.

They rode in double file. The stomp of hooves in unison evoked memories of marching to France surrounded by hundreds of soldiers.

"Welcome home, farmer. So, do you think yourself worthy to join the Enforcers? You think yourself superior now?" Patrick sneered.

Despite his irritation, he turned a tight smile on Patrick. He wasn't going to let this noble get the best of him. The captain was provoking him.

"Maybe I'll take your job," he joked.

Patrick's smirk was gone, and he fell back. Chuckling to himself, Thomas shook his head. He wanted nothing to do with the title 'Enforcer,' nor what it entailed, but seeing the smug look fade from Patrick's eyes was somewhat satisfying.

Lord Samson waited at the gate as everyone rode past. His eyes paused on Thomas.

"I want you with me," Lord Samson ordered. His eyes focused behind Thomas. "You, too."

His satisfaction faded when Patrick joined them. It was understandable that Lord Samson wanted Patrick to accompany him. But for Thomas, to be seen with Patrick would be difficult to live down. A seed of dread settled in his stomach.

"Looks like we're going to be working together," Patrick scoffed. "I've heard things; I'm impressed."

All of Thomas's nightmares tried to force themselves to the surface, and his skull heated up. As his sight blurred, a dark laugh erupted from the captain.

"Are you still trying to hide that? You can't be an Enforcer and maintain your honourable reputation. You were picked for a reason. You know this."

"I didn't choose to be an Enforcer." Anger unfurled in his stomach.

Everything about Patrick was immoral. To be cast in the same light was vile.

"Is that judgement? You hate us, don't you? So, it's yourself you're trying to hide from, then. This will be delightful to watch." Patrick laughed.

Chapter 13

After Philip's funeral, word of the killer spread through Kempschester, and fear with it. No one who had seen the mysterious murderer could say what he looked like, beyond the description of 'a shadow man'. The townsfolk whispered a name amongst themselves, The Shadow of Death. There had been two murders in two days, but no one had been killed in the last three. Thomas's impatience grew with each passing day as any possible trail grew cold. Not that there was a trail.

"One of our own came face to face with the killer as Wynnstan died, and I cannot get reason out of him."

"What did he say?" Thomas asked.

"All he can do is mumble about a shadow, and that it let him live when it had the chance to kill him. It was there one moment, gone the next."

"Perhaps he is an assassin." Patrick muttered. "They're spoken of as shadows all the time."

"Patrick might be right," Thomas agreed. "It is unusual for an assassin to leave witnesses alive, though."

"Unless he's doing that on purpose. Look at the fear that's spread of him already," Lord Samson said.

"Part of the hunt," Thomas said. "Like a cat with a mouse."

"Someone's seen what he looks like or could be sheltering him," Lord Samson said. "Start bringing in people to question. Anyone who might have laid eyes on him. Knock on doors in the areas where my father and Wynnstan were killed. Someone will know where or who he is."

"I suppose that means you won't be returning to your wife as quickly as you hoped," Patrick mocked.

"At least I have a wife to return to," Thomas said without hesitance, receiving a cold stare of hatred in response.

Dressed in black leather armour with the grey cloak, Thomas was accepted by the Enforcers without question, despite his status as a farmer. Other soldiers were quick to band together. Townsfolk, however, averted their eyes, moving out of his way as he passed by on horseback. Enforcers were known to revel in their reputation, but Thomas never would. He was not born into great wealth as most of the Enforcers were, and he would never cast himself above the people. Peasants with whom Thomas once traded were now as afraid of him as any other Enforcer. He had never yearned to be in Riverwick as much as he did then. With every familiar face, he sought out warmth instead of fear and hostility.

Thomas rode ahead of Lord Samson and Patrick as they spoke in low voices. He entered the marketplace. Many stalls had closed. Those who remained no longer called out to passers-by. A thriving market had come to a standstill since the arrival of the pestilence. The stench of death lay in every dark corner of Kempschester, all bearing signs of the black ailment.

"Graeme?" A familiar voice rose from behind him. "What are you doing on your brother's horse? He would kill you if he found out."

Nicholas. A welcome sight as he approached his friend's butcher stall. Chickens, pigs, and lamb carcasses hung from the stall; the gamey scent of meat overpowered everything else. Nicholas had left Riverwick years before with his wife, Catherine, to find a life in Kempschester.

"Wrong brother," he replied with a grin.

A smile lit up Nicholas's face. "Thomas! You're back! Why are you here and not home with your family?" Nicholas's eyes took in the black armour before darting to Lord Samson and Patrick. "You're with them? Why?"

Thomas let out a weary sigh. "I'm with them to hunt for the killer."

Nicholas lowered his voice. "People have called him 'The Shadow of Death.'"

The name was just as unnerving as the first time he'd heard it.

"You avoided answering my question. I didn't even know you had returned," Nicholas said.

"I arrived home a few days ago."

"Straight from war to this, then?" Nicholas gave an understanding nod before his forehead creased into a frown. "But why you?"

Thomas put effort into keeping his face expressionless, shrugging. *How am I supposed to answer that question?*

"Come on, Thomas, Lord Samson wouldn't pick people for no reason. You had to have done something deserving of such a title. He's keeping a close eye on you too, like you're his prized fighter."

Thomas's stomach tightened as he shot a look over his shoulder. Lord Samson and Patrick were in deep conversation, but their eyes were watchful in his direction.

"I'm a prisoner."

Nicholas gave him a sideways glance. "Do not become like them."

"Grim said the same thing."

"Your brother knows what he's talking about. You're respected by many. Don't let them—"

"Enforcer Blake! You're on the job! Don't make yourself too comfortable. You better be asking questions," Patrick's voice thundered across the market.

Nicholas paled and took a step back away from Thomas's horse, shaking his head.

"Please go. I can't have Patrick smashing my stall because you stopped to talk to me." Nicholas hurried away back to his stall, glancing back at him warily. When Thomas didn't move, Nicholas scowled, busying himself. Thomas sighed, returning to Lord Samson and Patrick.

Patrick had a habit of stirring up people around them out of boredom and amusement. They passed by a man carrying a basket of eggs. He stuck out his foot and pushed. The poor man fell in the mud, dropping the eggs. With a cackle, Patrick kept riding. Thomas climbed off his horse.

Lord Samson stopped when he saw Thomas wasn't behind them."What are you doing?"

"I'm helping him," Thomas said.

Eggs had been smashed, but Thomas helped pick up those that weren't broken.

"Why?" Patrick asked.

"Not all of us enjoy tormenting people for no reason," he glared.

Lord Samson's silence regarding Patrick's antics was no surprise to Thomas. The new title, 'Lord,' didn't change the fact that Lord Samson had once been an Enforcer himself. The only time Thomas had seen a different, more civilised side to Lord Samson was on the front lines. Patrick and Lord Samson had a lot in common. The son of a lord and a noble, born into wealth, with no idea how much people beneath them suffered.

"You're going to be the Lord of these people. Is this how you want to treat them?" Thomas asked. "They do not deserve this. For the sake of amusement?"

Lord Samson's expression darkened as he considered Thomas. After speaking out of turn, he waited to be reminded of his place. He had just challenged the Lord of the manor, with a peasant to witness it.

"You're right," Lord Samson said. "Patrick, help him." Lord Samson continued the way they had been going.

"What?" There was a look of pure hatred behind the eyes that Patrick turned to Thomas. He climbed from his horse, red-faced.

"No!" The man whispered to Thomas, a tremble in his voice. "Please stop. He will make me pay for this humiliation later. I don't need your help." The peasant ran before Patrick could get close enough.

Thomas's stomach twisted. He had become a pariah. Helping people was only met with suspicion and more fear.

"Stop trying to convince yourself you're still a farmer, loved by all," Patrick fumed. "You want to tell yourself you're not one of us, but I know what you did in France. You were a *weapon,* and Lord Samson will wield you as one, just as he did in France." Patrick motioned to the retreating peasant. "I do not care what Lord Samson wants. You pull something like that again, I will gut you myself and drop you at the feet of the wife you're so impatient to get back to. Now, get back on your horse, Enforcer. We have a killer to find. That is your purpose, not," Patrick swept his hand to encompass those around them, "these insignificant distractions."

A dangerous light shone behind Patrick's eyes. Thomas did not doubt for a moment that Patrick would kill him if given the chance.

Chapter 14

Kempschester buzzed with whispers of a murderer. The Shadow delighted in the name they had given him. Guards were posted at the gates that surrounded the town. Lord Philip and the other one, whose name he learned was Wynnstan, had been his *first* kills. He wanted more. The exhilaration that came with taking a human life called to him. He hungered to be released, the desire to kill burning deep.

The Shadow followed men who hunted him. Their efforts to capture him would be unsuccessful, as none held the ability to see beyond the veil. They were unaware as to what it was they hunted, nor did they know that a world existed alongside their own. But one mortal had seen him, watched him from within the dark fog. There had been no sign of him in the days since Wynnstan's death. The Shadow remained intrigued by the mysterious presence.

After three days of pushing at the veil, yearning to feel the pull, The Shadow got what he wished for. This time he stalked his prey from the shadows, preferring to stay within his realm as long as possible. Drawn towards the main entrance, he found himself staring into the faces of four guards. *All of them?* His first two kills had been one at a time. This would make for more of a challenge.

These men, whose job it was to protect Kempschester, were fated to meet his blade. But to appear among them would end in his own blood being shed this time. Townsfolk had not yet retired for the night, making it more difficult to find a way to kill four men without someone trying to step in. As he evaluated his options, lost souls surrounded the guards, as if they knew what was to come. *Drawn to death?* Among them, the faces of Wynnstan and Philip.

He chose an alley to conceal his entrance, emerging from the Shadow Realm, shivering as he stepped into the cold night air. The almost sweet, fruity odour of rotting flesh and decay set off the desire to retch. *I dislike this world!* If there was a way to kill from within the Shadow Realm, he would be done with this already.

The only way to complete his hunt was to separate the guards and draw them away from the gate. He stepped far enough out to the shadows, waiting for one of the guards to notice him.

"Who are you?" A guard with a crooked nose finally caught sight of him.

He stepped back, hidden once more by the shadows.

The other guards turned."Who are you talking to?"

"I thought I saw someone."

The others turned their backs again. The Shadow revealed himself a second time. As expected, footsteps echoed as the guard followed him.

"Where are you going?" a voice called out.

"I'm just checking something."

The Shadow waited at the far end of the alley as his prey stepped towards him.

"I knew it. Who are you? What are you doing here?"

"I am your death."

The Shadow finished off Crooked Nose with haste. There was no reason to draw this one out when he had three more kills waiting for him. The guard grasped his own throat, as if he could prevent what was only moments away. Choking filled the silence of the alley as the guard fell. A strong odour of urine filled the air.

"Adam? What are you doing down there?"

As he retreated to the Shadow Realm, a familiar presence emerged again.

"Do not be afraid, my friend." The Shadow took on a non-menacing tone to coax the figure forward. *"It is their time,"* he waited, holding out his weapon.

Piercing blue eyes rose to meet his before shifting to the sickle. *What if he wants to kill me?*

The second guard stood at the opening of the alleyway, squinting into the shadows. "Adam?"

"This kill is yours if you want it," The Shadow nodded to the blade in his hand.

Dark desire flickered within the eyes, the blue intensity darkening to black. *That's interesting.*

Finally, as the second guard walked into the alley, the dark figure stepped forward, accepting the sickle. As his fingers closed around the handle, they connected with The Shadow's hand. A jolt passed between the two of them.

Both of them pulled their hands back. *I know him. He is me. Is this the self I lost when I awoke here?* Questions for which he had no answers rushed around him.

"Who are you?" he asked.

His other self stepped through the veil, leaving him burning with curiosity.

He is mortal. Am I his shadow self? Is he the one who commands me?

The black-eyed figure whispered the words. "I am your death."

His mortal self killed from behind, gripping the forehead with a motion fuelled by bloodthirstiness, cutting deep, winding around the neck. A gash of red opened in pale flesh. The guard choked, thrashing on the ground.

The Shadow joined his mortal self in the other realm as the guard died.

"There is great Darkness in you," The Shadow said. *"You gave into it without hesitation."*

A smile formed. The black eyes returned his gaze. Wisps of black fog rose like smoke, curling around the figure.

"I am Darkness." The voice was similar to his own whisper, but spoken out loud and in his mind.

Footsteps approached. "Adam? George? What are you doing down there? Get back to the gate; you're on duty."

The pull towards the guards to kill them drew The Shadow forward. Side by side with his other self, they moved towards the guards.

"That's not Adam or George," another voice said. "Raise the alarm. That's The Shadow of Death. There are two of them!"

Chapter 15

The Shadow of Death had sparked a hunt and disappeared again. The fact that no more bodies had turned up should have been cause to celebrate. It only added to Thomas's growing sense of helplessness and desire to go home. *I'm going nowhere if we don't catch him, and that is not happening unless he kills again.* Thomas sat in his room in the Enforcers' wing, a tankard of ale in front of him. His room was plain, with a bed, wooden chest, and a table, yet still bigger than his back home.

Graeme's presence nearby, dark and empty, made him pause in removing his armour. *Nonsense! Why would Grim be here in the middle of the night?* Oh no, Emma! But before Thomas could reach out to his brother, the presence faded. Thomas shrugged it off. Their bond, even this far from Riverwick, still managed to force its way through. Graeme's presence was more likely to be his brother waking from a nightmare.

Voices filled the halls. Enforcers were yelling. Uneasiness set in as Lord Samson made his way towards Thomas's room.

"Get your cloak and your sword. The killer has struck again," Lord Samson ordered him.

Thomas wrapped his cloak around his shoulders and sheathed his sword before finishing the ale in one quick gulp. Less bitter, more filled with honey and fruit than the ale of Riverwick, it warmed him as he followed Lord Samson.

"He emerged from the shadows, only to become shadows." One of the guards who had attempted to arrest Thomas was in the dining hall, eyes glinting in fear. "He came after us."

"There were *two* of them," the other guard said, his voice low.

"Patrick and Thomas, let's go," Lord Samson ordered, on the move already with a lantern.

"Aren't they the guards who tried to arrest you?" Patrick asked.

The front gate was not far from Lord Samson's estate, so they walked. Lord Samson led him and Patrick to an alley next to a tavern. Odours of urine, ale, and rotting bodies were like a wave as he walked down the alley.

Lord Samson knelt over one, holding the lantern above the body. "Look at this," he said to Thomas. "What do you see?"

Thomas limped around the body. The guard had almost been decapitated. "His throat is cut deeper than the rest."

"Is that supposed to mean something?" Patrick muttered.

"Adam's body isn't like this. Neither were the others. The kills were calm; he took his time. This one..." He pointed to the throat. "Deep, savage."

Thomas met Lord Samson's eyes. "He gave in to the rage. Why was he so angry?"

"I know who would be angry at them," Patrick said.

"Patrick, stop. Your bitterness towards Thomas is wearing thin. If you're trying to imply this was him, don't. I've seen those who met the end of his sword. They didn't look like this." Lord Samson's words were hard, leaving no room for argument.

"I don't think it is a sword," Thomas said to the lord. He forced himself to kneel. Lord Samson reached for his arm, as if to steady Thomas. "The cut looks strange. It goes *around* the throat, more than a straight blade would."

"Hmm. You might be right." Lord Samson straightened, pointing towards the gate. "To take out the guards… looking for an escape?"

Thomas followed Lord Samson towards the gate, ignoring Patrick's glare. "If so, he could be anywhere by now."

"There are villages in which he would seek refuge," Lord Samson said. "Patrick, I want you to organise four hunting parties to spread out across the villages. Groups of six. Ensure to even out the numbers between soldiers and experienced Enforcers."

"Yes, Lord." Patrick ran off to carry out his orders.

"Thomas, you will know this better than any of us. Would villagers be likely to hide him?" Lord Samson asked.

"I don't think so. No one would want to risk Enforcers arresting them." Thomas tried to force away the rising panic at the idea the killer could be in Riverwick. "They just want to go about their lives, which are already difficult. Such things would only make it more so."

"You ride with me." Lord Samson turned from the gate. "We will cover Riverwick."

"Thank you," Thomas said.

"I need you focused. If that means letting you check in on your family, then so be it." Lord Samson passed his eyes again over the bodies. "Patrick raised a good point. You had good reason to be angry with these men."

"I can assure you, I did not sneak out of Enforcer quarters in the middle of the night to take on four guards. That would be a challenge with this hobble." He met Lord Samson's stare head-on.

"I suppose you're right. You stink of ale. So you were unlikely to be going anywhere in a hurry," Lord Samson laughed. "Remember when we ran out of ale before new supplies arrived? You and Aris stole wine from the French camp, dragging all those soldiers behind you. They were furious that you'd taken their wine."

A smile crept across Thomas's face. "Aris took an arrow to his shoulder, but it did not slow him down. He was right back in battle the next day."

Lord Samson had a fondness for reliving events from the war. In those moments, he spoke to Thomas as an old friend.

"That Aris..." Lord Samson shook his head. "Nothing kept him from battle. It's as if he lived for war. You, him, and Caleb were quite the trio."

"Enough war stories," Patrick grumbled, returning on horseback. Stable hands followed with Lord Samson and Thomas's horses.

The brothers-in-arms bond Thomas shared with Lord Samson visibly bothered Patrick. They had a shared experience that he resented.

Overconfidence spoke through Thomas. "It's all right, Patrick. *Some* of us had the courage to fight for our country, while you *bought* your way out of having to go." Thomas climbed onto his horse.

Patrick's face was a mask of fury. "You like to think you're better than me, farmer, but you're no different. You pretend you have honour and morals, but I know what you're hiding from and what keeps you awake at night. What you—"

"Patrick, that's enough," Lord Samson ordered.

Patrick didn't stop. "What you became on the battlefield is why you're here. The sooner you accept what you did, the sooner we can stop pretending that there isn't savagery in you that both frightens and excites you."

Patrick's words were suffocating. Breathless, with a tight chest, Thomas clenched his fists. Black spots danced before his eyes.

Before he could respond, riders approached.

"Finally. You three are with me. We're going to Riverwick." Lord Samson pointed to groups of Enforcers as he spoke. "You, Ashvale. Greenwick. Hazelbury. Anything suspicious, you follow it through."

"What if he's gone further than Ashvale?" Patrick asked.

"Then he's no longer our problem. Let's start with those villages. Question people. If anyone knows anything, it's your job to find it." Lord Samson mounted his horse. "Thomas. Riverwick may be your home, but you are still an Enforcer, and you are to behave as such. You will question the villagers, just as you would anyone else."

Chapter 16

The ride from Kempschester to Riverwick had never been so long. As they rode into view of the village, the first rays of dawn streaked across the clouded sky in red and orange. Thomas sought out his brother's presence, only to not find it in Riverwick. *Where is he?* He focused on Graeme's energy, and a breath of relief rushed from him when he found him. Probably at the river again. It would give him time with Emma first.

"Thomas, you do what you need to. I will speak with your uncle. When you've seen your wife, question your father and brother. The rest of you, spread out," Lord Samson ordered as they rode through the village. "If he is here, we will find him."

They arrived in the centre of Riverwick and dismounted their horses, tying the lead ropes to a hitch rack in front of the church. Patrick eyed the ruins but said nothing.

A light breeze tugged at Thomas's cloak, the cold air brushing over his face and neck.

"What is that stink?" Patrick asked, covering his nose and mouth.

Thomas breathed in the smell of ale and wood smoke, mixed with the distinctive, musky scent of goats, sheep, and cows.

"That is the smell of *home*," he said. "You might want to watch where you're walking." As he said it, Patrick's foot descended on the droppings of a horse. With audible disgust, he glared. Thomas held back laughter. "Do not blame me. You were not watching where you placed your foot."

"Remind me why we are here," Patrick demanded, turning to Lord Samson. "This is absolutely—"

"No different from the human faeces you walk through in Kempschester," Thomas retorted. "At least we don't have it raining down on us."

"No, you probably bathe in it." Patrick's hostility towards him was growing. His insults of Riverwick brought defensive anger out in Thomas.

"You two, enough," Lord Samson ordered as he walked in the direction of Thomas's house.

As Thomas followed, Patrick's annoyed grunt and muttering behind him faded. The clouds darkened the village, but people were outside, likely trying to get work done before it rained. As they passed by, their eyes took in his black armour and grey cloak, quickly looking away.

"Thomas?" James stopped in front of him as they approached his house. "That is a new look for you." James's tone suggested his dislike of it. His eyes fell to Lord Samson . "What brings you here, Lord Samson?"

Thomas left them to their conversation, hoping Emma was awake. The ache in his shoulders eased as he released the tension.

Inside, the cold, empty kitchen made the entire house feel abandoned. There was not one day Emma or Amelia had not lit that fire and filled their home with the aroma of hot food. Thomas raced up the stairs as much as his wound would allow him.

"Emma?" He burst into the room.

Emma sat up, blinking. Isaac opened his eyes but shut them almost instantly.

"Thomas? What is it?"

He nodded to Isaac. "Why is he sleeping in here? Is everything alright?"

"He's scared of sleeping alone, convinced the Enforcers will come and get him."

"It cannot have helped that I scared him."

Emma took his hand. "Spend time with him. He will forget about it soon enough."

Thomas sat on the bed and leaned in to kiss her. "The kitchen was empty. Where is Amelia?"

Her lips curved upwards. "Amelia rose early to meet Graeme by the river."

"She did?" Thomas laughed. "Oh, good for you, brother."

"Those two had a very long talk the day you left and then visited Mary's grave together. They've been out every morning since. It's not as it was, but there is improvement. They both love each other, and needed to grieve together."

"If they're sneaking out for alone time, that's more than an improvement," Thomas noted.

"They're trying." Her hand brushed his face. "You trimmed your beard."

"A requirement the Lord of Kempshire expects of all Enforcers."

"You're still an Enforcer? So, you haven't caught the killer yet?" she asked.

"Unfortunately, no. He still eludes us."

"Then why are you… Oh. You think he's here?" Her voice rose.

"I hope not. Lord Samson saw fit to allow me to come home, but I still have to work."

She cupped his face. "I give Lord Samson my thanks. The people of Riverwick will not take kindly to being questioned by one of their own."

Thomas rested his hand on her thigh. "Let's not talk about that. Are you alright? Is there anything you need?"

"Just find that murderer so you can come home to us." Emma laid her hand over her belly.

Thomas leaned over and kissed her again, placing his hand over hers. "I will be here for the birth, I promise."

He rose from the bed, wishing he could take Emma in his arms and never leave her.

"I will hold you to your promise," Emma said.

Thomas placed a hand over his heart and flashed a grin at her, overjoyed that the tension between them was gone. He opened the door.

"You're back?" his father asked from the bottom of the stairs.

Thomas said nothing as he made his way towards his father.

"Had enough of the Enforcers? Too much for you?"

"Ethan, I am an Enforcer, and you will address me as such." Thomas let anger slip into his voice.

"What did you call me?" Father demanded.

"You heard me. Get out of my way." He pushed his father as he stepped by. "Wait for me at the table. I have some questions for you when I return."

"I am still your father, Thomas—"

"Today, you're not. Today, you are a villager being questioned by an Enforcer. Now sit down! Wait for me." Satisfied at finally having the courage to speak to his father in such a manner, pride swelled in him.

His father stepped towards him with a murderous glint in his eye. "Think you can talk to your father like that, do you?"

Thomas took a step back reflexively before reaching for his sword. "I will draw," he threatened.

Father stopped mid-step, his frown deepening as he focused on Thomas's hand resting on the hilt. "You dare…in my house? Get out!" His voice gained volume, but the glint of fear was unmistakable.

He's scared. Of me? A strange sense of power gave Thomas bravery. "No, this is *my* house. *You* get out."

His father stood face-to-face with him, neither of them moving. Finally, his father gave in and stomped towards the door.

Thomas's hands shook as he made his way to the stable. The fresh, sweet scent of hay mixed with horse manure greeted him as he entered. His father's horse remained in his stall, the rest empty. Thomas searched each stall, one at a time, for signs that someone had hidden there. As he reached the last one, someone entered the stable on horseback.

"Amelia?" Amelia jumped at his voice, her rasping breaths and quivering chin setting off warnings in him. She wore a blue riding cloak, her blonde hair tangled. "What is it? Are you. . .is something wrong?"

"His eyes," Amelia whimpered. "There's something wrong with his eyes."

"Who?"

"Please, Thomas, he was not far behind me."

He's here. Thomas's hand rested on his sword. "Get in the stall. You're safe."

Thomas moved back with Amelia, watching the door of the stable. A white horse entered, his brother on its back. He removed his hand from the sword handle. "Grim?" He let out a breath of relief.

Graeme's brows drew down as he dismounted. "Were you expecting someone else?" As he approached, he knocked over a scythe.

"Are you going to pick that up?" Thomas asked.

His brother tore his gaze from the scythe. "Have you captured the killer?" He asked instead. "Is that why you're home?"

"No, he killed again. Good to see you, too," Thomas said.

A muscle twitched in Graeme's jaw. "Is Amelia here? I must find her."

"Why?"

"Something scared her."

Graeme's barriers were up, but not enough. Thomas frowned. The dark presence within his brother rattled him to the core. *It's spread! How is that possible?*

"I know when you're lying. What happened?" Thomas asked.

"Nothing happened." Graeme's attempt to keep his expression guarded was not working.

Thomas positioned himself so Graeme couldn't pass, folding his arms.

"Are you going to let me pass?" His brother's eyes were hard and cold, that of a stranger.

"Grim?" He no longer recognised his brother.

"Leave it be, Thomas." Graeme sighed. "Fine, you can put Willow away."

Graeme turned towards the door. Thomas grabbed his shoulder.

"Graeme, stop! What are you—"

"I said leave it be! Remove your hand!" Graeme thundered.

As he turned, Thomas gasped, pulling his hand away. His brother's eyes were black, Darkness emerging from within as if a shadow had broken free. It surged forward, cloaking Thomas in dark fog. He took a step back as a figure took shape before him. The form towered over him, resembling that of a man, tendrils rising from it. For the first time, Thomas stood face-to-face with the Darkness that lived inside his brother — and it terrified him. Then it was gone, Graeme escaping through the door of the stable. His hands shook.

"What?" His voice barely audible, Thomas's heart raced. "Grim?"

Chapter 17

"Amelia?" Thomas called out.

She stepped out from the stall. "Is he gone?"

"For now. Care to tell me what happened?"

Amelia took a deep breath to calm her breathing. "He's been having strange dreams lately. I think he was having another one. He was mumbling in his sleep."

"Did you catch what he was saying?"

"'Death is coming. Darkness is here.' Then he said, 'I see them all.'"

An icy breath slithered its way down his spine. Amelia massaged her wrist.

"I shook him awake and he grabbed me. His eyes were *black*." Trembling, a tear slid down her face. "What's wrong with my husband?"

Thomas pulled her into a comforting hug. "It's going to be all right. Go to Emma. Do not tell *anyone* what you saw."

"What will you do?" she asked.

"I need to figure that out. Talk to him? Go."

She hurried away, leaving Thomas alone in the stable. Willow snorted, nudging at him with her muzzle, her warm breath tickling him.

"I don't have food for you," he said, leading Graeme's horse to her stall. She found what she was looking for and lowered her head.

Trying to quiet the rush of panic, Thomas followed the path to his house. He walked through the empty kitchen, hesitating at the bottom of the stairs. *How many times do I have to climb these things?* He took his time, still not sure what he was going to say to Graeme.

Thomas had always known what hid inside Graeme; the nightmares of his childhood had shown him as much. Shadow creatures and dark worlds that had haunted him now held him frozen outside Graeme's bedroom. The echoes of Graeme's voice, whimpering about shadows and fog, and his own, promising he wouldn't let anything take his brother. He opened the door.

Graeme's back was to him, sitting hunched over the desk. Thomas inched towards his brother, the pounding in his ears getting louder. A single candle reflected yellow on the side of his face and the pages of a book. He wrote in the journal that Thomas had given him, the quill scratching over the page. Graeme had not yet reacted to his presence in the room. Forcing himself forward, he caught a glimpse of a list of names, Graeme adding to it.

"What are you writing?" he asked.

"Go away, Thomas."

He grabbed the journal, laughing. "What is this?" he asked. "A list of names? I thought I gave this to you for your dreams."

In the middle of the list, their father's name and that of Nicholas leapt off the page. His laughter died. A tightening closed around his throat. Graeme rose and spun around, his black eyes narrowed. Thomas let go of the journal.

"It is from my dreams," Graeme said. "I still don't understand them."

You're lying.

Graeme paled, clutching at his chest. Thomas gasped for air, and ice gripped his heart.

"What is that?" Thomas asked. "Are you all right?"

Graeme fell first. Before Thomas could help his brother, he lurched forward into darkness.

The black receded, and Thomas awoke on the hard floor. Surrounded by confusion, he struggled to remember.

He and Graeme had been pulled into darkness. Graeme had called out to him. Black fog had circled them, and a voice spoke in his mind. The very essence of the voice had awoken absolute terror within him, coming from a place of nightmares.

"Let him go," Graeme had requested. His eyes. . .There was something wrong with his eyes.

"Thomas?" Amelia whispered. "I'm sorry. You were both out cold. Ethan's bringing Lord Samson in."

Emma hovered in the doorway, Isaac behind her. Thomas sat up, his whole body aching, and he groaned. Graeme lay where he had fallen, eyes still closed. The leather journal lay on the floor between them, a page open to drawings. On one side was a shadow figure; its empty eyes seemed to bore right into Thomas. The page next to it was a man with a hooded cloak, eyes black, with a small smile curving the mouth.

Footsteps thudded on the stairs. Thomas closed the book, placing it on the desk.

"Thomas?" Lord Samson appeared at the door beside Emma. His focus shifted from Thomas to Graeme.

"I'm all right," he said.

"What happened?" Lord Samson asked.

"I am not sure," he admitted truthfully. "Can you help me get my brother off the floor?"

The two of them lifted Graeme and carried him to the bed.

"What's wrong with him? Your father said the two of you passed out." Lord Samson took a hasty step away from Thomas. "Are you sick?"

Am I? Thomas raised his shoulders, drawing his eyebrows together. "I don't know. I'm fit for duty."

"Look, why don't you stay and keep an eye on your brother until he wakes." Lord Samson made for the door. "The others are searching everyone's homes and questioning people. They are hungry since we left Kempschester before breakfast, so we will be at the tavern," Lord Samson left.

Thomas pulled a reading chair to the side of the bed. He motioned at it for Amelia, and she lowered herself into it.

"I'm going back to bed," Emma said. "Isaac."

"Is Uncle Graeme dead?" Isaac asked.

"No, he's just sleeping," Thomas said and turned to Emma. "I can watch Isaac. Have you eaten?"

"Susanna brought food over," Emma said.

"Good, rest. I will be here if you need anything."

Emma plodded back to their bedroom. Isaac sat on the chair with Amelia, and she placed an arm around him, her free hand holding Graeme's. Thomas paced the room.

"You're not scared of him anymore?" he asked.

"More afraid *for* him. What's happening?" Amelia asked.

"I wish I knew," he told her.

"Is it something to do with his dreams? Should we be getting the priest?" she questioned, with a frown.

"Father Rohan?" Isaac asked.

"No, Father Matthew," Amelia replied.

Something was happening to Graeme. Thomas stood next to Amelia, crossing his arms over his chest. "He's never dreamed before, so these dreams must be taking an effect on him. Maybe he needs the sleep."

Dark circles under Graeme's eyes and the paleness of his face showed Thomas just how tired his brother was. *Why can't I hear him breathing? Come on, Grim, wake up.*

"What happened? You fell, too. Why did you wake and not him?" Amelia made a good point.

Because the Darkness has him. It didn't want me. Unsure where the idea came from, Thomas rubbed at his eye.

A groan rose from the bed.

"He's waking up," Amelia said, standing. "Graeme? Can you hear me?"

Graeme's eyes fluttered open, darting around the room. Relieved that they were no longer black, Thomas rushed to the bed as Amelia stepped back.

"What happened?" Graeme asked, voice croaking.

"You fell," Amelia said, her voice quivering.

There was only emptiness where Graeme's presence should be. It wasn't as before when either of them put up shields from each other or shut off their connection. The smallest spark had always been there. There was nothing, as if he stood before a chasm.

"I remember. Thomas fell, too," Graeme said.

"I woke up before you," Thomas said. He sought out the bond again, finding nothing. "I cannot sense you."

Graeme sat up. A flicker of his presence emerged from the void before it returned, heavily shielded.

Chapter 18

Snow drifted around Thomas, but the chill came from deep in his gut. His fingers closed around the hilt of his sword as he paced. Unable to force out the image of Graeme's black eyes, his grip tightened. Something was wrong with his brother. That dark presence was very real and had revealed itself to him. Ideas of possession and demons seeped into his mind. *What does that mean for his soul?* The hair on his arms rose. *Does he still have one, if he's let that Darkness in? Did he let it in, or has it just claimed him for the sake of it?* Each question was followed by another. Black eyes. Darkness. It's always been there. Why is this happening now?

Thomas drew his sword, metal whispering against the leather scabbard. With nothing to fight but fear, he gripped the hilt, his knuckles turning white.

"Thomas," James called out walking towards him. "Is your brother feeling any better?"

Thomas had left Graeme to rest. Amelia had remained, despite her unease.

"I don't know," he said, his voice breaking, and he re-sheathed the sword.

James gripped his shoulder.

"Graeme has not had a single day of rest since you left for France," James told him. "He'll be back on his feet in no time. You can't keep him from what he loves."

"I'm sure he will," Thomas agreed.

"Where are your friends?" James asked.

"My friends?" Thomas frowned.

"The ones you arrived with."

"Oh. I think they're at the tavern."

"Lord Samson has an interesting way of asking questions." James said.

Thomas had been caught up in what was happening with Graeme, letting his duty slip.

"I was supposed to question Father, and Grim."

"That explains why Ethan is keeping his distance. Did you say something?"

"I may have told him to address me as an Enforcer and to sit down and wait for me in the kitchen," Thomas said, keeping the last part out.

James tried to hide a smile and failed.

"Your brother is making my job more difficult than it needs to be," Thomas grumbled.

"My brother? He's your father." James laughed.

"He was your brother before he was my father," Thomas grinned back.

"There's that smile I remember. It rarely reaches your eyes these days. You were always a cheerful boy. What happened to him?" James asked.

The urge to cry overwhelmed Thomas. He cleared his throat. "He went to war."

James squeezed Thomas's shoulder. The door opened and Graeme stepped out, a black cloak hanging from his shoulders. A crow flew overhead, cawing.

"I'll let you two be," James ambled away with a wave.

"What did he want?" Graeme asked.

"He was concerned about you, actually."

"There is no need to be. As you can see, there's nothing wrong."

"Grim, something is very wrong. How can you not see that?" Thomas grabbed his brother's arm, finding no warmth in him. "You're freezing!" he gasped, pulling his hand back.

"Yes, it's snowing," Graeme snapped, walking towards the stable.

"Your eyes were black," he said, following Graeme.

"Thomas, stop." Graeme glared.

"I'm worried about you. I'm your brother, talk to me."

Graeme spun around to face him. "Who's worried? My brother or the Enforcer? I saw your eyes in the stable; you were afraid of me. So was Amelia. I have no answers for you." He resumed his walk towards the stable.

Thomas winced. He needed to be brotherly. Not the soldier or Enforcer. But Graeme wasn't allowing him much opportunity to do so. It wasn't long before Graeme returned with his horse in tow.

"Where are you going?" Thomas asked.

"Why?" Graeme demanded. "Do you want to question me, Enforcer Blake? Or is this my brother trying to protect me again? The only thing I need protection from right now is you."

An awkward tension passed between them. Graeme climbed onto the back of Willow, his eyes boring into Thomas's. He let out a loud sigh. "If you must know, I'm going to see Father Matthew."

Thomas frowned at his brother. "Are you sure that's a good idea? If word were to get out about you. . . your eyes." — he paused. — "We could lose everything. Not just the farm. Our home, our reputation."

Graeme looked as if he'd been punched in the gut, his eyes hardening as he tightened his fist around the reins.

"I did not mean that," Thomas apologised.

"Yes, you did," Graeme fumed.

Chapter 19

Thomas pushed the door to the tavern open. Patrick and Lord Samson waited for him, glass goblets on the table in front of them. *Leo's using his good glassware.* The fire's warmth greeted him, banishing the cold from outside. Empty plates sat in the middle of the table.

"Finally. What took you so long?" Patrick raised his goblet, liquid splashing over the sides. "Have a drink."

"We're no closer to finding The Shadow of Death," Thomas muttered. "We can't find him sitting here."

Lord Samson pinched the bridge of his nose. "I wish you wouldn't call him that. It's enough that I hear that everywhere in Kempschester."

"'The Shadow of Death,'" Patrick snickered. "What a stupid name."

Thomas opened his mouth but shut it, unsure what to say.

"He might be somewhat drunk," Lord Samson rolled his eyes. "He has been here a while."

"What else is there to do here?" Patrick laughed. "Your innkeeper has provided me with plenty of liquor to keep me happy. He brought out the good wine." Patrick stood, snapping his fingers at Leo. "More wine. Pour one for Thomas! It's his first week as an Enforcer."

"Shouldn't we return to Kempschester?" Thomas asked. "I'd like to finish this hunt before my wife gives birth."

Patrick and Lord Samson exchanged glances. An ache began at the back of Thomas's throat.

Patrick stared at Thomas, lines appearing on his forehead. "You can sit down and enjoy yourself at least. Free wine. An advantage of being an Enforcer!"

Thomas sat next to Lord Samson as Leo poured three wines. The innkeeper's eyes narrowed at Thomas before he left.

"Drink," Patrick ordered.

"It's best you listen to him," Lord Samson advised, taking a sip of wine.

Thomas lifted the goblet, breathing in a fruity scent before taking a mouthful. The wine was spiced with nutmeg and cinnamon, among more flavours he didn't recognise. A sweet taste overpowered the bitterness he expected. "Willowdale wine," he noted.

"You know your wines," Patrick's eyebrows lifted.

"My brother's wife is from there," Thomas put the goblet down. "Where are the others?" he asked the lord.

"They've left for Kempschester. You're right; I'd like to get on the road too. Granted that you've spoken with your father, we can go.

I should have known it would come down to him.

Thomas intertwined his fingers around the stem of the goblet. "I don't think he was in favour of being questioned by his son."

"Thomas, if you can't interrogate someone, why am I paying you?"

Thomas's hand jerked, almost knocking over the wine.

Patrick roared with laughter. "He didn't realise you were paying him." Patrick thumped his palm on the table. Thomas tensed, aware of Lord Samson's flinch beside him. "You think we do this for free?" Patrick asked.

"When we catch the killer." Lord Samson stood, finishing his wine. "Where is your father now?"

"Probably in the stable, drinking," Thomas grumbled

"Have the horses ready. This will not take long." Lord Samson marched out of the tavern, leaving Thomas alone with Patrick.

"You heard him. Ready the horses," Patrick ordered.

Thomas pushed himself up, moving with care towards the door.

"Thomas."

He stopped, surprised at Patrick's use of his name.

"If she's what it takes, use it. Stop wasting our time and yours."

Thomas glanced over his shoulder. "What do you mean?"

Patrick let out an impatient groan. "If coming home to your wife is what it takes to give you that focus, use it. Lord Samson is being merciful on you, probably due to your shared time at war. But I'm tired of being burdened with an Enforcer who despises the job." He raised his arms wide, motioning around the tavern. "You want to come home? Then commit to the hunt."

Thomas's hand rested on the door, pushing it open. "I have been."

"No, you've been more worried about your reputation among peasants. 'Commit to the hunt' means *commit* to it." Patrick paused to drink. "You're holding yourself separate from us, hoping that you can elude what comes with being an Enforcer. It's too late for that. If you don't do what is required for this hunt, it will last longer than it needs to and more people will die. Do you want their blood on your hands?"

Patrick's words had a ring of truth, winding Thomas. "Is that the wise advice of the captain of the Enforcers?" he asked in an attempt to recover from the tongue-lashing.

"If that's how I'm going to get you to listen to me, then yes. You've already failed to complete the simple task of putting questions to your father. Now we must wait, thanks to you."

The door closed behind Thomas. He loathed Patrick and everything the

Enforcer stood for, but this rebuke had struck home.

Outside, Thomas found two of his stable hands leading their horses towards the tavern.

"They've been fed and watered," said the first stable hand, a boy of fifteen.

"Thank you," he replied.

"Is it true that you're hunting a murderer?" the other asked.

"Unfortunately, it is," Thomas replied, mounting his horse. "Don't worry, we will find him." He reached out a hand for the lead rope to Lord Samson's horse. "Wait for Patrick."

Thomas towed Lord Samson's white horse behind him. Outside the stable, he stopped as two voices came from inside.

"You sent *my son* to question me? Enforcer or not, it's an insult." Father's gruff voice was low, slurred.

I was right about him being drunk.

"When an Enforcer tells you to do something, you do it. I don't care that he's your son. An offence against an Enforcer is an offence against *me*," Lord Samson said. "I ought to have you arrested just for the disobedience. Maybe I'll have Thomas do it."

Glowing with warmth, Thomas shook his head in amusement.

"I'm sorry, Lord Samson. I will show Thomas the respect befitting of an Enforcer," Father said.

Thomas held back speaking aloud. The old man was deliberately being disrespectful.

"Good. Now, you know why we're here."

"James said you're looking for a murderer," Father grunted. "I don't know what this has to do with Riverwick, but ask your questions."

"Has there been any sign of new arrivals in Riverwick?" Lord Samson asked.

"None."

"If there were someone here, would you give shelter to him?"

"No," Father said.

"If the murderer were someone you knew, would you tell me?"

There was a pause. "And risk being arrested? I'm not a fool."

Thomas sighed inwardly, rolling his eyes.

"Yeoman Ethan, I expect you to address me as a Lord. I know you served my father for a long time. Treat me the same way you would him." Lord Samson's voice hardened.

"If the murderer were someone I knew, I would tell you immediately."

"What if it were your brother? Or your sons? Would you hand them over knowing you're committing them to a painful death?" Lord Samson asked.

The hammering in Thomas's chest filled the silence, his mouth dry. *If it were Uncle James, could I do that? Or Grim?* Cold dread rolled in the pit of his stomach.

"If my brother or my sons were taking lives in cold blood, it would be my privilege to put an end to such Darkness," Father said.

Darkness. The chill spread.

"Thomas," Lord Samson called out to him.

Thomas jumped. "Yes?" His voice croaked.

"Is your father telling the truth?"

Thomas guided Guinevere forward to scan his father's face. The old man swayed; Lord Samson's hand was around Father's upper arm as if to hold him up. They both turned towards him.

"I believe him," Thomas said. "He's not a man to lie about something like that."

Lord Samson gave Thomas a look of pity and released his grip. His father lost the ability to stand, sinking to the stable floor. "We're leaving," Lord Samson said, approaching Thomas. "Say your goodbyes."

He left Thomas alone with his father.

"This is what you want, to be one of them? You have turned on your village and brought shame to your family," Father accused, struggling to his feet.

"I have turned on no one," Thomas retorted. Unable to restrain himself, he dismounted, bitterness seeping through. "Would I have brought you more glory if I had died at war? Ethan Blake, the poor father whose son died on the battlefront?"

"If you had, I would not have to look at the son who ripped my wife from me to come into this world."

The words were a cruel blow, equal to being whipped. "I always knew you believed that, but you never said it. Why now?"

Father stood face-to-face with Thomas, the smell of ale overwhelming. "Because I cannot look at you anymore," he said, swaying. "I tolerate you and your brother because I'm supposed to. It is torment, and I wish I had drowned you both."

Thomas froze with horror. The alcohol had loosened Father's tongue. "Then why didn't you? It would have saved us the suffering you put on us."

"You talk of suffering? I watched Isobel die and raised her killer. Your ungodly brother should have died with her. No one else saw, but I did. *His eyes were black*. Every time I visit her grave, his very presence taunts me. I would rather she was here than the two of you. I ought to end his miserable life and yours."

"Do not threaten Grim." Rage seized Thomas and he drew his sword.

"Going to kill me, are you? For saying what you already know? I see what he is, and you protect him. You always have."

"I protected him *from you*. I took your beatings so he wouldn't have to," Thomas said.

Father's right about the Darkness in Grim, but to say he should have died, to threaten to kill him? I will kill him if he tries.

"Your brother is the Darkness Isobel feared. Her dreams of Darkness and death were a warning. She knew."

"You are drunk, Father. Go sleep it off."

"Just go. I don't want you here. Take your brother with you." Father took a swing at Thomas but missed. Losing his footing, the old man fell hard.

"I do not need to remind you that I am an Enforcer," Thomas declared. "Try that again and I will arrest you. You deserve to sit in a dank cell." Father tried to get up. "Stay down. You're an embarrassment." *How have I never noticed how pathetic he is?*

Thomas left his father lying in the stable. Outside, Patrick and Lord Samson were waiting on horseback. Patrick, with a smirk of triumph and Lord Samson, with a satisfied smile that Thomas knew from battle.

"You heard everything, didn't you?" he asked as they rode from the village.

"Most of it," Patrick said. "What was all that talk of your brother?"

"Nothing more than ravings," Thomas muttered. "He's drunk. Half of what he says is mad."

"You took my words to heart," Patrick laughed. "Threatening to arrest your own father? You're enjoying the benefits of being an Enforcer, I see."

"Your father is an unpleasant man," Lord Samson said. "I can throw him in a cell if you want."

"No, best to leave him in his drunken stupor," Thomas frowned. "Why would you, though?"

"You are an Enforcer. We protect our own. That includes new recruits who despise their role." Patrick turned in his saddle, casting a look back at Riverwick. "I don't know how you can live in such a sorry village. What a relief to leave that behind."

Thomas followed Patrick's stare towards his village. The Shadow of Death would continue to kill, and fear for his family and all of Riverwick would remain until they finished the job.

"What we're doing isn't working," Thomas told Lord Samson. "If we're to find the Shadow. . .the killer, we need to change our approach."

The horses' steps on the dirt road filled the silence as Lord Samson considered this. "What do you suggest?" he finally asked.

"Use the townsfolk to our advantage. Offer a reward for his capture. Not just money, but they'll be recognised as the one who led to his arrest. Hailed a hero. You'll have all of Kempschester looking for him. They will give him no shelter and will willingly help the very people they fear the most."

Patrick's head turned towards Lord Samson. "It might work," the Enforcer said. "He remains in the shadows for now, but we're going to hold light to every dark corner of Kempschester. He will have nowhere to hide. Peasants would hand over their own brothers for the sake of some coin."

Lord Samson's eyes remained on Thomas. "Patrick."

"Yes, sir."

"When we return to Kempschester, spread the word. Whoever is responsible for his capture will be paid for it. I will host celebrations in their honour." Lord Samson showed a faint smile. "I knew I could count on you, Thomas."

Chapter 20

The moment they arrived back in Kempschester, news of the remaining guards reached them. Dead. Murdered by The Shadow of Death. Thomas and Patrick waited by the church as Lord Samson spoke to Father Matthew in the cemetery. The priest's height was short in comparison to Lord Samson's. His eyes crinkled, full of kindness as he acknowledged Thomas.

Snowflakes drifted down; the weather had followed them from Riverwick. Nearby, a cart full of infected bodies had been discarded, the guards on top. One guard's death had been more violent than the other's. Eyes open wide, the throat a gaping, bloody wound, his chest shredded. Father Matthew handed a sword to Lord Samson before hurrying into the church.

"They were off-duty," Lord Samson said. He held up the sword, revealing dried blood on the blade. "It seems Michael fought back and may have wounded our killer."

"Good. So, we keep our eyes open for someone with fresh wounds," Thomas said. "Six people in a week. How many more will die before we can stop him?"

"He let them escape, only to go *back* for them." A quiet outrage had replaced Patrick's usual arrogance. "He really wanted them dead."

"Thomas, it's your brother," Lord Samson said.

"Excuse me?"

Lord Samson pointed behind him. Thomas turned to find Graeme watching them from the front of the church.

"I will be inside to talk to those who saw this," Lord Samson said, pointing at the bodies. "Patrick." He handed the sword to Patrick.

"You're still here?" Thomas approached his brother, trying to get a grasp on Graeme's mood. "I thought you would be on your way home by now."

"I went to see Nicholas and Catherine first," Graeme pointed at the bodies. "Another one?"

"Two, sadly. They had escaped him the first time."

"It was their time," Graeme murmured.

There was that lack of sympathy again.

"Graeme, be respectful of the dead. These men were murdered. Someone else decided it was their time. They didn't deserve that."

Graeme cast his gaze down. "Sorry."

His mental shield slipped; something was off. His presence flickered, the usual tense energy drifting in and out. There was a *calm* in his brother that Thomas had never felt before. An unnatural stillness. *This doesn't feel like my brother at all.*

"Are you all right?" Thomas grabbed Graeme's arm. "What happened at home? Do you want to talk about it?"

Graeme glanced down at Thomas's hand. "No."

"Grim, you've never hidden anything from me."

Graeme pulled his arm out of Thomas's grip. "You've never hidden anything from me, either. But you don't want to talk about war, so please understand that I don't want to talk about my nightmares." His tone was guarded.

"I *killed* people, Graeme," Thomas blurted, losing the battle to the warmth of tears welling in his eyes. "You want me to talk about that? How my first kill was removing a man's head from his shoulders? How much blood I spilled? Or do you want me to talk about how I held in a friend's intestines while he begged me to kill him?" Thomas choked, sorrow rising. The emptiness in Graeme's eyes only made it worse. "I hope you never know what it's like to kill someone. Please, I asked that you give me time. You talk about your nightmares when you're ready."

Thomas caught a glimmer of urgency, as if Graeme wanted to tell him something of importance. But it faded.

"I'm here to talk to the priest. You should go. You're on duty." Graeme moved around him, casting another look at the bodies before he disappeared into the church.

"Thomas," Patrick motioned him over.

Inside the church, a single shaft of light streamed through a window, the pews mostly empty. At the front stood a statue of Jesus on the cross, head tilted down. Candles had been lit and a sweet, woodsy scent of incense burning filled the air. Graeme took a seat in the front pew, his shoulders hunched. Father Matthew sat next to him.

Lord Samson was speaking with a woman in the back pew, while Patrick stood against the wall.

"Who's she?" Thomas asked Patrick.

"Elizabeth, Michael's wife. She was there, saw the whole thing. The killer didn't go after her at all." Patrick pointed at two men who sat nearby. "They ran to help Lucas. Same thing, he had no interest in them."

"It's as if he wants to be caught," Thomas said.

"Or he doesn't care," Patrick agreed. "We need to find out what they saw."

Patrick sat down in front of one of the witnesses. Thomas addressed the other, a man of low wealth in need of new clothes and a bath.

"What is your name?" Thomas asked, keeping his voice low.

"Archibald, sir."

Thomas laughed. "No, I'm not a sir. Relax, Archibald. I'm just here to ask you some questions." He took a breath. "You saw Lucas die? I'm sorry you had to see that."

"That's right." Archibald's hand trembled as he pointed to the other witness. "We heard what sounded like a fight and screams. We ran to help. By the time we got there, Michael was dead, and The Shadow of Death was telling Lucas that it was his time to die."

"Did you get a good look at the killer? Do you remember anything that can help us?" *We're finally getting somewhere.* Overjoyed, Thomas envisioned wrapping his arms around Emma, spending time with Isaac and racing Graeme on horseback.

Archibald shook his head. "I remember the black blade in his hand, I think it was curved. He was quick to kill. Just..." Archibald sliced the air at Thomas's throat. "It was over before we could help. We tried to grab him, but he vanished."

Thomas stroked his chin. "A man just disappeared?"

"He was there in front of us one moment, then the next, gone." Archibald glanced around the church and leaned forward. "But he wasn't a man; he was a shadow. He had the shape of and moved like a man, but he sounded different."

"Different?" Thomas asked.

"His voice was a strange whisper, and dark."

Thomas raised his head just as Lord Samson stood.

"Thank you, Archibald."

"His eyes," the peasant said. "I'll never forget his eyes."

"The shadow man?"

"They were like the eyes of the dead. Different from the one who was with him."

"Someone was with him?" Thomas leaned forward. "What did he look like?"

"A shadow. Do you have any more questions, or can I go?" Archibald asked.

"You can go."

"Cease this talk of shadows!" Patrick walked out, his steps heavy as he moved.

Thomas and Lord Samson followed, the three of them stopping when they were far enough from the church.

"Shadow men?" Patrick's mouth pressed in a thin line. "That was time wasted."

"Are you putting something in the water?" Thomas asked Lord Samson. "I'm not sure we can follow a shadow that disappears. That got us nowhere."

"She kept rambling about his eyes," Lord Samson placed his hands over his face, letting out a frustrated sound. "We're no closer to him now than we were in Riverwick."

"We know there were two of them," Thomas pointed out.

"Great, we have two killers," Lord Samson was unimpressed. "That doesn't help, Thomas. They killed in the middle of the day, and only three people saw them, but they saw *shadows*."

An Enforcer approached the church. "Lord Samson, I think I have something."

"If you're going to say anything about shadows and dark eyes, I will lock you in a cell for a week," Lord Samson grumbled and followed the Enforcer to speak in private.

Through the door, Graeme finished talking to the priest. As he passed the witnesses, his head turned towards them.

"You should know we're going to lock the gates tonight," Patrick said. "Tell your brother before he gets shut in."

"Grim," Thomas called out. "Go home."

"Yeoman Graeme." Lord Samson had finished speaking with the Enforcer. "Have you come to join the hunt?"

"No!" Thomas warned, shooting Lord Samson a meaningful glance.

While paying attention to Lord Samson, Thomas made sure his brother was leaving. The sharp sound of a horse's hooves on cobblestones faded.

"We're going to South End. There have been reports of suspicious movement there. It's time to start knocking on doors," Lord Samson declared.

Suspicious movements in South End? What does he mean by that? South End was not a wealthy neighbourhood and was least likely to cause any trouble.

As Thomas and Patrick readied themselves for the ride to the other side of town, Lord Samson's words froze him in his tracks. "Thomas, be ready for what comes next."

What comes next? The words buried themselves deep in Thomas's consciousness. Cold fear crawled across his arms, panic cutting off his ability to breathe. This was the reason Lord Samson had recruited him. To go home, Thomas would have to unleash something almost as dark as the killer itself.

Chapter 21

Lord Samson's words were clear that Thomas would be a part of the interrogation, and once word got out, he would not escape that reputation. As they rode towards South End, Thomas feared what came next. These were people who relied on farmers, such as his family. *Why would we chase the killer in South End? What did that Enforcer say to* Lord *Samson to bring him here?*

The snow stopped. Cloud cover hung over Kempschester, and the cold air meant more was on its way. All around them, the townsfolk were murmuring. Only some of their words were audible.

"The Shadow of Death. . ."

"A shadow cannot be caught. . ."

"Not human."

"Not of this world."

"Not of this world," Patrick laughed.

"The usual hysteria," Thomas said, but thorns of doubt had wrapped around his throat.

Talk of a shadow should have been a ridiculous idea. One to dismiss before it was given time to grow. In the company of Patrick and Lord Samson, he had been quick to judge the witnesses. But with the whispers about The Shadow of Death surrounding him, and what he had seen in the stable, the cold grip of fear had taken hold. *Is it possible that what they claim to have seen isn't the usual hysteria? Is there something unnatural stalking Kempschester?* Had he not spent his entire life aware of the Darkness inside his brother, Thomas would have shrugged off the very idea of it. This was something new, and it was likely none of them knew what they were truly up against.

"Lord Samson, may God guide you in your search for The Shadow of Death," a man called out.

"Thank you." Lord Samson gave a curt nod.

More voices rose from the crowd in response.

"They won't find him; he walks in the shadows!"

"He *is* the shadows."

"He brought the pestilence!"

"He *is* the pestilence!"

Lord Samson stopped to speak with guards, who soon started to close the gates. On the other side, traders looked on with dismay before the gates locked them out.

"Do you think shutting off the town is necessary?" Thomas asked.

"While we're hunting a killer, I'm restricting movement in and out of Kempschester," Lord Samson said.

"But you're locking out traders. Kempschester needs the trade, especially now."

"Who are you to question him?" Patrick demanded.

"Patrick, stop. Thomas, it falls on me to protect these people. If we cut off his escape, it will not be long before we find him."

This was not the Samson Thomas had fought alongside in France. There was desperation in this. *If he isn't careful, we will have a battle of a different kind on our hands.*

"We'll be locked in here with him, too," Thomas countered. "Not to mention the townsfolk when they realise they're shut in."

"There are fifty Enforcers hunting him; he will feel us closing in." Patrick pointed around them. "As for the townsfolk, they'll do what they're told."

"It could be us he hunts," Thomas said.

"One against fifty? I think we have the advantage," Patrick laughed.

In Lord Samson's silence, Thomas's uneasiness grew from a whisper to a thunderous roar, but this was not an argument he would win. Patrick would see no fault in it, and Lord Samson had his mind set. They reached South End, and his focus shifted to their purpose there.

A plume of black smoke rose above the town, and Thomas gagged. A nauseating, putrid smell filled the air, so thick it stuck in the back of his throat. He covered his mouth, and his eyes watered. Thomas had encountered this odour many times. Burned flesh.

"Who's burning bodies?" Thomas asked.

"They're hoping to burn the pestilence away," Lord Samson said.

"I thought they were burying them all outside the walls." Thomas shuddered.

People deserved proper burial rites. To be burned or dumped in a mass grave was uncivilised.

"They want the dead out of their homes, and the gravediggers cannot get to them fast enough," Lord Samson replied. "Now, pay attention. We have had confirmation of suspicious movement on the days of the murders. We are here to arrest those people, no exceptions." Lord Samson gave Thomas a pointed look. "No mercy."

No mercy. Thomas's hands tightened around the reins. Those words alone were enough to bring rise to all he was trying to suppress.

"Patrick, you go on ahead, we will meet you at Albert Square. The others are there, they know who we're after. Wait for me, though."

Patrick gave Thomas a sideways look before leaving the two of them. Lord Samson said nothing until the hollow sound of horse hooves on cobblestones faded.

"You know why you're here," Lord Samson said.

"Yes, I do," Thomas confirmed.

"You know how I feel about failure," Lord Samson reminded him.

Thomas had no need to respond but nodded. Lord Samson nudged his horse forward, closer to Thomas.

"I will say this once and only once," Lord Samson cautioned. His voice had a ring of authority. "Follow orders. You will not falter; you will not question me. Any failure to be anything other than an Enforcer right now, and I will put you in a cell with those we arrest. What we are about to do will draw anger, and I need a strong front. Am I understood?"

"Yes."

"I want to hear you say you will follow orders." Lord Samson's eyes narrowed. "Pledge to me that you will do your duty."

This was the Samson Thomas knew from France. Demanding obedience and removing any doubt in his superiority.

"I will follow your orders, Lord Samson." The last of Thomas's hope crumbled. There would be no return to whom he was holding on to. He was an Enforcer and there was no way out. "I will do as you command, as is my duty."

"Good. When we've finished here, I may consider granting you leave."

A flicker of hope reignited in Thomas. "You mean…"

"You can go home to your wife."

CHAPTER 21

The clouds darkened. Men yelled as they were forced into a wagon with wooden bars. A door was kicked in with a loud bang.

"I told them to wait for me," Lord Samson grumbled. "Patrick!"

A woman screamed, as Enforcers struggled to remove a man from his house.

"Please, let me go! I did nothing!"

Lord Samson dismounted, running to assist. "Thomas!"

Before Thomas could move, the man headbutted Lord Samson and tried to run. Jumping into action, Thomas tackled the runner to the ground, met by resistance.

"Stop," Thomas instructed. "Fighting will only make it worse."

"I know you; you're not one of them. Help me."

The words alone were a punch to his chest. *What am I doing? I don't belong here.*

Instead, Thomas pulled the captive to stand. "I'm afraid you're wrong," he said. "I am an Enforcer, and you just headbutted Lord Samson. I cannot help you."

"You know we did nothing. We're innocent."

A bitter wind rocked Thomas, numbing him inside and out.

Lord Samson marched over, a furious light in his eyes. "Think you can headbutt me, do you?" he demanded and punched the captive's stomach.

The man doubled over, gasping. "I ought to have you hanged for that!"

This was a side of Samson that Thomas had only seen in the heat of battle. Thomas lowered his gaze to the ground, fist clenched as the lord threw another punch. Lord Samson had made it clear that any opposition from him would have consequences. *Am I going to let him beat someone?* Waves of suffocating hopelessness crashed over him.

Finally, Lord Samson calmed down and pushed the beaten man to the waiting cage. Patrick dragged another forward. A crowd had gathered, their voices a combination of anger and confusion. Thomas faced the townsfolk and attempted to draw his sword.

"No," Lord Samson stopped him. "We're not here for them." He turned to the townsfolk. "Return to your homes immediately. We seek the murderer."

"But why in South End?" A voice called out from the crowd. "Please, no one here is a killer."

Patrick strode through the crowd, grabbing someone and pulling him towards Lord Samson. It was a peasant who often worked in the markets.

"Patrick, don't be so rough," Lord Samson commanded. "You. What's your name?"

"Elijah."

"You want to protect your neighbours, I understand that," Lord Samson said.

"Sorry, Lord Samson, but they are innocent men your Enforcers are arresting," Elijah said with a bowed head. "I don't understand. They have done nothing."

Murmurs of agreement passed through the crowd.

"We've received reports that these men were seen in the area of the murders. They will be interrogated. If they are innocent, there is nothing to worry about."

Elijah pointed towards the cage. Enforcers stood in front of the jail, hands on swords as if waiting for a reason to draw them. "That man there was the witness of the first murder. He saw your father die at the hands of another. We are working men. Anyone seen was where he was supposed to be."

Elijah moved towards Lord Samson. Thomas and Patrick moved to block him. Thomas rested his hand on the hilt of his sword, ready to draw. To use it on the peasants of South End seemed excessive, not something Thomas wanted to do.

"Please, for your own safety, go home," Thomas said.

"The Shadow of Death is killing *your* people, *not* ours." Elijah waved a hand at the crowd. "We have nothing to fear from him. We are safe."

The townsfolk were silent, nodding in unison.

"Go back to your homes," Lord Samson's voice rang out. "Let me and my men do our jobs."

No one moved. Patrick pushed Elijah, drawing his sword. Elijah lost his footing and fell hard.

The Enforcer stood over Elijah, sword extended. "He said to go home."

"Patrick, what are you doing?" Thomas blurted before he could stop himself.

"Patrick, no. Let him go," Lord Samson ordered. "I order you to return to your homes now. Otherwise, there will be more to arrest."

Patrick kicked Elijah. The crowd slowly dispersed. Night had fallen and with it, a biting cold. Thomas, Lord Samson, and Patrick returned to their horses.

"Patrick, why do you always have to do that?" Lord Samson asked in a tight voice. "You don't need to jump straight to brutality all the time."

Thomas opened his mouth to remind Lord Samson he had just beaten a man for headbutting him. Instead he remained silent.

The leer that seemed permanently plastered to Patrick's face faltered. "We keep them in line," he mumbled. "Your father—"

"I'm not my father. I would rather these people not fear their Lord." Lord Samson caught Thomas's stare. The Lord lowered his voice. "I need you with me in the cells. One of these men knows something or is involved in the murders. Time for the real work to begin."

Chapter 22

As they entered the estate's courtyard, Thomas's heart sank and his stomach churned. It would be a long night of violence and inflicting pain. So much for leaving all that behind in France. He had no choice but to fall in line and follow orders. A gust of wind swept past, making him shiver. He had no one to blame but himself for what lay ahead.

The pyre had been completed. Heat pricked his arms and under his skull. This would be a very public execution. Luckily, his brother had left Kempschester and would be on his way back to Riverwick. *Grim never has to hear of this.* There was nothing through their bond, although as of late it had not been the connection to which Thomas was accustomed.

Overwhelmingly strong one day, but flickering the next. *Is it Grim's doing, or mine?*

Activity around them was chaotic. Men hurried to clear carriages, carts of armour, and war supplies out of the way. An Enforcer carried an armful of weapons to Lord Samson: a mace, a knife and an axe.

Lord Samson nodded. "Take them down to cell one with the prisoners. I want one man in cell two next door. The one who headbutted me."

The Enforcer hurried away, and Patrick followed. Thomas's heart was in his throat.

"Please don't make me do this," he pleaded, his eyes on the carts.

Lord Samson's silence stretched out. Thomas turned to face the lord to find him contemplating the weapons and war equipment.

"Do you miss it?" Lord Samson asked.

The change in topic drew Thomas's confusion.

"Miss what?" Thomas asked.

Lord Samson motioned to the weapons.

Ice pierced through Thomas's chest. "No!" *Why would I miss that?*

Lord Samson's eyes turned to him. "You were different there. More prepared to do whatever it took. I know it was because of the vow you made, but you never hesitated, never held back. The perfect soldier. You, Caleb, and Aris were among my best. Why are you so scared now?"

Unable to meet Lord Samson's eyes, Thomas focused on the servants who had taken their horses.

"I was not proud of what I did in France. War brought out the worst in me," Thomas recalled.

Lord Samson crossed his arms. "You could have fooled me. You *unleashed* something in France. You need that here. You're an Enforcer now, Thomas, and I still expect you to follow my orders."

Thomas's heart quickened as his throat closed. "Why these men? They are not our enemy; they're Englishmen."

The last words should have had an effect on Lord Samson. After what Thomas had done, there should have been something, a flicker of regret. *Nothing.*

"The sooner we're finished here, the sooner you can return to your wife. I know you are close with your brother, too. Don't you want to go home, Thomas?"

You had to bring my family into this? Thomas rested his hand on the sword pommel as they moved towards the underground cells. There was no way out of this. Everything he had done was to keep Graeme from the brutality of war, and he would do it again, no matter the cost. But now he had to dig into the cruelty he had uncovered in battle.

A servant ran over before they could enter the tunnel. "My lord, someone waits in the hall. He's been here awhile."

Lord Samson let out a growl of frustration. "Who? Can this not wait?"

"No, sir. He said it's—" The servant stopped mid-sentence as he caught sight of Thomas. "Oh, he found you. My apologies for the interruption." He frowned at Thomas. "I thought...I saw you... I mean..." The servant's eyes clouded over.

"What nonsense are you talking about?" Lord Samson demanded, his tone sharp. "He didn't find me. He's been with me the whole time."

"Oh, no." Only when Thomas reached out did he find Graeme's energy. Lord Samson shot him a curious look. "It wasn't me; it was Grim." *Why didn't I feel him before?*

"Why would your brother be here? He should have left."

"That's why he's here, sir. The gates are locked," the servant said, his eyes still on Thomas.

Lord Samson started towards the estate. "Thomas, your brother is going to have to wait until morning before he leaves. We have too much work to do, and I'm not opening the gates." He addressed the servant. "Find an extra bed and have it moved to Enforcer Blake's quarters. I want some food brought there to him." Lord Samson stopped. "Follow me, Thomas. We'll speak to your brother."

"He cannot stay here," Thomas said, following Lord Samson. "Not now." He fought back the rising panic. "I cannot do what you need me to do with him here."

Lord Samson shot him a look of disbelief. "I'm afraid neither of you have a choice. He is locked in like the rest of the town. He can keep you company as you ride back to Riverwick in the morning."

As they entered the estate, Graeme's back was to him, staring up at a statue.

"Graeme, why are you here?" Lord Samson asked.

"I didn't get out before you had the gates closed." Graeme turned. "I have to get home."

"You'll leave in the morning. I have no spare quarters, so you'll spend the night in your brother's room. He will be working late, so you'll have privacy for most of the night."

Thomas avoided Graeme's eyes, slamming a door closed on their connection. Just as he had done for the last four years, he needed to prevent Graeme from feeling any of his emotions. There was a chance that by shutting his brother out, he would only be giving Graeme reason to find answers himself.

"Thomas, show your brother where he'll be sleeping."Lord Samson left, shouting orders at servants.

"Has something happened?" Graeme asked. "The courtyard was—"

"Why are you still in Kempschester?" Thomas demanded as he led Graeme towards his room. "I thought you left. Like I told you to at the church."

Graeme glared. "Why are you taking it out on me? I didn't make it out in time. It's not my fault Lord Samson decided to lock everyone in."

"He did it to make sure the killer couldn't leave."

"You're defending him?" Graeme stopped mid-step. "You've shut me out again. What don't you want me to know? Something's happening." He grabbed Thomas's arm. "You're in over your head, Tom, and I think you know that. I don't like this."

"So now that *you're* the one being shut out, you don't like it?" Thomas pulled his arm out of Graeme's grasp to avoid his brother picking up on anything. Contact only strengthened their connection. He lowered his voice. "You had *black eyes,* which terrified your wife, if you didn't notice. Some strange nightmares are affecting you, but now you want to talk?" He continued walking, Graeme a few steps behind him. The best way to keep

Graeme away was to show annoyance. He could not reveal any of the dread that had engulfed him. "I'm busy, Graeme. I don't have time for this."

They reached Thomas's quarters, and he pushed the door open. The fire had been lit, taking the chill out of the air. Graeme walked past him, taking a seat at the table, candlelight reflecting over his face. Thomas waited at the door.

Thomas moved aside as a servant entered the room with a plate of chicken, beans, carrots and cabbage. The aroma made his mouth water. Garlic overpowered all else, but he did catch a whiff of a sweet, spicy scent and the sharp smell of black pepper. Another servant entered with almonds and dried figs. They placed the food on the table. Graeme stared in amazement as the servants left.

"So, this is how the other half lives," Graeme muttered.

"I can get ale brought to you, if you want," Thomas said. "Lord Samson provides those who stay in his estate with high-quality food." He took in a deep breath. "I have to go."

"What work are you doing? I heard them talking earlier. All the Enforcers are here."

"We've arrested people. Hopefully we'll have answers soon."

"About the murderer?" Graeme asked.

Thomas sighed. "Yes, about the murderer. That's why I'm here. I'll feel a lot better when we know the murderer has been caught."

"You thought he was in Riverwick."

"No, we had to search all the surrounding villages to be sure. Lord Samson knew I'd be worried for all of you. I'll be relieved when he's gone. There is enough death here without him adding to the body count."

"If you find him, you'll put him to flame," Graeme picked up a fork.

"He's killed people. Don't try to tell me he doesn't deserve it."

Panic flared in Graeme's eyes. The same look from earlier at the church. "Tom, I need to tell you something." He lowered the fork again.

"What is it? I must go. You being here has already tested Lord Samson's patience. He will be expecting me."

"If I tell you..." Graeme's voice was thick with fear, and his whole body shook. "Tom, something's *wrong* with me. These nightmares are *dark*." He put his head in his hands.

Thomas sat on the other side of the table, his annoyance melting. Graeme needed him, and Thomas had been dismissive, caught up in what he needed to do. "Grim, what is it?" he asked again, his tone softening.

"I'm scared," Graeme raised his head again. There was raw fear in his eyes, his voice quiet. "I'm drawn to it, but it still scares me."

"What? Tell me," Thomas asked with an ache in his throat. He caught the hesitance in Graeme's eyes. "I'm asking as your brother." He leaned forward.

Graeme had only spoken this way when they were children terrified of shadows.

Before Graeme could say anything, Lord Samson returned. "Thomas, time to go. Your brother will be looked after here. My servants are seeing to that. You have somewhere else to be."

Thomas rose from the table, Graeme's eyes pleading with him. "We can talk later. Stay here."

As Thomas followed Lord Samson, he shot one last glance at Graeme. His brother had visibly slumped, head bowed.

The cell was devoid of any warmth. A single candle dimly lit the room. Stone walls and a dirt floor surrounded him. The faint smell of urine mixed with stale water and smoke. Shackles and chains, along with tools of torture, hung from the walls. Turning from the display, Thomas found Lord Samson watching him. A prisoner was shackled to the wall, a dark bruise showing around his eye. The man Lord Samson had beaten. Thomas kept his distance. Patrick leaned against the door frame, arms folded.

"Thomas," There was a tone of impatience in Lord Samson's voice.

"What am I supposed to do?" Thomas asked. "It wasn't exactly interrogations that I…" Unable to finish the sentence, he stopped.

"Torture, interrogation, it's all the same," Patrick said with a shrug. "They all involve pain and screaming, but lead to answers."

"Patrick, leave us," Lord Samson said.

Patrick closed the door, leaving Thomas in the cell with Lord Samson and the prisoner.

"The Blake touch is needed to get results for this," Lord Samson said. "What you do in here will ensure the rest are ready for questions."

Thomas suppressed a shudder.

"The Blake touch usually led to bad things happening," Thomas said. "People dying."

"That's what happens at war," Lord Samson said. "People die."

"In battle, with a sword in their hand. Not on their knees after hours of torment for the sake of names and information." Thomas turned his palms up, staring at his trembling hands. Dread gnawed at his insides, waves of panic rising. Unable to hold back, he leaned over and retched. Liquid splashed on his shoes and Lord Samson's.

"Are you finished? I'm getting impatient, Thomas," Lord Samson's eyes glinted.

Thomas wiped his mouth, disgusted by the bitter taste of vomit.

"Once I start this, you know there's no holding me back," he warned. "You can't interfere."

Lord Samson held up his hands. "I won't. I've seen what happens if someone steps in while you're — what did you call it — 'under the sway of battle rage'."

Thomas took a step towards the prisoner, with no choice but to do what was expected. *All right, let's get this over with.* He let out a shaky breath, bracing himself.

"What's your name?" His voice came out calm despite the turmoil.

"Warwick." Was the reply.

In the dim light, the whites of Warwick's eyes shone as Thomas advanced.

"Do you know why I'm here, Warwick?"

"Please. I didn't do anything. I beg of you, have mercy," Warwick pleaded.

Have mercy. The words repeated themselves over and over. *Have mercy*. Caleb's last words. But they merged with other voices. 'Sans pitié,' uttered by the French frequently. No mercy. The cell around him blurred, becoming a reflection of his memories. A field of the dead —a massacre. Burning villages. Beating a French soldier who had invaded their camp. Everything Thomas had done because of his vow. The rising storm of his battle rage.

Screams rang out, piercing the murk. The bright haze of the battlefield faded, bringing the dark cell back into focus. The war was far away, and he was kneeling, his sword on the ground. Beneath him, Warwick's breaths were shallow, his face bloodied. Thomas's knuckles were red and bruised. The brutality of the war had taken him, and he had failed to hold it at bay. He hadn't asked any questions, instead giving in to the violence.

"There will be no mercy," he muttered.

Chapter 23

Thomas slumped under the weight of what he had just done, his heart hollow. With his head bowed, the wooden table before him filled his whole vision. He clenched his fists to stop them from shaking.

"Thomas, you have a job to do." Lord Samson's voice pulled him back from his daze. "You're not finished yet."

"Why me?" he asked, lifting his chin to meet Lord Samson's eyes. "Why did you need me for this? Patrick or any other Enforcer would have happily done this."

Lord Samson took a seat on the other side of the table. "He was my father. There was a lot he did that I didn't agree with. But Kempschester was important to him. I'm told he was on patrol. Returning home to that, I would burn down all of Kempschester to find his killer."

"What does that have to do with me?" Thomas asked.

"In France you fought hard to get home. I hoped that your desire to go home would mean we'd find the killer quickly. After four years of fighting alongside you, I could think of no one else I trusted more to find my father's murderer." Lord Samson's eyes darted to the door, and he lowered his voice. "The rest of the Enforcers, especially Patrick, only saw it as a means to remind people of their status. He couldn't wait for me as I ordered him to, and was already busting down doors. You know how to follow orders."

Thomas stood, the chair falling over with a thud. "I just beat someone because you ordered me to, and you knew that I would suffer from this. We both know what comes next." He leaned on the table, seething. "I'm about to torture people to get answers they may not have. You're pushing me to a dark place, Lord Samson, and last time I gave in to that, it got me dismissed. Is that why you stepped in, stopping them from executing me? So you could wield me like your personal weapon?" Patrick was right. A jolt of fury shot through him.

Lord Samson pushed himself out of his chair, leaning forward, hands on the table. "Calm yourself, Thomas, or I will lock you in this cell until you do." He strode towards the door. "It's time, we're finished here." Thomas didn't move, and the Lord scowled. "That's an order, Enforcer Blake. Now."

Lord Samson took the candle with him. With no choice but to follow, Thomas left the cell, groans of pain behind him.

Patrick waited at the next cell door holding a torch.

"You were right. He is quite barbaric," Patrick said to Lord Samson as he eyed Thomas.

Is that admiration? Nausea washed over Thomas again.

Patrick pushed open the door, revealing a pitch-black cell. Whoever was in the room had been in the dark this whole time. What had just occurred in the cell over would have echoed through this one. As Thomas stepped through the doorway, he froze. Once word got out of his actions here, it would follow him. *Grim is not far away. If he hears about this...* An image of Graeme swam before him, eyes filled with loathing as he turned away in disgust. Then it shifted to Emma's tearful face. *I cannot do this. If I do, what will it cost me?*

"Is he panicking?" Patrick's voice pierced the fog. "Thomas, I thought you were having fun."

Lord Samson put a hand on his back, pushing him forward. He stepped past Patrick, forcing away the storm that threatened to overwhelm him. Lord Samson followed him in. The torchlight revealed four men shackled to the walls and a single table and chair. The back wall held a variety of weapons only used for one thing. The door closed, followed by a click.

Blood pounded in his ears; all eyes were on Thomas. He yearned to go home. Working the land, racing his brother on horseback, hunting, swimming in the river. But to get home he had to walk through his personal hell.

"Thomas. What are you doing?"

The voice was far away. He blinked. Lord Samson was sitting on the table, his head tilted and his eyes upward.

"Stop stalling." Lord Samson pointed. "Start with that one."

With a deep breath, Thomas braced his shoulders and stood over the unfortunate prisoner. The cell had a musty odour to it and dripping water echoed inside the room.

"Tell me your name," Thomas began.

The moment stretched out, his question going unanswered. He clenched his jaw as he stepped forward.

"Did you not hear me?"

The room closed in, his temple pulsing. *Just scare him.* Heat rose in his cheeks as he took in the weapons hanging on the wall. A mace, an axe, knives, and pliers. *No, too much.* The dagger on the table with a heavy hilt and a long blade. Lord Samson took that weapon everywhere. Did he place it there deliberately? With shaky fingers, Thomas grasped the dagger's hilt. Lord Samson made no move to take it from him.

Thomas held the tip of the blade to the prisoner's eye. "What is your name?"

Another prisoner gasped. "Give him your name!"

The reply was barely audible. "Jacob. My name is Jacob."

Good, that's a start.

"I'm supposed to ask you some questions. You answer them. Otherwise..." He nodded to the dagger. "There will be a lot of pain. Do you understand?" His voice was strange, calm. *What am I doing?*

Jacob was pale. His eyes bulged as they clouded over. "Yes," Jacob choked out.

"You're aware of the murders? Lord Philip was the first," Thomas pressed.

"Y-yes," Jacob stuttered.

"Did you kill Lord Philip?" Thomas asked.

"I'm not the killer."

Lord Samson stepped forward. "You were seen outside your neighbourhood the night my father was killed. What were you doing there?"

"Please, I didn't kill anyone," Jacob's voice was thick with fear.

"That was not the question," Thomas said.

"You want me to confess to something I didn't do. None of us did it." Jacob's chin trembled.

"But were you there?" Thomas asked.

He hit Jacob between his eyes with the hilt. Jacob's cry of pain sparked memories of those he had questioned in France. The familiar haze of rage settled over him. *Don't, not now.* He had already lost control with Warwick. He had to contain himself.

"I was working!" Jacob said.

"What work?" Thomas asked.

Jacob shook his head.

"What work?" Lord Samson repeated his question, approaching Jacob. "You're a shoemaker, and no one saw you with shoes."

Heart thundering in his ears, Thomas took in a deep breath, holding on to what little calm remained.

"Why that neighbourhood?" Lord Samson demanded. "Did you know my father would be there?"

When Jacob didn't answer immediately, Thomas raised the dagger again,."Answer the question."

"I told you, I was there for work."

Lord Samson forcefully grabbed Jacob by the jaw. "What work? Why were you out so early in the morning?"

Jacob turned his gaze to Lord Samson, beads of sweat lining his forehead. "We take what work we can. Please, I know nothing about who killed Lord Philip."

Thomas recognised the glimmer in Jacob's eyes. He was holding something back.

"Why won't you tell us what the work was?" Thomas asked.

Jacob shook his head again.

He knows something.

"Did you think with me at war you'd have a town with no lord?" Lord Samson demanded.

Lord Samson's emotions were getting the best of him. Jacob was not going to talk, which meant Lord Samson would not grant Thomas leave to go home. Thomas's mouth was dry, and his throat tightened. *I cannot do what he expects of me. This was supposed to be over when I left France.* Everything in him was prepared to step back and let Lord Samson take over. But that wouldn't get him home. Lord Samson would berate and threaten Jacob, but usually left certain tasks for others to handle. As the Lord, Samson was expected to maintain a refined manner. It would be up to Thomas to do the dirty work.

Just as he had done at war, there was a job to do. Fighting against it would not get him answers. He hesitated. Once he took that step, it would be like falling and the rest would follow. He would not be able to hold back his rage. He closed his eyes. *Why fight it? This is why* Lord *Samson wants me here. Emma. Isaac. Grim.* Thomas opened his eyes again and plunged the blade into Jacob's shoulder. Screams of pain mixed with the horrified cries of the other prisoners.

"Stop!" The other prisoners cried in unison.

Twisting the blade, Thomas leaned in. Jacob paled, trembling.

"Please, Jacob, tell us what you were doing."

"I'm telling the truth! I was working. I didn't kill anyone. Please take it out, I'm answering your questions."

"Did you have a fight with my father?" Lord Samson asked. "It was well known that you peasants hated him."

Frustration kicked in; Lord Samson was in his way.

"Your father was an unpleasant man. Many fought with him," Jacob gasped, wincing in pain.

"Why were you in that neighbourhood? Peasants don't work there. You had no business there," Lord Samson snapped.

Thomas grabbed Lord Samson's arm and pulled him to the other side of the cell.

"Get out of my way and let me work," he grumbled. "Your emotions are a hindrance. If I lose control, you're as likely as he is to get hurt."

Anger blazed in Lord Samson's eyes, but quickly died. Instead, he relaxed, giving Thomas a nod. Thomas returned to Jacob, twisting the blade again. Jacob grunted in pain.

Defiance shone past the fear like a beacon as Jacob lifted his eyes to Lord Samson. "Am I here because of The Shadow of Death, or because I was out of South End, scaring the elites with my lack of nobility?"

Thomas's resistance to the job slipped, replaced by calm. *Here it comes.* "Just tell him what he wants to hear."

"But he doesn't want to hear the truth. He wants me to confess to something I didn't do." Jacob turned his focus behind Thomas, on Lord Samson. "You are supposed to protect us. All of us!" Pain and fear were spurring Jacob's anger, something Thomas had witnessed many times. "Your Enforcers like to cause pain. They fought with him, too. Maybe it's one of them! Get them in here with your interrogator!" Jacob turned to Thomas then. "You're better than this. You're a farmer, not his personal tormentor! Your own brother would not recognise you."

His brother. Graeme. The name pierced the fog and shattered his focus. Thomas measured the distance to the door.

"Don't think about it," Lord Samson commanded. "You are here because of your brother. You made a promise. Do your duty." He pointed to Jacob. "Or I'll have you chained up beside him."

I will never be free from this. Thomas considered letting Lord Samson shackle him. At the limit before his rage took over, Thomas would lose himself. Being chained to the wall would at least hold it back. Hold *him* back.

"Do what you are here for, Thomas," Lord Samson ordered. "To get back to your family."

My family. Thomas let the rage wash over him. Just as it had at war many times. Before he could stop himself, the mace was in his hand. Its wooden handle was rough in his tight grip, the bronze head heavy. Emptiness cleared his resistance, rolling through him like a wave.

"What are you doing with that?" Patrick's voice was far away, the tone rising. "What is he doing?"

"Oh, I've seen that look before. Thomas? Don't go too far, I don't want him dead," Lord Samson said.

Thomas crossed the cell. Jacob's wide eyes bored into his with a glint of fear. He swung, intending to stop before making contact. A loud crack filled the room as the weapon connected with Jacob's right side. A pained shriek pounded against his ears. Grey spots danced before him as he realised he couldn't stop. He swung the mace again, smashing the bone in Jacob's right leg.

"What are you holding back?" Thomas asked.

"Thomas, stop!" Lord Samson yelled.

Hands grabbed at him mid-swing, but he shook them off. The distraction threw him off, and the mace slipped from his grip, hitting the wall. He pulled the dagger from Jacob's shoulder. As blood curdling screams echoed around the cell, an arm snaked around his throat before he could plunge the blade into Jacob's chest.

"Please, make him stop! I'll tell you what you want to hear," Jacob panted before slumping unconscious.

Intoxicated with dark joy, he fought as Patrick and Lord Samson pulled him away, laughter bubbling up from somewhere deep inside him.

"He's too strong," Patrick's voice was low.

"Get the others in here!" Lord Samson commanded.

It took five men to pull him away. With his back pressed against the far wall, the rage receded and dread spilled in. The dagger was removed from his hand.

"Thomas? Are you in there?" Lord Samson asked.

He groaned. The last few moments were still fresh, but as the actions of another. Thomas blinked and let out a breath. Empty, he wanted to be anywhere else but the cell.

"You weren't wrong about him. What was that?" Patrick muttered.

There was a glint of fear in Patrick's eyes. A look that had often followed Thomas in camp.

"He's coming out of it. Give him room." Lord Samson's eyes were right in front of him. "Thomas, are you all right?"

"Did I kill him?" Thomas asked in dread.

His eyes fell to Jacob slumped on the other side of the room. Supported by the shackles, unmoving.

"He passed out," Lord Samson told him.

Something in Thomas had fractured, and now he snapped back to reality. The other prisoners were mute with horror, their eyes fixed on him.

"I could have killed him," Thomas whispered.

"You didn't," Lord Samson said. "You got The Shadow of Death."

"He confessed?" he asked.

Lord Samson flipped the dagger before holding it out to him. "This is yours."

He frowned. Lord Samson grabbed his hand and forced the handle into it.

Breathless, he glanced at Jacob, at the damage he had done. He had nearly killed the man. For a moment, he'd *wanted* to. That feeling had passed, and all that remained was his savagery before him.

Lord Samson grabbed a fistful of hair, pulling back Jacob's head. Recognition swept over him as Jacob's face finally came into clear focus. How had he not recognised him before? Jacob and his wife, Cecilia, traded with the

Blakes. The urge to get out had him pushing past Patrick as he fled from the cell.

Chapter 24

Fresh air on his face, Thomas breathed in until the urge to retch passed. The light of the waning moon reflected off the pyre. Three prisoners were escorted out, glancing at Thomas as they passed. Only moments ago, they had watched him… He shivered, aching to go home, far from here. It wouldn't change what he had done, though. A scream threatened to tear itself from his throat.

A footstep behind him warned of Lord Samson's approach. Thomas pressed a hand to the stone wall, breathing through his anguish.

"You left your sword behind."

Lord Samson held out his sword. Taking it, Thomas re-sheathed the blade.

"You deceived me," Thomas said. Rage bubbled up again, his blood boiling. "You didn't need me at all. This was all a power play. Your new weapon. I cannot do that again."

"You knew what you were in for."

"You knew I didn't want to do this. You made me do it anyway. For my family? Now I must look them in the eye and live with this every day."

"Watch that temper of yours, Thomas. You forget your place. We're not in France; we're not brothers in arms anymore. You speak to me as a lord."

Thomas buried his anger. "What happens now?"

"Now, Patrick gets a confession. You did your part; go home. Spend time with your brother, get some much-needed rest. Be there for the birth of your child. It is a joyous time for you and your wife. Then, you will report for duty."

"As an Enforcer?" Thomas faced Lord Samson.

Lord Samson threw a leather pouch at him. It jingled as he caught it. "That's what you are now, Thomas. Accept it."

Thomas opened the pouch, and lifted a silver coin from the top. All freshly minted coins, and more than he got paid in a month for farm work.

"Lord Samson," Thomas called out. Lord Samson's expression was blank. "I'm leaving now with my brother." He pointed at the pyre. "He doesn't need to be here for this. He doesn't need to know I'm responsible for…" He couldn't finish.

"It's the middle of the night, Thomas. You can leave at sunrise. Have something to eat. Sleep. You will need it for the journey back to Riverwick."

Thomas rushed to his quarters. He needed to make sure Graeme was asleep, that he hadn't somehow felt what Thomas had done. The halls were empty; his footsteps echoed. Laughter came from the dining hall as Enforcers drank in celebration. Thomas reached his room and opened the door quietly. A spare bed had been placed on the other side of his room. Graeme's breathing was quick, his eyes closed. He paused in the doorway. His stomach growled; he needed food. With food, there would be ale.

Just before Thomas could leave again, Graeme sat up. "Please, not him!" he pleaded. "Tom?"

Black smoke rose from him as it had in the stable. The yellow flame cast an eerie, shimmering glow over Graeme's face, but the black eyes sent a shiver down Thomas's spine.

"Grim?" Thomas moved into the room, concern for his brother overriding fear. "I'm here. What is it?"

Graeme's eyes focused on something behind Thomas and then visibly relaxed. "It's. . .It was a nightmare," Graeme muttered as the black returned to blue.

"Again? This is starting to worry me. Oh, and the black eyes that you refuse to talk about are unsettling. Did you get answers from Father Matthew?"

Thomas removed the baldric, placing his sword and Lord Samson's dagger on the table. He then unbuckled the clasps to the leather cuirass, dropping it to the floor. It hit the stone with a soft thump. When he threw the purse on the table, coins spilled over.

"No," Graeme gave no more, so Thomas let it go.

But his brother's appearance as he awoke was more difficult for Thomas to ignore. He forced a smile, overwhelmed by the urge to leave.

"I need food," Thomas said. "With ale, a lot of ale. Do you want me to bring anything back?"

"You're leaving?" Graeme asked, eyes darting around the room.

"I'm hungry. Get some sleep. We go home in the morning."

Thomas closed the door behind him and made his way to the dining hall.

Three long wooden tables stretched from one end of the room to the other. Over the fire was a cooking pot still half-filled with pottage, with a cask in the corner. A group of eight Enforcers sat at one end of the table and lowered their voices when they noticed Thomas. As he helped himself to pottage, Patrick entered the room.

"There you are," Patrick said.

"Please, let me eat in peace, Patrick," Thomas said, wearily.

Patrick poured two tankards of ale and followed Thomas to the table furthest from the other Enforcers. "Truce?" Patrick reached his hand out, offering a drink to him.

With suspicion, he studied the captain's face. "Why?"

Patrick rolled his eyes. "Just take the drink, Blake."

Accepting the drink, he let the thirst-quenching liquid run down his throat before starting on the stew. Chewing on venison imbued with sage, he closed his eyes, taking pleasure in its rich, gamey flavour.

"Witnessing you at work made me realise you have potential. I judged you harshly."

Silver banged against wood as Thomas slammed the spoon down. *Why can he not leave me be?* "What are you doing?" he demanded.

"What does it look like?" Patrick's usual sneer was replaced by comradery. "I'm enjoying a drink."

Something about Patrick's smile, his eyes avoiding contact, reminded Thomas of a dog. "You're afraid of me," he said, the realisation spreading across his face. "You're trying to ensure I'm not a threat to you by making an ally of me." Thomas lifted the tankard and chuckled. "The great captain of the Enforcers is scared of a farmer."

Laughter resounded from across the room. The Enforcers were watching, having heard what he'd said.

Patrick leaned towards Thomas, his face red. "You want me as your friend—"

Unable to hold back any longer, Thomas finished the ale and banged the tankard down. He mirrored Patrick's movement, shifting forward in his seat. "No." He lowered his voice. "*You* want me as *yours*. I survived a war. You've seen what I'm capable of; best remember that."

Patrick sat back, his mouth slack. With satisfaction, Thomas couldn't contain a smirk. A hush spread across the room.

"Thank you for the drink. Now let me eat in peace as I asked," Thomas said.

Patrick left without a word, chin high. Dazed, Thomas revelled in the surge of joy at speaking to a noble in a way he never would have dreamed of. He caught the Enforcers watching him.

"He's going to make you regret that," one of the Enforcers called out.

"Good luck to him," Thomas muttered.

One by one, the Enforcers stood and walked over to sit around him. Among them, he vaguely recognised fellow soldiers from France. A full tankard was placed in front of him, and hands slapped his back. He finished one and another replaced that, the room drifting around him as alcohol's effects kicked in. In ale-induced bliss, his own laughter and stories of the front lines emerged. Just like at war, brothers in arms surrounded him, lifting his spirits.

It was just before dawn when Thomas staggered back to his quarters. The door crashed against the wall as he pushed it open. The bang woke Graeme up with a start.

"Get up, Grim!" Thomas bellowed. "We are going home!"

Chapter 25

The townsfolk whispered his name, praying that 'The Shadow of Death' wouldn't come for them next. Peasants and nobles alike peered into the dark, afraid for their own mortality. Their fear of him awoke a dark ache, and with it a need to hunt. Concealed in the Shadow Realm beyond their sight, he sought out his next kill. As men were arrested, he found a soul among the crowd who blazed with the black flames of an approaching death. Is he my next hunt? Nothing had pulled him from the Shadow Realm yet.

He observed the Enforcers. One stood apart from the rest, a man with a limp. It did not take The Shadow long to learn his name. Thomas. His energy was different, with dark threads that emerged from within and were not yet infused with Thomas's essence. The Darkness of another? The dark threads wound around a silver cord that appeared to come from the centre of his chest. While following the one nearing death, The Shadow kept his eye on Thomas, intrigued by the Enforcer's energy.

Thomas had a rage in him, as proven by how quickly he fell into violence. Beating one prisoner, almost killing another, yet horrified by his own actions. As he ran from the cell, The Shadow was drawn after him. Outside, Thomas stood alone, gasping in panic. He was alone. Ready for the kill, The Shadow advanced. A hand grabbed his arm, holding him back.

His mortal self had arrived. "Not him."

"Why not?" The Shadow asked. *"Are you not ready to feel the rush of the kill? It's time."*

His other self watched as the new Lord of Kempschester emerged from the tunnel to speak with Thomas.

"No."

"If you want to kill him…" The Shadow offered his other self the black sickle.

The blue eyes widened. "No. You cannot kill him. You must choose another."

"I do not choose," he said. *"I go where I am compelled to go."*

"Not him." His mortal self pleaded in the voice of Darkness. "Please."

Why is he so important?

As Thomas left, The Shadow followed again. His mortal self had never fought against the Darkness infused with his being. He was curious as to what made Thomas different. *Why does he not want me to kill this Enforcer?*

Thomas walked into a bedroom where his identical double slept. Twins. The sleeper had the same silver cord, connecting the two. But where Thomas had threads of Darkness, this one's being was immersed in it. Dark thorns were embedded in the twin's heart, twisting through his entire essence, wrapping around the cord connecting the two.

The Shadow's mortal self left the Shadow Realm. Thomas's twin sat up; black eyes met his. Darkness of the Shadow Realm rose from the man.

"Please, not him!" The dark mortal pleaded. "Tom?"

"Grim?" Thomas moved towards his twin. "I'm here. What is it?"

"I will find another, this time," The Shadow said.

The one called Grim visibly relaxed. "It's... it was a nightmare," Grim said to his brother, black eyes changing to blue.

"I will not resist the call, though. If it leads me to him, he will die."

The Shadow left the twins, denied of a kill. His dark desire reverberated through him as he waited to hunt. Tired of waiting for the pull, he sought out his own prey. Drawn back to the one Thomas had almost killed, The Shadow found Jacob worse than before. Someone had beaten him again. Pale, Jacob had one eye swollen shut, and his breaths were ragged. Blood soaked through his tunic, the mace still on the floor from where Thomas had dropped it. Though Jacob's essence burned a brilliant green, it had dimmed, the black flames spreading. Jacob had been there to witness Philip's death.

"You do not have long to live," The Shadow whispered.

Jacob lifted his head, glancing around the cell with one eye. "Who's there?"

He can hear me through the veil! Is that because he's close to death? Am I to relieve him from his pain? There's no pleasure of the hunt in that.

The Shadow revealed himself. Jacob's eye widened. "It's you, I saw you. You're the one they seek."

"I am the one they call The Shadow of Death," he replied.

"You should be in my place. I am being accused of your crimes, and at dawn they will burn me unless you speak the truth."

"I have no intention of replacing you on the pyre."

"Then kill me now," Jacob begged. "Give me a quick death. Release me from such a fate."

A tear fell from Jacob's eye, and The Shadow almost gave in to a twitch of sympathy.

"Your demise is your own doing. Why did you confess?" The Shadow asked.

"Thomas was about to kill me. I would have said anything to not die. Once they started to beat me, I just wanted to make it stop."

"Yet, if Thomas had killed you there would be nothing to fear right now. Instead, you await a much more drawn-out and painful death."

Jacob turned his head away. "If you are not here to help me, why are you here?"

"I have witnessed death at my hands. Yours will be the first by other means."

"But my death is at your hands. You may not be drawing blood, but you've still killed me."

"Then I will watch you die, knowing that I have given another to the Shadow Realm."

"The Shadow Realm?" Jacob's fear shone through the eye that was not swollen shut.

"It will be over soon. Your pain will cease."

The approach of dawn saw half of Kempschester crowding into the courtyard. As Jacob was dragged out, the crowd called for his blood. Word had spread quickly of his capture. The Shadow followed as the Enforcers led Jacob, barely conscious to the pyre.

"Jacob?" A woman reached for him as he was led past. His wife, perhaps.

"Cecilia," Jacob's voice was thin, almost drowned out by the crowd. "Go home. You should not see this."

It seemed their fear of the pestilence was forgotten in their eagerness to see a man suffer. Many townsfolk believed Jacob to be, 'The Shadow of Death.' They cheered for his death as he was tied to the pyre. Others pleaded with anyone they could find for Jacob to be set free. But the words claiming Jacob's innocence fell on deaf ears.

As the fire was lit, the flames spread in an instant, licking at Jacob's feet before engulfing the rest of him. Screams burst from Jacob. The crowd displayed a bloodthirsty glee. Jacob's words from earlier returned. This death was his doing, but it was not his way to watch such a morbid show of humanity. Those who died by The Shadow's hands suffered only for a moment.

With one quick motion, The Shadow pulled the essence of the dying man into the Shadow Realm. Jacob's body slumped, but his spirit form continued to scream.

"Jacob, stop."

Jacob's eyes darted around, confusion and fear crossing his face.

"Where am I? What did you do to me?"

The Shadow pointed through the veil. *"You're in the Shadow Realm. Away from the flames while your body burns."*

Jacob eyed his body and reached a hand towards himself, but he was unable to pierce the veil.

"How is this possible?" He turned his eyes back to The Shadow. "Who... *What* are you?"

There was no easy answer to that, so he didn't say anything.

"Why me?" Jacob asked. "I did not deserve this."

"Deserving has nothing to do with it. It was your time." The Shadow had never conversed in this manner with those he'd killed before.

"My time? You did this. You and Thomas."

Deep red flames surrounded them, drawn by Jacob's presence. Jacob backed away from them. As his body died, his essence became a part of the Shadow Realm, turning the same red of lost souls. The realm had claimed another.

"What are those? What do they want?" Jacob's voice was laced with panic.

"They are lost souls. They're drawn to those newly released from life."

Am I supposed to comfort him? That is not my purpose.

"Released from life?"

"You're dead, Jacob." The Shadow pointed to Jacob's body.

"Dead?" Jacob's voice had become barely a whisper.

The Shadow left the lost soul of Jacob in front of his body. There would soon be nothing left of the man, only the red flames drawn to the next soul that entered the Shadow Realm.

Chapter 26

"Thomas, wake up!"

Thomas opened his eyes. Disorientated by the rhythmic movement beneath him and the dull thud of hooves on a dirt road, he tried to get his bearings. His face was pressed into coarse, white hair. He breathed in combined scents of grass, dust, leather, his drowsiness and confusion cleared. I'm on horseback... Guinevere... on my way home? The joy that swelled was soon smothered by uneasiness. A *terrible* mistake had been made, one he could not undo. Overcome by deep remorse, he longed for the oblivion of more alcohol.

Thomas sat up to find Graeme laughing at him. The hood of Graeme's cloak was pulled over his head. Numb from the cold, Thomas pulled his own up.

"Stop," he grumbled, pulling Guinevere's mane hair from his mouth.

"You almost fell off that time," Graeme teased. "You're drooling."

Thomas wiped away saliva and scowled. "You're an idiot."

"Ouch. Why are you angry at me? You're the one who keeps falling asleep. Sot."

"Don't call me that, I'm not a drunkard," Thomas said, his mouth dry.

"You were up all night drinking."

"Leave it be," Thomas muttered.

"Very well. Are you going to tell me why they've let you leave? Or why you were in such a hurry to go to church beforehand?" Graeme asked.

Thomas yawned. "I needed solace." It was the first time Thomas had been to church since his return. Father Matthew had offered little relief from the burden of guilt, so he'd knelt in prayer until the sun came up. Nothing had shifted the remorse that hung over him. He had condemned himself to more torment. "Why did you have to sit so close, watching me the whole time? You could have sat in the back, or waited outside."

"Just making sure you were safe."

"Grim, I was in a church with my sword and a dagger. Why wouldn't I be safe?"

Graeme didn't respond right away, his attention ahead of him. "You're right; it was stupid of me to worry," he said. "You avoided my other question."

By now Jacob was likely dead. "The hunt is over," he muttered.

"The hunt for The Shadow of Death?"

Thomas left the question unanswered.

"Tom, what happened?" Graeme pressed.

He stopped. Graeme passed him and turned around.

"What do you think happened? There was a confession… and an execution."

"Someone confessed? Who?" Graeme demanded. When Thomas didn't answer, he asked again. "Tom, who?"

"Jacob," Thomas said quietly.

"Jacob? No, he's not the killer. Why would he confess? Is that why we had to leave the estate, so I wouldn't see?"

"Please, stop asking questions." Thomas frowned. "Wait, how would you know he isn't?"

The village came into view. "Look, we're home," Graeme said.

"Graeme."

"Because I know Jacob would not be capable of such a thing, any more than you or I. I must go, Father will be angry that I did not return yesterday, and I need to talk to Amelia."

Willow broke into a canter as Graeme made his escape. Thomas let his brother go. *Why is he behaving so strangely? Is he angry at me over Jacob?* Instead of following, Thomas took a different road. One that took him to Leo's tavern.

Inside, the voices of other villagers stopped when Thomas entered.

"You haven't brought those friends of yours with you again, have you?" Leo asked.

"No, they're back in Kempschester," Thomas said.

Leo eyed him up and down. "Are you here as a grey cloak?"

"If I was, do you think that's any way to address an Enforcer?"

All eyes were on him.

"Sorry, I'm tired. I did not mean that." Thomas pulled off the cloak as he claimed a table. "You can all relax, I'm off duty." He gave the villagers his warmest smile. "I'm only here for a drink." He removed the sword and dagger, placing them on the table.

The crackle of fire filled the silence. "What are you waiting for, Leo? Pour the man a drink," a voice called out.

Laughter and conversation started again.

"Will it be ale or wine?" Leo asked.

"Just ale today. Why are there so many people here this early in the morning?"

"Rowan's daughter is to be married. They've been here all night."

Thomas raised his drink. "Rowan, congratulations. Who's the lucky groom?"

Rowan's eyes lit up within his narrow, dark brown face from the corner table as he grinned, raising his tankard to Thomas. "Your cousin!" He said. "John's finally getting married?! I didn't know they were courting. Why is he not here celebrating with you? Or James?"

"They were. John cannot handle his ale, so James took him home before dawn."

Spirited laughter filled the tavern, and Thomas joined in. He pulled the pouch from his belt, throwing coins on the table. "A drink for everyone!" he told Leo. Cheers rose from the villagers.

"Is that coin from your new job?" a villager asked.

"It is," Thomas replied between mouthfuls of ale.

"It looks new."

"The nobles like their money to shine!" someone else laughed.

"Lords own the banks; they can make money whenever they like," Leo said as he poured another ale in Thomas's empty vessel. "All right, men, I'm going home. Some of us need to sleep."

A chorus of "No!"spread around the room.

"My cousin will be here to serve you in my place," Leo grinned.

Just then the door opened. A man who held a slight resemblance to Leo, but with more hair on his head, walked in. In his arms he carried a puppy. It was a grey bundle of fur, a breed that would grow into a large dog.

"No, get that runt out of my tavern!" Leo said. "Why did you bring it here?"

"I sold the rest in Greenwick, but no one wanted this one," Leo's cousin said. "Maybe someone here wants a pup."

"How did you get such a dog?" Thomas asked. "They're not common."

"He means among the common folk," Rowan laughed.

Chuckles burst from half of the men.

"Does it matter? The nobles of Kempschester won't notice."

"You stole puppies?" Thomas asked.

"Careful, he's an Enforcer."

"He said he's off duty. Today he's one of us. It's his cousin getting married, remember?" The voice was spoken from the corner.

"I didn't steal them, but Lord Philip's breeder was happy to sell them to anyone before the funeral."

"How much?" Thomas asked, reaching into the leather pouch again.

"Twenty-five silver coins," Leo's cousin said, eyes on the money.

"I'll buy him."

The puppy was promptly placed on the table in front of Thomas. It then dunked its head in the tankard.

"Get it off my table," Leo sighed.

Thomas pulled the puppy onto his lap as a fresh drink was poured. A wet tongue licked his hand. Scratching the dog behind the ears, he downed more ale. A haze of intoxication descended on him.

Thomas led Guinevere back to the stable. Carrying the puppy in one arm, he stopped under his brother's window. He caught silhouettes moving.

"Grim!" He called out. His brother's silhouette paused in the window.

Thomas was still gazing upwards when Graeme emerged from the house.

"What are you doing?" Graeme asked. "It's freezing out here!"

"Brother, you missed the celebration! Did you know John's getting married?"

"Is that why you called me down here?" His brother's frown ruined

Thomas's giddy happiness.

"Oh, are you in one of your dark moods?" he asked.

"I was in the middle of a serious conversation with Amelia," Graeme glanced up at his window.

Movement and a grunt came from Thomas's arms.

"Is that a puppy?" Graeme moved closer to inspect it. "A running hound? How did you afford this?"

"Enforcers get paid well." His laughter burst out again, this time heavy with bitterness. "Paid killers," he mumbled under his breath.

"Why did you buy a dog?"

"Why not? I think I will call him Hunter."

Graeme watched Thomas, a strange look on his face. Concern mixed with pain.

"What?" he asked.

"You have no control over what you shield when you're this drunk. Tom, I'm sorry."

Curse that damned bond. I must have opened the connection again.

"For what?"

"I can feel *everything*, Brother. You're drowning in your own pain. I've never known you like this." Graeme grabbed him by the arm. "I know you don't want to talk about it, but you can't go on like this. Your anguish is suffocating. Trying to drink yourself into nothing is the sort of thing Father does, not you. Please, Tom—"

"Let go of my arm," he warned. Graeme's arm dropped away.

Without a word, Thomas led his horse to the stable.

"What you're doing to Emma is... She doesn't deserve this," Graeme called after him.

"Don't you have your own wife to worry about?" Thomas shot back.

Chapter 27

An overwhelming need for his bed was catching up. The stairs swayed as Thomas stumbled towards the bedroom. Halfway up, he sat down hard before losing his balance completely. There were muddy footprints on the stairs. Emma wouldn't want them in the bedroom. Once he kicked his shoes off, they thumped their way down the stairs. Resting at the bottom with a final thud, just missing Hunter. He winced. The noise was not his best attempt at being quiet. Dizziness washed over him, the stairs out of focus. Trying to stand was like balancing on a ship deck on a stormy sea. He would have to crawl the rest of the way.

Finally reaching the bedroom and pulling himself up, he leaned on the door, gripping the frame. The door swung open and he went with it, hitting the floor. *That hurt.*

Uncontrollable laughter. "Ow."

"Thomas," Emma hissed from their bed.

He climbed to his feet again, hugging the wall.

"Emma! My heart!"

"Lower your voice, you'll wake Isaac."

"Why is he in our bed? It's the middle of the day," Thomas laughed.

Isaac sat up, blinking. His eyes were unfocused but watchful. Emma rubbed his back until his eyes fluttered closed again. Reaching his bed, Thomas kissed the belly that held a new life within. There would be a new arrival soon. Sitting on the side of the bed, he leaned forward, kissing Emma on the forehead. She closed her eyes.

A soft thump and a whine from the doorway. The little beast had climbed the stairs. Emma's eyes shot open again.

"What was that?" Her voice rose as she tried to sit up and turn towards the sound.

Hunter stumbled towards him with clumsy steps. Scooping the puppy up in his arms, he smiled wide, releasing the animal onto the bed. Narrow eyes took in the puppy before shifting to his face.

"Where did you get that?" she demanded as Hunter licked her hand. Her hand ran over the dog's head.

"Leo's cousin."

A frown creased her forehead. "I can't understand you."

"Leo's cousin," he repeated.

"You're not making any sense, Thomas."

He sighed. *How is she not understanding?* "Leo-pold's cous-in."

Hunter climbed over Emma's legs, tail wagging.

"Thomas, grab it before—"

Isaac sat up again, rubbing his eyes. Catching sight of the puppy, he glanced up at Thomas, beaming.

"Go on."

"No, Thomas," Emma huffed.

"He's all right."

Emma met his eyes. With the room spinning around him, Thomas threw her his best smile.

"Go on, my little darling," Emma said finally.

Isaac climbed off the bed. Standing in front of Thomas, arms held out, he waited for the puppy to be placed in his hands. Thomas removed his belt, cloak and tunic, taking the empty place on the bed next to Emma. Their son's happy giggles and the puppy's grunts filled him with warmth.

This was everything he had dreamed of. Relaxing into drowsiness, he lay on his side, facing Emma. He had come home and was with his family, where he belonged. In the cosy bed, echoes of war and the interrogation seemed to fade away. In that moment, all that mattered was now.

Thomas kissed her. "I love you, Emma." He caressed her cheek before kissing her again, his heart full.

Emma's lips gave way to his. "I missed you," she whispered when they pulled apart.

Emma winced and let out a small groan of pain.

"What is it? Are you alright?"

"The baby is close," Emma told him, rubbing her belly.

"I will soon meet my son," he murmured.

His eyes were heavy, so he lay back.

"We don't know that it's a boy." Emma's voice was far away. "We could be having a daughter."

Daughter? Thomas smiled.

Chapter 28

The harsh light of day shone into his face. Thomas threw an arm up, wincing. *Have I fallen asleep outside again?*

"You're awake," Emma said, her warmth against his side.

Emma. He was in bed, not camp. Pain crossed her face, but it passed, her smile returning.

On the battlefield, Thomas had longed to come home to his wife for this closeness. Taking her face between his hands, he caressed her cheek. "I'm dreaming."

"No, Thomas. You're not dreaming." She gazed into his eyes. "You're here with me."

Thomas kissed her forehead and wrapped his arms around his wife, pulling her close. She settled into his embrace, head resting against his bare chest. Warm and content, his stomach flipped at the happy sound she made as it vibrated through him. "I missed waking up with you," he whispered. There was nowhere else he wanted to be more than next to his wife. "If I could stay here with you all day, I'd be a happy man."

"That thought is appealing," she said. "We can stay here as long as you like. Now that you're home, there will be many days like this. Just you and me."

Thomas withheld from her that he would soon be called back to Kempschester. No need to ruin the moment. "I do like the sound of that. Where's Isaac?" he asked.

Emma lifted her head. "Amelia took him and the puppy outside. It snowed again, and Isaac loves being in the snow."

Thomas couldn't hold back the smile. "We're alone?"

"We're alone," she said, her eyes on his mouth. Emma's breath was warm, as her fingers traced along his jaw to his lips. "I love you."

He was floating, content. "I love you."

"Are you falling asleep?"

"No."

"Yes, you are. If you'd prefer to sleep…"

"Mmm."

Her lips pressed against his and her hand groped him through his trousers.

Thomas's eyes shot open and Emma smiled against his mouth. Her lips were soft and sweet, giving in to his as he kissed back. Desire sparked between them; her moan lit his arousal as their kiss became ravenous. His arms tightened around her.

"You do know how to wake someone up," he murmured, his voice husky. Thomas let out a growl, kissing her throat. "Start something like that, you'll get more than you bargained for."

"I know what I'm starting," Emma whispered, lust burning in her eyes. "That's the intention."

Thomas hesitated. "Are you sure? I mean, the baby. . ."

"I don't think you can hurt the baby. I will hurt you, though, if you don't—"

Thomas fumbled with his trousers. "Ugh, why did I fall asleep before taking these off?" He muttered and threw the trousers on the floor.

Thomas kissed Emma's inner thigh, moving his lips up her body as he rolled her night dress up. Each kiss elicited a gasp or shiver. Finally, he discarded the garment and kissed her jaw. Emma's sharp intake of breath sent a flutter through him. She tilted her head back, whispering his name. Thomas trailed kisses across her throat as her fingers dug into his back. Emma shifted, straining to get closer, and he pulled himself out of her reach, getting a groan in response.

"My wicked little wife," he whispered with a smile. "You're an impatient one, aren't you?"

Emma slid her hands over his abdomen and chest. Every nerve jolted at her touch, the haziness of lust clouding his mind.

"Why do you torment me s—" Emma's words were cut off by another kiss.

Everything melted away; there was only the two of them. Emma's hand pressed against the back of his neck, fingers gripping his hair. He cupped her face. Their kiss was soft and gentle at first, then with growing intensity became hungry, heated. Warmth flooded Thomas as he wrapped an arm around her, pulling her hard against him. He pulled his mouth from hers, catching his breath.

"I've wanted no other like I want you," Thomas traced his thumb over her lips, then caressed her cheek. "Tell me what you need, my heart. What you want."

Breathless, Emma's face was flushed. "I need you," she pleaded. "I want you. Your lips, I want them on my body." She groped him again. "I want this."

"Let me take care of you. I will give you what you want."

Thomas took his time, trailing kisses from throat to navel. He took pleasure in her small quivers each time his lips met her skin. His hands brushed across her body and her fingers through his hair.

"Emma," he murmured, raising his eyes to hers, kissing her bump. "My

Emma."

"Thomas," she panted. "Don't stop."

He lowered his mouth once more, kissing Emma between her legs, hands firmly on her hips.

Emma gasped, letting out a groan.

Thomas lifted his head. "Are you ...?" He grinned up at her. "I've barely touched you."

"It's...it will pass," she whispered, one hand at the nape of his neck, the other digging into his arm.

Her face contorted in pain. He waited for it to pass. She let out another groan and closed her eyes.

"Emma?"

"Nooooo. No, not now." Her voice was full of pain and annoyance.

"What? Not now? Have you changed your mind?" Thomas choked on bitter disappointment.

She whimpered. "No, uhhh, you might want to fetch the midwives."

"Why... Oh. Now?"

"Now." Emma sat up with a heavy sigh "Help me dress," she whispered.

"You look better without it." His words were met by an eye roll. Thomas leaned towards her belly. "You have awful timing, little one." He pulled the night dress over her head before moving towards the door.

"Thomas?"

"Hmm?" He half-turned.

Her eyes were focused below his waist. "Trousers."

Thomas stumbled for his trousers, pulling them back on. Frustration burned the back of his throat. He ran down the stairs despite the pain in his thigh.

"Amelia! The midwives."

CHAPTER 28

The midwives and Amelia had been in his room for hours as Emma's screams split the air. The kitchen grew stifling, so Thomas grabbed his cloak and walked outside. Night had fallen and more snow blanketed the village, the cold numbing his face. Graeme followed him out and they sat side by side on the porch, his presence reassuring. Before long, Isaac and Hunter joined them. Thomas wrapped his arms around Isaac, lifting his cloak around the two of them. Isaac pulled away, but only to drag Hunter under the cloak.

Emma's scream echoed out again, the sound reverberating in every part of his body. Memories of war stirred; screams of anger, pain and fear. The cries from the battlefield were all around. His body tense, his mood dark, the recollection transfixed him. Isaac let out a small cry and squirmed, trying to break free. Drawing in a deep breath and relaxing, he loosened his arms. *I am home, with my family. I am not there anymore.*

When Emma screamed again, there was intense pain behind the wail. Isaac whimpered.

"You don't need to worry, Isaac. You are soon to be a brother." Graeme's attempt to comfort the boy fell flat.

Isaac turned around, leaning into Thomas. Hugging tightly, he placed one hand on the back of the boy's head, his heart twisting.

Voices and screams faded in and out, followed by a stretch of silence.

How long have we been out here?

"Tom," Graeme's voice was soft.

Amelia stood in the doorway, and all eyes were on Thomas. Graeme reached for Isaac as Thomas stood. Heart in his throat, he made his way up the stairs. *Something's wrong.* With a bitter taste in his mouth, he froze halfway up. *There is no cry. Should the baby be crying?* Fighting the rising panic, he raised his eyes to the top of the stairs. *What will I find in there? Emma!* Released from his inability to move, he took two steps at a time ignoring the pain.

Thomas rushed into the dim room.

The two midwives were dressed plainly, in pale-blue dresses with white aprons, their hair covered. The older of the women, Margaret, had assisted with Emma's first childbirth, as well as Amelia's. Wisps of grey hair stuck out from beneath her wimple. The second, Kassandra, was in her mid-twenties, with an ebony complexion and strands of black hair slipped from their place. Margaret tended to Emma and Kassandra held a bundle in her arms. His heart skipped a beat as he rushed to Emma's side. Sweat-matted hair stuck to her forehead, her face was pale, her breathing laboured. She opened her eyes and tried to sit up but was too weak.

"No, rest," he said and leaned over her. He kissed her cheek and forehead, her skin warm against his lips. "Just rest."

"We had a daughter," Emma's voice was barely audible.

A daughter. Pride swelled before the dread twisted in his gut.

"Had?" *Not have.* The word pulled the air out of the room and stung his eyes. Emma's eyes reflected the same anguish as she let out a sob. Thomas squeezed her hand gently, pressing their foreheads together. The floor creaked. and Kassandra held the bundle towards him. Emma's eyes were on their dead daughter, and she gripped his arm. Taking the lifeless form, he placed her in Emma's outstretched arms.

Emma cradled the baby, her eyes wet. A storm raged inside, his heart breaking as he caressed her face.

"Oh, Em,"

"She must be washed," Emma told the midwife.

Kassandra nodded. "It will be done." She glanced at Thomas. "You need to let her rest."

"I am not leaving her." He left no room for argument.

Emma's eyes closed, and he lifted their dead daughter from her. Kassandra took the baby from him and left the room. Margaret lay a cloth over Emma's forehead.

"What are you doing?" He asked.

"She is warm, I'm cooling her down."

He sat back in a chair beside the bed. Emma's breathing and Margaret's whispered prayers were the only sounds in the room. Thomas stroked her hand, ignoring the midwife.

He wasn't sure how much time had passed when Kassandra returned.

"Where's my daughter?" he asked.

"Amelia has her." Kassandra grabbed another cloth from a bowl at the end of the bed to clean between Emma's thighs.

Thomas kept his eyes on Emma. Ashen-faced, with shadows under her eyes, she appeared to be worsening.

"She's so pale. Is she…" He couldn't finish the sentence as fear gripped his throat.

"It was not an easy labour," Margaret said. "She needs her rest."

"Margaret?" Kassandra's voice was quiet. Her dark eyes were wide as they darted in his direction.

Thomas stood. The linen under Emma and her nightdress were slick with blood. Kassandra held a bloody cloth.

Thomas swallowed with difficulty. "She's bleeding? Is that normal? She didn't bleed like that last time."

Margaret was stern. "Please, Master Thomas, let me tend to her."

"Then tend to her!" he shouted, legs weak. Ice spread outward from his chest.

I cannot lose her.

Grabbing Emma's hand and finding it clammy, he squeezed. "Em?"

"Don't disturb her," Kassandra said. "Please, you need to leave."

"No!"

Her eyes opened, fingers squeezing back. “Thomas?”

Flooded with relief he smiled. “I’m here, Em.”

She gazed at him with a slight upturn of her lips, and the midwives’ voices faded into the background. Planting a kiss on the back of her hand, he stroked her cheek, wiping away a tear. “You’re alright. Everything is going to be all right. I’m right here.” Unsure if he was trying to convince her or himself, Thomas took a deep breath to hold back his terror.

The hand in his went limp as her eyes fluttered closed.

“Em?” Pain stabbed his chest. “Emma?”

Chapter 29

"Help her!" Thomas bellowed. "Please!" He struggled to breathe. *This cannot be happening.* "Emma?"

"I'm sorry, she's gone," Kassandra said, tears sliding down her cheeks.

"No! I will not hear it."

The midwives clutched each other as he towered over them.

"Please, we cannot help her," Margaret pleaded, her voice high.

Pain and sorrow engulfed him, crushing him with a deep sense of loss. The room blurred.

"Tom, stop!" Graeme ran into the room and stopped dead when he saw Emma. He grabbed Thomas by the arm. "Calm yourself."

"Don't touch me!" He roared.

He struck Graeme. His fist made contact just under his brother's eye with a dull thump. Pain jolted through his hand. Graeme let out a grunt, releasing Thomas's arm. Margaret and Kassandra made their escape, their quick footsteps pounding down the stairs. Their cries of panic penetrated his grief. *What am I doing?*

Fury ignited in Graeme's eyes. Before Thomas could move, Graeme's fist connected with his cheek. Sharp pain tore through his face, but Graeme didn't stop there and swung his other fist. This time the punch connected with his eye. His face throbbed. Dizzy, he advanced on Graeme.

"Tom, stop! Hitting me won't bring her back. Stand down. Please, I know you're in pain. Rein in your anger; Isaac needs you."

Isaac. Thomas's head cleared.

"You hit me," he muttered, touching his check tenderly. "Twice."

"Sorry, I couldn't help it. You hit me first. I lost my temper."

Thomas's focus was drawn to Emma's face. Tears welled up as his legs gave out from under him. "She's gone, Grim." He sank to the floor.

Graeme knelt before him, hand on his shoulder. "I know."

He shook as he tried to suppress his sobs. Graeme sat with him. No words were needed as sympathy radiated from Graeme.

Thomas let out a shuddering breath, unsure how much time had passed. The wave of anguish receded enough to talk again.

"She's gone," Thomas said again. It was sinking in. *She really is gone.* "What do I do now?"

"We bury her and grieve her," Graeme spoke softly. "I will grieve with you. You're not alone in this."

Thomas nodded and grasped Graeme's shoulder. "I couldn't ask for a better brother." He pointed to Graeme's face. "Sorry I struck you." A red mark had formed with the beginnings of swelling.

"You were overwhelmed by sorrow. But you might have to apologise to the midwives."

Thomas groaned. "Was I that bad?"

"You were. They couldn't get out quickly enough." Graeme gave him a small smile. "You're a fright when you're angry. No one's seen *you* lose control before. That was always *my* problem."

Thomas shook his head. "Something's wrong with me, Grim. My anger—"

"Is understandable in moments of grief," Graeme told him.

"No, It's not. I shouldn't have lost control. As you pointed out, you're the one with a temper. I've never been this way. It's not just the midwives, I've scared Isaac too." Images of Jacob and Warwick resurfaced. "Since the war, I lose myself in rage, to find I've done..."

"You don't have to explain rage to me," Graeme held a hand to his chest, taking in a slow breath.

"You felt it, didn't you?" Thomas asked.

"The pain pulled me from a dream. I knew something was wrong instantly. Amelia told me you needed me."

There was a mixture of relief and disappointment as Graeme spoke of being pulled from his dream, but it was gone before Thomas could grasp what it meant.

Thomas pressed his lips together. "Sorry."

"Don't worry about that for now. Just focus on what you must do."Graeme rose and held out a hand.

Thomas grasped the outstretched hand, letting his brother pull him up.

"Wash her body. I will have Amelia pick herbs."

"She likes...*liked* lavender," Thomas murmured standing over the bed. "Lem..." He took a calming breath. "And lemon."

"I will tell her."

Thomas leaned over Emma; her scent of lavender and lemon still lingered. As he touched his forehead to hers, hot tears finally spilled over.

"Goodbye, my heart," he whispered.

Chapter 30

Thomas knelt to Isaac's level. *How am I supposed to do this?* As he pulled a small cloak around Isaac, a wave of heartache threatened to drown him again. Graeme's hand squeezed his shoulder, as if to remind Thomas of his presence.

"Isaac, I have something important to tell you," he said.

Isaac's chin lowered as he peered at Emma in the roughly made coffin. Her eyes were closed, and she looked asleep, peaceful. A blanket that Amelia had gifted to her was wrapped around the small body of his daughter. Thomas had cleansed her with lemon-and-lavender-infused water. Then, with Amelia's help, he had chosen a light blue dress and brushed out her hair.

Isaac's brown eyes, so much like Emma's, lifted to his. "Why is Mother still asleep?" He asked. "Should we get a cloak for her or my sister? They will get cold."

Thomas swayed. Amelia gave him an encouraging nod.

"God has taken her soul to heaven," his voice broke, "and your sister."

"But she's right there."

"When we go to heaven, we leave our bodies behind," Thomas said. "She is in an eternal sleep."

"When will she come back?" Isaac frowned.

"People who go to heaven don't come back."

"She isn't coming back?" Tears welled up in Isaac's eyes. "But I want her to wake up. Is she angry at me?"

"She's not angry at you. She loves you very much and will watch over you." Thomas laid one hand over Isaac's heart, the other over his own. "She will always be with us, *in here.* But for now, we have to say goodbye to her. To both of them."

Thomas didn't try to fight the tears that flowed. Isaac touched his face. Still hurting from where Graeme's fists had connected, Thomas pulled his son's hands away. "Don't cry, Father." Isaac wrapped his arms around Thomas's neck.

"We can," Thomas smiled. "We're going to lay them to rest now." He pointed at the coffin. "We're going to carry her to the cemetery by the church."

"Where we can visit her?" Isaac's face was wet.

"Every time we miss her," Thomas reassured him

A dark gloom hung over Riverwick, and it had finally stopped snowing. With the help of John and others, James had cleared a path for the cart. Villagers stood watching him with solemn expressions. Amelia held her hand out for Isaac, nudging him to stand by Susanna. Father waited, seated at the front of the cart.

"What is he doing?" Thomas asked, his voice low.

"He's going to be respectful," James whispered. "I made sure of that. Are you ready?"

"I'm never going to be ready for this," Thomas muttered.

"We'll be with you every step of the way," Graeme said.

An ache twisted his insides as he lifted a trembling hand, caressing Emma's cold, hard cheek. Graeme knelt beside him, followed by Amelia and James on the other side of the coffin. Amelia placed lilacs in Emma's hands, the flowers' fragrance reminding him of spring.

"You were a sister to me," Amelia said with a sob. "When I suffered loss, you offered me solace and sat with me for hours over my daughter's grave. I will never forget you. Be at peace now, Emma."

Amelia rose, taking Isaac with her to wait behind the cart.

"I remember when the two of you met," James said. "Thomas found any reason to see you, to spend time in Hazelbury. He was known for his fondness of many women, so you were an unexpected addition to our family." Thomas couldn't hold back the snicker, Graeme's shoulders shaking beside him. "Be at peace," James finished, and stood back, John beside him.

"You were one of the few who could tell us apart right from the beginning," Graeme said. "Like Amelia, I have lost a sister today. You made my brother happy and have left a hole in our family. Be at peace, Sister."

Graeme's words had been so heartfelt, surprising Thomas.

"Thank you," he whispered.

Graeme nodded in acknowledgement. "Do you want me to stay?"

Thomas was supposed to be alone to speak his final words with Emma. He couldn't bring himself to say no. They hadn't been apart since Emma's death two nights before, and Graeme's presence soothed his turmoil. No Darkness, no shutting each other out, just a silent communication of sympathy and shared grief.

"Stay," he choked out.

Thomas traced a thumb over Emma's lips. "I will never again feel your kiss or hear your voice." He laid his hand over her chest. "Nor will I feel your heartbeat against mine." His fingers caressed her cheek, and he leaned forward, pressing his forehead to hers. As he lifted his head, a tear landed on her cheek. Thomas whispered in her ear. "We had such a short time together. Rest now, my heart, be at peace. I shall see you again." He kissed her forehead.

When he stood, his brother placed the lid over the coffin. James and John came forward to each take a corner as he and Graeme took the front. Bearing the weight, Thomas stepped carefully, matching his pace to the others' as they carried Emma to the cart. He took his place behind the cart as it started to move, Amelia and Graeme on either side of him, with James and John behind him. All of Riverwick had shown up, with many from Hazelbury, Emma's village. Sobs and murmurs of villagers surrounded him.

"What?" James said suddenly. "Stop."

Everything stopped.

"Don't move," Graeme said to Thomas as he and James left the procession. A white horse approached, Lord Samson on its back. *What's he doing here?* Before Thomas could leave his place, John grabbed him.

"Let them find out what it's about," his cousin said.

Graeme and James turned in his direction. James shook his head and said something to Lord Samson, but they were too far away to hear. *What are they talking about? James does not look happy.* Lord Samson responded, his eyes on Thomas. A chill of foreboding stirred. Voices of the villagers broke the silence as they started to talk among themselves. When Lord Samson dismounted, James shook his head again, pointing towards Thomas. Those around Thomas moved to cut Lord Samson off as he approached.

"Lord or not, you have interrupted a funeral," Graeme said, his voice loud with an edge of anger. "My brother deserves to bury his wife without—" He stopped, silenced by James grabbing his arm.

Graeme's anger reached Thomas through their connection.

Curiosity got the best of Thomas, so he approached Lord Samson. "What is it?" he asked. "Why are you here?"

"It can wait," James replied. "Get back, Thomas. Lord Samson, you may join the back of the procession if you wish."

Surprised at James's tone, Thomas returned to stand next to Amelia. Graeme and James soon joined him.

"What's happening?" Thomas asked Graeme.

"Not important right now," his brother replied as they started to move again.

Lord Samson rode alongside the cart, and Graeme exchanged a look with James over his shoulder.

The cart stopped just outside the cemetery, and Thomas joined Graeme, James, and John in carrying Emma to her final resting place. Carefully removing Emma from the coffin, they wrapped her body in a black shroud, tucking the baby in. Father Matthew waited as they lowered Emma into the grave. Amelia's sobs gave Thomas fresh tears, raw grief spilling over.

Father Matthew spoke over the grave, the words far away as they washed over Thomas. John had ridden out the day before and brought the priest back to Riverwick. As Graeme and James started to fill in the grave, Thomas struggled to stand. Amelia squeezed his hand, whispering to him, her words faint. New snowflakes drifted from the sky. Tilting his neck back, eyes on the dark clouds, he silently called out to Emma. She was really gone. The priest finally stopped talking, and the villagers offered condolences to Thomas before moving away. One by one everyone left, all but Graeme.

Head bowed, eyes on the grave, Thomas released a shaky breath. Graeme hadn't moved either.

"You're still here," Thomas said.

"I told you I would be."

Warmth overwhelmed him. He turned and glanced up, taking in Graeme's swollen, bruised cheek.

"You think mine's bad; you clearly haven't seen yours." Graeme gave an apologetic smile. "People were whispering about it."

Of course they would be. The Blake brothers showing signs of a fight at a funeral was scandalous.

"Is he still there?" Thomas asked.

"He's just standing there, waiting."

"What does he want?"

"There has been another murder."

Heat spread throughout his body, replacing the grief. Lord *Samson dared come here with that news on this day?* His knuckles were still bruised from what he'd done to Warwick. Jacob, an innocent man, was dead, and it was his fault. He had forced a false confession, and everyone would know it was him. *How much longer can I do this?*

"One day. He can't give me one day!" It had been the same when he had arrived home from war, so this should be no surprise.

"I can go in your place."

"No!" He said it a little too quickly and forcefully. Graeme tilted his chin, eyebrows raised. "My life isn't mine anymore. There's no reason you should suffer the same fate."

"I'll ask him to give you a break today; you've just lost your wife." Graeme crossed his arms. "I thought he had given you leave."

"A fresh murder takes priority."

If he didn't go, Lord Samson would likely take it as his vow being broken and make Graeme go. He couldn't allow that. Grief-powered rage surged through him. Fists clenched and jaw tight, he left Emma's resting place.

"You put an innocent man to flame," Thomas said through his teeth.

Lord Samson rested his hand on the handle of his sword, lifting enough of the blade to be a threat.

"You speak to me in that manner? You forget your place."

"I have just buried my wife. Forgive my anger after you bring this news, interrupting her funeral."

"My condolences," Lord Samson said. "Now saddle your horse."

"Can he not grieve?" Graeme demanded. "He's given so much to the king and to you, but you deny him this? When it was your father, you were granted time to—"

"No," Lord Samson interrupted Graeme. "I wasn't. My father's death meant I was Lord of Kempshire. He was murdered, but I didn't have time to feel sorrow. I had my duty. Just as Thomas has his."

Graeme opened his mouth, but Thomas held up a hand. "Grim, don't. He'll probably make me arrest you." Thomas had no fight in him. With no choice but to obey, he trudged back towards the stable.

Chapter 31

As Thomas led two Enforcers on patrol, something drew him down West Street instead of continuing on Church Road. Stabbing cold seeped through to his bones, as their footsteps crunched in the snow. The Enforcer next to him carried a lantern, casting a small yellow circle of light around them. Bryce was a broad-shouldered man with pale blonde hair and deep blue eyes that stood out from his deeply tanned face.

"Why did we have to leave our horses behind?" Bryce asked under his breath.

"Easier to be undetected," Thomas responded. "Lord Samson thinks the horses give away our location."

"No one's out here," Bryce complained. "Why are we? We're out here walking around and freezing while Lord Samson relaxes in front of a fire. My face hurts."

"I'd rather be in front of a warm fire, too. With a bowl of pottage, in the arms of my wife." Pain stabbed at his already raw heart. "But while there's a killer on the streets, we patrol." He shot Bryce a warning look. "Maybe keep your complaints about Lord Samson to yourself."

"Can I complain about the cold, though?"

Thomas chuckled. "I see no problem with that."

The other Enforcer, Reynold, spoke up. "I can't feel my hands." Reynold had rich, brown skin with curly, black hair, and was a man that Thomas knew well from the front lines.

"I can't feel my testicles," Thomas replied.

Light laughter surrounded him.

A man ran onto the road, covered in blood. "Help! My wife! The Shadow of Death killed my wife!"

"Where is she?" Thomas asked, immediately alert.

The man pointed. "The bedroom. He's still in there. The other one told me to run."

He's here?! This is my chance. Tingling all over, Thomas drew his sword. Bryce mouthed the words, *We got him,* eyes gleaming in the yellow light.

"You, stay here. Reynold, Bryce, eyes open."

Thomas steeled himself and barged into the house. Heavy footsteps followed him in. The dark house was quiet, and Bryce's lantern cast a glow in front of him. A strong metallic taste hit as he entered the bedroom. A woman lay on the bed, eyes open, her throat and torso sliced open.

"Oh, no," Bryce whispered. "Thomas."

Two shadow figures stood in the room above the woman. One had white eyes, the other's as dark as the rest of him. One of them held a black sickle. Both exuded Darkness.

"Surround them," Thomas ordered, moving to attack.

Thomas raised his sword. The second figure let out an amused grunt and *disappeared.*

"Where did he go?" Reynold asked.

"Stay focused," Thomas said as he struck.

"No," the voice was deep, dark. Spoken both out loud and in his mind. "Stop."

Stop? Not likely! Blade hit blade as The Shadow of Death raised his weapon in defence. The expected clash of metal didn't come — instead a strange clank followed by a jolt through his sword hand. Thomas attacked again, pushing forward. *Why isn't he attacking?* Advancing again, he swung hard and as the sickle moved to block. Thomas drew Lord Samson's dagger, raised it, and stabbed down. A cry escaped The Shadow, and it swung wildly at Thomas.

Thomas grunted as pain shot through his shoulder. Blue eyes stared back at him, and he froze.

"Put down your weapon," Bryce ordered, stepping forward.

"Bryce, stop," Thomas called out, lowering his sword.

The Shadow slashed across with his weapon. The sword slipped from Bryce's hand, hitting the floor with a crash. Bryce fell.

"Get help," Thomas ordered Reynold.

Reynold ran without question. Thomas dropped his sword and dagger, rushing to Bryce's side. The Enforcer's eyes were wide with panic as he tried to speak. Thomas pressed his hand to the wound as Bryce gasped and gargled. It would be no use. He had seen too many die this way, just as Bryce would. Warm blood seeped around his hands, and Bryce started to choke. Hands grasped at him before falling away as Bryce's eyes closed.

Thomas cursed, removing his hands.

"**Thomas.**"

Lifting his head, he made eye contact with Bryce's killer. Icy fingers of fear closed around his throat. *How could I be such an idiot?* His weapons were out of reach, and he was unarmed. He waited for the killing blow, but it never came. The murderer disappeared before his eyes.

CHAPTER 31

Thomas was in the dining hall next to the fire. Surrounded by Enforcers curious to hear about his encounter with the killer, he kept his head low. Reynold and Lord Samson held him down on the seat while the surgeon cauterised his shoulder. Searing hot pain pressed against flesh, sizzling as his wound was sealed. He turned his head away, eyes watering as he fought against the urge to cry out in pain. A muffled grunt escaped from him.

"Now, explain what happened tonight," Lord Samson demanded as the surgeon spread honey over Thomas's wound.

Before he could answer, Lord Samson cut him off. "I let you lead two men, and you got one killed," Lord Samson roared, nostrils flaring. "Then you let the killer escape?!"

"I didn't 'let' him do anything, I had my hands full," Thomas said, showing Lord Samson his bloodstained hands.

The surgeon wrapped linen around his shoulder and left.

"You should have had your hands full of weapons. In war you don't throw your sword down to help a fallen soldier. You keep fighting or you die," Lord Samson said. "Four years and you didn't learn that?"

"I wasn't thinking about war; I was focused on Bryce," Thomas told him.

"You're lucky the murderer didn't kill you."

"He could have," Thomas said. "He had the chance to."

Lord Samson folded his arms as he looked down at Thomas. "He let you live?"

"He did." Thomas left out the detail that the killer knew his name.

"You saw and fought him, but lived?"

"I don't think I was his target," Thomas replied. "The woman was already dead and the man somehow escaped."

"He said one told him to run," Reynold spoke up. "There were two of them, but one got away somehow."

"Let me guess: He just disappeared," Lord Samson narrowed his eyes.

Reynold gave Thomas a fearful look. This was the part of the conversation Thomas had dreaded.

"Yes," he mumbled.

"Excuse me? I don't think I heard you." Lord Samson turned to Patrick. "Did you hear him?"

"I said 'yes,'" Thomas said louder. "He disappeared into thin air; both of them did."

A low rumble of laughter burst from Patrick. "Next thing you're going to say is it was a shadow."

"It *was* a shadow," Reynold said.

Lord Samson and Patrick's eyes fixed on Thomas. "It was," he confirmed.

A hushed silence descended on the room.

"Everyone out," Lord Samson ordered. "Not you, though," he said to Thomas.

The room cleared within moments.

"I'm starting to see this was a mistake," Lord Samson glared at him. "You've been patrolling for three days. I gave you leadership, Thomas. Was my trust in you misplaced?"

"No, sir," Thomas hung his head.

"Then why are you coming to me with talk of shadows? We are above the superstitious nonsense of townsfolk. I expect the same from my Enforcers, especially my Captain."

"Your Captain? What does Patrick have to do with this?" Thomas asked.

"I'm not talking about Patrick."

"Then what...?" Thomas frowned.

"Most of the Enforcers don't respect Patrick as they do you. I need someone they can trust. Patrick is too....smug. Half of the men are like you, returned soldiers. They relate to you," Lord Samson said.

"But Patrick's already the captain," Thomas pointed out.

Lord Samson scoffed. "Come on, I let him call himself the Captain. It doesn't mean he's actually the Captain." Lord Samson unfolded his arms. "You lost a good man tonight. Right now, you're a burden. I need you to focus on the job. Put your grief aside. Once we've ended this, then you'll have time for that."

"It wasn't grief but ambition," Thomas replied.

The reminder of his wife awoke the flood of pain he'd barely been able to contain. The aching emptiness took hold. Emma had been at the centre of his desire to get home. Now, with her gone, all that was left was to be there for Isaac.

"Ambition?" Lord Samson asked.

"Yes. I want to be the one to bring this killer to justice. It's my fault Jacob died, and now Bryce. Every death at his hands is on me. Only then can I think about my son."

Lord Samson studied his face.

"I think you should bring your son to Kempschester. Your focus is divided, and I think with him here, you can become the Enforcer I want you to be."

Chapter 32

The Shadow fumed. Instead of killing the one he was supposed to, Grim had struck the death blow to an Enforcer. That was not supposed to happen! Through their shared Darkness, he tracked this other self through the Shadow Realm. The Shadow found him and a woman seated at a kitchen table, tunic in hand. Dancing flames cast a flickering orange hue on their faces as the fire crackled. The blonde woman held a candle to his shoulder as if examining something. Her soul blazed gold with no hint of Darkness. The Shadow watched them from the Shadow Realm, keeping out of Grim's sight.

"It looks really deep," she said, keeping her voice low. "You need a surgeon."

"No," Grim shook his head. "I will have to explain how I got wounded in the middle of the night."

He got wounded? The Shadow smiled, his anger receding. He had left as the Enforcer had arrived. Did the twin get the best of him?

"That's a lot of blood, Graeme. You need help."

His name is Graeme? Why did the other one call him Grim?

Graeme turned to face the woman, grabbing her hand. "Then you have to do it."

"What?" She shook her head. "Noooo. I'm not equipped for that."

"But your kitchen is." Graeme pointed. "That knife over there. Put the blade in the fire." She didn't move. "Amelia."

She stared at Graeme open-mouthed.

"This isn't something you have a lot of time to contemplate," Graeme urged. "I'm bleeding."

Amelia's hand trembled as she wrapped her fingers around the wooden handle of a knife. "How do you know how to do this?" she asked, putting the metal end into the flames.

"I've had to treat animals."

"Graeme! You're not an animal. This is going to be painful."

"I know." He forced the sleeve into his mouth, nodding to Amelia.

The Shadow couldn't risk getting too close; Graeme could sense him at any moment. But the concept of taking that knife and stabbing him with it had appeal. *He took my weapon. Where has he put it?*

Amelia carried the knife towards Graeme. "Now what?"

He took the sleeve from his mouth. "Press the blade flat against the wound. I'll tell you when to stop." He shoved it back in.

Amelia held the knife with both hands, pressing it to Graeme's shoulder. As soon as metal connected with shoulder, he flinched, his eyes wide open. He gripped the table and let out a muffled cry. She turned her head away from the sight of burning flesh as she pressed the knife in.

Graeme's hand rose, signalling for her to stop. The knife clattered on the wooden table, and she sat next to him.

The Shadow eyed the weapon. *I should kill him for what he did.* But as much as The Shadow wanted to pick up the knife and drive it into Graeme's stomach, it wasn't his time to die. The urge to kill usually came with a clear command from inside his being. There was none, only his anger.

Graeme had broken into a sweat, groaning in pain as Amelia removed the tunic from his mouth. She leaned against him and he placed an arm around her.

Graeme kissed the top of her head. "You did well. My wife, the surgeon."

"Don't make me do that again," she complained, hitting at him.

"I don't plan on getting stabbed by my brother again," he joked.

"Good, I don't want him scarring this," she said, pressing her hand to his body.

Graeme grabbed her by the jaw and raised her face as he lowered his head.

Time to leave! Watching these two was not his purpose.

"I think I angered him," Graeme murmured.

"Who?"

"The Shadow of Death. I helped someone escape tonight and thought he would kill me there and then."

The Shadow froze. *So you're not an idiot after all.*

Amelia smiled. "You saved someone? I told you!"

She's the reason he's resisting, all of a sudden.

"But then Tom showed up with Enforcers," Graeme muttered.

The brother. I should have killed him.

"You shouldn't have gone against your brother with a sword. You're no match for him."

Graeme's eyes became black and his head turned, searching. "Shhhh. He's here."

It took him long enough.

"Who? Thomas?" Amelia peered around the room.

"No, The Shadow of Death."

She let out a gasp. "Why?"

"I don't know." He rose from the seat. "I know you're there; I can feel the Darkness."

The Shadow revealed himself to Graeme. *"The same Darkness you're trying to deny is a part of you."*

"I'm not denying anything. What are you doing here?"

"You let him go. He was supposed to die."

"Graeme, who are you talking to?" Amelia asked, reaching for him. "There's no one there."

"Shhh, Amelia, he's in the other realm," Graeme said, putting a hand on hers, his eyes on The Shadow. "You won't see him unless he passes through to our world."

"The other realm?" She looked around. "Wherever you are, please stop haunting my husband. He's not going to kill for you, so stop trying to tempt him." Her hands grasped Graeme's arm as if protecting him from The Shadow.

The Shadow laughed. *"I like her."* He stood close to Amelia. *"She's seen your eyes and still wants to believe the best of you. Does she not know what lies within your heart?"*

"Get away from her," Graeme growled.

"You killed the Enforcer before his time."

"You left me to face the Enforcers. My brother tried to kill me. He almost did."

"You should have killed him. Or let me do it."

"I told you, *not him*."

"The first time I saw you, I mistook you for a shade. But I am the shade, a reflection of you." The Shadow glanced at Amelia. *"But this one is yet to know the real you. I can show her. Maybe she will find her own temptation of Darkness."*

"I said get away from her." Graeme grasped the knife. "I will kill you."

"Graeme?" The waver in Amelia's voice revealed her fear, and she pulled away.

Graeme's eyes changed back to blue. "Sorry, Amelia, it's ... he threatened you." He dropped the knife.

Amelia paled. "If he is a part of you, as you say, why would he threaten me? Is that not the same as you threatening me?" She regarded Graeme, her chin high.

"No, you know I could never hurt you," Graeme took her hand. "Amelia, he is the darkest parts of me. His threats are meant to scare me, that's all."

"It looks like it worked," she muttered. "Now what? You give in because he threatened me?"

"No!"

"Is it not too late for that? You already did." The Shadow laughed. *"If that's your final say, this will be your only warning. Don't get in my way. Your brother and your wife will pay for your interference."*

The Shadow stepped through the veil, revealing himself to Amelia. She clapped a hand over her mouth to stifle a scream, backing away. The odour of burning flesh still lingered, mixed with wood smoke and ale. The warmth of the room wrapped around him.

"This was your doing," he said, and Amelia whimpered. *"Your life is in his hands. If he tries to stop me again, I'm coming for you."*

Chapter 33

Unable to stop contemplating his fight with The Shadow of Death, Thomas had left early in the morning to go home. When he returned to Kempschester, there would be consequences for abandoning his post. Lord Samson would probably make an example out of him.

I must know for sure if I saw what I think I saw. He said my name like he knew me. I should do my duty and have Lord *Samson and Patrick with me. What if I'm wrong?*

Thomas rode into the stable, breathing in the sweet-smelling fresh hay. Guinevere snorted as he dismounted. His foot kicked something solid, and he dug through the hay until he found a leather journal. He opened it, recognising Graeme's scrawl within the pages. *What's his journal doing out here?* The page he had opened it to showed a list of names.

"Graeme?" Amelia's voice called out from a stall.

Thomas opened the door. "It's me. He's not here?"

"Thomas, I didn't realise you were back," Amelia said, brushing down her horse.

"Father!" Isaac ran from another stall, Hunter at his heels. "You're back!" The boy wrapped his arms around Thomas's legs.

"For a short time." Thomas closed the book, his thumb keeping his place. He knelt in front of Isaac. "Are you behaving for Aunt Amelia and Uncle Graeme?"

Hunter pushed his wet nose into Thomas's face, licking his chin. Thomas pulled his face away from the dog's hot breath and scratched behind Hunter's ears.

"Aunt Amelia took me to see Mother," Isaac said.

"Thank you," he said to Amelia. "Isaac, why don't you take Hunter outside? I need to talk to Amelia."

Isaac led Hunter out of the stable.

"Thank you for looking after him. How is he?"

"He misses his mother, and you. Did they let you come home?" she asked, still brushing her horse. "Has The Shadow of Death been caught?" There was a twinge of hope in her voice.

"No, this visit is unauthorised."

She glanced over her shoulder. "Unauthorised?"

"Where is Grim?" he asked.

"I don't know, I woke up and he was gone." Her tone rose a pitch.

She knows something.

"Amelia, you were afraid of him that night. We've both seen his eyes. Is there anything you want to tell me?"

"I don't know what you mean," she said, turning away again.

"I think you do. Something is happening to my brother, and you know what it is." Thomas moved around Amelia, grabbing her chin. "Tell me."

"Is that why you've come home? To interrogate me?" She refused to meet his eyes.

"Amelia." She didn't respond. "Look at me, Amelia."

She finally looked up. Thomas lifted the journal to eye level.

Amelia paled. "No…"

Her reaction gave him what he needed. Prying about his twin was not the way he should do this, but he needed answers. He opened the book again.

"Don't!" Amelia pleaded.

There were names in the journal. Lord Philip. Wynnstan. Adam.

"Why is my brother writing the names of the dead? What are the other names for?"

Thomas read the list again. Father's name was in this. Jacob. Nicholas. He had seen lists like this before. Calming his breathing, Thomas fought against the rising horror.

"This is what he was writing that night, isn't it? The first time his eyes turned black?"

She hesitated.

"Amelia?"

"Yes."

"Amelia, that was before many of these people were killed. How did he…" Tendrils of fear wrapped around his heart. *No. That can't be it.* "Is he the killer?" His voice choked on the last word. *Not my brother. Please, not Grim.*

Frustrated by Amelia's refusal to answer his questions, Thomas sighed. "You were terrified of him that night. Now you're protecting him?"

Grim, what have you done? He broke into a cold sweat.

"Do you believe that he could do that? That he could be a killer?" Amelia asked.

There had been an emptiness in Graeme. Something dark. *Is that enough to make him a killer?* If Graeme had murdered, surely he would have felt that through their connection. Yet there had been times when nothing was there, just as there was now.

"I wouldn't have thought so," he muttered. "But now I'm not so sure." His own actions had proven that even moral men could be ruthless.

"What will you do?" Amelia asked in a shrill voice.

"I'm going to have a talk with my brother. I know where he is. Stay with my son."

Chapter 34

W*hy does he still come here?* Thomas would always know where to find his brother. All that Graeme had lost to the river, and this was still where he came for quiet. It would be better to confront him here, where Graeme felt most at ease. The conversation was either going to confirm his fears or bring them to an end. Holding on to hope that he was wrong, Thomas sought out the link with Graeme, finding nothing. The absence of his brother hurt. Will we ever just be the brothers we used to be, instead of shutting each other out?

Despite the biting cold, it wasn't the chill that sent shivers through Thomas's body. It was a deep cold that had settled over him, and the dread that engulfed him was hard to shake.

"Please, let it not be my brother," he whispered to himself. "I don't know how to help him, if it is."

Recent rain added a layer of slippery ice to the snow, so Thomas guided his horse through with care. Wood smoke clung to the air. The grey plume through the trees led Thomas to his brother. He dismounted to approach on foot, tucking Graeme's journal into his belt.

"This is pointless," Graeme's words broke the peace of the forest.

He had his back to Thomas, a black cloak pulled tight around him.

"What's pointless?" he asked.

Graeme stood, spinning around. Thomas smirked.

"Grim, it's only me."

"What are you doing here?"

Thomas sat in front of the fire, holding out his hands for warmth. "You always come here seeking to quiet the noise. Does it work?"

Graeme lowered himself to the ground. "Sometimes." His brother watched him with furrowed brows.

Thomas's hesitance drew out the silence. *What am I waiting for? Just ask him!* Finally, he turned to face Graeme, pulling the journal from his belt.

"Are you going to tell me about this?"

"This is why you came here? To ask me this? What happened to privacy?" Graeme asked, red-faced.

Graeme reached for the journal, but his twin pulled it from his reach.

"You left it in the stable," Thomas said.

"Liar. Give it back."

"Not until you tell me why you wrote those names."

Graeme's eyes narrowed. "If you're going to accuse me of something, say it."

"Are you...?" *This is it. I can't put this off any longer.* "Have you done something?" He blurted

He couldn't say it. The words were right there, and he still couldn't say it. *I'm an Enforcer, yet I can't ask my brother one simple question.* Fear of the answer was holding him back from doing his duty. As he struggled to push past his apprehension, Graeme offered no words. Pain clawed inside his stomach, with a weight pressing down on his chest. *Why isn't he saying anything?*

"I know it was you at the house," Thomas said. "You think I wouldn't recognise my own brother's eyes? Why did you attack me?"

"You were the one who attacked me. You almost killed me!" Graeme shot out and groaned, shaking his head at himself.

Thomas opened the journal and placed it on the ground between them.

Thomas pointed to the list of names. "Graeme, what have you done?"

"I'm not the killer, Tom." Graeme kept his attention away from the book. "But I am *connected* to him, somehow. I know you saw him disappear right before we fought."

"You're connected to him?"

Graeme stared at the fire. "It is The Shadow of Death that haunts my dreams."

"Your nightmares?" Thomas's voice rose. "You dream of The Shadow of Death?"

"I've seen *all* his kills. Every night, I'm pulled somewhere else, surrounded by Darkness. I cannot escape it."

"Like a dark room or a cell?"

"No. It's another world, made from shadows and fog. There is a presence watching me, a living being of immense Darkness. It's not just around me, but in me. Then I see The Shadow of Death. I see him kill."

"You're not making sense. The Shadow of Death is Darkness?"

"No, but he's made from it. I think."

Thomas's heartbeat echoed. "The names, those are his kills?"

"Yes."

"Why?"

Graeme turned his face towards Thomas. "Why what?"

"Why you?"

Graeme shrugged. "I don't know."

"Don't lie to me, Graeme."

"I ... " Graeme wavered. "The Darkness connects the two of us, somehow. It pulls me in, and I feel like I belong there," he admitted, words rushing out.

"No," Thomas said. "You don't belong there. You can't believe that." He closed the leather book. "That's what you tried to tell me at the estate. About the Darkness."

Graeme nodded. "There's something wrong with me, Tom. It's a part of me. I think it always has been."

"I know."

"You know? You never thought to say anything?" Graeme raised his voice.

"Why didn't you?"

"You had your duty; can you blame me?"

There was a long pause as the meaning of Graeme's words sank in. "You were afraid of me, because I'm an Enforcer?"

It had become easier to call himself an Enforcer lately.

"I was afraid you'd have to pick between duty and brotherhood. I didn't want to put that on you."

"Grim… I'm sorry. Duty or not, you know I've always looked out for you. You're my brother. But you're not the killer, so you have nothing to worry about."

The pop and burble of flames and river were soothing. Thomas threw more twigs on the fire.

"You came here *thinking* I was the killer," Graeme murmured. "Did you come to arrest me?"

"I'm not sure I could have if you were," Thomas admitted. "I'm always your brother first, before any duty. You must believe that."

"You still rode here in your Enforcer colours with your sword," Graeme said. "You say you're my brother first, but you're still an Enforcer. I think you've accepted that."

Thomas's stomach knotted at the hurt in Graeme's eyes and voice. Coming here in the black armour and grey cloak had been a mistake. He couldn't blame his brother for seeing that as a betrayal.

"The thought to come without it did not occur to me," he admitted.

The divide between them hurt. Graeme had kept things from him out of fear. *I'm as guilty as he is for keeping secrets.*

"Tom."

"Mmmm?"

"I've been distracted, but I have noticed that there is something bothering you. Is it about Emma?"

It would be so easy to say yes. Graeme would let it go if he did. The loss of his wife would explain the pain. But this was his chance to talk about his own nightmares. "It's not just Emma."

"Something happened, didn't it?"

A heavy silence hung between them. "I happened," he muttered. "I came here to ask if you were the killer, but I've done worse."

"What did you do?" Graeme repeated Thomas's question to him.

"I put an innocent man on that pyre."

Graeme absorbed this. "You knew Jacob was innocent?"

Thomas rose to his feet. "Lord Samson gave me no choice."

"For what, Thomas?"

"I was part of an … interrogation."

"You're the one who interrogated Jacob?"

Thomas met his eyes. "Yes."

"You beat him?"

"Beat him? No. If Lord Samson hadn't stopped me, I would have killed him. I almost did, but he still died."

"How could you do that? You knew Jacob. He didn't deserve that!"

The words seemed empty, as if Graeme was saying them because he had to.

"I was following orders, Graeme. Like I'm supposed to."

"Following orders?" Graeme's mouth slackened as he frowned at Thomas. "I've never known you to be cruel. You would never have done that before…" Graeme left the sentence unfinished.

Thomas finished it for him. "Before I was summoned to war. Even the most honourable of men are changed by battle."

"Is this why Lord Samson recruited you?"

Tell him. "Lord Samson saw… things," Thomas admitted. "At war."

Graeme stood. "What things?"

"I went … dark…" Thomas began. "He saw the worst of me."

"Dark?" Graeme asked.

All the years of pain and horror building inside him were overflowing. *I cannot deny what I did anymore. I cannot hide from the truth.* "There is no justification for what we did. It was inhumane."

"What did you do?"

Thomas hesitated.

"Thomas?" Graeme urged.

The burden of guilt was a weight he had not wanted to face or share with his brother. *Tell him.*

Thomas spoke towards the river to avoid Graeme's piercing eyes. "We raided nearby villages to draw out French soldiers. To lure them out, captives were put under distress."

"You're talking about torture?" Graeme asked quietly.

Thomas nodded. "When the soldiers came, it was a massacre." Phantom screams echoed, mixed with the faint cries as the French pleaded for their lives. "I was taken by battle rage and couldn't stop. I blacked out, and I came to covered in blood." A tremor had started. "There is so much of it on my hands." Hot tears streamed down his face. "I'll never escape that."

"I cannot claim I understand what you endured or what you did. But you're home now, Tom. You need to put the war behind you."

"I can't. Every time I close my eyes…"

"Nightmares. So, you try to drown out their screams with ale. I'm not sure that's the best way to face your actions. I think you should talk to Father Matthew."

"I've already tried that."

"You are a righteous man. Your actions at war cannot be held against you."

His twin echoed a lie Thomas had been telling himself since leaving France.

"God has already judged me. He took Emma from me."

Bitterness dripped from his words. *I sound like Father.*

"There is Darkness in both of us," Graeme said. "I cannot hide from mine any more than you can. Keeping secrets from each other has only led to a divide between us. I miss my brother."

Thomas had only told Graeme half the truth. "I'm right here," he said. "I'm not going anywhere."

Graeme finally reached for the journal, turning the pages over. Thomas caught sight of drawings again.

"You still draw," Thomas commented. "That's really good."

"Drawing helps give me quiet. I drew these from my dreams."

Graeme held the page up to him. On one page, a figure in a cloak with Graeme's black eyes, dark lines over his face. On the other, a form Thomas had seen.

"That's him?"

"It is."

"I'm curious, was it you who told that man to run?" Thomas asked.

Graeme flipped back to the list. "Amelia gave me that idea, that if I was to know their names I could help them. I'm not sure The Shadow of Death was very happy about that." Graeme cleared his throat. "He threatened Amelia. I don't know how to protect her from a shadow of another realm."

"I'll help you," Thomas promised, hand on sword. "He's still solid and can be wounded."

"He threatened you, too."

"Oh." Thomas read through the names. "Many of these have already died. I can help you protect the rest. Nicholas is in here."

"So is Father," Graeme said.

Ethan Blake. The name blurred. "All the times we hid from him in the fields. The orchard," Thomas reminded his brother, bitterness choking him. "James sheltered us."

"I remember."

"It's come to this? Saving the man who would kill us?"

"What do you mean kill us?"

Thomas filled Graeme in on the conversation from the stable. "I always knew he hated me, but to hear it out loud…I despise that man."

"I keep trying to give him a chance to be a better father, and all he does is disappoint me." Graeme shook his head. "So, we let him die?"

"I don't know," Thomas admitted.

"You need to stop following me." Graeme's eyes turned black. "He's here," he whispered.

Thomas froze. "Where?"

"Next to you."

The hairs on Thomas's arms rose. There was nothing there, but he couldn't deny the presence of something dark. He stood, hand on sword. *I can't fight something I can't see.*

Graeme jumped to his feet. "Move away from my brother." His voice echoed in Thomas's mind, a lower grumble than Graeme's usual tone.

Darkness emerged from Graeme, wisps of black fog or smoke rising from his body and curling around him. Dark energy crackled within Graeme's new shape, ripples of anger spreading out. A weapon took form in his hand, the same sickle Thomas had seen before.

While they both shielded themselves from each other, the Darkness ripped apart their barriers, flooding through the connection and engulfing Thomas. He fell to his knees as a furious roar erupted from Graeme's mind and throat.

"Grim, what are you doing?" Thomas yelled, hands to ears, yet unable to block out his brother's fury.

A second shadowy form appeared in front of Graeme.

"I know you think you fight against it, but for you to do that, you've already surrendered to The Darkness. You cannot use a power you want no part of." The Shadow's voice came out a whisper. It turned its head towards Graeme's journal. *"I will see you soon."*

A black haze settled over Thomas before he lost consciousness.

Chapter 35

Thomas floated in a sea of Darkness and fog. The link with Graeme was wide open, and his brother's mind was in his own. There was no sign of Graeme, yet his presence surrounded him.

I need to get back to Kempschester. Before Lord *Samson sends someone for me.*

"You don't have to worry about that right now." The words were thoughts, no voice. But it was Graeme.

"Grim? What happened?" he asked.

"I didn't mean to hurt you, Tom. I'm sorry." A deep regret rumbled through Thomas.

Flames of deep red approached him. A blue glow from the sky drew his eyes upwards.

"Is that a blue moon?" he asked. "Where are we?"

"You're in the Shadow Realm. You must wake up."

Thomas sat up on his bed breathing hard. "Grim?"

Amelia glanced up from beside the bed. "You're awake."

"What happened?"

"He brought you back from the river," she said. "He was really scared."

"Where is he?"

Amelia studied him. "Did you two fight again?"

"It's all right, Amelia. I would never do anything to harm my brother."

"No, just try to kill him."

Thomas climbed from his bed. "I didn't know it was him," he pulled back the top of his tunic. "He stabbed me, too." He showed her his wrapped shoulder.

Amelia lifted the linen from his wound.

"He's wounded, too." She put a hand to her hip. "Performing surgery on my husband in the middle of the night was not something I ever thought I'd see myself doing."

"How long was I out?" Thomas searched around his room. His belt and sword lay on the wooden chest. "Where's my armour and cloak? I must go." He pulled on his belt.

"Graeme went in your place."

Thomas spun around. "What?"

"Patrick arrived not long after you and Graeme got back. They left not long after."

"Why would Patrick take my brother?"

Thomas's stomach lurched at the gleam in Amelia's eyes. *No.*

"Amelia, please tell me Grim didn't just try to pass himself off as me. No one is going to believe that for long."

"It worked on Patrick."

Thomas raised an eyebrow. "Patrick is an idiot. He doesn't count."

"In your armour, on your horse, he did look convincing," she smiled.

"He took my horse?!" Thomas barged towards the door. "He knows the rule with Guinevere." Stomping down the stairs, he let out a groan. "You don't touch a man's horse without his say so."

"You can't go. If you do, they will see what he did," Amelia called after him.

Thomas stopped halfway down the stairs. She was right. If he showed up in Kempschester while Graeme was on his horse, it would cause a lot of trouble for his brother.

"But he left my sword behind? No Enforcer is going to believe I'd go without that."

"He took his own."

"Why did he take such a stupid risk?" Thomas asked. "Samson's not going to believe it's me. Grim will be lucky if he doesn't get locked up."

"The Shadow of Death saw Graeme's list, and Nicholas is next."

"If somehow they don't discover him, I left when I shouldn't have. If they don't arrest him for that, how does he plan to leave?"

"He will leave through the smuggler's gate tonight."

"The smuggler's ga—he's really thought this through, hasn't he?"

"He wants to protect people, Thomas. He is a good man, despite—"

Thomas scoffed. "Despite being soaked in Darkness?" He returned to the bedroom. "What's he going to do when he sees the killer? His black eyes are noticeable. I'm not sure Nicholas will be as accepting as you or me."

"Stop trying to find a problem with it and just have faith in him," Amelia said. "You have a day to yourself. Enjoy it."

"Very well, where's my son?"

"James has him. He's in the orchard."

"This is not going to work," Thomas grumbled, removing his sword belt. "They're going to march here any minute."

"It will work," Amelia left his bedroom.

"What will he do if The Shadow of Death comes after one of us?"

Amelia paused in the doorway. "You have your sword. After four years on the battlefront, I assume you know how to use it?"

Her footsteps led away down the stairs.

"I can't fight him if he's in the Shadow Realm," Thomas told her.

"Graeme has his weapon." Her voice was faint. "Maybe it will be useful against him."

"A sickle?" Thomas shook his head. "That is not an adequate weapon for a fight. He'd be better off with something bigger. A sword would be far superior to such a small blade. Or, if it has to be a farmer's tool, a pitchfork, even a scythe."

Why did The Shadow of Death choose the sickle in the first place?

Thomas knelt over Emma's grave, his first visit since her funeral. Flowers from Amelia's visits had been laid on the loose dirt. Other graves — Mary's, his mother's and his uncle's, showed the others his family had lost. No headstone had been made yet for Emma's grave.

Life is so short. We must make the most of our time with family while we still have the chance. Thomas wrapped his arms around Isaac, enfolding the boy completely in a full-body hug. Isaac leaned against Thomas, the two of them needing the reassurance as much as each other.

"I miss her," Isaac's voice wavered.

"So do I."

"Why did she have to go?" Isaac sniffed.

Isaac's question was one Thomas had been asking. Thorns of grief pierced his heart.

"I wish I knew," he admitted. "But you still have me, Son. We are both here to remember your mother. She's not truly gone."

"But you're never here," Isaac complained. "I don't want you to leave again."

Do you have any idea how much you sound like your mother right now?

"I have work. I have to go," Thomas released Isaac. "What if you could come to Kempschester with me? We could live there. Lord Samson has already told me I can rent a house from him. You would have tutors to school you when I'm at work."

Isaac stared up at Thomas. "Would I see you more?"

"Of course."

"How will I be a farmer if I don't live on a farm?"

"Who says you have to be a farmer?" Thomas laughed.

"Grandfather. He says it will be my duty to take over the farm when you and Uncle Graeme are gone."

He would say that. Already forcing that on my son?

"You can be a farmer if you want to be," Thomas said. "One day you might decide you want to be a baker or a blacksmith. No one can decide that for you, especially not your grandfather."

"Will you take Guinevere to Kempschester?"

Thomas grinned. "You think I would leave her behind?"

"You left her behind before," Isaac reminded him.

"That's because I didn't want to take her to France. It was not a good place for such a beautiful horse to be. Your other grandfather gifted me that horse when I married your mother."

"Can I get my own horse?" Isaac asked.

"What do you need a horse for at your age?"

Isaac's eyes lit up, and a slow smile spread across his face. "If we live in town, can I get a sword? Like yours?"

Thomas couldn't hold back his laughter. "We will talk about that later."

Isaac's smile faded quickly. "But I won't be able to see Aunt Amelia or Uncle Graeme. Or the village."

Thomas cast a look around him. As much as he hated farming, this was his home, the only life he had known. The only time he had been away from his family was for war, and being an Enforcer would only make it harder to return as much as he wanted.

"We can always visit them when I'm not working."

"And Mother?"

"Any time you want to," he promised. "But we haven't decided on this yet, so you cannot tell anyone."

"You mean it's a secret?"

Thomas ruffled the hair on Isaac's head. "For now."

"Do you have to go to work soon? With the Enforcers?" Isaac asked.

"Not today. You can thank your uncle for that."

"Is he an Enforcer now?"

"No, he's pretending to be me so I can spend the day with you." Thomas lifted Isaac's chin. "You're not afraid of Enforcers anymore? Of me?"

"I'm still afraid of them. But Aunt Amelia said you're a good Enforcer, and you would protect me from the rest of them."

"That's right, I'll never let anyone get you." Thomas hugged his son again. "It makes me happy that you're not scared of me, Isaac. A boy should not be afraid of his father. You never have to fear me. I want to be a good father to you, I'm trying."

"You are a good father," Isaac said into his shoulder.

I hope you're seeing this, Emma. Me and our son are bonding.

"Do you want to stay here longer?" Thomas pulled away, rising to his feet.

"No, we can go," he said. "I'm hungry."

Isaac put his hand in Thomas's as they left the grave. Thomas turned back once.

"Goodbye, Mother," Isaac said. "Goodbye, Sister."

Chapter 36

The Shadow found a way to show Graeme what he was. Graeme had given in to the Darkness to protect his brother. Such a display of power meant that there was no struggle; Graeme knew what lay within, embraced it. *Why, then, does he oppose me? For his brother and wife? I will kill them.* Understanding of why The Shadow had separated from his mortal self sank in. He held no memories, no humanity to cling to, no reason to resist. His only purpose was to kill, drawn by Graeme to each human meant to die.

How else would he have knowledge before I did, who my next would be? The Shadow only knew right before a kill who he was to hunt. Yet Graeme had a list of names in a book, his past kills *and* those he was *yet* to hunt. The brothers had spoken of Nicholas, whose name was next on the list, as if they knew him. But without being called forth to kill, The Shadow had no way to find Nicholas, so could do nothing but wait. It was not time yet for Nicholas to die, and he would know when it was. *Graeme* would tell him when.

Graeme's unexpected presence in Kempschester drew The Shadow to seek out his mortal self. He found him dressed in the black and grey of Enforcers. *What is he doing?* Those around him called him Thomas, but The Shadow recognised the Darkness that burned within. Imitation of his twin brother fooled all *but* the Lord of Kempschester. The lord's scowls were a clear show of suspicion as he let it play out. To take his brother's place meant that Graeme had somehow forced Thomas to remain behind.

He thinks he is here to stop me, but he will lead me to my next kill, to Nicholas. The Shadow let Graeme see him. Panic flitted across Graeme's face as he closed his eyes before anyone saw that they had become black. There was nothing he could do while passing for his brother, but there would be a time when he would go to Nicholas.

It wasn't until the sun began to set that Graeme broke away from the Enforcers.

"You took your time," The Shadow told him.

"Leave Nicholas," Graeme said. "He does not deserve this."

"I exist to take lives, and you keep telling me who I cannot kill. But you write the name Nicholas on a list among those who will die." The call came, drawing him away from Graeme. *"He is next, and I want my weapon back. You cannot stop his death."*

Graeme had the sickle. The Shadow only needed to reach out; it was his, after all. Somehow, Graeme had bound it to himself, hidden it in the Shadow Realm. But the dark blade knew its true owner, and The Shadow easily reclaimed what was his. Before his mortal self could say another word, The Shadow left him. It was time for Nicholas to die.

Entering a house, The Shadow found himself face-to-face with a man whose soul showed the same black flame of those not long for this world. Their kitchen was filled with the sweet tang of wine as a red-haired woman poured red liquid into goblets.

"Nicholas." The Shadow had no reason to hide himself.

Nicholas and the woman gasped at his presence in their home.

"Who are you?" Nicholas demanded. "How did you get in here?"

The woman had the familiar glint of fear deep in her eyes. "Nicholas, he is The Shadow of Death." Her words were almost a whisper. "He has come for us."

"I am not here for you. Only him."

Graeme's presence approached, telling The Shadow time was limited to separate Nicholas from his mortal tether.

"Catherine, run," Nicholas urged, reaching for a knife.

She dropped her goblet, wine spilling on the floor.

"No. Stay," The Shadow ordered.

The woman did not need much convincing as she backed herself into a corner, eyes glazing over, whispering prayers to herself.

There was a thud, followed by a sharp crack, as the door gave way under body weight. Graeme had arrived.

"Nicholas?" Graeme ran into the kitchen. "No." He froze. "Please, not him."

"Thomas?" Nicholas half-turned. "Graeme, help."

The Shadow unleashed fury, his blade singing as he cut deep. Graeme's horrified cries mixed with Catherine's sobs and the pained grunts of Nicholas as his blade slashed at flesh, tearing linen. Hot blood sprayed as he sliced throat, chest, and torso. Nicholas slumped to the floor, gurgling.

Chest heaving, the man turned his head towards Graeme, eyes wide with terror as they focused on black eyes.

"No," he rasped as Graeme knelt beside him.

"Nicholas, I'm sorry."

Nicholas could only make choking sounds as he recoiled from Graeme. His gaze turned towards Catherine as he died. The Shadow knelt in front of Catherine, whispering in her ear.

"Get away from her," Graeme drew his sword. "Catherine, are you hurt?"

"He isn't here for me," Catherine whispered.

"Let me do what you called me to do," The Shadow told Graeme.

"*You* did this?" Catherine cried. "*You're* the reason he came for my husband?" Her eyes shifted to Graeme. "Why are your eyes black?"

"Why are you doing this?" Graeme asked.

"He was on your list; it was his time to die."

"You have a list?" Catherine cried.

Graeme had a dangerous glint in his eyes. "I will kill you," his voice was filled with dark hate.

"I would much rather work with you than against you. Stop trying to convince yourself you are one of them. You are Darkness."

Catherine rose to her feet, hysteria emboldening her. "My husband is dead because of you." Her eyes darted towards the door behind Graeme. "He was your friend! Someone, help!" She reached for the jug of wine and threw it at him. Missing, ceramic smashed against the wall. As she picked up an hourglass, she caught sight of Graeme and froze.

The Darkness inside Graeme emerged once again, and he advanced on Catherine. A scream tore from her throat, cut off by Graeme's sword. The hourglass slipped from her hand as she dropped beside her dead husband.

"What are you?"

Her breaths rattled until finally, one last groan escaped.

"This was not as I expected."

"Why are you doing this?" Graeme asked again.

The Shadow pointed at Catherine, who was now empty, lifeless.

*"**You** did that. It was **not** her time to die. She was **not** on your list. Just as the Enforcer wasn't."*

Graeme dropped his sword and fell to the ground.

"Nicholas," Graeme whispered. "I'm sorry, old friend."

Chapter 37

Something is wrong with Grim. With a new strength to their connection, Thomas was unable to close himself off from Graeme. Blind rage burst through, but before Thomas could understand the reason, anger gave way to emptiness. Darkness. *No, what is he doing?* Then a deep sorrow. Pain like a hot blade pierced his chest. Thomas stopped the horse as he struggled to catch his breath. What just happened?

He arrived at the smuggler's gate that led into Kempschester, an entrance that hadn't been used in over ten years. Almost completely hidden in overgrowth, the wood was rotting, the metal hinges rusting. Thomas pulled the hood over his head, blowing on his hands to warm them. Graeme would meet him so he could take back his armour and horse. His heart hammered, fearful that Lord Samson had arrested his brother. He could do nothing but wait. *He's supposed to be here. What is taking so long?*

"Tom?" Graeme's voice hissed from the other side of the gate.

"I'm here," Thomas raised his eyes to the sky in silent relief.

The gate opened, metal screaming, sending a deep shudder through Thomas. Graeme rode through. They dismounted, and Thomas grabbed his brother by the arm.

"What were you thinking?" Thomas demanded.

"I wanted to help Nicholas."

"I could have—"

"No, Tom, there was nothing either of us could do," Graeme said, with regret in his voice.

Graeme might as well have punched him in the chest. Sick to the stomach, Thomas swallowed past the lump in his throat.

"He's dead?" Thomas asked, his voice hoarse. "That's what I felt, just before. You saw it happen?"

"I couldn't stop him. Nothing could have stopped him," Graeme's voice broke.

"No, I'm more skilled than you. I could have protected Nicholas."

"Tom, stop. He was dead on the floor before I could take a step."

Numb, Thomas wiped at his eyes and cleared his throat. "You have to go," he said. "Give me my armour. Don't you ever take my horse again."

Graeme removed the cuirass, bracers and cloak. As Thomas pulled the leather armour on, a horse snorted nearby. Thomas froze.

"Did you hear that?" Graeme asked in a whisper.

"That was not Guinevere or Willow." He peered into the dark. "Did anyone not believe you were me?"

"Everyone accepted it without question. Although I think Lord Samson was suspicious."

"You stinking idiot!" Thomas climbed onto his horse, armour unbuckled. "You have to leave, now!"

"Neither of you are going anywhere," Lord Samson's voice boomed.

Now we're finished. Thomas broke out in a sweat. Next to him, Graeme gripped his arm.

"Lord Samson," Thomas croaked.

"I knew you would use this gate. Give me one reason I shouldn't arrest your brother. Passing himself off as an Enforcer to gain unauthorised entrance to the town. Not to mention you leaving in the first place," Lord Samson raged. "Did you think I wouldn't recognise the difference in your eye colour? Or that he lacks the ability to talk to people the way you do?"

Say something before he arrests Grim.

"It was my idea," he blurted. "Please, he doesn't deserve to be arrested for something I made him do."

Surprise flared from Graeme.

"It was?" Lord Samson asked. "Why?"

"I wanted to spend the day with my son," Thomas said. "Since losing my wife, I want to be there as much as I can for him."

In the dark, Graeme's eyes burned into him. *Do not say a word,* Thomas willed silently.

"Is this going to be an ongoing problem?" Lord Samson asked.

"No, sir."

"Have you given thought to what we talked about?"

"Considering it, Lord Samson." Not wanting further talk about his move to Kempschester in front of Graeme, he changed the subject. "Can my brother leave?"

"No."

"No?" Thomas and Graeme asked at the same time.

Is he going to arrest Grim?

"You're going to ride back to Riverwick in the dark?" Lord Samson asked Graeme.

"I know the road well, sir, as does my horse."

"No, you can stay here for the night. What you two did was risky and stupid." Lord Samson turned his horse around. "Come. I'm sure you're both hungry."

"If you knew, why didn't you arrest him?" Thomas asked, following Lord Samson.

Graeme caught up, riding alongside Thomas.

"Patrick would have liked that after he punched him."

"He. . .You punched Patrick?" Thomas rubbed his eyebrow. "Why did you punch Patrick?" *Oh, this will not be good.*

"He was insulting me. . .you," Graeme explained. "I lost my temper."

"I would have liked to have seen that," Thomas uttered under his breath, and Graeme snickered.

"As it is, Patrick demanded I arrest you," Lord Samson said. "He already despises you; your brother has given him more reason to do so."

"But—"

"But I didn't arrest your brother or expose his lie, because of the lengths you would have gone to, to protect him. You and I both know you would have attempted to bust him out. I don't need my captain pulling stunts like that."

"Captain?" Graeme whispered. "You're captain? No wonder Patrick hates you."

"That is not something Patrick is aware of yet," Lord Samson said. "Nor anyone. I will let you announce that."

"Thank you, sir," Thomas said.

The main entrance was lit up with torches and guarded heavily. The guards acknowledged Lord Samson and opened the gate.

Lord Samson stopped, facing Thomas. "I've known a few twins, but none are more likely to cause trouble than the two of you. Please don't make me regret not arresting you." He eyed Graeme before shifting his hard stare to Thomas. "Go and eat. Graeme can leave at sunrise, and you will have patrol."

Lord Samson left, riding across towards the estate. Thomas and Graeme followed.

"I can't believe you punched Patrick," Thomas laughed.

"I can't believe you let him talk to you that way. I know he's a noble, but does he have to be so berating?"

"I don't let him. You're right; he's a noble. Their influence can reach Riverwick. I know my place."

"It's a shame he's not on the death list," Graeme muttered as they entered the estate.

"Grim! You cannot speak like that!" Thomas said. "You would wish death on someone? What is wrong with you?"

They dismounted. Met by servants, their horses were led away to the stable.

"I would wish death on those who deserve it," Graeme replied.

Thomas stopped mid-step and grasped him by the arm, pulling his brother to face him. "Is this you or the Darkness inside you? You cannot decide who does and doesn't deserve to die."

"This is me. It always has been. The Darkness is a part of me, Thomas, and you know that. You keep trying to control everything, make sure no one sees what's below the surface for your own reputation. But this is something you cannot control. Stop trying."

His skull prickled as Graeme pulled away and walked towards the Enforcer quarters.

God, please help my brother. Remove this Darkness from his heart. Thomas had pleaded these words many times.

He ran after Graeme. "Are you hungry?"

"Yes, food!" Graeme responded as if nothing had happened. "I hope there's plenty of ale, too."

Thomas laughed. "There's always ale; Lord Samson owns a brewery. It's better ale than we get in Riverwick."

"Don't let Leo hear you say that."

Thomas was met with a rich, gamey fragrance the moment they stepped into the dining hall.

"They have venison again," his mouth watered.

The dining hall was full. Enforcers talked among themselves as they ate and drank.

"I've never seen so many Enforcers in one room," Graeme grumbled.

"Thomas!" Reynold called him over. "Men, make room for Thomas and his brother!"

Enforcers shuffled around, and plates were set down at the empty places.

"Brother of Thomas…"

"Graeme," his brother said.

"Graeme, ale or wine?"

"Ale, thank you."

Tankards were slammed in front of them, spilling over the sides. Thomas raised the venison to his mouth, taking in the honey and wine flavour.

"How do you have so much venison?" Graeme asked while chewing.

Laughter surrounded them.

"Lord Samson cheats," Reynold said with a grin.

"Cheats?" Thomas asked.

"He pays men to steal it from village peasants who illegally hunt."

Graeme choked. "He what?"

Not here, Grim. Thomas urged. *Not now.* But Graeme's face reddened, his eyes glinting. Thomas ground his teeth, heat rising in his own cheeks. His anger rolled through him as he struggled to clear his head.

"Lord Philip started it a year ago," Reynold explained. "He suspected the forest was being illegally hunted and thought his scouts were useless. So he paid raiders to patrol the forest instead."

No one else seemed to notice the rage building in Graeme.

"Have some ale," Thomas urged his brother.

Graeme turned his flashing eyes to Thomas. "Did you consider that the peasants are just trying to feed their families?" he asked Reynold.

"They shouldn't be hunting in the forests," another Enforcer said. "They're stealing from land that doesn't belong to them."

"But the land belongs to the king. Why does the lord get the spoils?" Graeme said.

"Because he protects the land from would-be thieves." Reynold said. "This conversation got serious very quickly. No wonder you call him Grim," Reynold laughed, glancing at Thomas.

"My brother, uhhh, spends a lot of time with peasants. He sympathises with their pain," Thomas said.

"Speaking of pain, did Thomas tell you he punched Patrick?" Reynold asked Graeme to change the subject.

"He had that coming," a voice from the next table called out. "It's about time someone put him in his place."

Laughter spread around the room, then stopped. Patrick had entered, glaring at everyone. Bruises marked his face, similar to those currently fading on Thomas'.

"I punched him twice?" Thomas muttered.

Graeme shrugged as he reached for ale. Patrick's cold eyes landed on Thomas. "How did your brother get in here?" he demanded. "This is Enforcers quarters."

Thomas rose to his feet. "That looks like it hurts," he pointed to Patrick's face. "Are you sure you want to provoke me again?"

Patrick paled. "Are you threatening me, Enforcer Blake?"

The entire room had stopped eating, their eyes darting between Thomas and Patrick. Even the nobles seemed to be holding their breath.

Overconfident with an audience and tired of Patrick's superiority, Thomas raised his eyebrows. "It's *Captain* Blake to you."

Enforcers gasped, but many of the nobles exchanged looks, their faces darkening.

"Captain?" Patrick demanded, forcing a laugh. "You think you're captain?"

"I know I am," Thomas said. "Consider this the announcement."

"We'll see about that," Patrick left.

"You are nothing but a farmer. Why would Lord Samson promote you over nobility?" came a voice from the corner.

Those around Thomas stood, facing the nobles. "Are you questioning Lord Samson's decision?" Reynold asked.

Chaos erupted as soldiers and nobles yelled across the room at each other.

Thomas sat.

"I didn't realise how quickly this has become your world," Graeme said in a low voice.

"My world? What do you mean by that?" Thomas finished the ale.

"You enjoyed putting Patrick in his place," Graeme motioned around the room. "A promotion and men loyal to you? You never liked farming, but you belong here. Like it or not, you're an Enforcer, Tom."

Unable to deny Graeme's words, Thomas breathed in. "Does that bother you?"

Graeme's eyes moved around the room again. "It was always you, me, and Nicholas. We lost Nicholas when he left Riverwick, but now he's really gone. I never thought I might lose my brother, not like this."

Thomas faced Graeme. "Grim, what are you talking about? You're not going to lose me."

Graeme hesitated before returning his gaze. *"I already have."*

Chapter 38

"Thomas," Emma's breath tickled his ear. "You're going home."

He groaned.

"Thomas," Emma whispered again. "Captain Blake!"

Pounding in his head brought him back into his empty bed in the Enforcers quarters. He sat up in confusion. He squinted at the daylight that filled his room. The thumping came from his door, which shook with each thud. In the other bed, Graeme covered his own face with a pillow, growling into it.

Lord Samson called out from the other side of his door. "Thomas, are you still asleep in there?" Fists smashed against the door.

"Answer him," Graeme said, voice muffled. "That banging is hurting my head."

"I'm awake," Thomas replied.

The door burst open to reveal Lord Samson dressed in a red tunic of wool with a blue cloak. The Kemps' coat of arms was embroidered on the tunic, a grey shield with a white horse and sword.

Thomas jumped from his bed, relieved that he had not slept naked. If not for his brother's presence, he would have.

"Lord Samson?"

"I sent a servant for you. Why are you still in bed? Do you think I have time for this? I have the Lord of Thornesby arriving this morning."

His mouth was dry, the pain in his head throbbing. "You sent a servant?" he asked. "I didn't hear anything."

"Were you up all night again? Is that why half my Enforcers are still in bed?"

Last night had been a long night of drinking, most of it blurry. But Graeme singing and laughing along with everyone else stood out clearly. He had looked happy.

Thomas chuckled.

"I'm glad you find that amusing. Both of you are going home. A message arrived early this morning from your uncle."

"Is something wrong?" Thomas asked.

"It's your father."

Graeme sat up. "Is he dead?"

"Dead?" Lord Samson's brows drew together. "No, he's sick. *Go now.*" Lord Samson gave Thomas a tight-lipped frown. "Thomas, I grow weary of this back and forth. You must make a decision."

"Make a decision on what?" Graeme asked when Lord Samson had gone.

"Get up, Grim," Thomas pushed aside the question. "We need to go."

Thomas pulled on his cuirass and buckled it before reaching for the bracers. Going home meant he was off duty, but he had worn armour so long, it was a part of him.

"Why? To rush home for Father?" Graeme lay down again. "Neither of us will miss him, and we know he is going to meet The Shadow of Death.

We'll be rid of him. Everything we've endured at his hands will be over."

"Is that all you're thinking about? That he deserves to die, so let him?"

"Yes. You're not?

Yes. I hope he chokes on his own blood. Thomas shook his head. "What about Uncle James?" He demanded. "Did you think about him? As unpleasant as father is, he is our uncle's brother." Thomas pulled on his shoes. "James has already lost two brothers." He wrapped the belt around his waist and grabbed Graeme's cloak, the wool soft in his hand. "Our uncle is about to lose the last of his brothers. You really don't care?" He threw the cloak at Graeme. "Now get up so we can support the man who was more of a father than Ethan was. He's never let us down, Grim. We cannot let him down."

Thomas had the fur-lined hood of his grey cloak pulled up, head bowed against the biting chill. Graeme's black cloak was pulled tight. Snow drifted around them and covered the ground, crunching under the horses' hooves.

"It's beautiful," Thomas murmured.

Next to him, Graeme shivered as he lifted his head enough to show Thomas a red face and narrowed eyes. "You would be freezing to death and still say that."

Thomas's fingers were numb, his breath white. *Warm bed. Fire. Pottage.*

"We're almost home," he said.

"Liar," Graeme grumbled. "We're only halfway. Stop trying to make me feel better."

The snow became heavier, making it difficult to see the road. A deep shiver passed through him.

"This is getting worse," his brother complained. "If we had been able to leave last night, we would have missed all this."

"Think warm—"

"Don't say 'think warm thoughts'. We're going to be frozen before we get home."

"Grim, it's a little snow," Thomas laughed. "Be glad it's not a storm. We will be home soon."

"Stop. I know you're just as miserable as me in this."

"My face hurts, my hands are numb, and I need to piss. Is that what you want to hear?"

"Yes, I'm not alone in my frozen torment."

"Good, as long as you're happy."

"Who's Caleb?" Graeme asked.

Taken aback by the abrupt change in subject, Thomas lost his smile. "Where did you hear that name?"

"You were talking in your sleep last night. You kept saying his name and 'I'm sorry'. That was before you started talking to Emma."

Talking in my sleep? What else did he hear?

"He's dead," Thomas said, flatly.

"That doesn't answer my question."

Thomas hesitated. "Caleb was a brother. He's the reason I got discharged."

"Discharged? You held that back before."

"I hoped to avoid talking to you about that," Thomas admitted.

"Stop holding on to the war, Tom. It's consuming you. I tried to give you time, like you asked, but your remorse and grief are too great," Graeme said. "It's time to talk."

Graeme was right. He couldn't hide from this conversation anymore, no matter how much he dreaded it.

"I wanted to…" The memories were rushing at him, and the warmth of a tear slid down his cold cheek. "You're wrong though, I haven't been holding onto what happened in France. I've been trying to run from it."

Graeme said nothing, waiting for Thomas to go on.

"Our camp had been invaded by enemy soldiers…"

Cold water ran down Thomas's back and neck, and his hair was plastered to his head. Rain muddied the ground, mixing with blood as he knelt over a wounded Caleb. Warm blood spilled around his hands as he held them against Caleb's abdomen. His sword lay beside him in the mud. Thunder clashed from above.

Pale and breathing rapidly, Caleb lifted his blond head and groaned as he caught sight of his midsection. His green eyes widened. "Is that my guts?" His head fell back, hands shaking as he reached for his stomach.

Aris, a man of immense build, stood over Thomas. He was the only soldier in armour, a magnificent black-and-red cuirass, with black leather vambraces and greaves. With dark, wavy hair, olive skin, and brown eyes, Aris was a man who lived for war.

"Shhhh, don't move," Thomas said.

"Thomas. Please. Kill me." Caleb gazed up at Aris. "Tell him."

"Thomas, it's a mercy kill," Aris said.

"I cannot do that."

"You're not killing anyone who is not already dying." Aris put his hand on Thomas's shoulder. "You are only quickening his death, ending his torment. It is honourable."

"Please," Caleb pleaded again. "Have mercy."

"It's the right thing to do," Aris said.

Thomas drew his dagger.

Graeme's piercing eyes watched Thomas intently from under his hood.

"Aris was right. You gave Caleb what he asked for," Graeme said. "It isn't wrong to show mercy. Your guilt is unnecessary."

"Unnecessary?" Thomas scoffed.

"You're allowing the dead to haunt you. Let me help you put them to rest."

"Help me how?"

"When we were children, I always felt safe. You were always there, determined to be the big brother protecting me. It's my turn to do the same for you. Don't try to bear this burden alone."

Graeme's deep sympathy flooded through their connection, unrestrained warmth. Thomas couldn't hold back the burst of pride. His brother would *always* stand with him, no matter what they had to face. Darkness would never break that bond.

"I came back broken," Thomas admitted.

"You came back different. I would not say you're broken," Graeme told him. "I've heard James talk of war madness; perhaps you experienced that?"

"I'm not mad," Thomas said, his voice hard.

"I know that, but you are feeling the effects of war. There will be an adjustment. You killed people; that is not going to be easy to come back from."

Darkness in Graeme rose. The surge surrounded Thomas, but it was smothered before there was a chance for more.

"I know you felt that. I think I tore apart our mind shields," Graeme said. "I lost control of it yesterday. I'm sorry it hurt you."

So, we've finished lying to each other. Good.

"I remember the Darkness and what The Shadow of Death said."

"You saw him?"

"Yes, right before I passed out. Then you were talking to me in the Shadow Realm?"

A heavy silence fell over the two of them. Thomas studied what he could see of Graeme's face under the cloak's hood. A shadow of fear flickered between them.

"I know I must stop him, but I don't know how. Lord Samson and the Enforcers don't know what they're up against. I watched him kill Nicholas, and there was nothing I could do," Graeme blinked, his tears stinging Thomas's eyes.

"Well, if your journal is right, we know where he will be next," Thomas said.

"Father?"

CHAPTER 38

It was Thomas's duty to capture The Shadow of Death. He had gotten someone killed with his last attempt. This time would be different.

"I never thought I would hear myself say this, but we must protect Father. No one else has to die."

Graeme lowered his head," No one else has to die."

Chapter 39

Silence as dismal as the dark clouds above hung over Riverwick. The crisp smell of snow and woodsy smoke clung to the air. Few villagers were outside, but they bowed their heads as Thomas and Graeme rode by.

"That's strange," Graeme murmured.

"They've never done that before."

They approached their farmhouse, a light breeze ruffling their cloaks.

"We should have until nightfall," Graeme said.

"Are you sure? He has killed in the middle of the day before."

"That was a one-off. He was finishing what he started with those guards."

How do you know so much about this?

Amelia and Isaac were outside, the boy lying in the snow, Hunter at his side.

"You're back!" Amelia said to Graeme as they dismounted.

Graeme smiled down at Amelia, putting one hand on her waist, the other around her back, pulling her in. "Sorry, we got caught. Lord Samson knew the whole time. I missed you."

"I missed you too. I was worried something had happened. Our bed was cold without you."

Jealousy burned through Thomas. "Where is James?"

Amelia tore her gaze from Graeme. "He is upstairs, with Ethan."

"Come on, Grim, our uncle needs us."

Thomas marched inside without waiting.

He kicked off his shoes, and they hit the wall with a soft thud. Graeme's followed. Before he started up the stairs, he paused and straightened the footwear.

"What are you doing?" Graeme asked.

Unable to explain his actions, Thomas shrugged as he led his brother upstairs to Father's bedroom.

James turned as they entered, his face lighting up. "Nephews, you're here!"

Father's eyes were closed, giving no reaction to their presence, his face pale. An unpleasant smell half-hid beneath the sweet floral scent of jasmine and sharp rosemary that had been laid on his bed.

"Where else would we be, Uncle?" Graeme asked. "How long has he been sick?"

"A day. He had a headache first, then said he felt weak and tired. Amelia spoke to the physician from Hazelbury when he passed through yesterday. Henry recommended we put Ethan to bed. He will call in again tomorrow." James cast a look of pain over his brother. "He's already showing the lumps and is coughing up blood."

Thomas's arms tingled. "The pestilence is in Riverwick?"

They had been lucky to have gone this long without it.

"He's the first," James replied, his voice terse.

Thomas gave James a squeeze on the shoulder. "I'm sorry, Uncle. We came back as soon as we heard. Is there anything we can do?"

James passed his eyes over both Thomas and Graeme. "Yes, there is."

"Anything. What do you need?" Thomas said.

James glanced between them again and Thomas looked at Graeme, whose eyes narrowed with suspicion. "I want you to forgive your father," James said.

"Excuse me?" Graeme and Thomas asked in unison.

"I know your feelings for him, and all I ask is that you forgive him before he dies."

"You ask a lot," Thomas said, his voice tight. In his disbelief that James would make such a request, raw pain shot through him, becoming hot anger which roared in his ears. "You know we cannot do that."

"Thomas, you will have no reason to —"

"Stop, Uncle, we can't," Graeme said, stepping in front of Thomas. "Tom and I don't always agree, but we do on this. You were the one to shelter us, yet you ask this? Did you know he wanted to kill us? We were babies, and his first thought was to end our lives."

James's lack of surprise sent a chill through Thomas. "You knew?"

"I'm the one who stopped him," James let out a heavy sigh.

"But you demand that we forgive him for that? He would never want or ask for our forgiveness. He probably doesn't think he needs it. Nor does he deserve it," Thomas said. "We came here for you, but that is never going to happen."

"You should leave," Graeme warned, eyes flashing.

James glared at Graeme. "Ethan's my brother. If it were yours, nothing could tear you away."

Thomas moved away until his back touched the wall. The rising thrum of anger caused by years of hurt and fear took his words from him.

"Please, Uncle, you ask the impossible of us. Leave," Graeme said.

"You bring shame to my brothers' names." James left the room without a word, his heavy footsteps stomping down the stairs.

"Tom? He's gone." Thomas took in a deep breath. Piercing blue eyes stared into his as Graeme studied his face. A hand rested on his shoulder. "Are you all right?"

"It's not just the beatings," Thomas muttered. "But admitting that he wished he had drowned us and hating me for Mother's death. After constant humiliation and fear at the hands of drunken outbursts, I have no forgiveness in me."

"I know. I don't either."

"You were right."

"About what?"

"This is what he deserves." Thomas eyed Father. "When he dies, Uncle will grieve with his nephews at his side, but I will not mourn him. We will be free of the burden of being Ethan Blake's sons."

"The house, the farm will be passed down to you," Graeme said.

"To you," Thomas corrected.

"We are both the grandsons of Walter Blake, but you are Ethan's eldest son. Not by much, but still the eldest."

"I don't care. You are the one worthy of such an inheritance." Thomas meant it. He had no desire to own land and would happily pass it on to Graeme.

"I'm not dead yet," Father said, in a raspy voice. "Come to watch me die, have you?" He sat up, coughing.

"The Shadow of Death is coming for you," Graeme said.

"What are you doing?" Thomas whispered.

Graeme ignored Thomas and approached Father's bed. "It is your time, and you can do nothing to stop him. But it will be the sons you wanted to kill who will stand between you and him."

"I do not need you to protect me," Father coughed again. "Get out of my room."

"We're going," Thomas grabbed Graeme. "But when it's dark, you'll feel his cold breath on your neck. We'll return then."

Thomas dragged Graeme from the room, leading him downstairs.

"Cold breath? What was that?" Graeme asked as they took a seat at the table.

"I don't know. You just threatened him with The Shadow of Death. I felt I needed to say something, too."

The laughter bubbled up from Thomas as Graeme chuckled.

"I need a drink after that," Thomas said.

"We have plenty of time. I'll go with you."

"You don't have to do that."

Graeme raised his chin. "How long has it been since we had a drink together?"

Thomas grinned. "Last night?"

"And it was the happiest I've seen you since you returned," Graeme noted

"I could say the same for you," Thomas said. "There was a smile on your face, almost as if you were having fun. You were singing! With Enforcers, no less."

"I'm not going to turn my back on my brother. Even if you are an Enforcer."

"Whatever this is with you, I'll see it through, too."

Joy filled his chest, lightening the dread that had been hanging over him.

Chapter 40

His next kill awaited. The call of death was loud and demanding, drawing him to a village. Snow covered the ground, and gusts of wind howled through the trees. As he passed through the veil, his black cloak flailed around him. Frigid air chilled The Shadow to his core. He approached the house, leaving footprints in the snow. At the front door, he pushed and it swung open easily.

Inside, the warmth of a still-burning fire greeted him, the house silent. Thomas sat hunched over the kitchen table, head resting in his arms. A small puppy slept at his feet, its ears twitching. On the table were empty tankards and a sword with a scythe engraved in the blade. Graeme's presence emanated from upstairs, close to the one who was to die. Preparing himself for a fight, The Shadow called on his sickle, ready as he moved up the stairs. The next name in Graeme's list had been Ethan Blake. Eager for the kill, he followed the call.

An older man who resembled the twins, with grey lining his beard and hair, lay on the bed, his eyes closed. Ethan's life force was dim. Dark flames spread as the green of his soul faded, almost dead already. A rot filled the room. The smell of the dead and one he had come to know from the ailed.

Graeme sat in a chair in the corner, asleep. Across his lap was a sword marked with the same scythe as on Thomas's. The twins had clearly anticipated his arrival.

Candles lit the room, casting a yellow glow on Graeme and Ethan's faces.

The Shadow raised his sickle and approached Ethan.

"Step away from him," Graeme said, his voice cold.

With the sword pressed into his back, The Shadow held up his hands and turned to face Graeme. His mortal self was now an inconvenience.

"Why do you oppose me? I know the Darkness that lives in you. Drop your sword."

The Darkness that twisted around Graeme's essence rose to the surface, his eyes becoming black once more.

"I said, step away from him," Graeme repeated louder. "I'm not going to ask again."

A grunt and a gasp behind him meant Ethan was awake.

"What are you doing in here?" Ethan demanded.

"Father, shut up and go back to sleep,"

"I tire of fighting you." The Shadow half turned, pointing at Ethan with his sickle. *"Him or your brother. Maybe I'll visit your wife."*

"No," Graeme whispered, his knuckles around the sword turning white.

"Someone will die tonight. Make your choice."

Graeme's focus shifted to behind The Shadow.

"So much for you two protecting me," Ethan said, his voice seething. "Where is that worthless brother of yours? Still at Leo's?" He scoffed.

Graeme lowered the sword, decision made. "Not them," he said. "Kill him." The sword hit the ground with a clatter as he bowed his head.

Kill him. The order came from deep within.

"I found your journal," Ethan said. "That list of names. You set this thing on the world, didn't you? I knew the moment you were born that you brought a curse down upon this house."

"Grim?" Thomas called out from downstairs.

"Make it quick," Graeme urged.

The Shadow turned and raised his sickle, bringing it down fast.

Footsteps thumped up the stairs, and The Shadow handed Graeme his sickle. Laughter burst from him as he returned to the Shadow Realm.

Chapter 41

Protect Father. Arrest The Shadow of Death.

Thomas opened his eyes. With his head resting on his arms, the table beneath him smelled like ale. Sitting up, he straightened the tankard, wiping at the spilled ale with his sleeve. He'd spent most of the day with Graeme at Leo's, only to return home as nightfall approached. Unsure when he'd fallen asleep, or why his brother had left him, he stretched. Graeme's presence hummed in the back of his awareness, a constant energy that Thomas couldn't shut out. He was upstairs, probably watching Father.

Warm from the fire, Thomas removed his cloak, dumping it on the table. Voices drifted down the stairs. Graeme's dark fury burst through Thomas's chest. *What's he angry about this time?* He rose to his feet, and the room spun. *I need to slow down on drinking.* Re-sheathing his sword, he steadied himself as another wave of anger crashed over him.

Anger gave way to emptiness, and a spark of helplessness settled around his throat.

"Grim?" Thomas called out. *What is he doing? Has Father done something?*

A cold stab of fear spiked in the pit of his gut. He ran up the stairs and burst into Father's room.

Father's eyes were open, his throat bloody as he gasped his last breath. But it was the sight of Graeme, black eyes, gripping the sickle that chilled Thomas to his very core.

"He's dead," his brother said.

"I can see that." Thomas had no other words.

Questions raced forward, demanding to be asked, but Thomas couldn't speak them. The very idea hurt. *Not Grim. Please, no.* A gasp came from behind him. Thomas spun around to find Amelia in the door, a hand over her mouth. As her eyes darted from Father to Graeme to Thomas, she paled. Her horror reflected his own.

"Graeme, what did you do?!" she asked, her voice hitching.

Stomach churning, Thomas struggled to breathe. His heart raced as he turned his gaze to Father. He was dead, and the expected relief didn't come. Only a deep dread as Amelia's words roared through him.

"Please explain yourself," Thomas pleaded. "Tell me you didn't do this. Tell me you didn't kill him." *This is what I feared. Everything I did was for nothing.*

"Why would you ask that?" Graeme demanded.

Thomas's eyes dropped to the sickle and back up to Graeme's face. "Do you not realise how this looks?"

Graeme dropped the weapon. As it hit the floor with a dull thud, Thomas caught Amelia's surprised jerk. Tears glistened in her eyes as she continued to stare at her husband.

"Graeme, please," she begged. "Tell him you didn't do this."

"You really believe I killed him?" Graeme's eyes passed between Thomas and Amelia, shoulders drooping. "That I would—" His words cut off.

More than anything, Thomas wanted to believe Graeme hadn't done it. That he hadn't taken a life. But the presence of Darkness in his brother made Thomas doubt *everything.* It had always been there, and it was only a matter of time before he took a life, before he gave in completely and the Darkness claimed him. Thomas had looked past it, even grown comfortable with it.

"I don't know what to believe right now," Thomas said, his heart breaking. "You're the only one standing over our murdered father with a weapon bearing his blood." Thomas rubbed his chest. "You're the one with some unexplainable connection to The Shadow of Death, writing a list of his kills." *Was it you the whole time?* Unsure he wanted to know the answer, Thomas couldn't ask those words.

Amelia's hand left her mouth, but she was frozen in place. Her eyes were on Graeme, full of hope and fear.

Graeme's eyes shifted focus, half-turning. Father's bedroom closed in around Thomas as the presence of Darkness within Graeme unfurled. Suffocating, Thomas marched from the room. He needed fresh air.

Gusts of wind whistled around him, tugging at his tunic. Questions pounded against his head as he took calming breaths. He hadn't been this scared since the day he had seen the summons with his and Graeme's names on it. His actions had set him on a dark path, a vow to protect Graeme from becoming a killer. The words of the past echoed around him. *I did everything to prevent this. Was I always going to fail?*

Thomas arrived at the Lord's manor. Many soldiers were there, ready to depart to their post on the front lines. He found Samson supervising wagons being packed with weapons and supplies. He climbed off his horse, the message in his hand.

"You're early. You're not expected for another week," Samson said.

"Not Grim," he told Samson. "You need to recall this summons. Please, talk to your father."

Samson blinked. "You cannot recall the summons of a lord. I've been called to France, too. It is our duty."

"Please forgive me. I beg that my brother remains behind," he pleaded. "He has just lost his daughter. Now is not the time for him to leave. He would lack the

focus you need in battle. His grief would be his downfall."

Samson appeared to consider this. He turned to give commands,"You! Get that horse secured to a cart."

Thomas waited, heart pounding. No one else had seen the summons yet, nor would they. He had to get Graeme removed from it. He would do whatever it took to keep his brother from going to war. It wasn't for the grief as he claimed, but due to the Darkness inside him. War and death would only unleash something no one was ready for. Its presence had been there their whole lives. Instinct was screaming at Thomas. Graeme could not be exposed to the savagery of war. It would change him.

Finally, Samson turned back to him. "Wanting to protect your brother is noble, but we need the men."

"One less soldier will not affect the outcome,"

Samson studied Thomas through narrowed eyes. "You ***really*** *don't want him there."*

"No. Please, Samson."

"I've heard about this bond of the Blake twins. What will you do to make this worth my while?"

The glint in Samson's eyes sent chills through Thomas. He was enjoying this. He wanted Thomas to beg, to give a reason for Graeme's pardon from the war summons. This was the only way. I'm sorry, Grim. *His brother could never take a life, would never know about this. It would sting that he hadn't been summoned, but that was better than seeing his brother become a killer. With no way out of this, Thomas dropped to his knees before Samson.*

"If you see fit to excuse my brother from the summons, I will bring God's fury with me to the battlefield. Like a warrior of the old times, I will be the reason the enemy fears us. They will drown in their own blood, and we will be remembered by history."

His vow came from deep within his soul, the words torn from him the second he uttered them. This was a promise he ***shouldn't*** *be making, and Samson would hold him to it. This was probably going to get him killed. The delight that shone through Samson's face made his heart freeze. He grasped the hand that reached out to him, his vow wrapping around both of their arms, an energy that bound* *him to his words.*

"Do you swear?" Samson asked.

"I swear."

"Thomas?" Amelia's voice broke him out of his reverie.

"Amelia." He turned. "I—"

"Graeme, he's gone!" she cried.

"What do you mean, 'he's gone'?"

"Gone. He was there, and then he wasn't."

Thomas rushed upstairs, with Amelia following close.

"Where did he go? Did he say anything?" Thomas asked.

Their connection was still open, but Graeme's energy had retreated into the Darkness.

"He *disappeared* right in front of me," Amelia murmured. "He didn't say anything, but he could see something I couldn't. I think we hurt him."

"This is my fault. I shouldn't have said..." Thomas sighed.

"We both did this." She grabbed his arm. "What if he's in that other realm?"

Thomas pushed down the fear that clawed at his insides. Words seeking to be said aloud threatened to surge forth. He clamped down, refusing to speak them. He placed a comforting hand over Amelia's. "I'll get him back. I promise."

Chapter 42

Thomas had trouble concentrating on Father's funeral while Graeme was missing. He and Amelia had spent half the night cleaning the body and wrapping him in a shroud. Afraid James would direct accusations at him and Graeme, Thomas and Amelia had agreed it was important to keep their uncle from seeing their father's body. Luckily, no questions were asked, on account of fear of the pestilence.

The funeral passed in a blur as Thomas focused on his brother. If Graeme was in the Shadow Realm, as he'd called it, Thomas needed to find a way in, and he didn't know where to start.

James had chosen to have their father buried next to his other brothers. Thomas hadn't fought him on the decision, not caring where he lay. With his back to them, head bowed, James hadn't moved in some time.

Isaac stood between Thomas and Amelia, holding both of their hands. An icy breeze ruffled their cloaks. Thomas pulled his son's hood up before his own. The air was thick with burning wood, and villagers had left to return to their warm homes.

"Is grandfather with mother?" Isaac asked.

Thomas clenched his teeth together and gave Isaac's small hand a gentle squeeze. "Yes."

Resisting the need to seek out Emma's grave, Thomas held back a sigh, his grief tightening in his chest. It was too soon to be at the cemetery again. So much death; no wonder Isaac was afraid.

"Graeme's absence has raised many questions," Amelia said under her breath.

"I know," Thomas murmured. "There's no one who didn't notice. James is furious. After we refused to forgive father yesterday when he asked us to, I cannot blame him for taking offence."

"To not be at his father's funeral has people worried. Graeme has been a part of everything that goes on in Riverwick. There's no one he turns his back on. He's been the beating heart of the village since you left," Amelia said.

This was a surprise to Thomas. "He has?" Graeme's tendency to avoid attention and his inability to show compassion at times were the opposite of what Amelia had described. "It seems I don't know my brother as well as I thought I did."

"He learned from you," Amelia said. "As much as you hated farming, you were always a big part of the village. He found it challenging at first, but just followed what you would do. Unlike you, he *wants* to be a farmer. It makes him happy."

Thomas couldn't hold back the grin. *We are as different as we could get.*

"Let's leave James," Thomas said. "I think he will be here awhile." He nodded to John as they left the cemetery. "We'll get him back," he reassured Amelia.

Snow crunched underfoot, and they passed where the church once stood, its absence daunting. James had made good work of the church, the charred remains completely gone. As winter was settling in, it was likely that rebuilding wouldn't start until spring.

"How will you find him?" Amelia turned her head to meet his eyes.

"I don't know."

"Do you have a way to communicate with him?"

Thomas laughed and stopped walking. "I'm sorry, communicate with him?"

Amelia turned to face Thomas. "Everyone knows how close the Blake twins are, that you have a bond no one else can break. But Graeme's told me there's more to it. You feel each other's pain and emotions. You have a connection that isn't what people would call normal, and when you're apart you can still sense the other. He told me that you could shield yourselves until two days ago. So, can you speak to each other?"

"He told you that?" Thomas asked.

"When we first married."

Astonished that she had known the whole time, Thomas continued walking.

"No, other than the usual way, we cannot speak from afar," Thomas said. "We did try, though, when we were younger." As they reached the house, Isaac ran inside, the door slamming behind him. "The longer he's not here, the less I can sense him. Right now all I feel is cold, emptiness and Darkness. There is a sense of him, his energy, but it's faint."

"Darkness?" Amelia asked.

Before he could respond, a rider approached on a white horse. Lord Samson was dressed in a dark-blue cloak, its hood pulled up.

"I'll check on Isaac," Amelia followed Isaac inside.

"Lord Samson, what are you doing here?"

"I heard about your father. My condolences," Lord Samson said.

"You're a bit late for the funeral."

Lord Samson nodded to the house. "Where's your brother? I didn't see him."

"I… I don't know," Thomas admitted.

"He didn't go to Ethan's funeral?"

"Why do you care about my brother?" Thomas demanded, protective.

"Calm yourself, Thomas. I'm just surprised he's not here," Lord Samson dismounted.

Thomas approached the house. "That's not why you're here, is it? To ride all this way in snow—"

"Did you know Nicholas O'Shea? I believe he was from here."

Thomas stopped mid-step. He had forgotten about Nicholas.

"I…Yes, he's a friend of ours."

"He and his wife were slain in their home."

Catherine, too? Grim never mentioned her. A fresh wave of grief passed over him. Nicholas had been their closest friend, and Catherine was the daughter of a baker. Everyone knew everyone else in Riverwick. This would be another great loss for the village.

"He's dead?" He feigned surprise, but the tone of sorrow was real.

"Where is his family?" Lord Samson asked. "I thought it best I let them know. Their bodies will be brought back tomorrow. Father Matthew will remain here for the funeral."

"The O'Sheas returned to Ireland last year," Amelia said from the doorway. "Catherine's mother and father died a few years ago."

"Is there somewhere we can speak in private?" Lord Samson asked, dismounting.

Thomas led him away from the house, shooting an apologetic look at Amelia.

"You need to come back to Kempschester," Lord Samson said. "I have patrols all over town, but he's slipping through, somehow."

"You are never going to catch him," Thomas shook his head. "He's in the shadows, laughing at all of us."

"Your friend and his wife were murdered in a horrific way. Wouldn't you want to catch the one who did it?"

"Yes, but I don't think your method is working."

"You might be right. How would you propose we find him, then?"

Thomas considered the question. "He's not going to expose himself, and he knows we're hunting him. Stop the hunt for a few days."

"Stop the hunt?"

"He'll stop hiding. Like when a stag catches scent of us, he'll stay where he knows it's safe. When he loses that scent, he's out in the open."

"You want me to tell all my men to stand down?"

"Make up some reason you're pulling the Enforcers off the streets. Host an event to honour the fallen."

Lord Samson narrowed his eyes. "Patrick will fight me on this. Possibly the other nobles, too."

"Remind them you're the lord. Their dislike of the situation shouldn't matter to you, especially when people are dying."

Lord Samson raised his chin. "I knew you had potential. Patrick didn't agree with recruiting you. He prefers Enforcers to be nobility."

"Patrick would prefer that. They're more likely to agree with him than soldiers who have experience at war. His way is strength and force, nothing else. He thinks it's the only way."

"Isn't it?"

"You know it isn't."

Lord Samson glanced around the farm. "I gave you time to consider moving to Kempschester. Time is up. What will it be?"

Thomas bit back frustration. "It was never a choice, was it?"

Lord Samson folded his arms. "You buried your reason for returning to Riverwick. You and your son will have a home; he will be well taken care of while you're working." Lord Samson met his eyes. "I don't like having to come all this way. We need to have you close. I promoted you, Thomas, because many of the men trust you. The captain needs to live in Kempschester."

Back on his horse, Lord Samson left without a word. Snow crunched as Amelia approached.

"I'm sorry to hear about Nicholas," she said. "Catherine wasn't on Graeme's list, though."

"We need to find Graeme," Thomas said, worry rolling in his stomach. "I have to move to Kempschester. I cannot leave while my brother is missing."

Time was short and desperation sank in. *Grim, where are you?*

Chapter 43

Thomas passed between sleep and the waking world, restless.

A chill crawled up the back of his neck. Someone was watching him. Surrounded by Darkness and fog, he spun around.

"Grim?" His voice echoed back at him in the silence.

Whispers from the dark had his heart pounding. Thomas almost surfaced, but the dream dragged him back.

A baby, suffocating inside its mother's dead body as shadows and red flames closed in. Darkness wrapped around the baby. Piercing blue eyes turned black and dark lines spread across its skin. As the baby was pulled from the realm, it took a part of Darkness with it.

Once again, Thomas almost woke.

"Thomas," Graeme's voice echoed inside and out.

A blue moon glowed from the sky, and red flames surrounded him.

Graeme stood before Thomas, gripping the sickle. Dark lines twisted around his hands and arms, across his face and neck. Wisps of shadow rose from Graeme, tendrils curling around him, black eyes watching Thomas, his face blank.

"Grim?" He looked so different, as if it weren't Graeme at all. "Is this real, or am I dreaming?"

"You shouldn't be here," Graeme's voice pounded on the inside of his skull.

"Why do I get the feeling you brought me here? This is the Shadow Realm, isn't it?" Thomas asked.

"**Yes. You don't belong here.**"

"Neither do you. How do I get you out?" Thomas asked.

"**I don't want you to,**" Graeme told him.

"I don't believe that."

"**It doesn't matter what you believe.**" Graeme turned his back on Thomas. "**You need to leave.**" He walked away. "**Stop looking for me.**"

"Grim, you know I'll never stop," Thomas promised.

The shadows engulfed Graeme.

"It's too late," a voice in the darkness said. "Your brother is gone."

Thomas sat up in a cold sweat, breathing hard.

Have I lost my brother? Thomas's chest ached as he was seized by panic. Graeme's presence had diminished, along with his hope. Three nights had passed since Father's death and Graeme's disappearance. The growing fear that Graeme had not only killed Father, but also had something to do with Nicholas and Catherine's deaths had kept Thomas awake. The little sleep he did get was uneasy as he awoke from dreams of his brother.

Did he surrender to the Darkness inside him? If he killed Nicholas, what about the others? *Grim, what have you done?* Heart thundering against his chest, Thomas climbed out of bed. Trying to sleep would only lead to more nightmares. He needed a distraction.

CHAPTER 43

Thomas pushed open the door to Father's room with an axe. A soft yellow circle of light shone around the candle he placed on the wooden chest. He opened the window wide, and bitter-cold air blew in.

Start with the bed. Thomas and Amelia had removed bloody linen from the bed already. He raised the axe high and swung hard. Wood splintered, and he swung again. To channel his pain, he continued, his muscles aching. At each swing came moments of his life. Father's disapproval. *Thud.* Father beating him. *Thud.* Father busting the door down to get into Thomas's bedroom. *Thud.* His vision clouded as he swung again and again. Him and Graeme hiding in the field, and Father's voice getting closer as he sought them out. A wave rose within him, and pain tore out of him in a guttural cry, his throat raw.

"Thomas?" Amelia appeared at the doorway, yawning. "What are you doing?" Her blonde hair was messy from sleep.

Thomas threw the axe down with a loud thud and picked up pieces of the broken bed, throwing them out the window.

"Thomas," Amelia's voice was both gentle and firm. "It's the middle of the night. Do you have to do this now? Where's Isaac?"

"He's asleep," Thomas said, throwing more pieces out. "I can't sleep. I don't know how to find Grim, and I think he's trying to tell me to stop looking."

"How? I thought you couldn't speak that way," Amelia said. "Why would he tell you that?"

Only emptiness remained where his brother should be, a void of nothing. "Because he's gone," he shouted. "There is nothing left of him," Thomas choked, the words bringing heat to his eyes. Sorrow enclosed around him.

"You don't know that," Amelia pleaded. "He wouldn't leave me. Or you."

"I don't want to believe it either. I fear it isn't just Father he's killed. His dark nature got the best of him."

"He is a godly man," Amelia's chin trembled. "He's not a killer."

Bitter laughter burst out of Thomas."A godly man? He was taught to be. Going to church doesn't change what he is. But I know my brother, I know what lies deep within his soul. I've *always* known." Thomas placed a hand over his chest. "When we were children, I felt a shadow over my own heart. and I knew it was Grim. He told you about our bond. Did he ever tell you he saw shadows, that they wanted to take him? Grim didn't dream, but I did, and my nightmares weren't my own. I dreamed exactly of what he saw. I know you want to think the best of your husband, but there is Darkness in him and it's always been there."

Amelia said nothing, her silence prompting him to go on. After years of not telling anyone, the words flowed easily. "As we grew, it worsened. I began to fear what he was capable of."

"If you feared him so much, why protect him?" Amelia asked.

"Whatever is inside him, he is still my twin brother. I feel everything he does. I promised Grim the shadows wouldn't take him when we were only eight. I gave him my word I would always be here to fight for him."

"But you weren't here. You left and were gone for four years."

"Believe it or not, that was to protect him, too. Why do you think he never got summoned?"

The realisation glinted, and she nodded in understanding. "You did that?"

"Yes," Thomas sat on the chair, brushing a hand through his hair. "I don't know how to protect him anymore. I'm scared for my brother, but I don't know what we'll find if we do get him back."

"Do you really believe that?" A tear glistened in her eye.

"I do," Thomas hesitated. He didn't want to say the words, and Amelia wouldn't want to hear them. "Father was on the list. He wrote that list. How else do you explain it? I think it's time we admit Grim is The Shadow of Death. He said so himself — he's connected somehow."

"What will you do when you find him? Are you the Enforcer or his brother?"

Chapter 44

A heavy snowfall had made roads difficult to travel, trapping Thomas in Riverwick for three weeks. But it would not be long before he was expected to move to Kempschester. Three weeks since Graeme's disappearance, and Thomas was no closer to finding his brother. No longer able to sense Graeme, he feared the worst.

The nutty aroma of breakfast pottage filled the kitchen. As Thomas finished eating, Isaac's laughter drifted down from upstairs with Amelia's voice. To avoid gloomy thoughts of his brother's absence, Thomas had promised to take Isaac outside. His absence for the past few years meant he had a lot to make up for. Isaac's attachment to Thomas had only grown in the time he had been home. The two of them had grown closer, a father and son relationship that brought joy to Thomas.

Hunter lay at his feet, head on paws. As Thomas waited to take Isaac outside, he relished in the warmth and crackle of the fire. Isaac's love of the snow meant they would likely be outside for hours.

His light patter on the stairs brought a smile to Thomas's face. The boy appeared in the doorway, a brown cloak wrapped around him with the hood pulled up. Isaac's eyes lit up. Thomas rose.

"Go on, out you go," Thomas said, following Isaac.

The blue sky and crisp air greeted him as he walked outside, his breath white.

Isaac ran around with Hunter. Thomas smiled, warmth in his heart as he gave chase. Isaac's delighted peals of laughter pushed away his dark mood.

"Watch out, Isaac, I'm coming to get you!" he called out.

"Nooo, you can't catch me," Isaac shrieked, running away.

He caught up easily and wrapped his arms around his son as they fell to the snow. Hunter sniffed their faces and barked, tail wagging. Lying on his back in the snow, Thomas couldn't hold back his laughter as Isaac struggled to get out of his arms. Snow seeped into his clothes, but he didn't care.

James approached on horseback, John beside him. Thomas sat up.

"Race Hunter to the stable and back," Thomas said. "I need to speak with James."

James dismounted. "Any sign of your brother yet?"

"No," Thomas snapped. "Please stop asking, Uncle. I don't know where he is, and every time you ask, I—"

James put a hand to his shoulder. "I know, I'm sorry. We're all worried for him, Thomas. This isn't like him."

"You don't have to tell me that," Thomas said.

John joined them on foot.

James pointed to Isaac. "He looks happy."

"He is," Thomas watched Isaac.

"As do you."

"I get to spend time with my son. What more can I ask for? I do have a lot of catching up to do with him," Thomas chuckled as Isaac tripped over in the snow. "You're all right, Isaac, get up." Isaac lay on his stomach and bit into the snow. Thomas shook his head. "Don't eat the snow. Amelia!"

Amelia walked outside holding a basket.

"Can you watch Isaac for a while? He's eating snow again."

James and John laughed.

"Perhaps have him help you collect the eggs," Thomas said.

Amelia nodded as she moved towards the stable, stopping to talk to Isaac. With excitement visible on his face, he trailed after Amelia with Hunter beside him.

"For someone who's only known his son for a few weeks, you're good with him. He adores you," James said.

Familiar sorrow closed his throat. "I must be. I'm all he has left."

"When do you two leave for Kempschester?"

"It should be safe to take the cart in two or three days."

"You're really leaving us," James said. "It's like watching my own son leave."

"You were good to us, Uncle. I'll never forget it."

"I should hope not. I expect you and your boy to drop by when you get time off. How is he going to get used to living in town? He won't be able to run around the farm."

"Isaac's excited for the move. He will have tutors to keep him busy," Thomas said.

"How do you feel about the move?" John asked.

Thomas weighed up his answer. "It's no secret that I'm not a farmer." He grinned. "But Riverwick is my home. I never thought I'd leave for somewhere like Kempschester. I'm going to miss being here."

"Be careful, Thomas. You'll be in the centre of it. The pestilence still claims many in Kempschester," James warned.

"Do you have anything to report?" Thomas asked, getting to the purpose of their conversation. "Have you found anything? Has the pestilence spread?"

"Gabriel is dead," John whispered. "The one you hunt is here."

Thomas's scalp crawled.

"Here? Are you sure?" Thomas asked.

"Gabriel had locked himself in his house; we had to break down the door," James said. "When we got inside, we found his body, throat cut."

John signalled a slashing motion across his own throat. "But when we looked closer, he had signs of the pestilence, too."

"Are you sure he didn't cut *his own* throat?" Thomas asked.

John shook his head. "There was nothing around to suggest that. The wound went around his throat, like that of a curved blade."

"Let's keep this quiet for now, to avoid panic," Thomas said.

The last thing any of them needed was a panicked village. Thomas and James had been working to contain the growing hysteria. Word of Ethan falling ill had spread quickly, with many shutting themselves in their homes.

"How will we explain his death?" John asked. "He needs to be buried."

James stroked his chin as he looked around. "No one knows he's dead yet. No one saw us break down his door."

The house Gabriel had lived in was on the outskirts of the village. A man in his late thirties and unmarried, he had chosen to build a house a little apart from everyone else.

A flicker of something in James's eyes made Thomas's stomach churn.

"I get the feeling I am not going to like this."

"You're not," James hesitated. "I can't say I'm happy to suggest it."

This does not sound good at all.

"We burn his house."

Cold spread through Thomas's entire body. "We can't do that! How can you suggest such a thing?"

"He's already dead," James said. "People burn bodies of those who were ailing. It's no different from that."

As much as I hate to admit it, he's right. It still stirred dread inside Thomas as he considered James's suggestion.

"Another fire is going to scare people. We don't have a church. Many are scared by the absence of God. You want people to believe Gabriel died in a fire? They'll believe He has condemned them," Thomas said.

"This may be our only choice, Thomas. It will stop the fear of the murderer and the pestilence, and it may be our only way to stop more from getting sick."

Thomas nodded slowly. "Very well. This is on you though, Uncle. I cannot do it."

Thomas changed out of wet clothes, helping Isaac out of his soaked tunic.

"Thomas?" Amelia called out.

"We're in here, I'll be out in a moment."

Thomas gave Isaac a dry tunic.

"Father?" Isaac peered up at him. "Where's Uncle Graeme? Will he come back before we leave? I miss him."

Thomas knelt to Isaac's height. "So do I. Graeme had to be somewhere else, but he'll be back."

"I hope so. Otherwise, Aunt Amelia will be all alone."

Thomas ruffled Isaac's hair. "We can't have that. Go downstairs, there's some bread waiting for you."

Isaac beamed and then ran from the room, his footsteps thumping down the stairs.

"Amelia, where are you?"

Amelia appeared at the door to her bedroom, holding Graeme's journal.

"What are you doing with that?" He asked.

"I was cleaning, and it fell on the floor." She held out the book to Thomas. "There are more names than I remember."

He accepted the journal, running his hand over the soft leather before flicking through pages. "This is a lot of names," he said. "When did he do this?" He blinked: Gabriel's name jumped out of the page at him.

Amelia pressed her lips together, a glint of fear in her eyes. "I don't know," she said. "Look at the last page."

Thomas did as she said, and his blood ran cold. Patrick Harrison, Samson Kemp. The names below theirs were mostly unfamiliar. By the end of the page, the ice was now in his heart. Isaac Blake.

"He's going after *my son*?!" Rage pounded through Thomas like thunder.

"He wouldn't do that," Amelia's eyes were big. "He loves Isaac."

"Then what is this?" Thomas flipped the pages back. "These are people killed by The Shadow of Death. Why would Isaac's name be here?"

Mouth dry and heart pounding, he turned more pages. A drawing. Graeme had always been talented, ever since they were children, but the scene before him was horrific. How did Grim know to draw this? He wasn't there. Flames consumed a man as a crowd watched. In the corner, a man with a black cloak pulled over his head reached for Jacob. On the next page was a church. A cemetery on one side and the trees bare. Large wooden doors stood open, with a single shadowed figure standing between them.

"That's the Kempschester Church," he realised.

"He drew that a few days before he left," Amelia told him. "He saw all of them in a dream and had to draw them."

A dark figure on the yellowed parchment paper stood out. Turning back to the list, he gaped at the name under Gabriel's. Matthew Bennett. Dizzy, his hand trembling, he dropped the book.

"What is it?" Amelia asked.

"I'm getting my armour. Stay with Isaac." Thomas marched back to his room.

"Your armour? What are you doing?"

Should I get Lord *Samson?*

"Stopping him. Enough people have died. *This ends now.*"

Chapter 45

Kempschester was cold and quiet as The Shadow followed Graeme through the double wooden doors. The scent of burning candles and dried roses greeted him.

"**This one is mine,**" Graeme said.

The Shadow handed Graeme his sickle and moved down one side. Father Matthew turned, Bible in hand, his face lighting up as he laid eyes on Graeme. Graeme's hood remained over his head as he smiled back at the priest, keeping his head bowed.

"Graeme, I did not see you at your father's funeral. Nor that of Nicholas and Catherine. It is pleasing to see that you are still among the faithful, though. So many have lost their faith and turned to superstition and flagellation."

"Father Matthew, you are mistaken," Graeme's dark voice boomed within the church.

Finally, he raised his head, pulling down the hood, revealing black eyes and dark lines on his face. The priest's gaze clouded over as he backed up.

"This is the house of *God*; you are *not* welcome here!" The priest shook as he crossed himself. "Get out!" The Bible dropped from Father Matthew's hand. *"What are you?!"*

Graeme stepped forward and raised the sickle. "I am Darkness. It is your time."

Footsteps announced an arrival, The Shadow turned to find a silhouette in the doorway.

"Please help me," the priest pleaded. "Demons walk among us!"

"**Not demons,**" Graeme said. "**Your death.**" He glanced at The Shadow. "**Hold him, I'll take care of this.**"

The Shadow moved towards Father Matthew, pinning him to the wall. Father Matthew whimpered, struggling against the grip. With one hand to the priest's chest, The Shadow tightened his other around his throat.

"Try to escape, you'll hit the ground before you take a step," The Shadow warned, turning to keep an eye on the person at the door.

Father Matthew stopped his struggles. The new arrival stepped forward, revealing a grey cloak and black leather armour.

"Enforcer," The Shadow warned.

"**You should leave,**" Graeme said.

"Graeme, stop. What are you doing?" The Enforcer advanced again, candlelight falling on his face. *Thomas.*

Thomas's eyes darted from Father Matthew and The Shadow to Graeme.

"**Have you come to arrest me?**" Graeme asked.

Thomas gripped the hilt of his sword, not yet drawing it. Desperation shone in his eyes, his knuckles white.

"If I had, do you think I would be alone?" Thomas asked.

"**You've come to kill me, then.**"

"I've come for my twin. Grim, please. Stop what you're doing and come home."

"I am home," Graeme told him. **"The Shadow Realm is where I belong."**

"No," Thomas insisted. "Your home is Riverwick."

"Stop wasting time," The Shadow said. *"Kill him. Or I will."*

"It's not his time," Graeme threw back at him.

Thomas ran forward, shoving his shoulder into Graeme and pushing him down. The sickle slid across the ground. Overwhelmed by a rising desire to kill, The Shadow eyed his sickle. *I can finish the priest and then the brother.*

Graeme tried to get up, but Thomas pinned him down under a foot, drawing his sword.

"Stay down, I don't want to hurt you," the sword pointed at Graeme, pressing in between his shoulder blades.

The priest's life force called to The Shadow. Kill him. *It is his time.*

"Did you come here for me, or to save the priest?" Graeme demanded. **"The Shadow of Death will kill him if I don't. I know you don't want that on your hands."**

Thomas's hand trembled. "Grim, stop, this isn't you."

"I'm not doing anything. You're running out of time, Brother."

Thomas raised his eyes to Father Matthew, meeting The Shadow's gaze.

"Let him go," Thomas ordered.

The Shadow let go of the priest and advanced on Thomas. *"Your time is up,"* he said. This one had interfered enough.

The Shadow gripped him by the throat, intending to kill. Thomas paled and grunted in pain.

"What are you doing to me?" he choked out.

A flicker within the Enforcer came from his life force, as if it were fading. Thomas's sword clattered on the ground, his eyes turning white. The Shadow let go, and Thomas fell to his knees, gasping for breath. The strength of his life force returned his eyes blue once more. The Shadow studied his hand and reached for Thomas again. His touch weakened the Enforcer. *How am I doing this?*

Graeme rose to his feet, retrieving the sickle.

"Run," Thomas croaked at Father Matthew, his whole body visibly straining against The Shadow's touch.

As the priest ran past, Graeme swung wildly with the sickle, making contact. The priest hit the ground. Dead.

"Grim," the word was almost inaudible as Thomas gazed up at Graeme. "Brother, I'm sorry."

"What are you doing to him?" Graeme asked.

"Killing him."

"I haven't seen his death, it isn't his time."

"I don't care, he needs to die." The Shadow unleashed a dark energy, aiming it for Thomas's life force. *Could I do this the whole time?*

Thomas grunted, defiance bright in his eyes before they became white again.

Graeme groaned in pain. "Stop."

"I'll stop when he's dead."

"Stop!" Graeme begged again, his voice weak. Another groan as Graeme took a step towards The Shadow. "Get away from my brother!"

Black eyes changed to blue, and the Darkness twisted around Graeme as if trying to maintain its grip on him.

"I said let him go!" Graeme boomed. "Release him now!"

A sharp pain started inside The Shadow, as if someone had gripped his heart. *If I kill Thomas, it is possible Graeme will die.*

The Shadow stepped away from Thomas. *"He will continue to seek you out."*

Graeme knelt in front of Thomas. "Tom?"

Thomas's hands dropped to the ground, his shoulders heaving. "Grim, what. . .?"

Graeme glared at The Shadow. "He was killing you. I told you to stop looking for me."

Thomas panted. "You know I could never do that."

The dark lines on Graeme's face faded as he helped Thomas to his feet. Retreating to his realm, The Shadow burned with fury. Once again, he had been denied killing the Enforcer. From behind the veil, he pressed in close to Graeme. "You will lose this fight."

Graeme ignored him. "Are you alright? Can you walk?"

Thomas took a step away from Graeme, straightening. "The pain's almost gone. What was that?"

"Something I didn't realise he could do," Graeme muttered.

The twins turned towards Father Matthew.

"He's dead. You killed someone," Thomas picked up his sword.

"Are you going to arrest me?"

"I should. You're the killer, it's my duty to capture you."

"But I'm your brother. You said you'd choose me over duty."

"Grim, you killed *our priest*! I don't know if I can protect you from this."

A gasp from the doorway turned both their heads. The Shadow smiled. A woman wearing a green cloak had walked into the church, her hand over her mouth. Her wide eyes on Father Matthew's body before shifting to the brothers, she took a step back. Without a word, she ran.

The brothers stared at each other.

"Tom?"

Silence passed between the brothers.

"Run," Thomas told Graeme, re-sheathing his sword. "You must run! I will try to stop her, before..." He didn't finish the sentence as he ran after the woman.

Chapter 46

A tight knot formed in his stomach as he raced from the church. Thomas ran in the direction she had gone. The sight of Graeme standing over Father Matthew's body with a sickle would be impossible to explain. Not that either of them could deny that Graeme had killed the priest. There was only one way that Thomas would be able to stop word from reaching the Enforcers or Lord Samson of what Graeme had done.

What am I doing? Am I prepared to kill for a murderer because he's my brother? Doubt snaked its way through Thomas long enough for him to stagger, hesitance slowing his step. *If they arrest him, they will kill him.* Thomas kept his eyes on the green cloak in front of him. As he forced himself forward, the woman ran down an alleyway.

He followed her into the alley, met by the stench of rotting meat, faeces, and urine. He gagged, searching for the woman, but she was nowhere in sight. With too many footsteps in the snow to track her path, a flash of cold terror paralysed him. *It's too late. I'm too late.* Once news of Father Matthew's death reached Lord Samson, or any Enforcer, they would call for Graeme's arrest. In all his life, Thomas had never experienced such fear. Icy fingers curled around his spine, cutting off his breath.

What do I do? Grim. Get Grim out of Kempschester. Finally able to move, Thomas charged back to the church, breathing heavily.

"Grim? We must go *now!*" His voice was met by silence, with Graeme nowhere to be seen.

I told him to run. Where would he go? Thomas returned to his horse, scanning the streets. Nearby, Kempschester markets were almost bare, a small number of people, but none in a black cloak.

Heavy footsteps crunched in the snow as three horses surrounded him, Enforcers on their backs.

"Captain Blake," Patrick sneered. "Where is your brother?"

"I don't know," he admitted. "What do you want, Patrick?"

"You had the murderer in your sights and let him go?" Reynold asked.

"It's his brother —of course he let him go. He's probably been protecting him this entire time," Patrick said, a hard gleam in his eyes. "Get the shackles," Patrick dismounted. "What is it you call him? Grim? I'd say things look grim for you right now. *Both* of you."

Reynold climbed off his horse, retrieving a pair of shackles.

Thomas clenched his fist around the reins, the metallic clang reverberating through him. They had come for Graeme. *Wherever you are, Grim, stay hidden.*

"You don't need the shackles, he's gone," Thomas said.

"Get off your horse," Patrick commanded. "Remove your sword and dagger and drop them on the ground, now. Reynold, arrest him."

Reynold's head jerked in surprise. "Arrest him? I thought we were here for Graeme."

"Thomas Blake!" Lord Samson's voice boomed as he approached. "You stand with a murderer. I command you to get off your horse now and get on your knees."

With no choice, Thomas climbed from his horse, kneeling in the wet snow. Patrick grabbed the shackles from Reynold, his face a mask of triumph as he advanced on Thomas.

"Take his weapons," Patrick ordered Reynold.

Thomas drew his own sword, throwing it to the ground at Reynold's feet before doing the same with his dagger. More Enforcers arrived, drawing the attention of townsfolk. People came from their houses and the market to watch. Cold metal closed around his wrists, the shackles heavy. Patrick grabbed Thomas's hair and dragged him to his feet.

"Why do you arrest him?" A voice called out. "One of your own?"

"He is not our own. He is the brother of The Shadow of Death," Patrick bellowed.

Angry voices rose. Patrick disappeared into the crowd, leaving Thomas with Reynold. *This cannot be good.*

Thomas took a step forward, but Lord Samson gripped his arm.

"You stay with me." Lord Samson snapped his fingers at Reynold. "Bind his feet with irons, too."

"Samson..."

"It's *Lord* Samson. I think I've had enough of you telling me what I can and cannot do. You made yourself into something unrecognisable for the sake of your brother, but he is worse than you. Nicholas O'Shea is proof of that. He almost gutted the man. You saw the bodies; Nicholas's chest was cut to shreds. It takes a lot to mangle someone like that. Then to stab *his wife?* Your brother is a monster. He must be put down."

"Graeme Blake!" His brother's name was barely audible, but it was enough to quiet the crowd. Patrick had their attention.

This was going to get out of control — fast. Thomas's shoulders were tight, his stomach rolling as Patrick put on a show for the crowd.

"He killed a lord. He killed guards. He killed his own friend! Now a priest." Patrick was inciting rage from those surrounding him.

Lord Samson pushed Thomas, forcing him to walk. Guinevere had a lead rope attached to her, connected to Lord Samson's.

"Father Matthew was a friend to you all. He was a beacon of hope. To kill him is to renounce God. It is an attack on all people of Kempschester. He has taken something from you all. The only way to get that back is with his death!"

Thomas half-turned, trying to catch Patrick's words.

"Move," Lord Samson pushed him.

The murmuring throughout the crowd was growing in volume and anger.

A voice rose above the noise. "Lord Samson, what are you doing to protect us? You arrest his brother, but where is Graeme?"

Lord Samson turned, facing the townsfolk. "Graeme Blake must be brought to justice. Let no place be safe for him. He will not escape capture."

The anger became a roar. Thomas hung his head, eyes burning. *I'm sorry, Grim. I can't help you now.*

"You should know, Patrick is going to kill your brother, and he wants you to burn, too. If you help us find Graeme, show your loyalty, maybe you'll walk away from this."

The crowd's energy was that of a pack of wild dogs foaming at the mouth.

"You know what you're asking of me?" Thomas whispered.

Thomas caught a glimpse of Patrick. There was a glint in his eyes, a small smile. He was enjoying this. Thomas shook, and the chains rattled as he flexed his wrists.

What had been a spark of fear erupted into an inferno as focus turned towards him. They would consider him, as Graeme's brother, just as guilty.

"Stop! While we hunt his brother, Thomas will remain under my guard," Lord Samson addressed the crowd, giving Thomas a hard stare. "I promise you we will find him. Any man that gives Graeme refuge will burn with him."

A lump rose in his throat, his heart heavy. He lowered his gaze. Dizzy with pangs of guilt, he prayed silently they would not find him.

"He calls his brother 'Grim'. Grim the Reaper is The Shadow of Death. Hunt him down!" Patrick's voice rang out again as Lord Samson shoved

Thomas to move.

"Hunt him down! Burn him," people repeated with vehemence.

The crowd grew as other townsfolk came out to see the commotion. They took up the cry for Graeme's blood.

"For the King's Justice!" Patrick called out.

"For the King's Justice," the crowd repeated.

It was a mob, and Patrick had no control of it. If they found Graeme, he would be torn apart.

Chapter 47

Parched, Thomas let the water pour into his mouth and down his chin. Refreshing and soothing his thirst, he reached up for the leather flask. Chains rattled as he moved, keeping his hands from reaching the pouch. Lord Samson pulled it away. Thomas had been chained to the cell wall for five days, with Lord Samson questioning him morning and night. The only source of light was through the top of his cell and the lantern Lord Samson brought with him.

"You were at the church with him. Why didn't you bring him in?" It was not the first time Lord Samson had asked this.

Unable to explain himself, Thomas remained silent, as he had each time Lord Samson walked into the cell.

"You're trying my patience, Thomas. Where is your brother?" Lord Samson knelt in front of him. "Stop protecting a murderer."

He turned his head, avoiding Lord Samson's cold stare.

"I've closed the gates again, and every house in Kempschester is being searched. They will find him."

"*If* he's still here," Thomas blurted, his voice raspy.

Lord Samson straightened, glaring down at him. "I have Enforcers stationed in Riverwick, so he has nowhere to go. Your uncle is very cooperative."

Uncle James. He forced down bitterness. He could not blame James for doing what he was told.

"I notice you've kept Patrick out," he said.

"Thomas, if I let Patrick in here, you would be worse off than Jacob was," Lord Samson paced the cell. "Not only does he want to break both your legs, but he's got your sword and would take great pleasure in gutting you with it." Lord Samson's feet stopped right in front of him. "The longer you are in here, the less I can help you. Don't you want to go home to your son?"

Isaac. "I know you're not letting me go home after this," Thomas croaked. "I *can't* tell you where my brother is because *I don't know.*"

"Reynold," Lord Samson called out, and metal creaked as the door opened.

"Father?"

Thomas raised his head in disbelief as Isaac entered the cell. "Isaac?" He glared at Lord Samson. "Why did you bring him here?"

Isaac ran towards him, and he raised his arms, wrapping them around his son. Over Isaac's shoulder, Lord Samson stood in the doorway, arms crossed.

"Are you all right?" Thomas asked. "Did they hurt you?"

"No, they didn't hurt me," Isaac said into Thomas's chest. "You promised the Enforcers wouldn't take me."

A lump formed in his throat. "I know. I'm sorry I wasn't there."

Isaac pulled out of his embrace. "Why are you in chains? Did you do something wrong?"

"I did," Thomas whispered, holding Isaac by the arms.

"What did you do?"

Thomas raised his eyes to Lord Samson's.

"I didn't stay home with you," Thomas said. "I'm sorry, Isaac."

Isaac leaned in to hug Thomas again. He held a hand to his son's back.

"Can you come home now? Aunt Amelia is sad, and Uncle Graeme's still gone."

"I can't right now."

"Why not?"

"Because your Uncle Graeme has done something really bad, and they want to find him," Thomas whispered into Isaac's ear. "So until they do, I have to stay here."

"Is he a bad person?" Isaac questioned.

He started to say 'no' but paused. Graeme was a murderer, and there was nothing Thomas could do to change that. As he held his son, the image of Isaac's name in Graeme's scrawl forced its way into his mind. Unable to shake free of it, he let his shoulders slump. "I don't know *what* he is," Thomas said finally, his voice flat. "He's lost himself."

"That's enough," Lord Samson said. "Let him go."

"You have to go with Lord Samson," Thomas advised.

"I don't want to, I want to stay with you," Isaac's voice trembled.

"You can't stay here. You go with Lord Samson. I'll be home soon," he promised. "We have a house in Kempschester waiting for us."

Lord Samson grabbed Isaac's hand, leading him away.

A tear slid down Isaac's cheek as he turned around. Warmth welled in Thomas's eyes, and he blinked away tears. The door closed behind his son.

"This is your last chance to prove where you stand," Lord Samson returned, to crouch in front of him.

"You're asking me to betray my twin brother."

"No, I'm asking that you *let go* of him. He will be dead soon. You don't have to share his fate. Choose loyalty, and you walk out of here with your son. He's already lost his mother; he doesn't have to lose his father, too. Do you want him to suffer?"

Thomas eyed the door Isaac had just walked through. "I know what you're doing. Using my son like that?" He shook his head.

"I can see it in your eyes, Thomas."

"See what?"

"Surrender. Let me know when you're ready to talk."

When he was fortunate enough to sleep, Thomas searched for Graeme in his dreams. Every time, he ended back at the church, a pool of blood at his feet and Father Matthew dead. Instead of Graeme, Darkness stared back at him.

"Fight it, Grim. You have the strength," he woke himself up talking.

The empty cell taunted him. Unable to escape the constant cold, he drew his cloak around him. He'd lost track of the days he had been locked up; and on Lord Samson's last visit, Thomas had clung to the whisper of Graeme's presence.

"Tom!" Whispered urgency interrupted his dark contemplation.

Thomas blinked, a face coming into focus. *No!* Darkness showed, not just in Graeme's eyes, but around them.

"Grim?" He eyed the locked door. "What are you doing? I told you to run! How did you get in here?"

Graeme disappeared.

Shafts of light shone through the hole in the roof of his cell, and voices drifted down from above. Dawn had arrived. Thomas stood, dusting himself off, eyes on the spot he had seen Graeme. Just a dream.

"Hold on, Brother. I'm going to save you and Isaac, somehow," he whispered to the empty cell.

Chapter 48

Hands lifted Thomas to his feet, pulling him from sleep. He groaned, opening his eyes. Three Enforcers helped him to the table. On the table were a lantern, a leather flask, a tankard and fresh clothes.

"What are you doing?" Thomas asked.

"You need to be presentable," Reynold said.

"For what?"

"Lord Samson has requested your presence."

Thomas frowned. "He knows where I am."

"It's all right, I've got him," Reynold nodded to the other Enforcers. "Bring in the wash basin."

As they left, Thomas studied Reynold's face. "What does he want?"

"Thomas, you've been in here for twelve days."

Twelve days?

Reynold held up a tankard pouring water from the flask. Thomas held the vessel in both hands, shackles and chains clanging as he tipped back the water.

As it ran down his dry throat, he gulped, greedy for more.

Reynold pulled the water away. "Don't drink too fast."

"Where's my son?"

"He's in safe hands."

"Is this Lord Samson's new interrogation?" Thomas asked. "Why has he sent you?"

"This isn't an interrogation, Thomas. You need to wash, you stink. I brought you fresh clothes. Then, I'm to escort you to Lord Samson. We're your guards."

"My guards?"

"Most of the nobles want you dead. To them, protecting your brother makes you as guilty of the murders as he is. Lord Samson put men at your door who he knew would do their job."

"Why don't you want me dead?"

"Soldiers stick together."

"Come on, Reynold, you know what I did on the battlefield. You know I was dismissed. What separates you from the nobles in wanting me dead?"

"I think you made a mistake. You let Graeme go because you still saw him as your brother, and twelve days in a cell gave you time to re-evaluate that."

Thomas forced a laugh. "You think after all this, I would turn on my brother?"

"Why would you continue to protect him? You know what he's done. How can you think this is the right thing to do?" Reynold asked.

Before he could answer, four Enforcers returned, carrying a deep, round, wooden wash basin between them. Reynold stood. Servants followed them in, pouring steaming water into the basin. A sweet, earthy smell rose from it.

Reynold removed his shackles. "We'll give you privacy. But we're right outside your door."

The Enforcers left, a click of the door sounded as it locked.

Thomas dipped his hands into the water, relieved at the warmth. He brought the water to his face, eyes closed. Tearing off his tunic, he sniffed at the garment and grunted. "Reynold was right about the smell," he muttered. Removing the rest of his clothes, he climbed into the basin. He let the hot water wash over him, his aching body screaming with relief.

As he scrubbed, voices outside the door reminded him that he wasn't alone. The idea that he needed guards for protection from nobles bothered him. Missing his sword and the familiar black armour, he sighed. Realisation hit him that he had to completely rely on Reynold and the others.

Thomas finished and climbed from the basin. As he dried himself off, he pulled on the fresh clothes.

"Reynold," he called out, fastening a dark-brown cloak around his shoulders.

The door opened.

"Word of advice. Address him the way a peasant would address a lord," Reynold instructed, placing the shackles around his wrists and ankles again.

"Why would I do that? I'm not a peasant," Thomas grumbled.

"There's talk of Lord Samson removing your and Graeme's status as yeomen. Your uncle and cousin have taken over your farm. Right now you're a prisoner, Thomas. You stand to lose *everything*."

"Very well, take me to him."

Reynold walked beside him with two Enforcers leading the way, another two behind him.

CHAPTER 48

Lord Samson walked beside Thomas through the gallery of the estate. Reynold remained, but Lord Samson had dismissed the other guards.

The sun shone through the windows, and sage and lavender filled his senses.

"Your son misses you," Lord Samson said. "He cries for you at night."

Thomas swallowed back the anguish that arose. Defeated, he remained silent.

Suddenly, pain exploded inside Thomas and he stumbled. Holding a hand to his face, he groaned in pain. More pain followed, as if he had been struck in the face. A sting sliced across his back.

Lord Samson frowned at him. "What is wrong with you?"

Pain and fury burned deep within. *Grim?* Something was happening. The stone walls spun around him as another wave of pain tore a cry from him. That Graeme continued to elude capture had given him hope. Now, deep sorrow replaced what little hope he had. Fire burned along his back, again and again, forcing Thomas to his knees. Tears stung his eyes as the pain blurred everything around him.

Their shared connection had brought them close over the years. But feeling each other's pain had always been a downside. Though Thomas had taken the beatings from Father to protect Graeme, his twin had still felt the pain through him. Now, someone was hurting Graeme, and Thomas's protectiveness burned through him. But with shackles, he could do nothing.

As he reeled from the sting of a whip, Darkness surged, threatening oblivion. Graeme's presence flickered. *He's about to give in to it. No! Grim, don't. Hold on, Brother.* Thomas reached for his brother's energy, willing him to not give in to the Darkness.

Reynold helped Thomas to his feet. "What happened?"

Someone ran towards them; a man appeared. He whispered to Lord Samson, who then waved him off. Thomas straightened, bracing himself for more pain.

"Come with me," Lord Samson said. "I have something to show you."

Thomas followed Lord Samson and Reynold into the courtyard. "What are we doing out here?" He asked. His question went unanswered, Reynold appearing as confused as him.

Cold wind chilled him to the core, his face and lips numb.

Whatever had happened to Graeme was over, but his back still stung. Everything hurt. Enforcers rushed into the courtyard, standing nearby. No one moved or spoke. Many men rested hands on their sword hilts.

The rattle of chains drew his focus to the gate. A figure limped forward, heavy shackles around their neck, wrists and ankles.

"No! Grim!" Thomas stepped forward, instantly pulled back by two sets of hands.

Graeme lifted his head, and Thomas gasped. One eye was swollen shut, the other black instead of his usual blue. Half of his face already showed discolouration from bruising. Five Enforcers walked close behind, with their swords drawn on Graeme. As he met Thomas's gaze, Graeme faltered in his step. Patrick pushed him hard, and he fell.

"Get him up," Patrick commanded.

Enforcers pulled Graeme to his feet. Patrick grabbed his arm, pointing at the pyre. "See that?" Patrick asked.

Graeme stared at the shackles on Thomas, until Patrick forced his face around towards the large pyre.

"You will burn for what you did."

The vitriol and pleasure Patrick held for Graeme's suffering stung like ice.

"To take such pleasure in someone else's death, to boast over it, you deserve to be on that pyre," Thomas growled.

"Get him in the cell," Lord Samson ordered Patrick. "Stop tormenting him."

Patrick muttered under his breath and led Graeme into the tunnel.

Chapter 49

Reynold chained Thomas next to Graeme. The cell reeked of vomit and urine. Men surrounded them, swords drawn.

"We can't protect you anymore," Reynold whispered as he crouched in front of Thomas. "You're on your own, I'm sorry." He glanced over his shoulder. "Just say the word. I can make it quick."

"I have no intention of making it that easy for them," Thomas countered. "I will stand with my brother to the end. You're a good man, Reynold. Thank you."

Reynold stood. "They're both secure, Lord Samson."

"Out," Lord Samson ordered. "All of you."

Feet shuffled over dirt as Enforcers filed out. The door creaked, slamming shut, metal clicking into place. Patrick remained in the cell, standing next to Lord Samson.

"Thomas Blake, you stand accused of shielding a murderer. Graeme Blake, you stand accused of murder. What do you say to these charges?" Lord Samson asked.

"What are you doing?" Thomas scowled.

Patrick cracked his knuckles. "This is when you confess to your crimes, you idiot."

"You want me to confess? Why?" Graeme asked.

Lord Samson strode across the cell, standing over Thomas and Graeme.

"Both of you have a choice. Make it easier on yourself," Lord Samson said. "Thomas, your brother will burn. *You can still return to your son.* I don't want to make your boy an orphan. Remember, you still have a house waiting for you here."

"Leave Isaac out of this," Thomas glared. "Why are you bothering with a confession?"

"I want to hear him admit what he did," Lord Samson said. "He killed my father. Did you know?"

Patrick's icy stare moved from Thomas to Graeme.

"I don't know how you're doing that with your eye, but stop." Patrick demanded, sword to Graeme's throat.

"Get away from my brother," Thomas warned, rising to his feet.

"Or what?" Patrick taunted ambling over to Thomas. "There's not a lot you can do. You're in chains."

Thomas lunged forward until the chains stopped him, and Patrick flinched, backing off. With a forced smirk of superiority, Patrick whispered in Lord Samson's ear, eyes on Thomas.

"Thomas," Lord Samson began as Patrick took a step back. "You once came to me, begging to have Graeme removed from the summons of war."

Graeme's head jerked towards Lord Samson, eyebrows furrowed. "What?"

"What are you doing?" Thomas asked in disbelief.

"You vowed to serve with ferocity, and you showed a ruthlessness I have rarely seen. Show your murderous brother what you did for him. Show him what you became."

The world stopped.

"You think I would interrogate my brother?" Thomas asked.

"Look at him. He's not even your brother anymore," Lord Samson pointed. "He's murdered people. How can you justify protecting that?"

"No."

Lord Samson's eyes hardened. "You're disobeying an order."

"Stick your orders. I don't care what you say. I am not interrogating him," Thomas declared.

With a slack jaw, Graeme turned his swollen face up towards Thomas, one eye still closed, the other its usual piercing blue.

Patrick punched Thomas hard in the gut. Sharp pain shot through his stomach as he doubled over. Heaving and gasping for breath, he forced down the urge to retch. With a hand against the rough stone wall, he waited for the pain to pass.

"No," Thomas said again.

"Tom," Graeme murmured, eyes closed. "It's all right."

"What? No!"

"Isaac," Graeme whispered, opening his eye again, regarding Thomas. "Amelia. Do what you need to. You don't have to protect me anymore. He's right; I'm going to die. There's no reason you can't go home; they need you." Tears fell from his eyes. "Look after her."

At a loss for words and light-headed, Thomas gaped at his brother.

"You don't know what you're asking of me. I can't."

Graeme's shoulders heaved. "I did it," he confessed to Lord Samson. "I am The Shadow of Death, and I murdered those people. Let my brother go."

"Grim, no."

The whites of Lord Samson's eyes were visible, his face flushed. "You killed Lord Philip." His voice was low.

"I killed—"

"Stop," Thomas lurched forward, met once again by Patrick's fist to his stomach.

A groan escaped Graeme's lips as burning pain erupted through Thomas. Gasping for breath, Thomas tried to hold on to consciousness. The cell spun and went black.

Thomas jerked awake, chains rattling as he sat up, trying to remember where he was. Next to him, Graeme's head was slumped, chin against his chest. They were alone, their cell quiet. A lantern on the table threw a circle of yellow light around it.

Worried about Graeme's silence, he turned his head. "Grim?"

His brother groaned in acknowledgement, lifting his eyes. The sight of Graeme's face was like a blow to the chest. Graeme looked around the room before frowning at him.

"You're an idiot," Graeme said.

"I'm sorry. I couldn't interrogate you. Why did you confess?"

"I'm going to die anyway. The only thing you've done is secured your spot next to me in the flames. Isaac already lost his mother."

Thomas clenched his jaw. "He has Amelia." The words themselves came out with effort, inflicting pain. "Once they found out I was with you at the church and let you go, it was over for me."

"I deserve what's coming for me, but you don't. I killed people, Tom. There's no absolution for me."

"What I did at war wasn't much better," Thomas said.

"Why did you have me removed from the summons?"

Thomas's jaw tensed. "You weren't supposed to know."

"Why?"

"You had just lost your daughter. I was trying to save you from more pain. You needed to be with Amelia." It was the same line he had fed Lord Samson all those years ago.

"Mary? This is not about her; don't lie to me. I should have been there alongside you, fighting for England. Why would you take that from me?"

"Because I was afraid of this. Of what Darkness you'd embrace when you took a human life. That my brother would become something dark and unrecognisable."

"So, you shut me out and embraced your *own* Darkness, instead?" Graeme's voice rose. "You sacrificed your own humanity, Thomas, and for what?" Graeme rattled the chains, loud metal clanking, jarring in the quiet cell. "Look where that got you! How does it help me that you're chained up, too? We're *both* going to die. You understand that, don't you?"

"Would you rather I interrogated you?" Thomas asked. "I don't think you understand what that means." Thomas pointed towards the weapons on the far wall. "That mace is broken from my last interrogation. I smashed it into his ribs and his leg. It took five of them to drag me away from him. You want me to do that to you? To break you down by smashing a mace against you?" The very idea of it turned his insides to ice.

"It can't be any worse than what Patrick's already done."

Thomas's eyes narrowed. "I'll kill him."

Graeme's laugh was full of bitterness. "How will you do that? Stare him to death? Your anger right now is meaningless!"

"Grim, you have one eye swollen shut and half your face is purple. Every time you breathe, I know it hurts, and your back feels like it's on fire right now. I think my fury is justified!"

"What of my anger? That my brother is going to die because of what I did? This was never going to end any other way for me. As grateful as I am to have you stand with me, I'd rather you were with your son. This should never have been your fate."

The lock of the door clicked, bursting open, and Patrick marched in.

"What are you two bickering about?" he demanded, hand resting on the hilt of his sword. "If you keep it up, I'll finish you off now." His eyes flashed, shifting from Graeme to Thomas. "Although, from what I saw before, you both feel each other's pain. We'd only have to kill one of you," Patrick smirked at Thomas. "You'd watch your brother die and feel it. There's more suffering in that than what I could ever hope for you."

Fury burned through Thomas, pulling him to his feet. He spat at Patrick as he strained against the chains. Trying to get at the Enforcer to wrap his hands around Patrick's throat. Patrick wiped the spittle from his face.

"I'm going to kill you," Thomas growled, losing control of his rage.

"It's true, what they say about twins," Patrick observed. "One is cursed to be a shadow of the other. But I think you're drowning in the evil inside your brother."

Patrick left them, locking the door again. The need to bury a blade deep within his chest overpowered Thomas. Seething, he fought against the shackles. A raw cry escaped his throat as he pulled the chains tight, metal clanking every time he thrashed his arms.

"Tom, stop," Graeme said. "You're going to hurt yourself. I know what you're feeling."

It wasn't anger burning through him, but something like battle rage. *Darker.*

"Tom, that's the Darkness. What you're feeling, that desire to kill, *that's me.*"

Dizzy, Thomas let out a breath, leaning against the wall and sliding down. "What are you talking about?"

"Look at me."

Thomas shook his head. "No, that makes it worse. Why did you let him capture you?"

"Let him? You think I let him do this?"

Stinging pain blazed across Thomas's back as Graeme groaned in pain again. Breathing hurt, and Graeme's small gasps broke the silence.

"I told you to run. Why would you come back?"

"I was never gone, just hiding. They caught me when I came out of hiding."

"Hiding? Where?"

Graeme hesitated. "I was in the Shadow Realm. I hid in the shadows until I couldn't stay there anymore. I held on to your presence to hold off the Darkness."

"I felt that!" Thomas said.

"When Patrick was kicking and whipping me, no one tried to stop him. I wanted to kill them all. I almost let go, Tom. There was a black scythe; I could have grabbed it. But I heard your voice telling me to hold on. You reached for me *right* when I was about to give in to it."

Graeme fell into silence. Hollow and hurting from the pain inflicted on his brother, exhaustion of the last twelve days caught up with him.

"I don't know how to get us out of this," Thomas said.

Chapter 50

Thomas awoke with a jolt. He had been dreaming of Isaac. The dark room around him held no warmth, and he was sitting with his back to the cold stone wall. Next to him, Graeme's eyes were closed.

"I don't want to die," Graeme panicked. "I'm scared, Tom."

"I know, so am I," Thomas admitted

Graeme's eyes shot open. "You?"

Thomas gave his brother a sad smile. "Don't tell anyone."

"I'll take that to my grave," Graeme said, and flinched, then groaned.

"What?"

"I didn't say goodbye to Amelia; I just left her."

A heavy silence passed between them.

"I wish I could fix this," Thomas mumbled, with an ache in his chest.

Graeme said nothing.

Thomas twisted his wrist around, trying to free his hand. But it was no good. He would have to break his thumb.

"What are you doing?" Graeme asked.

"Being hopeful."

"You're still holding on to hope that we'll get out of this somehow."

Thomas eyed the axe on the other side of the room. So close, but not close enough.

"At least I'm trying something," Thomas grumbled. "Unless your Darkness can help, let me have my hope."

"My Darkness? That's what you're calling it now? I don't think it exists to help us escape."

"Well, unless you can pull something out of thin air, find something more useful."

Motion from Graeme caught his attention, and he straightened. Shadows wrapped around him, a slow, twisting fog.

"What are you doing?" he asked. Graeme's eyes were closed, his bruised face still. "Grim?"

A black sickle took form in Graeme's hand.

"Will this help?" He held the weapon out to Thomas.

"What is that? How did you do that?" Thomas inspected it. "You killed Father Matthew with that thing, I'm not touching that."

"You killed people with your sword."

"I didn't kill a priest. It is cursed."

"Fine, then we'll stay here until dawn. That's when they're coming for us, isn't it?"

Nothing about this is right. That blade spilled holy blood. His brother had pulled it out of thin air.

"Where did it come from?"

"The Shadow Realm."

"You can do that? Just pull weapons out of there?"

"The Shadow of Death didn't need it anymore, and it seems to be mine now."

"He really is a shadow, like they say he is."

"He is *my* Shadow. Now stop being prudish and take it."

"How is it supposed to help? Will it break a chain? Couldn't you have pulled an axe out instead?"

Graeme stared at Thomas. A muscle twitched in his jaw, and a flare of amusement flickered in his eye.

"Are you laughing at me?" Thomas asked. "This situation is hardly amusing."

"I just pulled a weapon of solidified Darkness out of the Shadow Realm, and you're telling me it's not good enough. I'm sorry, you try and do better."

Thomas couldn't resist the chuckle that broke from him then. Graeme was smiling and it lightened his heart.

"Is this better?" Graeme asked, his fingers around the handle of a scythe, the sickle gone.

"Why is it always farming tools?"

Graeme's face was blank. "I'm a farmer."

Thomas reached for the scythe but stopped. "A weapon of Darkness? Will it ... hurt me?"

Graeme rolled his eyes. "Lord Samson is going to come in here and see me holding this. Hurry up! We're out of time."

Thomas's fingers wrapped around the handle, and it responded to him, Darkness humming through the weapon. Energy ran from the scythe, and a jolt passed through his entire body. Heart racing, he almost dropped it. "What was that?" What could only be Darkness surged over his hand, his arm tingling. Cold filled his heart.

"It recognises you," Graeme's eyes lost their amusement. "Maybe because we're twins?"

Thomas pulled it out of Graeme's grasp. "This isn't normal metal; what is it?"

"Darkness, I don't think you can break it."

"Why didn't you do this earlier?" Thomas weighed the scythe. "This could easily kill a man with enough weight behind the swing. Even through armour."

"Forget about killing Patrick, Tom."

Thomas returned to the chain and swung the scythe hard.

"It's not going to work, they're going to hear us," he muttered, eyeing the dent in the wall.

Graeme gasped then, and Thomas glanced over. The Shadow of Death was in the cell with them. The scythe slipped from Thomas's hand, hitting the ground with a dull thud. He was back in the church, The Shadow standing over him. Its touch had sent pain through every part of him, and he'd known he was dying.

"Get away from me!" *Is it here to try to kill me again?*

"You don't need help then?" The Shadow moved away towards the far wall.

"Why would you help me? You tried to kill me."

"Tom, stop. Just accept help from him."

"We're in here because of 'him', Grim."

"No, we're in here because of *me.*" Graeme watched The Shadow.

The Shadow picked up the axe, pausing at the broken mace. *"You know, I was here during the interrogation. You have potential."* The Shadow moved over to Thomas, holding the axe high. *"Hold your hands apart."*

"Potential for what?" Thomas's eyes were glued to The Shadow's hands. It raised the axe high and brought it down hard. A loud clang echoed around the cell. Thomas winced as it lifted the axe again. The second strike broke the chain apart. He grabbed the axe, aiming for the chains at his feet.

Once Graeme was free, Thomas helped him up. He lifted Graeme's arm over his shoulder to support him.

"Turn around."

Graeme turned and he pulled the shredded tunic and cloak away from the angry red bloody welts on his brother's back.

"How bad is it?" Graeme asked.

Patrick's savagery with the whip had left his brother's back in a raw mess. A white-hot rage burned through Thomas.

"They're deep, it'll heal," he assured Graeme. He pulled away, gripping the axe tight. "They would have heard that. Can you fight?"

"Can I … what?" Graeme asked in disbelief.

"Stay behind me. We might have to fight our way out." Thomas readied himself.

"Against armed Enforcers? Are you mad?" Graeme's voice was on the verge of hysteria.

Graeme was right, they had no way of getting out past Lord Samson and his Enforcers. The only way out was up the stairs. Footsteps descended into the cavern. Too many. It was too late. This was a lost cause. Thomas held the axe in front of him, eyes on the door, taking on a fighting stance.

"Get this door open," Lord Samson's voice had a ring of impatience to it.

Thomas's hand tightened on the axe as he braced himself.

Graeme grabbed his arm. "Tom, stop, there is another way out of here."

"What other way?"

"You might not like it."

"Right now, I don't see any other way out. I'll try anything," Thomas said with a sigh.

Shadows shifted around him and Graeme as something seemed to open. A curtain? A shroud? On the other side was nothing. Graeme's open eye became black as he smiled. "It's working."

The shadows inched towards him like rolling fog, Thomas took a step back.

"Don't be afraid of it. Just don't listen to it, either." Graeme picked up the scythe.

"Listen to what?"

The lock in the door turned, and the door burst open. The cell shifted, as if smoke parted them from the place in which they had just been. Lord Samson and Patrick entered the cell. Thomas raised his axe. Graeme placed his hand over the blade, pushing it down. He shook his head.

The Shadow left us.

Darkness crept towards Thomas, curling around him like living fog. This was not a good place, devoid of humanity. It was as if he stood between life and death, and the realm *knew him.* It *wanted* him. His heart was still. *Am I dead?*

"This is a locked room; how did they get out?" Lord Samson's eyes flashed, his voice far away.

How am I seeing them, and they can't see me?

You're seeing them through the veil. I'm holding on to it so we don't get lost.

Graeme's voice was in his head.

Your voice is also in mine, Graeme's voice laughed.

How? We've never been able to talk like this before.

I don't know. I think it's strengthened our link somehow, Graeme replied.

Patrick's mouth slackened and he rubbed at his eyebrow. Thomas's chest swelled with satisfaction, and a smile tugged at his lips. Graeme's mind laughed in his.

"Find them!" Lord Samson demanded.

Patrick's eyes darted around the room again, almost as if he were hoping to see them.

He's right there. It would be so easy to kill him.

No, Graeme urged.

Something in the dark responded to his anger, feeding it.

I will kill him. He whipped and beat you.

Not now. We need to escape first.

Escape, yes. We need to be alive to kill Patrick.

"The Shadow of Death took them," an Enforcer declared.

"Don't be foolish," Lord Samson marched from the room. "Graeme confessed to being The Shadow of Death."

"So did Jacob," Patrick reminded Lord Samson. "Interrogated by your soldier."

Patrick's eyes paused on the back wall. A scowl slid across his face. "Lord Samson."

"What?!" Lord Samson's voice echoed from outside the cell.

"They have weapons."

Lord Samson cursed. "Find them! Now!"

Chapter 51

"Thomas," something whispered to him from the shadows.

That voice... It came from behind him. *Emma?*

Graeme pulled him back. *It's not her. don't listen to it. We must stay connected.* He tightened his grip on Thomas's arm.

Not her? But it was her voice. I'd know that voice anywhere.

"Thomas," the voice called again, lemon and lavender surrounding him. "I'm here." Emma's voice urged him forward, loss tearing at him.

Em?

Tom, no. Emma's dead. You buried her, remember? I stood with you over her grave. Graeme's urgent voice in his mind created confusion.

How am I hearing her, then? I can smell lemon and lavender. It's her! She's here, Grim.

Tom, please trust me. It's not her. It's this realm. You're hearing the dead. If you walk towards the voice, you'll get lost. It's what the Darkness wants.

What the Darkness wants? Why would it want me? "We have to get out of here," he said aloud. "I can't stay here, Grim, not if it's trying to pull me in with her voice."

"Where do we go?" Graeme asked. "We can't go home."

Thomas considered this. "We find somewhere to lay low for a few days."

"What about Amelia…and Isaac?" Graeme's eyes bored into his. *We can't leave them.*

"There's going to be too much attention on them. For now, we wait." Raising his arm, he pushed at the shadows. "How do we get out of this… Shadow Realm?"

"We're safe in here. We can hide here."

Thomas's stomach twisted. *Grim is too comfortable in this place.*

I heard that.

"I want to put distance between us and Lord Samson. My horse is in the stable."

The truth was that the Shadow Realm unsettled Thomas. It was starting to get a firm hold on him, and if he didn't leave, he wasn't sure he would.

"Walk through it," Graeme instructed.

"Can't we leave the cell before returning to…our realm?" Thomas asked.

"You're going to be uncomfortable with that."

"Why?"

"Because I need to let go of the veil. You can't break contact with me, Thomas, no matter what you hear or see. I can get us to your horse, but if you let go, I'll lose you." Graeme turned towards the door. "The dead will whisper. You have to ignore it."

"You know a lot about this realm."

"I've been in here for at least a month."

The dream of Graeme as a baby flashed through his twin's mind. "All right," Thomas said.

The cell faded, Darkness surrounding them. A blue moon hung in the sky above them, and red lightning flashed. Whispers emerged from the dark. Graeme's grip on Thomas was equally as tight as his. A presence brushed against his arm, black fog swirling around his feet.

It's not black fog, Graeme told him silently. *That is Darkness. Let it pass through you.*

What? Why would I do that?

Don't ask questions, Tom. Please, just trust me.

Graeme's open eye was black, the dark lines moving across his face and neck. As Thomas studied his face, he pushed away all doubt.

I trust you.

It knows where we want to go.

The Darkness moved in closer, curling around his body, surrounding them completely. Empty nothingness engulfed him, wrapping a cold grip around his heart.

Red flames surrounded them, familiar faces within. *Jacob? Nicholas?*

They won't recognise you.

Why not?

They've lost themselves. I saw Nicholas just after he died. It didn't take him long before he became this. Catherine too. They're drawn to the living.

Why are they here? Thomas asked.

I think they're trapped.

Trapped? They didn't go to Heaven? Thomas watched the souls around him. *Is Emma trapped here, too?*

I've seen her a few times. I don't think they can. Ready? This might be jarring.

They stepped into biting cold, the wind going straight through him.

"We're right out in the open." Thomas let go of Graeme, seeking cover.

"Sorry, I thought this would be better than in the stable and surprising anyone in there."

Thomas held the axe out in front of him. "I'm ready for them." He eyed the scythe in Graeme's hands. "You're really going to use that thing as a weapon?"

"You have your choice of weapon, I have mine," Graeme grinned.

"You wear it well," Thomas chuckled.

The courtyard was empty with a deafening silence.

"I don't like this." Thomas led Graeme behind a cart. "It's too quiet. We just escaped—this courtyard should be heavily guarded. Keep your eyes open."

Graeme knelt beside him. "There are five in the stable."

"How do you know this?"

"The Shadow told me."

The Shadow. "So now it's *helping* us?"

"If it weren't for him, you'd still be chained to the wall in that cell," Graeme reminded his twin. "He's *not* your enemy."

Thomas grunted in disgust. "Your shadow tried to kill me. That makes it my enemy. How do we get out of here, then?"

"Wait here."

"Wait here? What are you—" Thomas bit down on a groan as Graeme disappeared into the Shadow Realm. "I'm the soldier with combat experience. Why am I the one being left out of the action?"

In the silence that followed, Thomas's impatience got the best of him. Stepping out from behind the cart, he advanced on the stable.

"Thomas, drop your weapon."

He let go of his axe and it hit the ground with a clang. "Reynold."

"There's no escape for you. Hand yourself in."

Thomas turned around as Reynold drew his sword. "You know I can't do that."

"Where's your brother?"

"He's behind you." He smiled at Reynold.

Reynold spun around. Thomas wrapped his arm around his throat. Holding the back of Reynold's head, he used enough pressure for him to pass out.

"Sorry, Reynold," he whispered as his friend slumped against him.

After dragging the Enforcer behind the cart, he picked up the fallen sword and axe.

Thomas walked into the stable in time to see Graeme swing the scythe at him.

"Grim, stop, it's me," Thomas raised his weapons instinctively.

Graeme stopped before making contact. The Darkness that wrapped around him had ceased to shock Thomas. Black eyes, dark lines and wisps of Darkness were as familiar as his usual self. The bodies in the stable, however, were comparable with a battle scene. Two of the five Enforcers had their throats slit, while the other three had been slashed deeply across their chests.

"Tom, what are you doing in here? I told you to wait." Graeme's scythe disappeared.

"What a mess," Thomas stepped over a body. "You've really embraced your instinct to kill, haven't you? Were you trying to cut them in half?"

"You wanted your horse," Graeme glanced down at the Enforcers' bodies. "The gates are going to be more heavily guarded than this. How do you hope to get out?"

A burst of energy gave Thomas the spark of battle rage he was all too familiar with before going into a fight. *There is only one way through those gates.*

"Kill anyone who gets in our way." He opened the stall to let Guinevere out. "Try not to let them kill you first."

Graeme turned an empty expression towards him. "Now you *want* me to kill people?"

He handed Graeme the axe and sword and climbed onto his horse. "This is war, Grim. Neither of us can afford to hold back right now."

"War?" Graeme passed the weapons into his outstretched hands.

Thomas tucked the sword and axe handle through his belt. "It's all I can see right now. If we hope to live through this night, the Enforcers are our enemy. They will not hesitate to put us down. Get yourself a horse, and let's go."

Thomas nudged Guinevere and waited at the door for Graeme. Graeme rode into sight on a white horse. Thomas suppressed a groan.

"Lord Samson's horse?"

Graeme shrugged. "You said, 'Get a horse.'"

"I didn't mean to get the one horse that belongs to the Lord of Kempshire,"

Thomas rolled his eyes.

"You want me to get another horse?"

A shout rose from the courtyard. Damn Reynold. "Too late for that now." Thomas tapped Guinevere on her side with his foot, forcing her into a gallop.

They passed through the archway to Lord Samson's estate as more voices joined Reynold's. Two Enforcers tried to intercept them as they rode past. The sharp beat of her hooves, followed by Graeme's stolen horse behind him, broke the peace of the night. Thomas drew his sword, separating from Graeme. As he approached the gate, an Enforcer threw himself out of Guinevere's way. Another drew a sword. Thomas raised his own, but The Shadow of Death appeared, slicing with the sickle. Blood sprayed, and the Enforcer dropped.

"Clear a path for us," Thomas told The Shadow.

An Enforcer pulled Graeme to the ground. Graeme groaned, not moving.

Dark anger swirled within Thomas, and he scrambled off the horse. Sword ready, he faced Graeme's attacker, lunging forward. His blade pierced the Enforcer's throat.

"Grim?"

"I'm all right," Graeme sat up, and Thomas pulled him to his feet. "Now I'm ready to kill."

Enforcers charged at them. The Enforcers caught sight of Graeme's scythe and stopped. Thomas advanced, his brother beside him. The Shadow appeared next to him. Pushing down his unease, he attacked the Enforcer closest to him. Sword struck sword, the metallic clang ringing through his teeth as he pushed forward. Energised, he let battle rage take him.

Cries of anger and pain pierced the haze. His sword sang through the air, and he forced his opponent back. Two already lay dead on the ground, their torsos sliced open. Thomas's sword got past the Enforcers' defence.

"Tom, more are coming," Graeme's voice came from behind him, the gate open.

"How did you…" The sounds of approaching footsteps and horse hooves stopped Thomas mid-sentence.

"*Go.*" The Shadow pushed him towards the gate.

He stumbled.

Graeme had the horses waiting. "We have to go."

More Enforcers approached. The sky lightened as Thomas retreated through the gate after Graeme. Dawn had arrived. He climbed onto his horse.

"Ride!" Thomas checked behind him. "Don't stop."

He led Graeme towards the forest.

Chapter 52

"Keep moving, Grim," Thomas urged.

The sun had risen, and above them was a clear blue sky. Sheltered from icy wind only slightly among trees, Thomas pulled his cloak around him. With their retreat slowed by the forest, the voices of Enforcers were not far behind.

"Where are we going?" Graeme inquired.

"Willow Grove. They cannot follow us there; it's outside of Kempshire." Lord *Samson will have to ask the Lord of Thornesby permission before he can hunt us there.*

Graeme groaned. "That's half a day's ride."

A familiar whistling hiss passed by Thomas, and an arrow struck the tree ahead of him. Graeme ducked as another flew past.

"They're firing on us?" Graeme turned in his saddle. "Tom, they're close."

Lord *Samson must have given a kill order if they're firing arrows.*

"We go deeper into the forest. Away from the river. They won't be able to get a clear shot."

"That's wolf territory."

Another arrow whistled past, just missing Thomas. "Would you rather face arrows?"

Thomas followed Graeme as he veered off the path.

The forest became dense, darker. Panic flared with every sound as Thomas kept watch around them. The smell of damp moss and wood filled the air. An eerie silence hung over them.

"Ride to the rise," Thomas whispered. "We can get a better view."

He and Graeme climbed from their horses, ascending the rest of the hill on foot. A twig broke, and he spun around, hand on sword.

"It was just the horse," Graeme said.

"Who did you hear?" Thomas asked the question that had been burning inside him since their escape.

Graeme's good eye clouded over. "Hear when?"

"In the Shadow Realm. You warned me not to listen to it. What did you hear?"

Graeme gave him an empty stare, lines appearing in his forehead, but said nothing.

An ocean of sorrow threatened to overwhelm him as echoes of Emma's voice from the Shadow Realm pulled him into deep despair. Forcing back his anguish, he shut himself off from it, as if closing a door. Now was not the time to drown in renewed grief. As short as his time in the Shadow Realm had been, he couldn't shake the dread that clung to him.

Thomas scanned the forest, listening for any hint of being followed.

"Mary," Graeme said at last. "I've heard her cries every morning, the moment I wake up, for four years. She's what Darkness pulled me in with. Her laughter, her voice."

"I'm sorry I wasn't there when you needed your brother."

"I'm sorry, too," Graeme said. "I know what you gave up for me." Graeme took a deep breath. "Tom, I didn't kill Father."

"Then why did you run? You gave in to Darkness."

"I didn't know if you'd believe me. With the looks you and Amelia gave me, I thought I had lost you both. I gave in because I was tired of fighting it. The two of you were the only reason I was holding on."

Thomas turned to his brother. "You didn't lose us, Grim. We spent weeks not knowing how to get you back. Amelia cried every night, regretting what she'd said to you." He studied his brother's face. "I know it was always there, but I never knew what a battle it was for you."

"I've really made a mess, haven't I?"

"Just hold on to me and Amelia, if you have to. I won't let you give in to that again." Thomas said. "How does your back feel?"

It was a stupid question. Stinging pain still zigzagged across Thomas's back as if he had been the one whipped.

"It hurts," Graeme said. "I've never been whipped before. I never could have imagined pain like that." He pointed. "I think they've turned back."

Three Enforcers had turned, riding back towards Kempschester.

"Let's keep going; we're not far from Greenwick. I can find something to help with your back."

Thomas started back down the hill.

"You're going to walk right into a village in the middle of the day and ask them to help?" Graeme asked.

"No, I'm going to wait until night falls and steal what I need."

"Since when do you steal? The only thing you've ever stolen was Uncle's pears."

"Since we're fugitives, and no one in their right mind would help either of us with the risk of being executed or arrested," Thomas said.

I'm a fugitive. The very words sent shock through him. Deep in the forest, alone with his brother, he was on the run. *I've lost everything. My honour, my home, Emma, Isaac.* Thomas clenched his jaw tight. Rising frustration closed around his throat. Emptiness, desperation and crushing defeat had replaced what should have been hope.

"I don't know what to do," he admitted. "Nor how we're going to live through this. Just because they've turned back today doesn't mean they won't try again. Lord Samson will never stop hunting us."

"It's not over yet. We can run," Graeme said.

Since when is he more hopeful than me?

"Where?" Thomas demanded.

"Where Lord Samson won't find us. London? Scotland?"

Pain throbbed in the right side of his head. He massaged his temple to ease the headache. "That means leaving behind everything and everyone we know. Are you prepared to—"

"I'm not leaving without Amelia," Graeme said.

The truth sank in, tearing at Thomas. If he could get to Isaac, he would always be looking over his shoulder. *Is this the life I want for him?*

"Amelia and Isaac may be better off without us. What life can we offer them now? We're fugitives bound for execution. You want to put that on your wife? Force her to leave Riverwick and put her in danger?"

Graeme sighed. "You've given up. I can feel it. You fought to get back to your wife and son, only to give up?"

Unable to hold back, his anger and grief overflowed, like a dam breaking.

"My wife is dead!" Thomas said. "I fought for nothing, because now, Emma is gone, and I think Isaac is safer away from the both of us. Especially with his name on your list!"

Graeme's chin lifted, and his eye narrowed as he studied Thomas's face. "You saw that?"

"Did you think I wouldn't find out? You wrote my son's name on a list of people fated to die. I will always protect my son. I just never thought it would be from you."

"I would never hurt him, you know that."

"Whether it's you or your shadow, I won't let you kill him."

The horse's steps filled the silence. Birds chattered in the trees above, and wind whispered through the leaves. Thomas remained alert, watchful for wolves and Enforcers.

"After all this, maybe it's you who stops me."

"Do you need to be stopped?" Thomas asked.

"I don't know. I feel it, hear it whispering. There's going to be a day when there is more Darkness than me. Each life I took pushed me closer to losing myself." Graeme let out a deep sigh. "I've already given in to it once. I killed people and I *wanted* to. Maybe I'm already lost."

A lump formed in Thomas's throat. "It's not over yet," he said. "How do we fight it?"

Graeme scratched his jaw. "You want to fight Darkness?"

"Yes."

"I'm not sure you can."

"I want to save you and Isaac."

Graeme gave him a pained look. "What if you can only save one of us? Would you kill me to protect your son?"

Chapter 53

I *need to get back to Grim.* Footsteps thundered behind Thomas as the owner of the house gave chase. An angry voice followed him. The door in front of him opened, and Thomas froze. They had him surrounded.

"I know you," the older man before him was a farmer who traded with Riverwick. Oliver, father to the one behind him.

"He's trying to steal from us," his pursuer, Mason, grunted.

"You're one of those Blake twins from Riverwick," Oliver's eyes were hard. "Didn't Lord Samson arrest you both? What do you want with us?"

"I'm not here to hurt anyone," Thomas said, clutching a bundle to his chest. "Please, let me pass. You never saw me."

Cornered, heart thundering in his ears, Thomas fought to hold off the battle rage bubbling up.

Oliver moved towards Thomas. "Is your brother here too?"

As he backed away, the urge to draw his sword grew.

"Why are you stealing from us?" Mason demanded.

"Don't come any closer," Thomas warned. "Just let me get back to my brother."

"Your brother?" Oliver shook his head. "You should both hand yourselves in."

Mason grabbed Thomas from behind, arms snaking under his own, fingers intertwining behind his head. The bundle he carried fell from his arms. A surge of energy burst through him, the need to escape raging from deep within.

"Let me go!" Thomas said through clenched teeth, struggling against Mason's grip.

"Easy. Don't struggle," Oliver took Thomas's sword, holding it on him. "Now, tell us where your brother is."

Thomas had told Graeme to leave for Willow Grove if he didn't return. But Graeme would come looking for him. The idea of his brother walking into a trap terrified him. He reared back, smashing his head into Mason's. His own vision blurred as Mason grunted, letting him go.

Oliver glared. "Don't move. I will kill you with your own sword." He eyed Mason. "Are you all right?"

Thomas advanced, the sword on him wavering. "If you kill me, my brother will come looking. You do not want him here."

Oliver's eyes widened, and he dropped the sword. A gasping breath behind Thomas made him turn around. The Shadow stood in front of Mason, hand against his chest. Dark energy engulfed Mason and The Shadow. The man's eyes turned white as he paled, falling to his knees. All too familiar with the painful effects of that touch, Thomas sympathised with him.

"What are you doing to him?" Oliver bellowed. "Release him."

"Why are you here?" Thomas demanded.

"I am here for them." The Shadow said as Mason's body hit the ground.

Thomas retrieved his sword. "I'm sorry about your son," he said to Oliver. "I'm going now, please don't follow me."

"You killed him," Oliver's eyes darted from Thomas to The Shadow. "Help! Someone—"

Thomas cut off Oliver's call for help with his sword pressed across the farmer's throat. "Don't," he warned, heart pounding. *How am I going to get away from this?*

"Kill him," The Shadow instructed. *"He cannot be allowed to live."*

Oliver's eyes bulged, and he swallowed thickly against the blade. He whimpered, his whole body trembling. "Please, don't."

Calm emanated through him, The Shadow's words taking hold. *Kill him.* Unable to resist the rising wave of battle rage that engulfed him, he gave in, the command surging from deep within. He cut deep, and Oliver's body dropped to the floor with a thud. Standing over the body as blood pooled around Oliver, Thomas re-sheathed his sword and grabbed the dropped bundle.

"Did Grim send you?" he asked, turning away from the sight of Oliver's and Mason's lifeless bodies.

"He did not," The Shadow said.

"Then why did you come? I didn't need you."

"But you did, you called to me."

"Why would I call you? Me and Grim are in this mess because of you."

Without another word, Thomas left the house. The Shadow did not follow him, nor did anyone see his escape. He fled Greenwick, leaving behind a deathly silence. It was time to return to Graeme.

The forest was rich with life. Wolves howled from afar, and a crow's cry somewhere in the trees above echoed around him. Leaves brushed his arms as he passed by.

Thomas approached where he had left Graeme, catching sight of his brother pacing.

"You're late," Graeme said. "What happened?"

"I got what I needed," Thomas held up the cloak bundle. "Sit down. Remove your tunic and cloak."

Graeme folded his arms. "What happened in Greenwick?"

"Nothing."

"Liar."

Uneasiness crawled across his arms. "I don't know why you bother asking if you already know the answer."

"Tell me what happened," Graeme said.

"Why? It won't change anything," Thomas said. "Now turn around, I need to dress your wounds."

"Tom, you need to say it."

"No, I don't! Stop pushing me," Thomas said through clenched teeth.

"I'll say it, then."

"Don't."

"Why don't you want to hear it?" Graeme asked,

"Because I know what happened. I do not see any need in discussing it," Thomas sighed. "Graeme, please, turn around."

"You killed someone."

You killed someone. Three words strong enough to pierce through his very being, turning to stone in the pit of his stomach.

"Damn it. Why couldn't you leave it be?" Thomas asked, heat rising in his face.

"You killed someone," Graeme repeated.

"I SAID STOP." Anger had Thomas reaching for his sword.

"What are you going to do with that?" Graeme said.

The Shadow appeared between them, white eyes narrowed as it regarded Thomas.

"Oh, good, he's back with his awful eyes," Thomas backed away. "It's bad enough he was in Greenwick. Now this." He massaged his head to ease the painful pounding.

"He was in Greenwick?" Graeme asked.

"Don't do that. Don't pretend you didn't send him," Thomas scowled.

"I didn't." Graeme addressed The Shadow. "Why are you here?"

"I was drawn here," The Shadow replied.

Thomas's arms prickled. "Am I next on your list?" He glared at Graeme. "Or is it *your* list?" Chest puffed out, he advanced on The Shadow. "Get on with it, then. Is that what you're here for? To finish what you started in the church?"

"There was a time I sought to kill you, but no, I am not here for that now. You need not fear me unless you intend to strike." The Shadow half-turned, casting a look towards Graeme.

"He needs no protection from me," Thomas said. "Nor does he need you here. Your presence is unwelcome."

"If that were so, I wouldn't have been drawn here. It seems you both require my presence."

"He might be useful," Graeme said.

"He's a killer. How can he possibly be useful?"

"I'm a killer, as are you," Graeme pointed out.

He's right. The things I did. . .I just killed a man in his own home. He had no more strength to fight.

"Fine, let him stay, as long as he's out of my way. Can you sit down now?"

He unwrapped the cloak, revealing bread, a leather flask, wine in a green bottle, dried meat, honey, linen strips and woollen tunics. Graeme turned, doing as instructed. Thomas examined his brother's back. Deep welts marked the skin, open and raw.

Thomas uncorked the wine. "This is going to hurt."

"You're drinking? Now?!"

"Shhh! The wine isn't for me, you idiot." He poured the wine on Graeme's back. "Not all of it."

A scream burst from Graeme before he bit down on his torn tunic. Agony burned across Thomas's back, piercing him to the core. He took a mouthful of wine and handed it to Graeme, then opened the honey jar.

"Is that honey? What are you doing?" Graeme asked, turning around.

"I'm dressing it. Stop moving."

Thomas dabbed honey on Graeme's back, covering the welts, before laying linen strips over the top.

"Did you learn this at war?" Graeme asked.

"That's right. I had to."

Finished, he gave Graeme a fresh woollen tunic and cloak, breaking the bread in half.

"Eat and get some rest."

Thomas leaned against a tree, a deep cold settling over him. They needed a fire for warmth but couldn't risk lighting one. He bit into a strip of meat, its taste infused with salt and smoke, then washed it down by drinking from the leather flask.

"Ugh, water? Why would they keep water in this?" he muttered, but his thirst compelled him to drink more of the refreshing liquid.

Thomas pulled his knees up in an attempt to contain body heat. Nearby, Graeme winced as he pulled the cloak around himself and leaned sideways against a tree trunk.

"I'll take first watch," Thomas offered.

CHAPTER 53

It was going to be a long night.

Chapter 54

In the cloudless night, there was nothing to do but sleep while Graeme kept watch. Every time Thomas closed his eyes, Caleb's face swam before him. His face soon became Graeme's, swollen and bruised. His back, torn up by a whip, pain which had flared through Thomas. *Patrick did this.* Breathless and seething, he desired revenge. *Patrick and* Lord *Samson, I will kill you both for what you did to my brother. To both of us,* he swore silently. He had made a vow to Lord Samson once before, for the sake of his brother. Now another one took hold. Battle rage stirred inside, his hand twitching to grasp the sword and strike hard at his enemies. He longed to give in to his rage, to let it burn away all that he held close. Honour and righteousness had gained him nothing but pain. Anger felt good, and he would cut out their hearts.

"Tom, please calm yourself. You're giving me a headache. I thought you were supposed to sleep while I kept watch." Graeme's voice pierced the quiet night, breaking into his plot of revenge.

Restless, Thomas climbed to his feet.

"Where are you going?" Graeme asked.

"I can't sleep, I'm going for a walk."

"In the middle of the night?"

"Sorry, Grim, I just need to walk it off."

An owl called overhead, followed by a second nearby. The forest was calm, still. A contrast to the chaos that swept through Thomas. Moonlight reflected dim light over the forest floor as he made his way through the trees. He took in a deep breath.

"You know of the Darkness that lives in your brother, but you still fight to protect him." The Shadow had followed him.

"I told you to stay away from me."

"No, you told me to stay out of your way."

Thomas groaned. "What do you want?"

"Why?"

"Why what?"

"Why do you fight for him? You're an Enforcer. It is your job to—"

"I'm not an Enforcer anymore," Thomas interrupted The Shadow. "But if you must know, he's my brother. I'd never turn my back on him. Why does this matter to you?"

"In doing so, you've allowed yourself to be corrupted."

"Corrupted?" Thomas stopped walking.

"You have gone from Enforcer to someone who kills for his brother."

"No, *you* made me do that. I don't know how you did it, but I know it was you."

"There is a thread that connects the two of you." The Shadow reached a hand towards Thomas's chest. *"Here."*

Thomas took a step back. "Don't touch me." He knew all too well what the Shadow's touch could do.

"The silver thread that binds you is no longer silver. His Darkness will become your Darkness."

A cold knot tightened in his gut. "That will never happen."

"You want to kill those who wronged your brother. You want them to suffer. That is why you cannot sleep. I can feel your desire to kill, just as I could sense Graeme's."

Thomas continued walking again, wishing The Shadow would leave him be.

"Do you deny this?" The Shadow walked alongside him.

He couldn't. "No," he admitted. "I cannot deny, you speak the truth."

"I will seek them out for you."

Before Thomas could say anything, The Shadow was gone. Alone again, he yearned to forget about everything. Darkness, killing, that he was a fugitive, and all that he had was lost. Nothing in his life was as he had planned. *What am I supposed to do? I've abandoned my son, only to freeze in a forest.* He leaned against the trunk of a tree, its bark rough on his hand. The plan was to go to Willow Grove to escape Lord Samson's reach. *Where do we go after that? No lord will protect us.* Graeme's suggestion of London or Scotland was appealing, but his brother would never leave without Amelia. Nor could he leave Isaac, either.

"I have found them. They are in the village you call home," The Shadow said from behind Thomas.

Thomas spun around. "They're in Riverwick? What of my son?"

"The child is there, with your brother's wife. They are under heavy guard."

Thomas marched back to where he had left Graeme. Revenge was within his grasp; and in that moment, nothing else mattered.

"Grim, we're going back to Riverwick."

Chapter 55

Whispers in the dark woke Thomas from a deep sleep. Fog had descended upon the forest, blanketing the trees.

"Grim, did you hear that?"

Graeme's slow breathing in response gave him a smile. *You need it, Brother.*

"Thomas," the voice was vaguely familiar, yet he couldn't place it.

Thomas followed the whisper, drawing his sword.

A dark shape moved within the fog.

"Show yourself," he ordered.

The figure stepped forward, and Thomas recoiled in shock. A man with green eyes and blond hair approached him.

"Caleb?" He gasped.

"**Hello, Thomas.**" Caleb smiled.

"But you're ... you... I thought...." Thomas broke into a cold sweat. "This is impossible. How are you. . ."

"**Alive? I'm not,**" Caleb said.

"I'm dreaming," Thomas muttered, putting away his sword.

"**This isn't a dream, Thomas.**"

"Are you haunting me?" Thomas asked.

"**I'm here to remind you what you did. You need to accept what you are.**"

"What I am?" he asked. *What is he talking about?*

Angry voices, pained cries, and the clang of swords emerged from the dark. In the middle of a war camp, cold hard rain fell from the sky. Drenched, Thomas spun around.

"Caleb? Where are you?"

"**Remember,**" Caleb's voice echoed inside his mind.

An enraged scream burst forth. His spine crawled as a soldier strode into view, barefoot, wearing only trousers and a cloak. The attack had caught them by surprise, and Thomas hadn't bothered with a tunic, or shoes before grabbing his sword.

No. Not that. "Stop," Thomas whispered. "I don't want to see this."

Face-to-face with the soldier, he stared into his own face, gasping. Like an echo of the past, but unrecognisable and covered in blood. His eyes were white, not blue.

He fell into the memory, becoming his past self.

The pain of the arrow radiated through his leg, but energy surged as he gave into battle rage driving him forward. Unburdened and unrestrained, he stalked through the camp. Any remaining French soldiers fled, muttering, "L'assassin de l'ombre." The Shadow Assassin. A title they had given him out of fear.

"Thomas, stand down." A blond man stood in his way, trying to stop him. "Aris, I don't think he sees me."

Thomas slashed at the one in his path, dark joy bubbling up as the man fell.

Strong arms wrapped around him from behind, an unbreakable hold. "Stop! You've defeated the enemy. They've retreated, it's over." The voice penetrated his consciousness, and battle rage pulled back in response.

Thomas blinked. "Caleb? Aris, let me go."

Aris released him and Thomas dropped to his knees, hands trembling.

Pale and breathing rapidly, Caleb lifted his head and groaned as he caught sight of his midsection. His eyes widened. "Is that my guts?" Caleb's head fell back, hands shaking as he reached for his stomach.

Kneeling over his brother in arms, Thomas prayed to be released from the dark rage in which he'd lost himself. Unable to face what he had just done, he closed his eyes, willing to sever himself from the brutality and violence.

A dark energy burst out of Thomas. A loud crack boomed across the battlefield, reaching through the veil of another realm. A shadow stood over him and was gone.

"Shhhh, don't move," Thomas said, pressing his hands on Caleb's stomach.

"Thomas," a voice pulled him from his living nightmare.

The war camp faded. Blue light shone down from the sky, and Caleb's presence shook Thomas to his core. "You're not Caleb, are you?" he asked.

"**I am not. He is among the lost**," the being pointed, losing Caleb's shape.

Bright red souls of the dead surrounded him. Familiar faces of those who had died. Father, Emma, Nicholas, Jacob, Lord Philip. Caleb. None recognised him as they closed in.

"I'm in the Shadow Realm. How did I get here?" Thomas asked.

"**You followed a familiar face.**"

"You led me here. Why?" Thomas demanded.

"**To show you what you are.**"

"What I am?" *I am cursed with the same Darkness inside Grim.* "No," he whispered.

"Tom?!" Graeme called out to him.

Thomas sank to his knees. *Am I like Grim? The Shadow. . .No.*

Graeme rushed to his side. "You already claimed me. Not him, too," he pleaded with the Darkness.

"**He already surrendered his humanity for you.**"

"Tom, I'll get you out of here," Graeme whispered in his ear. "Does Darkness have a hold on you? Focus on me, on my voice. Don't let the

Darkness in."

Unable to answer, Thomas could only hold his trembling hands out in front of him. *It was all me.*

Tom. What happened? Graeme's voice inside his head was gentle. He addressed Darkness. "What did you do to him?"

"He has seen the truth."

"What truth? Let him go."

Graeme groaned, the Darkness inside him emerging.

Grim? What's happening? Are you hurt? Thomas came out of his daze.

Graeme's eye held no recognition. The scythe formed in his hand.

"Do not challenge me, mortal. I will make you take his life just to remind you what you are."

"*Please* don't," Graeme pleaded, his voice echoing. "Not him. *Please,* let him go."

"In time, he will not care. Neither of you will. He is free to leave if he wants to."

Graeme knelt beside Thomas, hand on his shoulder. *We have to go. If you've given in to Darkness, it will be harder to leave. Have you given in?*

No.

Do you want to leave? Graeme asked.

Yes.

The swirling fog around them faded. They were back in the forest.

Thomas bowed his head. "How did you find me?"

"It's hard not to when we're linked the way we are. What happened?"

"I saw Caleb," The ground beneath him was steadier as he stood.

"Caleb? Your friend from war?"

"I need to ask you something," Thomas began. "Why do you believe The Shadow is a part of you?"

"Because every time he killed, I was drawn to it. As if his presence called me forth. But dreams started to show me who was to die *next.*"

"Then you wrote their names in your journal."

"Yes. Why do you ask this now?"

To say the words out loud would make it real. But he could no longer hide from the truth.

"He's not of *you,* Grim. He's the darkest part *of me*. I was so afraid of the darkness inside you, I couldn't see that, by living in its presence for so long through our connection, it had taken a hold in me. My actions at war only strengthened that grip. Everything that's happened, it was *me*."

Chapter 56

A shadow of a rider behind them caught his attention. It was gone before he could tell who it was.

Thomas hissed between his teeth.

"What is it?" Graeme asked.

He searched the forest again. "We're being followed."

"Do you think it's Enforcers? How long have they been following us?"

"I don't know, let's stop here. Dismount, you stay with the horses."

"Me? What will you do?" They both climbed from their horses.

Thomas led Guinevere to the river. "I will keep us safe." He tensed at the sideways look Graeme gave him "What?"

"Nothing."

"Liar. You've been giving me strange looks since I told you about The Shadow. I'm not delicate, Grim. Do not treat me as such."

"Very well. But what does keeping us safe mean to you now? Are you sure you're still suited for that?"

The words hit Thomas like a blow to his stomach. "Just stay here," he growled.

He left Graeme beside the river, yet uneasiness coiled deep within. Graeme was right: Something had changed. The burden of his actions settled over him, making him afraid for The Shadow's return. *I unleashed it on the world. How do I stop it? Can I stop it?*

A twig snapped behind Thomas and he spun around.

"Reynold."

"I've been following you since Greenwick. How did it take you so long to notice?"

Greenwick?

"You're on your own, so I didn't think you were a threat." He lied to cover his surprise.

"But now?"

Thomas shrugged. "I grew bored. Are you here to arrest us? By yourself?"

"You should know by now we've been given a kill order. Reinforcements are on their way from Thornesby. Every village is under heavy guard, especially Riverwick."

"Greenwick wasn't."

"It is now. You should know I'm from Greenwick. I knew Oliver and Mason."

Thomas drew his sword, sinking into his stance. Weighed down by regret, he let out a heavy sigh. "I'm sorry, Reynold. I take no pleasure in your death."

"Nor I in yours," Reynold drew his own sword. "But you know how it is."

"Duty above all else," Thomas quoted.

Reynold hesitated. "Your brother is the killer; you spared my life at the estate. Step aside, let me kill him, and I'll spare yours. Maybe on your own you stand a chance of fleeing England."

"I'd be careful about threatening my brother," Thomas warned as he advanced in quick movements, slashing across.

Reynold blocked, retreating as he did. Metal clanged against metal. Then Reynold advanced, striking hard in a downwards motion, and Thomas deflected. He returned the attack without hesitation, only for his blow to be blocked. He didn't wait before he swung again, advancing, forcing Reynold back.

His vision narrowed as he focused only on Reynold. Movements blurred as the two of them struck at each other, both aiming to kill. Strike followed by block. Slashing down and across, steps to advance and retreat. They were evenly matched, their fight to survive driving them both.

Reynold got past his defence.

"Drop your sword, Thomas," Reynold pressed the blade against his throat.

"Why would I do that?"

Thomas kicked hard, pushing Reynold back, following through with his sword. He laughed as the thrill of battle kicked in, his strikes faster and harder than before. An energy and Darkness rose, swift and blinding. Thomas lost himself, giving in to his rage. Their swords met, ringing out through the forest. Reynold's eyes glinted with fear, his blocks desperate against Thomas's barrage of blows.

Reynold fell back. Thomas raised the sword, bringing it down hard, knocking his friend's sword to the ground. Thomas pushed the Enforcer back until he was pressed against the trunk of a tree, blade to throat.

"What's wrong with your eyes?" Reynold asked, his shoulders and chest heaving. *"You're not human."*

"How do you want to die?" Thomas asked. "You know I cannot allow you to live, so I will give you an honourable death. A quick one."

He let Reynold guide the blade down, stopping when it rested against his ribs, then pointed at his heart. "Finish it," Reynold closed his eyes.

Thomas angled his sword up, driving it in hard through the leather. Reynold groaned in pain. "You fought well, my friend," Thomas whispered, plunging the blade in deeper. "Unfortunately for you, not well enough."

Sweat formed on Reynold's brow. "Lord Samson will throw everything at the two of you," he grunted.

Lord Samson and Patrick. An all-consuming need for revenge took Thomas, feeding his rage.

"Then I will take them with me." He pulled his sword out. "They won't see their death coming."

Reynold slid to the ground, breathing heavily. A hand touched his shoulder. Without thinking, Thomas spun, bringing the sword up.

Tom, a voice called from another place as he met his new challenger. A blade blocked his. Without waiting for a counterattack, he drove forward again. His opponent made no attacks, using only defence.

A stabbing pain brought Thomas back to himself. In the middle of the forest, his frenzied cry echoed around him. He gripped his sword tightly, panting. His blade buried deep in Graeme's stomach and searing agony pierced his core. Graeme stared at him, brows drawn down and mouth slightly open, gasping.

Thomas's knuckles turned white. He drew in a gasping breath. A black sword Thomas had never seen before slipped from Graeme's hand and hit the ground with a dull thud. He withdrew his sword and threw it down. Graeme clutched at his stomach, and pain blazed through him through their connection. Graeme swayed. Thomas rushed forward, only to be pushed away by a bloody hand. His brother opened his mouth. Only sounds escaped, no words. Deep betrayal burned in his eyes.

"Grim?" Thomas's heart pounded hard, gripped by ice. "No!"

Graeme stumbled. Thomas lunged forward, sinking to the ground with him in his arms. The forest darkened, fog surrounding them. Day had become night, with an always full blue moon. *The Shadow Realm?* Lost souls encircled them, waiting.

A long moan burst from Graeme, tears in his eyes. He tried to speak again, his mouth forming the word, *Why?!*

Thomas fought against the urge to cry out, his eyes stinging.

"I'm sorry, Grim. I didn't..." His hand hovered over Graeme's stomach, trembling. "I don't... I can't." Unable to find words he shook his head. *I'm sorry*.

A second chilling groan sent a shiver through him, along with a wave of pain. Graeme's body heaved, and he let out a retching sound.

Gasps and groans were the only sounds Graeme could make as he tried to speak. He formed the word *Please*, fingers tight around Thomas's arm. *Tom, don't leave me, I don't want to die alone.*

Thomas pulled Graeme into a sitting position against him and held his hand. Graeme's fingers tightened around his.

"I'm not going anywhere, you're not alone," Thomas could barely speak. *I'm right here.*

The sound Graeme made was halfway between a whimper and a moan. The anguish in Thomas mixed with the agony radiating from his brother as Graeme heaved again. He put his free hand on Graeme's stomach over the wound, warm blood seeping through his fingers.

"Grim, I'm sorry." Hot tears flowed freely, and it hurt to breathe.

He fought against the shuddering sob that tore through him, and his stomach clenched around an icy fist. *He is losing colour. He doesn't have long.* Graeme went rigid with agony. "I never meant for this." Speaking hurt. *I was supposed to protect you. I'm sorry, Grim, I'm so sorry.*

Graeme retched violently and vomited blood down his front, his lips and chin dripping red.

"I kn…hhmmmmm," Graeme took in a breath, whimpering as he did. *I know.*

This is all my fault. My battle rage—

Stop. Graeme groaned again, deep shudders tearing through him. *I forgive you.* A lump formed in Thomas's throat. He pushed the hair from Graeme's eyes, leaving a trail with his bloody fingers. *It's not battle rage, but Darkness. I saw your eyes, they were white. You gave in, after fighting for me to not do the same*. Graeme leaned his head against his chest. *It hurts.*

"I know, I feel it too."

Graeme's grip loosened, so Thomas squeezed his fingers tight.

Tom? Fear flickered in his open eye, the other still swollen. For a moment, the Graeme Thomas held was as he had been as a child, crying out to him, afraid of the shadows. *Don't go.*

"Sshhh, I'm here," Thomas whispered, suffocating. *I'm not leaving you.*

Will you feel my death?

It was a question they had both asked many times, and the excruciating pain burning through Thomas meant that he would. That he already was feeling it.

Don't worry about that right now.

I want to go home. Please... take me... home ... Amelia. Graeme's voice in his mind grew weaker, yet he strained to meet Thomas's eyes. *She must know ... I didn't leave her ... Promise me. Bury me next to my daughter.*

I'll take you home, he promised. *I'll take you to Amelia. Be at peace, Brother.*

A tear ran down Graeme's cheek, his life dimming. *Will I know oblivion, or is there something else waiting for me?* His gaze darted to those waiting for him. *I don't want to be a lost soul, trapped like them.* The words were barely a whisper, but Graeme's fear rumbled from deep inside as he took a deep breath.

You won't be like them, Thomas lied. There was no way to know that, and Graeme's eye met his with a slight smile before it closed.

Graeme breathed out, his energy and pain extinguished.

Thomas gripped his brother's hand. "Grim?" His voice echoed in the silence.

Graeme's presence faded, and the quiet ripped at his heart. There was peace in his brother, but the separation of their bond was not peaceful. Graeme's death reverberated through Thomas, the deep pain of a hundred blades piercing his chest. Agony and sorrow tore into him, clawing his insides, twisting. Where Graeme had been, only emptiness remained. His soul was ablaze while being wrenched apart. His vision dimmed and everything went black.

Chapter 57

Thomas stared up at a blue sky and empty trees. He lay in the snow, chilled to his core. Graeme's head rested on his abdomen.

"Grim," he said, pushing Graeme away. "Move. Use your cloak for warmth if you're cold." Dull pain pounded against his temple. *Have I been drinking again?* Thomas sighed at the silence. "Are you in a mood?" His brother didn't move, his eyes remained closed. "Grim?"

He's dead. His recollection returned with force, and he struggled to breathe. He pulled Graeme into his arms, tears streaming down his face. An ocean of anguish crashed over him, squeezing his chest. His brother's absence pressed in, a cold void of nothing. *I'm sorry, Grim.* Thomas bowed his head. He had taken the life of his twin.

Thomas pulled Graeme's cloak tight to wrap around the body like a shroud. "All I have endured, and I never knew suffering until now." He pulled himself away from Graeme. "Yes, brother, I felt your death, and it felt like I was dying too. I hope you find peace. I'll take you home."

His sword lay nearby, tainted with Graeme's blood. Thomas strode to the river and threw the sword in. It hit the water with a splash, ripples spreading out. He washed his hands. When he returned to Graeme's body, his knees buckled. Unable to move, Thomas closed his eyes, taking deep breaths. A sorrowful moan broke free.

"*What happened?*" The Shadow was back.

Bitter laughter broke through rising grief. "What do you think happened?"

"*The Enforcer?*"

Reynold lay where he had fallen, slumped against a tree, eyes closed. *I'll send someone for you after this is over.* "He didn't do this." Thomas slid his arms under Graeme's body.

"*What are you doing?*" The Shadow stood over him.

"I have to take my brother home."

"*Those who hunt you are still in Riverwick,*" The Shadow said. "*If you go there now, they will kill you.*"

Patrick and Lord *Samson. I swore to kill them.* A spark of anger pushed back his grief. *They did this.*

Thomas lifted Graeme's body, straining under the weight. "I promised to take him home, he needs to be buried." He carried his brother back to the horses.

"*You will not get that far. You cannot keep a promise if you're dead. Do not let your emotions be the end of you.*"

He's right, I will kill them first.

Thomas lowered Graeme's body to the ground again, kneeling beside him.

"I'll take you home as I promised. Just not yet. I will finish this first." He placed his hand over Graeme's chest. No heartbeat, no rhythm of breaths, just an empty body. "They will suffer for what they've done." He let the sight of Graeme's swollen eye and bruised face feed his rage. *Darkness. Let it in so I can kill my enemies.*

"Help me," he asked of The Shadow. "Help me kill them all."

The Shadow held out a hand to Thomas. As he grasped the outreached hand, gloom plunged the forest into pitch black. Darkness appeared in the sky and swallowed the sun. Voices echoed from the depths of shadows. Whispers of those he'd killed surrounded him. Their faces flashed before him, their deaths. People who had fallen to both sword and sickle. Graeme's. *I killed my brother.* Four words he had been trying not to accept.

The Shadow pulled Thomas to his feet. "They'll be begging for their death."

Daylight returned. Thomas retrieved both Graeme's fallen sword and Reynold's."We attack after dark."

Chapter 58

"Where are you?"

Thomas had been calling his Shadow self unsuccessfully. He waited at the tree line.

"Come to me now."

Nothing.

"I summon you, heed my command."

The silence taunted him. The muscles in his jaw tightened, and a drum pounded in his ears. *Grim had better luck connecting to it than me, and it's my shadow. How did he do it?* Agony returned at his own mention of the name Grim.

"**Do you not grow tired of fighting?**" Darkness whispered to him.

Yes. All his life, he had been aware of the Darkness and fought to keep Graeme from its grasp. Always present at the edge of his consciousness, it had inched closer to his heart each time he sacrificed his own humanity for the sake of protecting Graeme, only to lose him.

All I have left now is Isaac. Thomas clung to a vision of his son. Isaac's name was on Graeme's list, and all attempts to save those fated to die had been failures. *How do I save my son from myself?*

The answer was right there. *No!* The truth sank in. *He is not safe with me in his life. I can never see him again. Once I'm done here, I will leave. Isaac is better off with Amelia. Far from me..*

The last of his hope to see Isaac ceased. Too exhausted to fight anymore, he didn't resist Darkness as it seeped in. Cold penetrated his heart, taking hold. The spark of dark energy inside Thomas ignited, spreading through his entire being and burning away his humanity. Free of pain, fear and grief, Thomas revelled in a lightness that filled his chest.

"My Shadow from within, you will listen to me!" Thomas's voice boomed, heavy with menace. "Show yourself."

Just like that, The Shadow was there, standing in front of him as if it had been there the whole time.

"Where were you?" he demanded. "Why didn't you come when I called out to you?"

"You needed to use your connection to Darkness to call me. I see you have given in completely."

"Be ready to attack," Thomas ordered. "As soon as the sun goes down."

"Who is La Mort?" The Shadow asked.

"Where did you hear that name?"

"Who is it?"

"A name the French gave me," he said.

The question took Thomas to the first time he'd heard the name.

He was in a small French village, which was silent as a grave. Sword and dagger in hand, Thomas was under the sway of what he'd thought to be battle rage.

Aris and Caleb next to him as they stood over villagers. Murmurs among the villagers, their eyes wide.

"Qu'es-tu?" a villager asked, his eyes darting among the three of them.

"He wants to know what you are," Caleb translated.

"L'assassin de l'ombre," a villager whispered.

"La mort," another villager murmured.

"What are they saying?" Thomas asked.

"They've given you names," Caleb said. "The Shadow Assassin and Death."

Thomas knelt before the villager. "Me? You want to know what I am?"

All eyes on him, some villagers cried' others were too scared to move.

Thomas raised his sword, scythe engraved on the blade.

"I am your death."

Thomas held two swords, ready to kill, but neither were his—his brother's black sword, humming with energy, made from Darkness, and the weapon he had claimed from Reynold's body.

"Go, I want to know exactly what to expect," he ordered.

Thomas saw through his Shadow's eyes. That had never happened before, but he adjusted to the double sight quickly. The Shadow entered Riverwick, hidden behind the barrier.

Inside the house, Amelia sang to Isaac in the kitchen.

Outside, Enforcers were on full alert, looking around them.

Five Enforcers guarding the house, The Shadow's voice whispered inside. *More scattered throughout the village.* Lord *Samson and Patrick are standing by with your uncle and others.*

As The Shadow scanned Riverwick, Thomas studied who he would be facing. There were faces he didn't recognise, and the Lord of Thornesby stood with Lord Samson. They're his Enforcers, just like Reynold said.

A flicker of energy drew his attention away from Riverwick. What is that? He spun around, but nothing was there.

Thomas, The Shadow called, his voice urgent. *For you to get to* Lord *Samson and Patrick, you'll need a clear path. It will be difficult.*

I'll have to strike fast. Thomas replied. *The rest of them will move in the instant they see us.*

You can use the Shadow Realm for cover.

I don't know how to get into the Shadow Realm. He frowned. *My brother or Darkness was my way in, last time.*

A spark of energy made him turn around again. Immersed in the presence of Darkness, someone was close by. Thomas dropped into a fighting stance, swords ready.

"Show yourself," he said.

No one stepped forward. A jolt of consciousness within the Darkness sent a shock through him. That presence.

"Grim?" he asked in disbelief.

There was recognition within the presence, but no answer.

Come back, he said to his shadow.

The Shadow returned.

"I'm going for Patrick first, then Lord Samson. I want them dead before anyone realises I'm there."

Before The Shadow could respond, raised voices drifted across the fields, drawing their attention.

"Get me closer," Thomas said. "I want to see what's happening."

The Shadow pulled Thomas into the Shadow Realm. He'd once held fear of the idea of getting lost, but now his urge to kill drove him forward. Fog coiled around him, and again his brother's presence.

"Have you seen my brother among the lost souls?" Thomas asked his shadow.

"No, he is not among them."

Thomas searched the fog around him. "He's here. I feel him."

"How? He's dead. If he were a lost soul, there would be nothing of him."

"I don't know."

The veil emerged from the fog. Men moved towards his house, holding torches.

"Are you sure about this?" James's voice echoed through the veil.

"I'm tired of waiting. If this doesn't work, I don't know what will," Lord Samson said.

Being this close to Lord Samson and Patrick awoke his bloodlust. *I'm so close. I can step through the veil, and they won't know what hit them.* Thomas tightened his fingers around the swords.

At Lord Samson's signal, torches were thrown into his house. It caught fire quickly. Thomas lowered his swords, stunned. Flames engulfed the building. Fire roared and crackled.

Thomas didn't care about the house. All he wanted was to kill Lord Samson.

"Let me out," he told his Shadow self. "Stay here."

The shift between realms was as jarring as it was the first time. Thomas faced Lord Samson. The air was thick with smoke and burning wood.

"I hear you're looking for me," he said.

"I knew you would come." Samson looked around. "Will your brother be joining us?"

"Not this time."

Enforcers circled Thomas, blocking him from Lord Samson, drawing their swords.

"He looks different," Patrick said.

Thomas. Graeme's voice rumbled from both inside, and all around. Everywhere and nowhere all at once. *It is not their time yet. You must wait.*

"Wait for what?" Thomas asked.

"I want him alive. We can use him to draw his brother in," Lord Samson said.

Thomas prepared for the first attack, swords ready.

Stand down. Graeme instructed him. **Let them capture you.**

"Why would I do that?" Thomas demanded. "I'm here to kill them."

"Who's he talking to?" James asked.

Not yet. You will have your chance. If there is anything in you that remembers our connection, listen to me. Trust me, hand yourself in. They will not kill you. Not while they want me too.

They don't know he's dead. Thomas dropped his swords and lowered himself to his knees, hands up in front. "I hope you're right about this," he relented.

Enforcers closed in, their swords on him as Patrick approached, his face lit up with triumph.

"I never thought you would be stupid enough to come back for your son and your brother's wife," Patrick said. "Too bad you wasted your time; they will perish with your house."

"What?!" Thomas turned his eyes to the house. "They're in there?!"

"Patrick," Lord Samson warned.

Finally, Thomas caught sight of Graeme through the veil. No longer bearing the discolouration or swollen eye, he was as he had been before his arrest. But he no longer appeared human. Part human, part Darkness, with the smoke like essence rising from him. Dark lines traced over his face and neck, also twisting around his arms, eyes black. A cold smile twisted his lips as he gazed at Thomas. Black fire burned from within.

Patrick's fist struck Thomas in the jaw, knocking him out.

Chapter 59

Pain flooded in through the void, and Thomas groaned, flexing his jaw.

"He's waking up, get him in those irons," Lord Samson ordered. Chains rattled and cold metal closed around his wrists.

He's within reach, kill him. Unsure if the voice was The Shadow's or his own, Thomas opened his eyes. Patrick's presence awoke his bloodlust; the Darkness in him surged forth. He reached for Patrick. One hand gripped Patrick's shoulder, the other on his chest. A jolt passed between them, with dark energy wrapping around them both. Thomas put all his will into his desire to kill Patrick, calling on his Shadow. Patrick gasped for breath, his eyes turning white, his life force darkening.

"Help," Patrick croaked, trying to push Thomas from him. "Get him off me."

Thomas, stop. Graeme told him. **Not yet.**

He ignored Graeme, fixed on killing Patrick. The door opened and men tried to pull Thomas away.

Tom.

"Don't let him touch you," Patrick's warning was barely audible before he lost consciousness.

Thomas was released immediately, and a dagger pressed against his throat. "Remove your hands," Lord Samson ordered from behind him. "You, secure those chains. Someone get Patrick out."

Patrick was removed from the wagon, and Thomas was chained to the floor.

What was that? Thomas examined his hands, the fingers black.

You've become one with your shadow; I can see it. Graeme said. **Remember in the church?**

How can I forget that? The pain was excruciating. I felt like I was dying. I can do that? I can kill with touch?

It seems so.

"That's new," Lord Samson said. "What did you do to Patrick? How did you do that?"

"What's wrong with his hands?" an Enforcer asked.

"His eyes," another added.

"There is something very dark in you," Lord Samson said. "I saw it at war and when you interrogated Jacob. But what I see now is unnatural."

"You would be an idiot not to fear me," Thomas told Lord Samson.

"I want extra guards now, but no one touch him."

"I thought you had a kill order," Thomas said.

"We do, but we need your brother first."

Thomas chuckled. "You won't draw him out."

Flames roared and crackled behind him. Smoke burned the back of his throat. *I forgot about that.*

"Did you have to burn my home?" he asked. "Does it not seem a waste?"

"You don't get a say in that anymore," Lord Samson said. "I have publicly denounced your status as Yeomen. Right now, you're nothing but a peasant. But as a prisoner, you're lower than them."

Thomas shifted around to follow what Samson was pointing at. Villagers gathered, watching his house. Many crowded around him from a safe distance. James approached, staring at Thomas.

"Hello, Uncle."

James shook his head. "You're not the man I thought you to be. Neither of you are. Tell them where your brother is, Thomas."

"Oh, don't act so disappointed. From what I hear, you gained a lot from our disgraced reputations." Thomas addressed Lord Samson. "Do you have any ale? I'm a little thirsty, send someone to Leo's for me."

Lord Samson's eyes hardened, glinting. "You're asking for ale?" he asked. "Have you completely lost your mind? You're a prisoner, Thomas, lined up for execution. Ale should be the furthest from your mind right now."

"Execution, yes, I know. Terrible. But you want Graeme, too. You're not getting my brother. So, while we sit here and wait for him to not show, I'd like a drink."

"Where's my horse?" Lord Samson demanded through the bars. Thomas gave him a small smile but said nothing. "Why did you hand yourself in?"

"My brother told me to," Thomas replied truthfully.

"He told you to hand yourself in?" Lord Samson asked.

"Yes, I think he has something planned. I wish he'd share it with me."

"Where is your brother?" Lord Samson demanded.

"I don't know, but I think he's around here somewhere," Thomas grinned.

"He's close?" Lord Samson asked.

"Yes, closer than you think."

Patrick had awakened and was shaky as he stood next to Lord Samson.

"He said it himself, Graeme's close by," Patrick said. "Do you think he'd come forward if we make this one scream?"

Thomas laughed. "Try it." He leaned forward, holding up his hands.

Patrick backed off.

"There will be no torture of prisoners," Lord Samson stated. "We already did that. I won't allow it again." He pressed his face towards the bars. "We burned his home; we have you. He will show."

I have no need for a house, I'm dead. Graeme's voice boomed from beside him.

"They don't know that," Thomas said to Graeme.

Patrick looked around the cell. "Who are you talking to?" he asked Thomas. "What don't we know?"

Thomas caught the smile on Graeme's face and was unable to hold back his own.

"Is there something amusing about this?" Patrick asked.

"Yes. Your fear is. You can barely look me in the eye."

Patrick drew his sword. "I'll show you fear," he growled.

Lord Samson stopped Patrick with a hand over his sword, shaking his head.

"What's wrong with you?" Lord Samson asked.

"Are you feeling left out? Don't worry, Lord Samson, you're next on my list."

"Threatening an Enforcer is one thing, but now you've directly threatened a Lord," Patrick said. "Are you trying to lose your head?"

Voices called out for Lord Samson as men rode towards him, towing three riderless horses behind them. Lord Samson strode over to meet them.

"Isn't that your horse?" Patrick asked.

Beside him, Graeme cursed. **If they've found the horses...**

"I know."

"Can you stop talking to no one?" Patrick demanded, turning to watch the new arrivals.

An Enforcer climbed off his horse and walked to Reynold's black mare. With Lord Samson's help, the two of them pulled Reynold's body from the animal's back, lowering it to the ground. Then, Graeme's body was pulled from the back of Guinevere.

You were supposed to bring me home, Graeme said.

I know. But I would have walked into this, so I thought I'd kill them first, Thomas told Graeme silently.

That didn't work out, did it? Graeme's voice was heavy with annoyance.

A woman's cry pierced the air. Amelia ran into view, falling to her knees and sobbing over Graeme's body.

"Yes, I lied about her and the boy perishing in the fire," Patrick shrugged. "I was hoping for more of a reaction from you. Even now, at the sight of your brother's body, you show nothing."

"I grieved him when he died," Thomas said. "No need to drag it out."

"I think your brother's death did more than you're letting on," Patrick mused. "There is nothing in you. *This* you would have made for a great Enforcer," Patrick pointed at the bodies. "Did you kill Reynold?"

"Yes."

"Do you have any remorse over that?" Patrick asked. "You killed a man you worked with."

"Why would I be remorseful? He was trying to kill me."

"When did he kill Graeme? Did he surprise the two of you?" Patrick frowned through the bars.

Thomas shook his head. "Reynold didn't kill Grim, I did."

"Lord Samson!" Patrick called out. "He killed his own brother."

Amelia froze. A sob tore from her throat. Lord Samson and Amelia spoke and then she gave him a book. Lord Samson opened it.

She gave him my journal, Graeme said. **What is she doing?**

Lord Samson walked over and held the book open to a list against the bars.

"Your brother had quite the list he was keeping," Lord Samson said. "That is a lot of names. We've both seen lists like that before. I believe you kept a few of them. Why did he write those names?"

Thomas glanced at the journal. "That was Graeme's list," he said. "I don't know why he wrote those names."

"But you knew about it," Lord Samson prompted.

"Are you done asking me stupid questions?" Thomas asked.

"What was it the French called you?"

"You know what they called me."

"L'assassin de l'ombre," Lord Samson frowned. "You were The Shadow

Assassin. Is this what you've been doing this entire time? Your brother wrote the list, and you killed them as a shadow, just like in France."

Patrick grabbed the book, flipping through the pages. "We're in here," he muttered. "So is his son."

Lord Samson crossed his arms. "You would kill your own son?"

"Would you believe the reason I'm here is that I'm hoping to prevent that? Where is he?"

"Your crimes have earned him a lifetime of servitude," Lord Samson told him. "He will never know freedom again."

What?! "My son is not a servant! He is a Blake. Blakes are free men."

"He will know what his father was. He will know it was you who cost him his freedom."

Amelia. Graeme's voice contained no affection, only surprise that she would be here.

She gave Thomas a hostile glare, her face a mask of hate.

"Is it true? "she demanded. "Did you kill him?"

"I did, by accident; I'm sorry, Amelia."

"You don't *look* sorry." Tears streamed down her cheeks. "Your own brother. Why?"

"I never meant to kill him," he told her. "He wanted me to bring him home. So you knew he didn't leave you."

The words had an effect on Amelia. She paled, fresh tears falling.

"Prepare the ride back to Kempschester," Lord Samson ordered. "Someone load Reynold onto his horse, he's coming back with us. The boy comes, too; put him on my horse."

"I want his horse," Patrick said.

"What of my nephew?" James asked.

Lord Samson moved towards his horse. "There will be no funeral for him. Burn the body."

Isaac was lifted onto Lord Samson's horse, silent as Thomas's wagon began to move.

"We have what we came for," Lord Samson said. "Congratulations, men, we finally have The Shadow of Death. There will be a celebration tonight."

The Enforcers around him cheered.

"Wait," Amelia called out, running towards Thomas. She lowered Hunter into his cage. "You cannot expect me to keep him."

Lord Samson peered into the cage from horseback. "This is not going to be a comfortable ride back to Kempschester for you. Tomorrow, you'll be executed."

Chapter 60

Fifteen-year-old Thomas and Graeme raced their horses through Riverwick. Darkness burned within Graeme, snaking around a silver thread that connected them. The sun shone down on them, their laughter carrying on the wind. Villagers moved out of their way.

The dream changed. Two men stood before him. Graeme, as Darkness. Black eyes watched him from beyond the veil. A dark fire burned within, his essence bound to the Shadow Realm. The other, himself with white eyes, his hands and forearms black. They were connected by a black thread: The same Darkness inside Graeme had spread to Thomas.

The jarring of the road jolted Thomas back and forth as he leaned against the bars. Hunter had curled against his side, asleep.

You saw it, Graeme was beside him still.

I did. Around them were Enforcers on horseback. *Was this always our fate? You told me I wouldn't die.*

You won't.

Thomas had believed in the King's Law. Now it would be his end. His death was closing in.

I think it's time to admit I'm not getting out of this one, Brother. I'd say I'll be joining you in the Shadow Realm, unless I become a lost soul.

"It was good while it lasted," he murmured.

It is time for one last hunt, Graeme said.

"How do you suggest I do that?" Thomas asked, pulling on the chains.

Call upon your Shadow within.

In Shadow form, Thomas stood in an empty street.

"Where are we?" he asked.

Kempschester. Give the townsfolk a reminder of what The Shadow of Death can do. Send Lord Samson a clear message that he is powerless.

With Thomas locked up, Lord Samson would not be expecting more deaths. Unburdened by his mortal body, the urge to kill flared in him again.

This time he wasn't just seeing through The Shadows' eyes; he *was* The Shadow.

"I don't have your journal. How do I know who to kill?"

Can you not feel it? Graeme pointed at a woman who sat against the town's walls. She coughed.

"Her? She looks like she's going to die anyway," Thomas scoffed.

The woman's eyes darted to the space Thomas stood, her face blank.

I can see her life force, it dims.

"Then let her die."

Graeme's black eyes gleamed as he turned towards the woman. **It is her time. Release the woman from her mortal tether.**

"You kill her, then. This feels like a pity kill."

I don't think I can, while I'm bound to the Shadow Realm. Brother, it has been a while since we hunted together. Start with her. This is your kill. Kempschester will know fear tonight. Lord Samson's turn will come, as will Patrick's.

"You're him. The Shadow of Death. Grim the Reaper," the woman had recognised him.

Grim the Reaper? That name better not stick. It doesn't bring fear at all.

Thomas knelt before the woman. Fine shivers ran through her body. *Why is she out here?*

"I am. Are you not afraid?" he whispered.

She coughed. "There are some who do not fear you. Is that why you are here? Is it my time? I am ready."

She wants to die! Thomas hesitated.

"What is your name?" he asked the woman.

"Christiana Baker."

Graeme's smile stretched wide, teeth showing. *It is her time.*

"I do not fear death," Christiana whispered. "Release me from my suffering."

Can't you see? Graeme answered his question. **She's ready.**

Graeme reached out to him. Despite being on the other side of the veil, the hand that grasped his shoulder was solid. This was not his usual kill, but it would draw attention.

Thomas held out his hand, waiting for Christiana to take it. He placed his other hand against her back.

"Will it hurt?" she asked.

Many had died painfully by his hand, yet there was no reason for her to not go peacefully. He didn't want her screaming or bringing a crowd just yet.

"It might hurt for a moment. But it will be over soon. It's just like going to sleep. My brother will welcome you to the next world, where you will be free."

"Your brother?" she asked, looking around.

"He is here, waiting for you," Thomas told her.

She closed her eyes, gripping his hand as if for dear life.

It did not take much of his deathly touch to separate Christiana from life. Her soul entered the Shadow Realm, a brilliant blue glow. Graeme reached for her, and the two disappeared.

"Grim?"

His brother returned without her.

"What did you do?" Thomas asked.

I released her.

"Where?"

To a realm where she will know peace. She does not need to remain here. Graeme motioned to the lost souls. **None of them do.**

"You want to free them? I thought we were here to hunt."

Graeme smiled. **Very well, let's show them who The Shadow of Death really is. Find your next kill, Tom.**

Pain exploded in his side, then a second time. Thomas groaned as his cage came into focus and into a stable. Patrick's foot connected with his side again, and Thomas spit up blood.

"You enjoy handing out pain," Thomas grunted. "Come here, I will show you pain."

He stared at his outstretched hand. Now thick black lines twisted around his hand and forearm. *What's wrong with my hand?*

Patrick stepped back, out of reach. "It's dawn. Townsfolk are filling the courtyard to watch you burn. I will be the one to lower the flame."

"You are indeed a cruel man," he rasped, still gaping at his hand. "You will know a cruel death."

Patrick ignored his comment, content with tormenting him instead.

"Your son cries for you. He's here, you know. He will watch you burn."

Isaac cannot be here. Graeme said. **He will die.**

Thomas growled as he lunged at Patrick, only to be jerked back by the shackles. The Enforcer, out of reach, only laughed at his rage.

"I see where your dog got his nature from. He is a wild beast, isn't he?" Patrick said.

"No, he just doesn't like you," Thomas replied.

"It will not matter; he's gone. He ran as soon as we reached Kempschester."

Triumph lit up the face before him, a sneer that only fuelled Thomas's desire to kill.

"Why do you taunt me, knowing what I can do?" The Shadow's power burned within. A flicker of fear behind Patrick's cruel eyes satisfied him. "You're wise to be afraid."

"Enough," Lord Samson had arrived. He held his dagger to Thomas's chest. "Try it, Blake. I will end you right here and drag your body to the pyre so they can watch you burn."

Thomas's show of power had visibly thrown Patrick. Sweat beaded his top lip. "What took you so long? Where are the others?" he asked.

"He killed again. Five dead," Lord Samson shot Thomas a scowl. "You've been busy. I've been getting reports all night of sightings of The Shadow of Death. All those who died are from your brother's journal."

Thomas shot a look at Graeme.

They are yet to find the rest.

"How do you kill from in there?" Lord Samson asked.

Why am I going along with this? I can kill both of them.

No! Wait. Let them lead you to the pyre. Graeme said quickly.

What? But they will set it on fire. I will burn.

I have seen the flames, but they will not be your demise. Graeme pointed around the stable as Enforcers marched in, **You will be theirs.**

Lord Samson turned to Patrick,."It's time. Get him ready."

Enforcers trained their swords on Thomas as Patrick reached for the shackles, his hand trembling. Patrick had experienced his touch, and it was satisfying to witness the effect it was having on the Enforcer.

I really hope you're right about this.

Patrick was careful not to make contact with Thomas as he attached new shackles to his ankles and wrists.

"Be careful," Lord Samson warned as Thomas's hands flexed. Lord Samson held his sword to his back. "Move."

Thomas took pleasure in Patrick's fear and that it took five Enforcers to escort him. The joy soon faded as he was marched from his cell. *I am going to die.*

Thomas, do not fear your own death. It will be as I have seen it.

Thomas stopped and half-turned. The tip of a sword prompted him forward again, chains rattling with each step.

Graeme walked beside him. **Trust me.**

The angry murmurs of the crowd rose as soon as the stable door opened.

Amelia waited in the doorway, her eyes cold as she caught sight of Thomas.

"Amelia. . ." Thomas began, turning his gaze to Graeme.

She is not supposed to be here.

"I'm here to make sure you get what you deserve," Amelia said.

Amelia, you need to leave. It is not your time. Graeme urged. **Tom, she cannot die here.**

"Keep moving," Lord Samson was not wasting time.

"Amelia, leave here now," Thomas urged.

"I will leave when you are dead."

Graeme's pleas for her to leave went unheard. Thomas had no choice but to move through the angry crowd, yet they moved away from him.

A drop fell from the sky before it opened, and a downpour saturated everyone. They weren't deterred, though. They were there to see Thomas burn. A low clap of thunder sounded in the distance.

Patrick tied Thomas to the pyre.

I don't know what you have planned, Grim, but you better hurry.

Thomas searched the crowd. Graeme was still trying to send Amelia away, and the face of his son looked up at him.

"Father!" Isaac cried out and ran to Thomas. Enforcers caught him and he screamed in their grasp.

The anger of the townsfolk rose above them as they called for his death. The world slowed down.

Amelia, ruuuun! Graeme's voice boomed in his head.

Isaac turned towards where Graeme stood, as if he had heard him.

Lord Samson and Patrick, side by side, each lowered torches to the pyre. The flame took, its heat racing towards Thomas.

Kill them. Graeme told Thomas. **Kill them all.**

Lightning cracked across the sky. A jolt hit Thomas in the centre of his chest. A burst of dark energy and Darkness burst forth just as red lightning from the Shadow Realm struck Graeme. His world plunged into Darkness.

Chapter 61

Screams of the dying echoed all around. A sharp ringing sounded off in his head.

Thomas. *Can't move.*

Graeme. **Not alone.**

Pinned down, he tried to take a deep breath. Pain flashed through him. Isaac. Amelia. Fragmented memories tore him apart. Lightning had struck a man on the pyre, and dark power had blasted outward.

There was silence in the dark.

Trapped. No, *bound* by the shadows. Darkness. Death. The confusion cleared. Someone was speaking to him, whispering. The light was coming from above him. Unconsciousness started to close in, and he fought against it. He started to surface. The shadows were receding, but a wave of darkness crashed over him, pulling him back, not willing to let go.

Shadows were closing in. Lost souls. Neither alive nor dead. *You are Darkness. You are Death.*

His face hurt. Hot pain surged through his entire body. Something pushed down on top of him. Rain drummed loudly from above, and water seeped through. With all his strength, he pushed at whatever was on top of him. Am I buried? He pushed out, and everything fell away. He stood in the remains of the pyre. Flames surrounded him, doused by the rain. As he reached up for his hood, his gaze fell on his left hand. The flesh was charred on his thumb, index, and third finger. Burned away completely, revealing blackened bone. The bindings to the Shadow Realm were gone, but black lines branching around his arms and hands remained. Wisps of Darkness rose from him like smoke, curling around his arms and body. Pain subsided.

A thick scent of smoke and burning hung in the air, joined by a sweet and sickening odour. Charred bodies surrounded him. At his feet, Samson had been hit directly by the surge of dark energy. His face, arms and neck were blackened, and his eyes were wide open and clouded white. Patrick's body was the same. Emptiness swirled where rage had been as he closed the corpses' eyes.

Both the memories of Graeme and Thomas merged, making it difficult to grasp where one ended and the other began. Their minds whispered, *Graeme. Grim. The farmer. The human embodiment of Darkness. Born from the dead, connected to the Shadow Realm.*

Thomas, the soldier. The killer. Possessed the touch of Death. After years in the presence of his brother's Darkness, he embraced his own.

Brothers. Twins. Two halves. Death and Darkness had become one.

Lightning had hit the two parts, and Darkness had exploded out of Thomas. Those in the courtyard had been hit by the shock wave. Death's power.

Their charred faces and eyes were the same as Samson's - white, dead. New souls awaited him in the Shadow Realm. The face of a child stared up at him with lifeless eyes. One side of his face was marked with black lines, as he had turned away before the lightning hit. He knelt before the body, taking the tiny hand in his.

"Isaac."

His voice echoed, Graeme and Thomas's. Whispered from both sides of the veil. The boy had meant something to him. A young life taken too early. Only one remained to mourn the child.

I need a horse.

A black horse with a white mane, his horse. He moved through the dead towards the stable.

"Thomas?" A woman's voice called out. Blue eyes widened at the sight of him, and she strode forward. "I saw what happened. How are you alive? Why are your eyes like that?"

"Amelia."

"Lightning hit you in the chest. No one survives that; you should be dead." She looked around at the bodies. "*I* should be dead. How did I know to run?"

"Graeme told you to."

"That was him? I thought I was hearing things."

"You were not hearing things."

Amelia narrowed her eyes "Where is he?"

He fought the desire to take her in his arms. To let her know everything would be all right. The memories of a past life were overwhelming. Holding her.

With her chin trembling, she gazed at him. "Thomas, you killed everyone in this courtyard."

He turned from her.

"Thomas and Graeme Blake are no more," he said.

"Then who are you?"

A reflection caught his eye. Black clouds above him cast a dark shadow over a puddle at his feet. His reflection gazed back at him. The same dark pattern on his arm covered the left side of his face and neck. His left eye was clouded, white, like that of the dead. His right, black, reflecting Darkness.

"I am Death," he said. "Live a long, happy life far away from here. Do not return to Riverwick. Forget about Graeme and all that happened here. Know that I loved you."

She reached for him. "Wait."

The power inside emerged to forge him into a new shape. One of Darkness and Shadow, meant to frighten her. The hope in her eyes faded, her mouth open as she took a step back.

"I said leave!"

The horse lifted her head as he approached, after returning to the human form of Thomas. Once he mounted the horse's back, he steered her towards the archway. Many would not see him coming, and many would run from him. But none would escape him.

He had once carried a sword with a scythe etched into the blade. It had been the tool of the harvest, the tool of his trade. Now, a scythe took form in his hand, one made from the shadows and Darkness of the Shadow Realm. Hunter ran to his side with a low growl. Dark fog twisted around him and his companions. The veil to the Shadow Realm closed behind them.

Epilogue

France 1944

From within the Shadow Realm, Death rode across the battlefield on the back of a white horse. Once a remarkable black mare with a white mane, she had lost her colour over the centuries. Still the loyal companion she always had been, her eyes burned black, an effect of the Shadow Realm. By his side, Hunter, a massive beast, faithful and savage. The Irish wolfhound often announced his arrival with a hair-raising howl that forced terror into men's hearts. Bombs dropped around him, yet he was beyond their explosions. Men screamed for their mothers as they lay dying. Overhead, a plane started to burn as it fell from the sky.

War in his time had not produced death of this magnitude. The whole world had gotten involved, and weapons had advanced. Bodies were ripped apart and burned beyond recognition. The world had changed. Cries through the Shadow Realm drew him to a mortally wounded man in a French uniform. He no longer kept lists of names for those to die, for the dying called him forth. It was time to help this one to the other side. Hunter let out a mournful cry that echoed across the battlefield as they emerged from the Shadow Realm. The soldier's eyes darted from the horse and dog before meeting his fearfully. Death knelt by the soldier, whose eyes glinted with recognition. After six hundred years, there were not many who didn't know him. Death. The Grim Reaper. The Pale Rider. The Angel of Death. The Reaper or the Harvester of Souls. He had collected many names over time, and it was known that to catch sight of him meant he was there for them. Dark energy surged within as he shed his shadow form. As he shifted to his human shape, the tendrils of Darkness that twisted around him remained, and the dark waves of his power emanated from him. Black veins branched from his fingers and hands and around his forearms.

"What's your name?" His voice was thick with Darkness, still reflecting the voices of both Thomas and Graeme.

"Non," the French soldier murmured, terror radiating from him. *"Non, je t'en prie."*

"Do not be afraid. It is your time to die."

The soldier was not ready to go. Most weren't. He fought Death's grip, struggling to get away as much as a dying man could. His strength was spent quickly, and he collapsed back. The whites of his eyes showed as he looked up at the figure over him.

"Je m'appelle François," he switched to English, his accent heavy. "I am not ready to die."

"No one ever is," Death said.

François surrendered; all fight left. "Will it hurt?"

"Only for a moment. Then, it's just like going to sleep."

François grasped his hand in a tight grip and nodded, bracing himself. He placed his hand over François's chest. Dark energy flowed. From the Darkness, the Shadow Realm, his own power, the touch of Death. The soldier gasped as his heart absorbed the jolt, and a groan escaped his lips. Calm passed over his face, and he smiled. Darkness gripped François's heart. It slowed. His essence, his spark, dimmed along with the light in his eyes. A tear escaped as he let out his final breath and his eyes fluttered closed.

Death guided the soldier's soul to where he belonged before returning to the battlefield. There were many more that lay dying in the mud. Eyes were on him. It was not unusual; he was often sighted after taking a life before he returned to the Shadow Realm. They would whisper about the Grim Reaper walking the battlefield, reaping souls. He scanned the field to find a man in the middle of it all, eyes on him. The man approached without fear. The olive skin and black, curly hair hinted at Mediterranean origins. This man was no stranger to him, though. Those watchful dark eyes woke a memory long since buried. The memories of a young, frightened soldier determined to prove himself. From another war. Images rose from deep inside him.

"I know you," he said.

1344

Rain. Blood. War. Swords clanged and men fought. English against French. Cries of rage mixed with screams of pain. The dying became still. A soldier advanced on Thomas, shouting in French. Unable to get the upper hand, Thomas broke into a sweat. It was the first day on the battlefield, and he was about to die. A sword struck down his opponent. Blood sprayed over him as he slipped over in the mud.

"Thank you!" Thomas said.

A man in black-and-red armour smiled down at him from atop a chestnut horse. Fellow soldiers spoke of this man and his ability to stir others to battle.

He was already highly respected and a great soldier. Watchful eyes remained on him. For a moment, it was as if he were speaking to Thomas, a silent command. A jolt drove through him. Fight! Kill! No words had been spoken out loud, but something inside of him responded. A savage need awoke. The need to fight. To win. Any last uncertainty was ripped away, ready to kill and to die. He was invincible. Victory! Death to the enemy! Sword gripped tight and covered in blood and mud, Thomas let out a battle cry. It was as if the embodiment of war itself had spoken to him, unleashing an ancient warrior.

1944

Aris's eyes ran over his face. "Hello, old friend. This is a new look for you," he spoke in a German accent, the English accent from six centuries before long gone.

"Aris?" A brother in arms from the French war stood in front of him, six hundred years on, unchanged.

Aris glanced at François's body. "Still killing the French, I see. Some things never change."

"French, German, American, or English —I take no sides in this war."

"I've heard stories of you. You're the new Thanatos, but with a lot more titles," Aris said.

"The god of death?" he laughed. "I am no god."

"But you are, Death." Aris smiled. "The Shadow Assassin *and* Death, as it were."

"I am. I free them from their mortal tether and take their souls to where they belong."

"So, you are Charon, as well. Why do you converse with them?"

"To calm them. They accept their fate quicker and put up less of a fight."

"Have you had to fight many?" Aris asked.

The weapon he had once selected as a nod to his former life was always close by. He called upon his scythe. "Not for a long time. Some do want to fight, but once they see this, they give up."

Made from Darkness, the scythe had as frightening a reputation as he.

Aris eyed the black scythe.

"I never imagined that Death would be Thomas Blake from the Hundred-Years War."

Death shrugged off his human form, taking on the appearance that drew terror. He was made completely out of shadow and Darkness, with wisps twisting around him like smoke.

"I was once known as Thomas, and as Graeme. Now, I'm known by many names."

Aris exhibited no fear, only awe.

"There are two of you in there? Graeme? The brother? That must be the reason for the eyes. I recognise the white," Aris paused. "I knew there was Darkness in you—in Thomas—when I pushed you. You were a terrified soldier, likely to die if I hadn't inspired you to fight. After your battle rage emerged, I suspected I had pushed you too far. This is not what I ever would've expected."

"Inspired me to fight? You did that?"

"It's a speciality of mine," Aris smiled widely. Flames burned deep within his eyes.

A round of fire rang in the distance. Another explosion, closer as a plane droned over their heads.

"Tell me Aris, how are you still alive? What are you?"

"That, my young friend, is a long story."

This story Continues with *Death's Shadow.*

Learn War's story in *The Whispers of War* & *The Echoes of War*...Coming soon.

About the Author

Serra is an author of dark historical fantasy and paranormal romance books with stories that draw you in from page one. Within these worlds that she created, you will find unbreakable family bonds, darker aspects to humanity, shadow realms as well as passion, lust, strong FMCs and men who would risk anything for the women they love.

Serra's journey to becoming an author started from a young age, when her first creative writing attempt—a poem titled 'The Mighty Oak Tree,"—was published in her primary school newsletter. An avid reader with a vivid imagination, her Mum always encouraged her to keep writing. She proceeded to write poetry and short stories before discovering a deeper passion for novel writing and screenplays.

In 2021, she adapted a screenplay she'd been working on, into her debut novel 'The Shadow Within,' which was published in November 2023.

Serra is a Melbourne-based author from New Zealand. As a reader and a writer, she's drawn into the dark fantasy and paranormal romance genres. Like many authors, she balances her writing alongside a day job in which she works in the communications part of a marketing and digital team; by night, she's a weaver of words, creator of worlds bringing forth stories that hold readers captive.

If you wish to subscribe, please visit:

www.serrarosewrites.com

Be the first to receive updates and sneak peeks at character art, quotes, chapters, next projects and early access to pre-orders.

Also by Serra Rose

The Horsemen Chronicles:

The Shadow Within
Death's Shadow

Upcoming Titles in The Horsemen Chronicles:

The Whispers of War
The Echoes of War
The Scourge of Famine
The Plague of Humanity

The Bloodsong Series:

Bloodsong
Consumed

Upcoming Titles in The Bloodsong Series:

Bloodking

The Bloodsong Series Spin-offs:

Eternity
Lovestruck
Lovesong

www.ingramcontent.com/pod-product-compliance
Lightning Source LLC
Chambersburg PA
CBHW030352310726
48979CB00001B/268

* 9 7 8 0 9 7 5 6 1 0 2 0 6 *